Margaret Thornton was born and bred in Blackpool and has lived there all her life. She is a qualified teacher but has retired in order to concentrate on her writing. She has two children and five grandchildren. Her previous Blackpool sagas, *It's a Lovely Day Tomorrow*, *A Pair of Sparkling Eyes*, *How Happy We Shall Be*, *There's a Silver Lining*, *Forgive Our Foolish Ways*, *A Stick of Blackpool Rock*, *Wish Upon a Star*, *The Sound of her Laughter*, *Looking at the Moon*, *Beyond the Sunset*, *All You Need is Love*, *Sunset View* and *Don't Sit Under the Apple Tree*, are all available from Headline and have been highly praised.

'A heartwarming tale of romance and heartache . . . guaranteed to light up the bleakest winter day'   *Northern Echo*

'A gentle novel whose lack of noise is a strength'
                                                     The Sunday Times

'A smashing holiday read'   *Lancashire Evening Telegraph*

'A brilliant read'   *Woman's Realm*

'A most charming, cheerful and funny book which I cannot imagine anyone not enjoying'   *North Wales Chronicle*

'A compulsive page-turner'   *Coventry Evening Telegraph*

WEDNESDAY'S CHILD

Margaret Thornton

headline

First published in 2004
by HEADLINE BOOK PUBLISHING

First published in paperback in 2005
by HEADLINE BOOK PUBLISHING

2

Cataloguing in Publication Data is
available from the British Library

ISBN 0 7553 2101 4

Typeset in Century Old Style by
Letterpart Limited, Reigate, Surrey

Printed and bound in Great Britain by
Mackays of Chatham plc, Chatham, Kent

Headline's policy is to use papers that are
natural, renewable and recyclable products
and made from wood grown in sustainable
forests. The logging and manufacturing processes
are expected to conform to the environmental
regulations of the country of origin.

HEADLINE BOOK PUBLISHING
A division of Hodder Headline
338 Euston Road
LONDON NW1 3BH

www.headline.co.uk
www.hodderheadline.com

Monday's child is fair of face,
Tuesday's child is full of grace,
Wednesday's child is full of woe,
Thursday's child has far to go,
Friday's child is loving and giving,
Saturday's child works hard for its living,
But the child that is born on the Sabbath day
Is bonny and bright and good and gay.

An old rhyme.

For my dear daughter, Elaine Marguerite, another 'Wednesday's Child'. A modern version of the old rhyme states that 'Wednesday's child is free from woe'. I pray, from now on, that this may be so.

of the local mills, Percy Harding did not intend to spend any of his vastly increased leisure time in doing household chores. Yes, he would dig the garden, fetch in the coal and – very occasionally – see to such things as unblocking a drain or knocking in a nail or two. But that was as far as he was prepared to go. His mornings were now spent in reading the daily paper from cover to cover and doing the crossword puzzle, then he would turn to his library book, invariably a spy novel or a murder mystery – what his wife called 'blood and thunder'. He spent his afternoons playing bowls or taking longish solitary walks into the countryside.

He looked up and smiled at Rachel now as she opened the sideboard drawer and took out the blue and white checked tablecloth, then spread it over the gate-legged dining table. 'It won't be long now, love,' he said, a little self-consciously. 'You're a brave girl.'

She guessed he was rather embarrassed, as he always was, at the mention of bodily functions and women's problems. Brave! She thought, as she laid out the three knives and forks and the wooden table-mats. She didn't feel brave at all; in fact, she was scared stiff at the thought of the ordeal that lay ahead, but she knew it was something that had to be endured . . . and then she would have her baby.

When it was 'Pancake Day', all they ate at their midday meal were pancakes, two each, or three if they could manage them, but two were usually sufficient. This ritual had gone on ever since Rachel was a little girl, coming home from school at dinner-time. Her father, then, had been out at work during the day and special pancakes were made for him in the evening. Rachel fetched from the kitchen the castor sugar in the fancy glass shaker with the silver top and the saucer of lemons cut into quarters.

'Come on, Dad,' she said. 'Mum's just tossing the first lot of pancakes. We'd better go and sit at the table.'

She knew her mother would want to enter proudly, bearing the dinner plates holding the crispy golden-brown pancakes with their delicately frilled edges. In spite of her stomach feeling empty and a mite peculiar, Rachel suddenly felt a pang of hunger at the tempting aroma as the plate was placed in front of her.

'There; those should go down very nicely,' said her mother. 'Put plenty of sugar and lemon on. You carry on, the pair of you, and I'll have mine in a little while.'

'By Jove! That looks grand, Lizzie,' remarked Percy, as he invariably did when a meal was placed in front of him, whatever it might be. He was nothing if not predictable, and he was certainly not unappreciative of the way his wife pandered to his every need. But that was what she was there for, wasn't she? That was his attitude, along with most menfolk of his generation, and as far as her mother was concerned, Rachel knew there was a certain tendency towards martyrdom in the way she fussed around him. But he was what was termed 'the breadwinner', or had been until recently, and, as such, was entitled to his wife's deference.

Lizzie Harding belonged to a generation of women who did not go out to work after they were married, at least not if they were in the social class to which Lizzie belonged. Lizzie's father, Herbert Ransome, who, along with her mother, had now been dead for many years, had been an under-manager at one of the few local mills in the small Yorkshire moorland town of Melcaster. Lizzie, on leaving school at fourteen, had also worked there, not in the weaving shed as did many of her contemporaries – both before and after they were married – but in the office.

She had met Percy Harding, who was employed at one of the other mills in the town, when she was twenty-seven years old, at which age she had believed herself to be well and truly on the shelf. She had seen Percy as a knight in shining armour come to rescue her from the humiliation of spinsterhood. He had been a good enough catch, in her parents' eyes as well as her own, having worked his way up from a lowly position as a weaver to that of overseer and, finally, under-manager. They had courted for three years before getting married in 1926 when Lizzie was thirty and Percy

4

almost forty years of age. And it had been another five years before their only child, Rachel, had been born.

Rachel had realised at an early age that her parents were rather elderly compared with those of her school friends. She had not minded at first. She was a contented girl, taking for granted her sheltered and somewhat restricted upbringing. She had always been well clothed and well fed, even throughout the war years, which had left the little town of Melcaster virtually unscathed. She had plenty of friends and she knew that her parents loved her in an undemonstrative sort of way.

It was only when she reached her mid-teens that she began, if not exactly to rebel, then to question her mother's rigid control of her life. When she had turned sixteen she was allowed to go to the dances at the church hall which were held fortnightly on a Saturday night, and to the youth club once a week. But whereas most of her friends were allowed to stay out until ten-thirty, or even eleven o'clock, Rachel's curfew was ten sharp and her mother refused to budge despite her pleadings. Admittedly, she did not plead very hard; it had become second nature to her to do as she was told. Church on a Sunday morning, accompanied by both her parents, was, of course, obligatory. It would have caused ructions if she had dared to suggest that she might not go, especially as she had become a confirmed member of the Church of England at the age of fourteen.

It was only when Rachel became friendly with Derek Watkins at the age of sixteen that Lizzie began to relax her rigid control, if only a little. Rachel knew it was not because her mother liked Derek all that much; it was more a question of better the devil you knew. Derek went to the same church, he lived in the next street, and his parents were what Lizzie termed 'nice respectable people', his father being a clerk on the railway and his mother a housewife, like herself. She had always worried about Rachel going to the Saturday dances because, some thirty miles to the north, was Catterick Camp, and the khaki-clad National Servicemen were often to be seen at weekends in the streets of Melcaster, as they were in other neighbouring Yorkshire towns. It was far better for Rachel to be friendly with a boy from her own background than with one whose breeding and upbringing were unknown.

Rachel's friendship with Derek, therefore, if it was not exactly welcomed, was tolerated. Besides, he would be going away soon to do his own National Service, and Rachel, to her mother's great pride, was going to a teacher training college. If her mother had hoped that the courtship would fizzle out as a result of their separation, then she was doomed to disappointment. As soon as Rachel had turned twenty-one and she had been teaching for only a few months she announced to her parents – the bravest thing she had ever done – that she and Derek intended to get married.

Her news had been greeted with the shocked silence she had expected, until her mother found her tongue and asked if she were pregnant. Rachel assured her this was not so; she and Derek loved one another and they wanted to be together. What was more, Derek had the chance of a small rented house, quite close to both sets of parents, and such an opportunity in those days of severe housing shortages was not to be sniffed at.

Lizzie had given in then, although she had really had no choice – Rachel had reached the age of consent – and she had thrown herself into the task of organising her daughter's wedding. As for Rachel, she could not wait to get away from her parents and into her dear little home with her new husband.

She believed they had been happy at first although it was hard work, teaching all day at the school on the outskirts of the town, and then coming home and doing all her household chores. Derek did not offer to help, nor did she ask him to. In some ways Rachel was her mother's daughter, brought up to believe that it was a man's prerogative to be waited upon and a woman's privilege to do so.

When they had been married for almost a year she

realised there was a baby on the way. And that, she believed, to her slight regret, would put an end to her teaching career, almost before it had started. Still, what was done could not be undone, and a baby might be just what was needed to complete their marriage. She was well aware that there was something missing in their relationship, but she was not exactly sure what it was. Her mother, of course, would be very quick to tell her that they had been far too young to get married, and maybe that was true. Certainly, much of the fun they had enjoyed together had now flown out of the window and their lovemaking had become a ritual rather than a pleasure. But a baby was always a reason for rejoicing and she hoped their love for this child would help to set their slightly shaky marriage back on course.

Rachel decided, in the middle of the afternoon, that she had better go home.

'Do you really need to?' asked her mother. 'Stay here, then I can look after you. You don't know when your pains might start, and your dad will be able to run you to the hospital.'

'But my case is at home, all packed and ready,' she replied. 'Anyway, Derek will take me, won't he?'

'If he's back in time. I don't want you starting with labour pains and being there on your own. Stay a little bit longer, love, just in case.'

So Rachel, against her better judgement, was persuaded to stay until five o'clock, and then she knew she really had to go. Her father ran her home in his Morris Minor, and when they turned the corner she could see – as, deep down, she had feared – that Derek's car, the large Ford he was allowed for his work, was standing outside.

'Oh, crikey! Derek's home already!' she exclaimed, grabbing at the door handle as soon as her father stopped the car. 'Bye, Dad. Thanks for the lift. We'll let you know when something happens. I must go now and see to Derek's tea.'

'Can't that husband of yours see to his own tea for once?' asked her father. She thought that was priceless, coming from him, and she wondered if he might be joking, but no, his face was deadly serious.

'No, probably not, Dad,' she said. 'You know what men are like.'

'Aye, mebbe I do. Well, take care, lass. Let us know if you want owt.'

'Yes, I will. Cheerio then.' She ran up the path as fast as her bulk would allow and thrust her key into the lock.

The door was pulled back before she could get her key out. 'Where the hell have you been?' Derek's habitually florid face was redder than usual. 'No, don't tell me. Let me guess. You've been round at your flippin' mother's, haven't you? As usual!'

Rachel knew she was in the wrong; she should have been at home. Every man had the right to expect his wife to be there to greet him when he had done a hard day's work. But surely, just this once, there was a good reason for her absence? She was not going to let him get away with it this time.

'Well, that's a nice greeting, I must say,' she retorted, pushing past him into the hallway. 'Yes, as a matter of fact, I have been to my mother's. She went to the hospital with me this morning, or had you forgotten that was where I was going?'

'No, I hadn't forgotten. But most women I know would manage all right on their own.' He threw his briefcase on to the floor before flopping down in one of the low-sprung contemporary armchairs which had been their pride and joy when they were first married. 'They wouldn't need Mummy with them to hold their hand.'

'And most husbands I know would be there to support their wives.'

'Support you? Good grief, Rachel! I'm working every hour God sends to support you. Do you expect me to take time off work as well, to come to the damned hospital?'

'No . . . I suppose not,' she replied grudgingly. Then, 'Forget I said it,' she added, much less aggressively. 'Of course you couldn't get time off work.'

She realised there was no point in antagonising him further. Their first child would be born in a few hours' time and she would need his support, as much as he was prepared to give. She knew that, like her father, he would be squeamish about the gory details surrounding childbirth. Not that fathers were allowed anywhere near the scene when their wives were giving birth. She sat down, tentatively, on the other G-Plan armchair and leaned forward. This was an uncomfortable position, though, with the weight of her abdomen pressing downwards; it had become very noticeable today.

'Don't you want to know what they said at the hospital?' she asked. 'About the baby?'

He glanced at her bulk a mite distastefully. She knew he found her pregnancy unattractive and he had not wanted to make love to her for several months. He did, however, smile briefly now and she saw his eyes soften a little.

'Well, you've obviously not had it, or you wouldn't be here, would you? How much longer, then? Did they say?'

'It will probably be today, later tonight, I mean. I've taken a massive dose of castor oil, so my mother thinks it'll be born tonight.'

'Oh, she does, does she? Trust your mother to know everything. Castor oil, you said? Why on earth did you do that?'

'Because they told me to, at the hospital.'

'And what good will that do?'

'Well, I suppose it's to lubricate ... everything inside there, you know.'

His repugnance at the idea showed on his face again.

'Oh well, we'd best have our meal then, hadn't we, before anything happens.' He smiled at her now, coaxingly. 'Go and make us a cup of tea, love. I'm parched.'

She stood up, not just because she was being obedient; she could feel the baby kicking strenuously. She had asked Derek to put his hand there the first time it had happened, several months ago, believing he must be as thrilled as she was. But he had seemed unimpressed, even slightly repulsed, and she had never asked him again.

'What are we having to eat tonight?' he continued. 'I know I'll have to wait a while for it, whatever it is. You haven't even taken your coat off yet.'

'No, sorry.' Why she was bothering to apologise she didn't know, but it had become automatic, somehow, to put herself in the wrong. 'I've got some bacon that's still quite fresh. I'll make some chips to go with it and I'll fry you an egg. I won't want very much.'

'Well, I do; I'm starving. Get a move on, there's a good lass.'

How on earth would he manage for the rest of the week when, all being well, she would be in hospital with the baby? It took Derek all his time to boil a kettle, let alone make toast or boil an egg. This thought passed through her mind as she edged her way around her small kitchen. She was so enormous now, from front to back, that there was scarcely room for her to squeeze past the formica-topped table to reach the gas stove. Of course she knew the answer to the query in her mind. Derek would go to his mother's, and she would cook his meals and do his washing and ironing just as she had done before his marriage.

He grumbled continually about their home, his and Rachel's, being too near to those of their parents, although it had seemed to be an advantage when they were planning to get married. And it still was, when it suited him. Rachel, too, sometimes wondered about the wisdom of living so close to one's parents. She knew, in a sense, that she had never really got away from home, from her mother in particular who still tried, kindly but determinedly, to exercise a control over her life. She sometimes thought that she and Derek would be better if they moved right away from the area, but there was little hope of that. They were now having to rely solely on Derek's wage and the rent of the small house was very reasonable. Now she was hoping and praying that the birth of their child would bring about some sort of a miracle.

She could not complain about Derek's concern, however, when her pains started in earnest. She had washed the pots and they were listening to *The Goon Show* on the radio – at least Derek was listening, chortling with laughter at his favourite programme – when she realised that this was something that could not be ignored. She had had minor twinges before, but this time it was for real. The pain that gripped her was so severe that she could not help shouting out loud. To give him his due, Derek immediately switched off the radio and started to fuss around her in a way he had never done before. He dashed upstairs to get her suitcase, ready packed for the stay in hospital, and to fetch her coat. She realised, of course, that he wanted her out of the way as quickly as possible, for fear she should give birth there and then on the carpet.

'Come on, Rachel; we'll have to hurry. I'll carry your case out to the car and get the engine going. Put the guard round the fire and switch off the light.' He stopped at the sight of her amused smile. 'What's up? It's not another false alarm, is it?' There had been a few of those during the last week, the pains starting and then subsiding again. 'Well, you're going to hospital this time, whatever it is. I'm getting sick of all this waiting.'

'And don't you think I am?' she said through clenched teeth, not smiling any more as another pain gripped her. 'No, it's not a false alarm, Derek,' she gasped when she was able to stand upright again. 'They're coming every ten minutes now and getting stronger.'

'And what's that supposed to mean?'

'I'm sure I don't know,' she sighed. 'It might be ages yet or it might be soon. How should I know? Just get me there, for God's sake!'

She had never known him to drive so fast, but fortunately there was little on the roads at that time of night. The hospital was an Edwardian building dating from the early years of the century. It was situated on the outskirts of Melcaster with a superb view of the nearby moors, a scene that Rachel usually loved. Tonight, however, the sky was dark with heavy clouds obscuring the stars, and the hills appeared stark black and menacing. She felt a frisson of fear as Derek took the case from the boot and they entered the portals of the grim-looking building.

When she had checked in she was told to sit in a wheel-chair and a porter wheeled her along to the maternity ward, with Derek trotting along at the side, looking abnormally subdued and self-conscious. He sat in the corridor whilst Rachel was examined by the midwife on duty.

'Yes, baby's on his way,' she said heartily. 'You were right to come in, Mrs Watkins, but I don't think he will be born for quite a while yet. Your husband might as well go home.'

The relief on Derek's face was transparent when he heard this and he stood up hastily. 'Right, I'd best be off then.'

'I'll leave you for a moment to say your goodbyes,' said the midwife. 'Don't worry, Mr Watkins. Your wife is in capable hands here.' But Rachel doubted that Derek had given a thought to the possible dangers of childbirth. It was far safer than it had been in the past, to be sure, but still not without its hazards.

'Yes . . . thanks,' he had the grace to say, and he did go so far as to put his arm hesitantly around his wife as the midwife disappeared into her room. 'You'll be OK, Rachel; I'm sure you will.' He kissed her cheek in a perfunctory manner. 'I'll . . . er . . . ring up in the morning, shall I, from t' phone box on t' corner, and see how you're going on? That nurse said it would be a while, didn't she?'

'Yes.' Rachel nodded. 'That's what she said.'

'And they don't want fathers hanging around, do they? She made that quite obvious.'

It would be all the same if they did, thought Rachel. Derek clearly wanted to be anywhere but there. 'No, you go now, Derek. Perhaps you could call at my mother's on the way home and tell her what's happening? I promised to let them know.'

'You and your bloomin' mother! No. Why should I? They've got a phone in the house, haven't they? That's more than we've got. Let 'em ring up if they want to know.'

Rachel felt tears spring to her eyes. She would never have believed that Derek could be so unfeeling. She would have liked to kid herself that his outburst of petulance was as a result of his concern for her, but she doubted that this was so. The truth was that Derek Watkins was concerned with nobody but himself.

'But they don't even know I'm here, do they?' she protested, trying not to let her tears overflow. 'Please, Derek. It's the least we can do.'

'Oh, all right then. I might. I'll see if I have time.'

'You've nothing else to do. Call and tell them now, Derek.' She almost spat the words at him, through gritted teeth, as another pain caused her to double up again.

'OK, whatever you say.' He glanced at her fearfully for a moment, then turned away and hurried off down the corridor.

Rachel burst into tears and an uncontrollable sob racked her body. In that moment she felt that she hated her husband. No, maybe hatred was too strong a word, but she knew that she disliked him, and the thought came to her, not for the first time, that her marriage to him had been a mistake.

The midwife came bustling out of her room. 'Now, now, Mrs Watkins, we can't have all this. I know you're upset at your husband leaving you, but there's no need for all this fuss. Now, get undressed and put this nightgown on, then pop into bed and we'll come and see to you in a little while.'

Rachel noticed there was a bed standing in the corridor outside what she guessed was the main maternity ward. 'Aren't I going into the ward?' she asked timidly. 'And . . . and I've brought a nightdress of my own.'

'You can go into the ward when your baby's been born. All

13

the other mothers are settling down to sleep and we don't want them being disturbed.' By her cries, Rachel supposed, if her pains became too severe to bear. 'And you must wear this regulation gown just for now.' It was an ugly shift-like garment which looked as though it was made from unbleached calico, with tie fastenings at the back. 'You can wear your own pretty nightie when you have your baby and your husband comes to visit you.' The midwife, a buxom middle-aged woman with a round rosy-cheeked face, looked more human when she smiled. 'Come along now, dearie. It won't be so bad.'

Rachel, feeling scared and miserable, did as she was told. No sooner had she climbed into the high bed than the midwife appeared again with another, younger nurse. They were carrying an assortment of funnels and bowls and rubber tubing. For a moment Rachel felt like laughing hysterically. She was reminded of 'water play' and how her class of infants had loved to splash around with jugs and bottles and tubes in a huge tank of water. It was believed to be educationally beneficial, although most teachers complained about the mess it made. These nurses, however, were bent on something much more sinister. She knew they had come to give her an enema.

'But I don't need an enema,' she cried. 'I took a big dose of castor oil. I've been to the toilet. I mean . . . I've been lots of times. I must be . . . empty.'

'We have to make sure, dear, and it will make the baby come faster.'

Oh, the indignity of it all! That was what Rachel knew she would never forget. Then the frequent dashes to the toilet along the corridor; the shock as her waters broke and soaked the bed sheet; the stainless-steel bowl shoved under her chin when she called out that she was going to be sick. And, every few moments or so, gathering momentum now, the unescapable pains.

They seemed to go on for hours as she lay there, alone, in the dark empty corridor. The night nurses, three of them, were in their own little sanctum. She could hear them laughing and she caught a glimpse of them through the doorway drinking tea. She even imagined she caught a whiff of cigarette smoke. It wasn't that they didn't care, but there was little they could do at the moment. They had seen it all before, many times, and pain in the first stage of labour was what women had to bear.

Finally, when she felt she could stand it no longer – it must have been in the early hours of the morning – the midwife appeared and gave her an injection. She did not know what it was, nor did she care. The pains subsided, temporarily, and she drifted off into semi-consciousness, feeling much more tranquil and unworried. The next thing she remembered was being wheeled hurriedly along a long corridor on a stretcher bed. She was fully conscious again now, but she no longer felt so afraid. 'Where are you taking me?' she asked.

'To the labour ward,' said a disembodied voice behind her. 'You've some hard work to do now, Mrs Watkins.'

The voice belonged to a nurse she had not seen before, a little dark-haired girl with an elfin face and a trim figure. Her waistline, accentuated by the broad black belt with a silver buckle, looked to be no more than twenty inches, marvelled Rachel as the young woman bent over her. 'Oh,' she said in surprise. 'I've not seen you before. Where's the other nurse? You know, the fat one?'

Rachel realised afterwards, to her acute embarrassment, that it must have been the effect of the drug injection that had made her speak so tactlessly. She would never, normally, have been so rude. But the new nurse just smiled. 'That was Sister Bradley; she was on the night shift. We've swapped over now and this is the day shift. I'm Sister Kennedy and I'll be with you until your baby is born. It shouldn't be long now.'

This second stage of labour was, indeed, hard work, as the young sister had said it would be. Rachel had been naïve, knowing very little about the actual procedure of birth except, of course, from where the child would emerge. First

15

stage, second stage; she would be able to speak about it with authority afterwards. You had to experience it yourself to know about it. Even this clever little midwife with her efficient manner and her dexterous hands would not really know what it was all about until she went through it herself.

'One more big push, Rachel.' She had become Rachel now, not Mrs Watkins, in the intimacy of the labour room. 'That's it! Good girl! You've done it. It's a girl!'

For a second or two Rachel had felt as though she was being ripped apart, and then it was all over. She felt a flood of relief and happiness. She had her baby and, what was more, it was the girl she had hoped for. She had not dared to say so when anyone asked her, as so many people had done, what she wanted. But she knew, in her heart, she had wanted a girl. As she looked down for her first glimpse of the child, she found herself crying out in astonishment. 'Good grief! I can't believe it. She looks just like my mother!'

She found it amazing that this tiny baby, at the very moment of birth, should bear such a close resemblance to its grandmother. Rachel was the image of her mother; everyone said so. And this baby, too, had the same high cheekbones, longish nose and finely sculpted features of both Rachel and her mother, Lizzie. Rachel had believed that all newborn babies were alike; red and wrinkled and resembling no one in particular other than a monkey. But this baby was different.

'Can I hold her, please?' she asked.

'In a minute, Rachel. Be patient, dear. I have to clean her up a bit first. And there's something else for you to do. One more little job.'

She had not known about the afterbirth; it was surprising, really, how little she had known. That was dealt with deftly by the assistant nurse, and then her baby was placed in her arms.

'There now. Isn't she beautiful?' said Sister Kennedy. 'What are you going to call her? Have you decided on a name?'

'Yes – Lorna,' replied Rachel. They had perused a book of babies' names and that was one that she and Derek had agreed that they liked. But she was not thinking of Derek at that moment, only the precious little bundle in her arms with her tiny starfish hands and the golden fuzz like chicken down on the top of her head. She had heard the child give her first cry as the nurse cleaned her and wrapped her in her cotton nightgown. They had to cry to get the air into their lungs, so Rachel's mother had informed her. But baby Lorna was not crying now. Her blue-grey eyes were staring up at Rachel, although she knew they were unfocused and could see very little but vague shapes and colours.

'What day is it?' asked Rachel, suddenly feeling disorientated and out of kilter. She could see through the window that it was daylight and the sun had already crept from behind the moorland hills, its radiance highlighting the variegated greens and browns, the drystone walls and the outcrops of rock.

'Wednesday. Ash Wednesday, to be precise,' replied Sister Kennedy. 'And it's eight o'clock on a lovely sunny morning.'

Wednesday ... Yes, of course. Ash Wednesday. She recalled now how it had been Shrove Tuesday – Pancake Day – when her pains had started. So little Lorna was a Wednesday's child. The old nursery rhyme flashed into her mind. How did it go?

Monday's child is fair of face,
Tuesday's child is full of grace,
Wednesday's child is full of woe ...

Goodness me! She hoped not. Not if she, Rachel, had anything to do with it. This child would be loved and cherished and would know nothing but happiness.

Suddenly the sky grew dark as the sun disappeared behind a cloud, and the next moment there was the pattering of heavy rain against the window; a climatic change which was a frequent happening in the Yorkshire hills. And the

17

child, at that instant, opened her mouth wide and gave a loud, agonising wail. Not just one cry; her yells went on and on and Rachel was powerless to stop them. 'She's crying!' she said, turning in distress to the midwife.

'Of course she is,' smiled the nurse. 'All babies cry. It's perfectly normal. Give her back to me now, Rachel. The doctor's coming to have a look at you.'

Rachel handed her back reluctantly. Sunshine and rain, happiness and tears, she thought. They were the lot of everyone who passed through life; they could not be avoided. And this little child, no doubt, would experience them too; she would have her share of sadness as well as joy. It was foolish to wish that all her days would be carefree and sunny. Yes, she was a Wednesday's child – Ash Wednesday of all things – but Rachel hoped desperately that her life would not be 'full of woe'. She even found herself looking ahead to the time when this little girl would be old enough to be married. How she hoped that her daughter would choose more wisely than she, Rachel, had done.

Chapter 2

'Oh, isn't she delightful?'

'What a gorgeous little girl!'

'You must be so proud of her, Rachel.'

Rachel was well accustomed to such comments about her dear little daughter. At two months old baby Lorna was, indeed, delightful and gorgeous, plus all the other effusive words which admirers used to describe her. She was beginning to smile now, proper smiles, not just windy ones, which transformed her face and caused people to say what a happy child she was. Rachel knew that Lorna recognised her now when she leaned over the cot or pram. There was that light of understanding in her brown eyes – they had changed to brown now, like Rachel's, rather than a muddy bluish-grey – and she would even stretch out her chubby hands and arms towards her mother.

This latest group of baby worshippers were the staff of Kilbeck Infant School where Rachel, until a few months ago, had been a teacher. At the invitation of the headmistress she had gone along that afternoon to take part in the festivities that had been arranged for the crowning of Queen Elizabeth II. The school would be closed, of course, on the actual day, so that the children could celebrate at home with their parents, watch the ceremony on the television, maybe, if they were fortunate enough to have a set, or listen to the wireless, or just have a general knees-up with lots to eat and drink. Rich and poor alike seemed to be affected by the air of expectancy and optimism that had gripped the heart of the nation. Most people would be celebrating in one way or another, except for the small minority of anti-royalists who were choosing to ignore the event, and others who regarded it as a waste of time, money and resources.

Kilbeck Infant School's celebration was taking place in the week prior to the Coronation. Rachel, with baby Lorna sleeping peacefully on her lap, had watched the five- to seven-year-olds, some of whom she had taught earlier that year, performing on the makeshift stage in the assembly hall. The hall was packed with friends, parents, mainly mothers – there were very few fathers to be seen – and a good smattering of doting grandmothers.

A little dark-haired girl with vivid blue eyes – eyes such as, it was said, Queen Elizabeth possessed – was crowned with due ceremony. Her white satin dress had probably been made specially for the occasion, but her golden cloak and train looked suspiciously like one of her mother's damask curtains. Several small boys in knee breeches and red velvet tunics bowed before her, whilst her ladies in waiting, in an assortment of white dresses and with glittering coronets on their heads, stood dutifully at her side.

Rachel recognised the queen as Samantha, a very helpful little girl who had been in her own class; a very apt choice for such a high honour. Rachel doubted that there would have been any jealousy or animosity at her election, at least not amongst her peers, although there might well have been some mutterings from the mothers. It was only when they reached junior-school age that the rivalries and back-biting started between pupils. Halfway through the ceremony Samantha's eyes began to wander around the faces in the audience. Catching sight of her former teacher sitting in the second row, she smiled delightedly and lifted her hand to wave. Then, no doubt remembering the dignity of her position, she lowered it again, trying to recapture her former solemnity.

Rachel smiled back at the child, finding, suddenly, that her eyes were moist. She had not realised she would miss the

20

children so much. She had her own baby, of course, and she knew that Lorna was more precious to her than anything or anybody else in the world. But there were still times when she was lonely, when she missed the companionship of the teachers, a couple of whom had become good friends, and the friendliness and exuberance of the children. For the birth of baby Lorna, sad to say, had done little to bridge the gulf that was widening between herself and Derek.

The older children sang a medley of patriotic songs, including 'There'll Always Be An England', 'Rule Britannia', 'Rose Of England', and a song which was continually being played and sung on the wireless at that time, 'In A Golden Coach', written especially to celebrate the Coronation.

The concert was followed, after the parents and most of the guests had departed, by a tea party for the children. They wore red, white and blue paper hats and made short work of the sandwiches, buns and dishes of red jelly prepared by the dinner ladies. This sterling group of women, worth their weight in gold, stayed on afterwards to do the washing-up whilst the teachers gathered in the staff room for their own private party.

It was then that baby Lorna was passed round from lap to lap. She did not seem to mind. She had woken up in a good temper and made no murmur of dissent as the unfamiliar ladies cooed over her. Rachel was relieved, though, when she finally put her back in her pram. Even then she did not protest. She was a remarkably placid baby.

'We are so pleased to see you again, Mrs Watkins,' remarked the headmistress, Miss Lacey. 'Aren't we, staff?'

Miss Lacey, one of the 'old school' of headmistresses, would never have dreamed of calling any of her staff by their Christian names. Even more outrageous was the idea of them ever calling her Matilda, although she was often referred to as 'good old Mattie' behind her back. Despite her somewhat forbidding appearance and her strict adherence to the formalities of yesteryear, she was an understanding head who showed a genuine interest in her teachers as well as the children in her charge. One of her peculiarities was to refer to them, collectively, as 'staff'.

They agreed unanimously now that it was, indeed, great to see Rachel again. Christian names were used quite freely amongst the rest of the staff, although not in front of the children.

'We still haven't filled your vacancy,' said Miss Lacey. 'We had to wait, of course, to make sure that everything turned out satisfactorily.' What she was referring to was the fact that Rachel had not officially resigned from her post, but had taken a leave of absence as a safeguard, just in case anything should go wrong at the birth and she should wish to return to the school. Such a precaution was common practice. 'I will have to do something about it before the end of term,' she continued, 'although it's doubtful that we can interview before September.

'I don't suppose . . . You wouldn't consider coming back, would you, Mrs Watkins? Mrs Metcalfe here has been taking your class – and making a very good job of it too; we're very grateful to you, Mrs Metcalfe – but she doesn't want a permanent position, do you, dear?' The said young woman agreed that that was so. She only filled in as a supply teacher from time to time.

Rachel, too, had been dilatory about sending in her firm resignation. She knew she should have done so, but something had kept holding her back. So her post was still open? And she did have quite a lot of time on her hands . . . She had heard other young mothers say how a baby kept you busy every minute of every day. In the first week or two maybe that was true, but Rachel was finding now that there were times when she was not exactly bored, but anxious for adult company and a stimulus which, alas, could not be found in her home and marriage. The improvement she had hoped for in her marriage had not taken place. Derek, in fact, seemed to be spending more and more time away from home, either working overtime or going out with his mates. The thought of returning to her teaching post was very tempting. She was breast-feeding little Lorna at the moment, but she could foresee no problem in weaning her on to a bottle. Her supply of milk was already decreasing, and Lorna was such a good, contented baby that she was sure she would adapt well to the change.

She found herself saying, 'I'm not sure. I certainly didn't intend coming back, but . . .'

'You mean you might consider it?' It was clear from the expression on Miss Lacey's face that she was pleased at the idea. Rachel had always got on well with her. On leaving college she had still known very little about the real nitty-gritty of teaching – training colleges tended to theorise too much – and she had learned a good deal from Miss Lacey. She was the sort of head who knew exactly the calibre of all her members of staff. Without openly interfering she knew, nevertheless, just what was going on in each and every classroom. And she had liked Rachel's common-sense approach to the children, and the way they responded to her.

'It is so difficult to get really good teachers nowadays,' Miss Lacey continued. 'There is quite a shortfall in some areas – in the big cities like Leeds and Bradford, for instance – in spite of the emergency training after the war and the recruitment programme now. We don't do too badly here; Melcaster is a pleasant place to live and work. It would be wonderful, dear, if you could find a way to coming back. I know there's your dear little baby to consider, of course. She's such a good little thing that you might even be able to bring her with you. I know of one or two instances where young teachers have gone back to work with their babies.' She looked thoughtful. 'On the other hand . . .'

Rachel smiled. 'No, I don't think that's a very good idea, Miss Lacey. There would be a clash of interests, surely, and somebody would be sure to suffer, either the baby or the children. No, if I do consider coming back – and at the moment it is rather a big if – I would have to make sure that I left Lorna with someone who would take very good care of her.' And the obvious person, the only person in Rachel's mind, was her mother.

'My mother might be willing,' she said. 'And my father has retired now, so maybe it would give him more of an interest in life.' Not that her father had ever had anything to do with her own upbringing. Like most fathers of the era he had left the child-rearing to his wife. But his increased leisure time, which had been a novelty at first, was now beginning to be irksome. Her mother had told her that he even helped to wash up now and assisted with the hoovering and dusting. So it was not beyond the realms of possibility that he might welcome the idea of looking after his little granddaughter. He loved her to bits, as did her mother.

'I'll ask them and let you know,' she told Miss Lacey. 'When I've decided myself, of course. It's a big decision.'

And what would Derek think about it? she pondered as she pushed Lorna, now asleep again in her pram, the mile or so to their home. Although relations between herself and her husband were still not good, he doted on his baby daughter. His care for her did not go so far as to change her nappies, or get up in the night when she cried, but it was obvious that he loved her very much. He nursed her from time to time, handing her back when she was wet or crying, but there was a look of wonderment on his face that was unmistakable. She knew that he loved his little daughter far more than he loved her, Rachel.

She did not know exactly what had gone wrong between them. She had come to the conclusion that it had never been right; they should never have got married in the first place. They had been too young. Rachel had never had a real boyfriend before, due to her mother's strictness, and Derek had been far too immature to shoulder the responsibilities of marriage. She had not been unhappy at home, but she had felt hemmed in and restless, especially after the two years away at college which had given her a taste of freedom. She had viewed marriage as a wonderful adventure, leaving home for good and moving into their own little house. Now, less than two years later, she knew she had made a mistake. Already she and Derek had grown tired of one another. She guessed that Derek knew it as well, but it was something they never talked about.

She broached the subject of her returning to teaching over their evening meal. She was surprised when he made very little objection to the idea of leaving Lorna with her mother, if her mother was agreeable, of course.

All he said was, 'I thought you wanted to cut loose from the apron strings, Rachel? God knows, it's time you did, and now you're talking about leaving the baby with her. We don't want your mother interfering. You know what she's like; give her an inch and she'll take a mile.'

'She's been very good to us, Derek,' replied Rachel. She did, in truth, sometimes feel annoyed when her mother presented her with a batch of buns or a fruit loaf she had made – as though she, Rachel, was not capable of doing her own baking – but she knew that she meant well and did not consider for a moment that she was interfering. 'Of course, if you really object to me asking her . . .'

'No. Why should I?' said Derek. 'The child won't come to any harm with her, I know that. And we might as well make use of the old girl if she's willing. Aye, you get back to work, Rachel. You'll be home afore me of an evening, though, won't you?' He answered his own question. 'Of course you will. Teachers work such short hours, don't they? It's nobbut a part-time job really.'

She did not rise to the bait as she knew he wanted her to do. They had had this sort of conversation before about short hours and long holidays. At one time he might have been teasing, but that was something Derek did not do very much now. All the fun had gone out of their relationship, if there had ever been any there in the first place; she sometimes wondered.

'I don't fancy the idea of coming home and cooking my own tea,' he added. 'But you'll be back soon after four, won't you? You'll have loads of time.'

'Don't worry, Derek.' She gave an inward sigh. 'I'll see to your teas, like I always do. You wouldn't have a clue anyway. You can't even make toast without burning it, can you?'

He actually chuckled. 'Aye, that's true.' He was tucking into the steak-and-kidney pie, homemade, that she had placed in front of him, with relish. Very rarely, however, did he comment on her culinary achievements. He had used to do, once in a blue moon, but now he took it all for granted.

'This is homemade,' she said. She, also, was enjoying the tasty dish of tender meat and rich gravy. 'By me,' she added meaningfully. She knew she was a good cook, having watched her mother, ever since she was a little girl, preparing nourishing meals – nothing too fancy – for the three of them. 'If I go back to teaching I may not have time to do my own baking. I'm just warning you, Derek.'

'Oh, you made it, did you?' he replied, with his mouth still half full.

'Of course I did! Where did you think it came from?'

'Well, I dunno, do I? And I don't care, neither, so long as it's good and hot and filling.' He wiped his hand across his mouth and gave a loud burp. 'Aye, it were good, I must admit.'

'Well, your steak-and-kidney pies may have to be shop bought in future.' She snatched his plate away from him before he had a chance to scoop up the remaining gravy with his dessert spoon. His habits – nothing too disgusting, admittedly, but annoying all the same – were beginning to get on her nerves.

'It doesn't matter. Doubt if I'll know the difference any-road,' he called after her as she went into the kitchen to fetch their pudding, the remainder of a trifle she had made the day before.

The appetising meal had put him in a more affable mood than he had been in for some time, but as they continued to talk – yes, to her surprise they were having a real conversation – she realised that it was more likely to be the idea of her returning to work that was causing him to be so buoyant.

It was not, of course, just the returning to work, but the fact that she would be making money.

'We'll be able to save up and get away from this dump,' he said, waving a derogatory hand at his surroundings.

'It's not a dump, Derek,' Rachel felt aggrieved. She was very proud of her little home, even though relations there might not be as congenial as she had hoped. 'You didn't say that when we were getting married. You were thrilled to bits that you had found us a house to rent.'

'Aye, mebbe I was,' he nodded. 'But I never intended it to be a permanent thing. I've always wanted to own my own house, but it's not possible on the pittance that Whittakers pay me. That's why I've been doing so much bloody over-time. Happen I won't need to if you go back to work.'

She had noticed his use of the possessive pronoun and it annoyed her. My own house, indeed! '*Our* own house, Derek,' she corrected him. 'I shall have a share in it as well, won't I?'

'Yes, we'll soon be able to save up enough for a deposit,' he went on.

She did not know whether or not he had grasped the significance of her interruption or if he had even heard her. Equal shares in their marriage; that was what she would have to insist on. She did not mind so much doing all the work, but she was damned if she was going to let him get away with sole ownership. Her name was going to be on the mortgage book, when they got one, or her name was not Rachel Watkins! She occasionally found herself looking back, with some regret, to the time when she had been Rachel Harding, but then the thought of little Lorna made her count her blessings. Her baby was the most wonderful thing that had ever happened to her, and she had her marriage to thank for that.

'Yes, I rather fancy one of those semis on that new housing development,' Derek was saying now. 'You know, Coronation Close; that's what they're calling it. I was driving past the other day so I got out and had a peek through the window –

of one that was empty, I mean. Gardens back and front, three big bedrooms, nice big lounge, and a smashing view over the hills from some of 'em. I know you like to see the hills, don't you, Rachel?'

She was surprised, and rather touched, too, that he should remember this. She never tired of the landscape in which she had always lived, the dale on the northern fringe of industrial Yorkshire, and she could not imagine ever living anywhere else. Derek, too, was Yorkshire born and bred. That was something they had in common, something, maybe, that they must cling to. And it might well be that this common goal, saving up to buy their own house, might prove to be the turning point in their marriage, giving them a second chance for loving and understanding one another.

He was not, however, being very considerate with his choice of Coronation Close. The houses, indeed, did sound lovely, if a bit out of their reach, but they were miles away from Kilbeck Infant School where Rachel, all being well, would be teaching. She told him so.

'Yes, it sounds very nice, Derek, but it's impractical. For a start, it's right at the other end of town from the school. Don't forget I would have to take Lorna to my mother's and then go on to school. It wouldn't be possible.'

'There's a bus, isn't there? At least we don't live out in the wilds. Melcaster's pretty well on the beaten track. Or perhaps your dad could run you to work. He's nowt to do now.'

'Just get back to reality, Derek. We won't be able to afford one of those posh houses. Anyway, we don't know yet what my mother's going to say. How much do you reckon we would need, though, for a deposit? On an ordinary little house, I mean. Something like this?'

'We want summat a bit better than this, Rachel. Oh, a couple of hundred, I'd say. Two hundred and fifty, mebbe, at the most.'

'Mmm ... that's not bad. We might manage that in a couple of years or so. In the meantime we're all right here. Yes, we are, Derek,' she added firmly.

'OK, if you say so,' he shrugged. 'When are you going to ask your ma?'

'As soon as I can. On Sunday, perhaps. Or maybe not. I can't really ask her in church, and she's always busy afterwards talking to her friends. And I have to get back to see to our Sunday dinner.'

'And I've got me weekly date with Charlie,' he reminded her now. 'Don't forget that.' It was, in point of fact, more than a weekly date, as he went out two or three evenings a week as well, to sup with Charlie in the local pub.

'I won't forget,' said Rachel. 'Do I ever? I'll be seeing my mother on Tuesday anyway – well, we'll all be seeing her – so maybe I'll wait till then.'

'Tuesday?' queried Derek.

'Yes, Coronation Day. Surely you haven't forgotten? We're going round to my mother's to watch it on her new television set.'

'Hey, wait a minute, Rachel. You might be going, but you can count me out. If you think I'm going to spend all day in the company of your ma – and all her cronies, no doubt – then you've got another think coming.'

'But you knew she'd invited you.'

'Aye, but I didn't say I'd go, did I? And I'm not doing, so there! Your mother can put that in her pipe and smoke it!'

'Don't be so horrible, Derek! You might at least show your face, for a little while at any rate. Especially as we want to ask her a favour.'

'Oh, come on, Rachel. It's far better coming from you than me. And you know she's not exactly my favourite person . . . and neither am I hers.'

'I don't know why. You used to get on well enough.' She remembered that he had made quite an effort, when they were courting, to get on the right side of her mother, but he no longer bothered to do so.

'I'm not good enough for you. I never was. At least, that's what your ma thinks.'

'No, she doesn't.'

29

'Of course she does! I can tell by the way she looks down her long nose at me. I'll show her, though, when I'm able to buy my own posh home.'

'Our house, Derek.'

'Yeah, whatever. She won't be able to look down on me no more.'

'You are forgetting, aren't you, that we won't have a house at all if she doesn't agree to look after Lorna?'

'OK, OK, I know. You don't really mind, do you, if I don't come on Tuesday? It's not really my scene.'

'But what will you do? This is one time when I won't be dashing back to see to your dinner, Derek. My mother will be putting quite a spread on and—'

'Oh yes, I'm sure! Trust your mother. She'll do anything to impress the neighbours. New telly an' all.'

His interruption made her even more determined that on this day of all days she would do exactly what she wanted to do for a change. '. . . and I don't know what time I will be back home,' she continued. 'In time to put Lorna to bed, of course, but you might have to fend for yourself, just for once.'

'Huh! There's no chance of that. If you're going to make a day of it, watching this blasted Coronation, then so will I. I'll see what Charlie's doing. If I know Charlie he'll be wanting to escape, same as me. He's got an ogre of a mother-in-law an' all.'

She deliberately ignored the insult, but she could feel the hurt of it, like a stab of pain at her heart. So much for the friendly conversation they had been having a little while ago.

'Oh. So where will you go?' she asked, in a tone of voice that indicated she did not much care.

'To the pub, I daresay. Where else?'

'They'll be closed, won't they? It's a public holiday.'

'Oh, you can bet quite a lot of 'em'll be open. They're not going to miss a chance of raking in the lolly. I've heard that some of 'em have even had tellies put in to attract the customers. We'll do all right, Charlie and me, you can be sure of that.'

He looked at her steadily, his bright blue eyes – his only remarkable feature – boring into her own. She looked determinedly back at him. She knew that neither of them was going to budge an inch. On that auspicious day they would each please themselves. After a few moments he gave a sardonic smile.

'Just make sure you talk your mother round, there's a good girl. And don't forget to give her my love!'

Rachel set off from her home at half past eight on Coronation Day, leaving her husband in bed. He had refused to get up 'so bloody early' on his day off. 'Then he can damn well get his own breakfast,' she had muttered to herself as she dashed around making toast for herself, getting Lorna ready for the day, and packing the pram with a supply of nappies and bibs and the rest of her baby paraphernalia, not forgetting the large ginger cake she had baked as her contribution to her mother's feast; she could not go empty-handed. Then, like the fool she was at times, she made two extra slices of toast, spread them with butter and marmalade and took them up to Derek, with a mug of strong tea, just the way he liked it. At least he did have the grace to emerge from beneath the bedclothes and thank her.

'Enjoy yerself,' he said, grinning. 'Here, give us a kiss before you go.'

She dutifully kissed his stubbly cheek, then lifted up baby Lorna from the cot where she was lying, all dressed and ready to go in her pram. Derek held her for a moment, very gently kissing her cheek before handing her back to Rachel.

'Be a good girl for your mummy and don't cry all through the Coronation. Have a good time, both of you. And love to Grandma. Don't forget!'

'Give over, Derek,' said Rachel, but good-humouredly. 'OK then, we're off now. You have a good time as well. So . . . I'll see you when I see you. Cheerio then.'

31

She had hung a Union Jack in the front window, as had many of the neighbours, just to show her loyalty to the Queen. When she reached her mother's street, however, she found that signs of patriotism were much more in evidence there. Red, white and blue bunting was stretched from lamppost to lamppost and almost every house sported flags or streamers or photographs of the Queen and her husband. As Rachel might have expected, her parents' home surpassed them all.

Her mother must have decided that red, white and blue was rather too ordinary. Her window was decorated with streamers of purple and gold, the royal colours. As well as the photos of the Queen and the Duke of Edinburgh taking pride of place in the centre of the window, there was a picture of the royal coat of arms with the lion and unicorn, and, in each of the four corners, small paintings of a rose, daffodil, shamrock and thistle. These, Rachel knew, were her mother's handiwork. Lizzie was very talented at all kinds of arts and crafts.

She could imagine Derek's comment, were he to set eyes on this extravaganza. 'Trust your mother; keeping up with the bloody Joneses as usual,' or words to that effect. Lizzie Harding was a very enthusiastic and energetic person who entered into all she did with a spirit of gusto and exuberance. And if she went one better than everyone else, then that was all to the good.

Her excitement was clear to see as she opened the door to her daughter and granddaughter. Her cheeks were flushed and her eyes shining with delight. She was wearing a royal-blue dress with white trimming at the collar and cuffs, partially covered by a red, white and blue apron. Rachel had not seen the dress before; she guessed her mother had made it specially for the occasion.

'You're nice and early, Rachel love. I wasn't expecting you just yet, but you'll be able to give me a hand, won't you? I'm busy making mounds of sandwiches.'

'That's what I thought, Mum. I've come early to help and . . . perhaps we can have a chat as well?'

'Of course we can. And how's my little pancake, eh?' That was what she often called Lorna, remembering the trauma of the day before the child's birth. She peeped into the pram. 'Ah, she's fast asleep, bless her! We'll lift the pram into the hallway, because it looks as though it might rain. Oh dear! I do hope it isn't going to rain on our lovely Queen. Percy, come and give us a hand with this pram, will you? Steady now, we don't want to wake our little treasure, do we?'

The kitchen was a hive of activity. Lizzie had already made a pile of egg-and-cress sandwiches and was starting on the salmon-paste ones. Rachel could also see a plentiful supply of boiled ham, corned beef and Spam, plus tomatoes, lettuce and cucumber waiting for attention on the kitchen table.

'Goodness, Mum!' she exclaimed. 'It looks as though you're going to feed an army! And this lot must have cost you a bob or two.'

'Oh, don't you worry about that, love. The folk that are coming have chipped in. Mona gave me the ham, Gladys the stuff from her husband's greenhouse. I shall make a big bowl of salad for them to help themselves. And – oh, I can't remember exactly – somebody else gave me the corned beef, and some of them are bringing cakes with them, and scones. I've made an enormous trifle and baked a special Coronation cake.'

'And here's a ginger cake,' said Rachel, placing her offering on the table. 'Now, what can I do?'

'Let's see . . . yes, you do the ham sandwiches and I'll finish off these salmon ones. We'll wrap them in greaseproof paper and they'll keep fresh for ages. What's the matter, love? You're rather quiet. There's nothing wrong between you and Derek, is there?'

'No, nothing like that, Mum.'

'I thought, happen, with him not coming with you . . .'

'No. He said he hoped you would excuse him,' Rachel muttered the white lie with her fingers tightly crossed, 'but it's not much in his line. He thought the room would be full of women and he'd be like a fish out of water.'

'Most of them'll have their husbands with them. And he could have helped to look after our little Lorna.'

'Well, never mind, Mum. We're all right, honestly. Actually, I wanted to ask you something; a very big favour.'

'Now you know I'm always ready to oblige, dear, if I can, whatever it is.'

To Rachel's relief, Lizzie raised no objection to the request that she should look after her granddaughter whilst Rachel returned to her teaching post. A beatific smile spread across her face after she had thought for a moment and she clasped her hands together in delight.

'I shall be only too pleased to help and I know your dad will be as well. Come here, Percy, and listen to this. He's getting on my nerves, to be honest, love,' she added in an undertone. 'I hadn't realised he'd be under my feet so much when he retired. It'll be an interest for him, looking after our little treasure. And you'll be able to save up, like you say, you and . . . Derek.' There was always a slight hint of disapproval whenever Lizzie uttered his name.

Her father, also, smilingly nodded his head. 'Aye, we'll enjoy looking after your little lass. She's not much trouble, is she? And it's not as if you'll be working long hours. Schools finish at four o'clock, don't they? I've seen some little 'uns coming home even earlier than that.'

Not their teachers, though, thought Rachel, but it would be best not to say too much at the moment.

'Lorna won't interfere with your activities, will she, Mum?' she asked. 'Your whist drives and your Mothers' Union meetings? I've only just thought about that.'

'Of course she won't! I shan't let her. I shall take her along with me, won't I, when your dad can't look after her. She's as good as gold, our little pancake, and all the ladies will love her. They'll be quite envious, I can tell you.'

Oh dear! thought Rachel, already imagining her mother boasting and possibly boring all her friends. Still, if she wanted the help she would have to leave her mother to her own devices.

'Right, that's settled then,' said Lizzie resolutely. 'We can talk about the details another time, can't we? Today it's our Queen's day. Oh, dearie me! I do hope the weather is going to improve for her.'

It was a tight squeeze in the Hardings' sitting room for the twelve guests – neighbours and friends who did not possess a television set of their own – plus Lizzie, Percy and Rachel and, of course, baby Lorna, who took up no extra room and was happy being passed from lap to lap. The room measured no more than fifteen feet by twelve and every chair in the house – even the kitchen stools – was arranged in rows facing the nine-inch television screen. This was contained in an oak cabinet almost as big as a sideboard. Lizzie had decided that if she was going to have a set, then she would have a good one, never mind the expense or the space it took up. The curtains were drawn to darken the room, although there was, in fact, no sunshine in Melcaster either, only dark clouds and the threat of rain.

It rained on and off all day in London, but the weather did not appear to have dampened the enthusiasm of the crowds who lined the route to and from the Abbey. It was a wonder that Lizzie saw anything at all, as she was busy for a great deal of the time, dashing in and out of the kitchen with plates of food and pots of tea, but, Rachel knew, loving every minute of it. She did manage to sit down for the actual crowning, and watched the Duke of Edinburgh bow and swear allegiance to his wife.

One of the most memorable sights of the day was that of the Queen of Tonga, a huge black lady, smiling and waving to the crowds from her open carriage. She was soaked to the skin, but refused to put up the carriage hood, and the crowd went wild, admiring her exuberance and her unselfish gesture.

Queen Elizabeth, with her husband at her side, looked radiant as she drove back to the palace after the ceremony. The smallness of the television screen and the fact that the picture was in black and white did not detract from the

35

brilliance of her smile and the glitter of the gems at her throat and in her crown.

At last it was all over. Rachel stayed until all the other guests had gone, and after another snack meal with her parents, to eat up the sandwiches and cakes that remained, she wheeled her baby home again. As she had expected, Derek had not yet returned.

Charlie Fleming and Derek Watkins had been friendly, on and off, for many years. They had been at school together, then had started work at the same Melcaster mill, Whittakers. Their two years' National Service had separated them, but on being demobbed they had returned to Whittakers, Charlie to the job of warehouse manager and Derek as a commercial traveller.

Melcaster, on the fringe of the industrial belt, had never had as many woollen mills as the towns of Leeds, Bradford and Halifax to the south, nor had it tried to compete with these giants. The air had always been a good deal cleaner up in Melcaster, and now the woollen industry, both here and in the larger towns, was in decline. Whittakers now produced ready-made clothing from material made from the synthetic fibres which were superseding wool and cotton; such fibres as nylon, Acrilan and polyester.

Charlie had married Marlene, his childhood sweetheart, on his demob from the army and they now had a one-year-old boy. He still went out with Derek on a couple of evenings each week and had not demurred when his mate had suggested they should spend Coronation Day together. Derek suspected, though, that Charlie's heart was not entirely in it when they went off on these 'lads only' outings. He teased him that he was henpecked, but Derek knew, to his slight shame, the truth of it – that Charlie was more contented in his marriage than was he, Derek.

Their usual drinking place, the Coach and Horses, was closed when they arrived there at midday. They had spent the last hour or so watching the procession on the television screens in the window of Listers, the electrical shop in the high street, along with a small crowd of twenty or thirty others, mainly men.

'That's a bloody let-down and no mistake,' said Derek, rattling at the pub door. 'What the hell do they think they're playing at, closing the place on a day like this?'

'They probably want to watch it all in peace,' replied Charlie. 'You can't blame 'em. Look, there's a notice in t' window. They're opening tonight as usual. Not that that's much good to me. I promised Marlene I'd be back before then. Come on, let's try our luck elsewhere. There's sure to be somewhere open.'

'Oh, flamin' hell! I thought we were going to make a day of it,' grumbled Derek as they walked off down the street. 'And now you say you've got to go home early. Didn't you tell me you wanted to get away from your ma-in-law, same as me?'

'So I do, but Marlene'll be going back home at teatime to get the little 'un to bed. She'll have had enough of her mam an' all by then. I assumed you'd be doing the same, getting back to help with the bairn.'

'You're joking!'

'Why? I thought you were thrilled to bits with that little Lorna of yours?'

'So I am, but I leave all t' messing about to Rachel. You'll not catch me changing mucky nappies and cleaning up sick.'

'You've got to take the rough with the smooth, mate.'

'OK, OK, you do it your way, but don't expect me to follow suit. For God's sake, let's not fall out about it.'

Derek was narked because his favourite pub was closed. Goodness knows why they hadn't bothered to find out before they set off, he fumed to himself. He had been so pleased at the thought of having a whole day on the loose that he had not really considered just how he was going to fill in the hours, only that he was going to throw off the shackles and get away from his wife for a while. He cracked on to Charlie that she was a nagging wife, but he knew that that was not true. Rachel was not a nag, not by any means.

They found a pub on the outskirts of Melcaster – the Queen's Arms, which was very appropriate – which was not only open but was serving sandwiches and pies; cold snacks which had been prepared beforehand and could be eaten whilst watching the television screen, with as little inconvenience as possible to the bar staff. Neither Derek nor Charlie was particularly interested in the Coronation as such, apart from it being a day for celebrating in the way you thought best. They dutifully watched the solemn crowning ceremony in silence whilst munching away at their cheese-and-pickle sandwiches, meat pie and crisps, and quaffing their pints of foaming bitter.

Derek found his thoughts wandering to Rachel. He knew he was doing her an injustice by suggesting to Charlie, or to anyone, that he was henpecked; moreover, he guessed that Charlie knew it was not true. She had never nagged at him, although he knew, if he were honest with himself, that she might – just might – have had cause to do so, occasionally. In fact she was, he supposed, a good wife to him, inasmuch as she washed and ironed his clothes, cleaned his shoes, looked after his baby daughter and cooked his meals – very appetising meals too. They had been happy at first . . . at least, he had told himself they were happy. So what had gone wrong? Why was he feeling so restless and dissatisfied, not only with Rachel, but with himself as well?

He knew one of the reasons was what the older generation – her parents and his – had told them right from the start, that they were too young to get married and settle down. Derek knew, of course, that her parents, particularly her mother, had said he was not good enough for their precious daughter. What was more he knew, deep down, that this was true. Rachel had been, and still was, a cut above him.

Why had he been so keen to marry her then? he asked himself. Possibly in order to get one over on that awful mother of hers, to prove that he was as good as anyone else. And because . . . well . . . he had always fancied her like mad. He had been stunned at first when Rachel Harding had agreed to go out with him. She had always seemed so aloof and unfriendly when he had seen her at the church youth club. But he had chanced his arm and had discovered she was a really nice lass, albeit a little shy. She had blossomed, though, under his tutelage. He had felt proud to be seen out with her. She was pretty, petite and fair-haired and she always dressed smartly and in the height of fashion. He supposed they had fallen in love; at least he had told her he loved her, asked her to marry him, and she had said yes. But that was before . . . and this was now.

'D'you want another one, mate?' Charlie's question broke into his reverie.

'What? Oh, yes please. Same again, eh?'

'Wakey, wakey. You were miles away. I bet it weren't the Queen you were thinking about?'

'Eh? No, it wasn't actually . . .' When Charlie came back with his pint he said to him, 'D'you ever find yerself having second thoughts – you know – about . . . you and Marlene?' When Charlie stared at him open-mouthed he knew, as he had really known when he asked the question, that his mate was horrified at such a suggestion. 'No, you don't,' he said quickly. 'Forget I asked. You and Marlene, you're . . . well, you're as happy as pigs in muck, aren't you?'

Charlie laughed, but he did not sound very amused. 'I don't reckon much to the comparison, but – yes – we're happy right enough. And it's been even better since our little Jeremy came along. For heaven's sake, Derek, you want to stop feeling so bloody sorry for yourself. You don't know how lucky you are. Your Rachel's a lovely lass – real classy an' all – and that baby girl, she's a little smasher. What's up with you, anyway? Have you and Rachel had a row?'

'No, we hardly ever do. But we don't seem to – I dunno – get on as well as we did at first. Things are not right, but I can't really put me finger on it. She's a good wife. I can't complain about—'

'Although you do, don't you?'

'Aye, I suppose so. But it's par for the course, isn't it, to have a moan about the wife? All fellows do it.' All except Charlie, he now realised. Charlie never – well, hardly ever – criticised Marlene. 'She's not as . . . well . . . as adventurous as I might have wished,' he went on. 'A bit . . . not exactly prudish, but she never lets go, not properly. I feel I'm missing out on summat.'

'I take it you're not talking about the meals she cooks?'

'Am I heck as like! You know what I mean. I hadn't been around very much before I married Rachel, and I'm thinking now that maybe I should have – you know – sown a few wild oats. How do you find it, in that department?'

Charlie's face took on a closed look. 'That's something I don't discuss with anybody. You should know that by now, Derek. When have I ever talked about Marlene like that?' No, he never had, mused Derek. Charlie was not beyond listening to, or even telling, the odd risqué joke when he was out with the lads, but his loyalty to his wife was unquestionable. 'I will tell you, though, that everything's fine, couldn't be better. And if you're having problems . . . in that department, then the fault most likely lies with you.'

'Hey, come on! That's not fair. It's not my fault; you don't know what she's like.'

'I know she's a bit on the posh side. That's what you said when you first met her, didn't you? That she was a classy bird. Maybe she finds you a bit – what shall I say? – insensitive, immodest maybe, compared with her, I mean.'

'I'm as common as muck. That's what you mean, isn't it? I know damn well that's what her mother thinks, always has done. I was never good enough for her precious daughter.'

'Hey, steady on. You know that isn't true. Of course you're not common. You're just an ordinary bloke, same as me. We didn't go to the grammar school, like Rachel did – and neither did my Marlene – but we're none the worse for that, and I'm sure Rachel doesn't think so neither. She wouldn't have married you if she hadn't wanted to.'

Derek gave a sardonic snigger. 'Oh, I can put on an act when I want to, talk posh like Rachel and her mother do. I have to talk proper in my line of business anyway, to impress the clients. The thing is . . . I find myself behaving just the opposite when I get home and I don't know why I do it. To annoy Rachel, I suppose.'

'You'll have to pull yourself together, mate. You don't want your marriage to head for the rocks, do you?'

'Aw hell! It's not as bad as that.'

'Your glasses, please, gentlemen,' said the barman, putting the empty tankards on his tray. 'You're welcome to stay a while if you wish and watch the television, but we have to stop serving now. Rules and regulations today same as any day.'

'I suppose we've nowt else to do,' said Derek, a shade grumpily. 'You won't go dashing off just yet, will you? Happen I'll try and sort things out with Rachel when I get home. Don't know what's up with me really.'

'You want putting in a bag and shaking up,' laughed Charlie. 'That's what my mother used to say.'

'Aye, mebbe I do. Summat o' t' sort.'

Derek glanced around at the small group of people who were still sitting on bar stools or on the chairs to the rear of the pub, ostensibly watching the Coronation proceedings. It was beginning to pall a little now – if you had seen one marching soldier or guardsman on horseback you had seen them all – and the crowd in the pub had dwindled considerably. There were two young women sitting on a red plush sofa near the window. One of them, a striking dark-haired girl, smiled as she saw Derek looking at her and she gestured to the two empty seats at the small round table. 'Come and join us,' she mouthed.

'Charlie.' He turned to his friend. 'There's a girl over there that I know from somewhere.' It was a lie – he didn't know her from Adam – but Charlie would certainly not be game for a pick-up. 'I can't quite remember who she is, but she obviously knows me. Look – she's beckoning to us.'

'Pull the other one; it's got bells on it!' said Charlie. 'She hasn't a clue who you are. They're most likely a couple of . . .

you know whats.' But Derek was already on his way over there, so Charlie reluctantly followed him.

As it happened, they were not ladies of ill repute, but two very nice girls who, nevertheless, were not backward in coming forward, particularly the more attractive dark-haired one. Derek soon gave up the pretence that he knew her – Charlie was not fooled anyway – and they introduced themselves. The dark one, who clearly had her eye on Derek as he had his on her, was called Babs and her fair-haired friend was Elsie. They were both shop assistants in Melcaster, Babs at a sweet and tobacconist's shop and Elsie at the local Woolworths.

They chatted about the happenings on the television screen, watched now by only half an eye, the weather, the lack of entertainment in the little town of Melcaster, and their various jobs. Derek's disclosure that he was a commercial traveller for Whittakers brought about the usual comment about 'travelling in ladies' underwear'. He had heard it many times before, but laughed dutifully. Whittakers did, indeed, produce underwear, both for women and for men, and other items of clothing as well – skirts, blouses, shirts, pyjamas and overalls.

By the middle of the afternoon Charlie was growing restless. Derek was not surprised when his friend stood up and said it was time he was going. He raised a quizzical eyebrow at Derek, but Derek shook his head. If Charlie wanted to play the dutiful husband then that was up to him.

'OK, see ya then.' Charlie raised his hand in farewell and quickly left the pub.

'Has your friend got a date then?' asked Babs. 'He seems in a hurry.'

'No, he's got a family,' replied Derek nonchalantly. 'He wants to get back to his wife and baby.'

'Oh, I see.' He was relieved that Babs did not ask about his own circumstances, and he did not intend to tell her.

A few moments later Elsie said that she, too, must be going. 'She has an invalid mother,' said Babs as her friend departed. 'She's a widow and Elsie's ever so good to her, but there was a crowd of neighbours there to see to her today.'

Derek nodded. 'So that leaves you and me.'

'So it does,' said Babs. She smiled at him questioningly.

Everyone, in fact, was leaving the pub now and the landlord was looking pointedly at the few who were still lingering. Derek started wondering, frantically, what he could do. He knew that Babs was expecting him to make some sort of suggestion, and as for him, he didn't want to say goodbye to her, not just yet.

'Would you like to ... er ... have a drive out into the country?' he found himself saying. 'I could go and get the car and we could have a bite to eat somewhere ... if you like?' The trouble was he did not want her going home with him. He had decided not to use the car that day, knowing that he might drink rather too much, but he would have sobered up by the time he reached home.

'Lovely,' she replied. 'Ta very much. Where do you live then?'

'Oh ... the other end of town. It's too far for you to walk. Shall I meet you somewhere, in half an hour, say?'

'That suits me fine,' replied Babs, to his relief. 'I'll have to pop home and get a warmer coat anyway. It's turned really chilly, hasn't it? I only live round the corner. So I'll see you back here, shall I, in half an hour?'

'I'll look forward to it,' said Derek. 'See you later then.'

He walked off jauntily, feeling very pleased with himself, but his footsteps slowed a little when he realised just what he was doing. Supposing Rachel was already at home? It was not likely, but if she was, then this little assignation would be stopped before it had even started.

But Rachel was not at home. He drove away, hoping that none of the neighbours had seen him; he would pretend to Rachel that he had had the car with him all day. And if Babs had thought better of it and didn't turn up ... well, he would just put it down to experience.

She was there, however, half an hour later, looking very

43

pleased to see him, in a cherry-red coat and a red, white and blue headscarf to keep the wind off her hair. She whipped it off as soon as she got into the car.

'I was afraid you might have had second thoughts,' she said, grinning at him.

'What, me?' he replied. 'Not on your life.' He squeezed her hand. 'Now, where shall we go?'

Chapter 3

Lorna was six months old when Rachel returned to her teaching post at Kilbeck Infant School. Her working day started early, before seven o'clock, although it was usually some forty minutes or so later that Derek rolled out of bed. She didn't mind because it meant that she was able to get on with her morning activities – bathing and dressing Lorna and giving her her bottle, then making the breakfast – in peace. Breakfast was just cereal and toast and she had usually finished hers before Derek, often bleary-eyed, put in an appearance.

To her amazement, however, he had actually agreed – no, he had done more than agree, he had offered – to wash up in the mornings, knowing that she had to leave the house quite a while before he did. She wheeled Lorna round to her parents' home before catching the bus at eight-thirty to take her to school. Whittakers Mill was in a different direction, so it was not feasible for Derek to give her a lift – not that he had ever suggested it.

They were jogging along reasonably well, though, she supposed. His offer to help with the breakfast pots did not extend to the evening meal as well, when there were often pans to be scrubbed and casserole dishes left to soak in the sink. She would sometimes prepare a casserole the night before, then heat it up in the oven in time for their evening meal.

Life was hectic at times, but on the whole she felt she was happier than she had been when she was at home, alone, with baby Lorna. She was not sure whether she was really getting along any better with Derek, or whether she was so preoccupied that she scarcely had time to consider the state of their marriage. She did feel, however, that he was more agreeable, and that this amiability seemed to date from Coronation Day.

He had arrived home that day at around nine o'clock in the evening, saying that he and Charlie and a couple of other lads had decided to make a day of it, and he hoped she didn't mind too much. That, in itself, had puzzled her. When had he ever cared about what she thought? They had driven out towards Skipton, he had told her, and had had a meal in a country pub. He had even suggested that he and she should do the same sometime, if they could get a baby-sitter, but so far they had not done so. There never seemed to be time, but at least he had made the offer.

She would have thought no more about the happenings of Coronation Day had she not happened to meet Marlene Fleming, Charlie's wife, in Melcaster one Saturday afternoon. After they had duly admired one another's children – Jeremy was a grand little lad, fifteen months old and already toddling and trying to talk – they had casually mentioned their husbands.

'It sounds as though the lads had a good time on Coronation Day,' said Rachel. 'I know Derek was full of it when he came home; the slap-up meal they'd had and everything. "It's all right for some!" I told him.' She laughed. 'What do you say, Marlene?'

'What? Oh yes, I suppose so. Charlie didn't mention any meal, actually. He was back home at four o'clock, from what I can remember; it's quite a while ago.'

Rachel opened her mouth to reply, then she thought better of it. What did it matter anyway? She was only making conversation with a young woman she didn't really know all that well. As Jeremy was growing restless they parted company, but Rachel was thoughtful. She was sure Derek had said that Charlie was with him when they went for that meal . . . or maybe she had just assumed he was there? He had said there were a few other lads as well. Maybe Charlie had not been one of them; according to his wife he had been at home.

Anyway, it was not worth making a fuss about. Rachel was only thankful that her life – her married life, that was – was reasonably peaceful, if not exciting. She and Derek each pursued their own interests, but she supposed that that was the way it was when you had a child and could not go out together. Derek still went out a couple of nights a week with Charlie. Or so he told her, and she had never thought to doubt him.

As for her, Rachel, she was grateful for the companionship of the staff at school. Apart from that, the only adult company she enjoyed was that of the Young Wives' Group at St Matthew's church.

She had attended St Matthew's ever since she was a little girl, going through the Sunday school, youth club, confirmation at fourteen, regular attendance at Sunday services and, finally, membership of the Young Wives' Group.

Rachel sometimes wondered why she went along so regularly, hardly ever missing a meeting. She knew, though, that if it were not for her good friend, Pauline Jeffreys, who was also a member, she probably would not bother to go at all. Pauline, at thirty-five, was one of the oldest of the young wives; she was also a colleague of Rachel's at Kilbeck Infant School. The name of the group was, in truth, a misnomer as there were a few single ladies as well amongst their number. That had been the idea of the vicar's wife as she, like her husband, the Reverend Michael Laycock, did not want anyone to feel neglected. Kathleen Laycock, however, did not attend the meetings herself. At fifty she considered herself to be no longer eligible as a young wife. But Rachel often thought, as she sat listening to the chatter at the end of the meeting, that the poor woman's ears must be burning.

The leader of the group was Judith Prendergast, the wife

of the lay reader, Nathan, who took over the pulpit every few weeks and often assisted at Sunday services.

The Young Wives' Group meeting, on that Wednesday evening in October, had followed the same pattern as usual. An opening hymn, accompanied very loudly and confidently on the piano by Norma Shuttleworth, an unmarried member of the group who, nonetheless, had plenty to say for herself; prayers, led by Judith; then a time of silence in which members could express their own prayers. 'Out loud if you will, but within your hearts if you prefer it,' Judith never failed to remind them. Rachel always had the feeling, though, that if you did not pluck up the courage to pray out loud – something she never did – then you were, somehow, inadequate. She did pray in those silences, but only for her own concerns – for her husband and little daughter – but she was sure God could hear her.

Judith had given the talk, too, that evening, although they sometimes had a visiting speaker or a discussion. She had spoken authoritatively about the Power of the Holy Spirit in One's Life, mainly, it seemed, in her own. Judith never doubted that she was right and her often blunt pronouncements were always prompted, she would say, by the Spirit working within her.

They were obsessed with sin. Rachel sometimes felt when listening to Judith and her cronies going on about the wickedness in the world – and, moreover, at the heart of every man and woman – that there was little to choose between her, Rachel Watkins, and Adolf Hitler! Now he had been a truly evil man, and so had John Reginald Christie who had only recently been hanged for the appalling murders at 10 Rillington Place in London. But Rachel believed there were far more good people than bad in the world. Great Britain, with the young Queen Elizabeth on the throne – and with Winston Churchill at the helm again – was entering into an era full of hope and optimism, a new Elizabethan age. Everest had been conquered, and, nearer to home and of more importance to thousands of youngsters, sweet rationing had at long last come to an end! The government had announced that income tax had been cut and the programme of house building was approaching record levels. Surely it was a time to look on the bright side?

It seemed to Rachel that her own greatest sin, according to these crusaders from the Young Wives' Group, lay in leaving her baby daughter with her mother whilst she went out to work to earn more money. For that, it would appear, was a grievous sin; to lay up treasure on earth instead of looking towards the rewards of heaven.

The two women whose turn it was on the tea rota poured out the dark brown brew – always far too strong – from the enamel pot and the dozen or so young wives gathered round to collect their cup and saucer and a biscuit.

'Custard creams!' remarked Pauline, Rachel's friend. 'My, my! We are pushing the boat out tonight, aren't we? You never know, we might even have choccy biccies one of these days.'

'I doubt it,' said Rachel. 'They'd make a mess in the saucer.' She surreptitiously added a little more milk to her cup, hoping that she was not being watched. Such an action might be considered extravagant.

They sat down, balancing their cups and saucers on their laps. They were joined almost at once by Judith and her great friend and ally, Miriam Curtis. These two women were both in their early thirties, several years older than Rachel, but a couple of years younger than Pauline. It was difficult, however, to guess their ages if you did not know. They both dressed in a decidedly middle-aged manner – tweed coats, brogue-type shoes, and felt hats pulled down over their foreheads and ears, which they did not take off during the meetings. Judith's hair was an attractive shade of auburn, but it was rarely seen – only on the hottest of summer days, and even then it would be pulled back in an unfashionable bun. Miriam was dark-haired, already greying at the temples, as one could see from the wispy bits poking out. Both women had shining faces, devoid of make-up, rosy cheeks, and, it had to be admitted, glowing smiles and cheerful voices.

'And how is that dear little baby of yours?' asked Judith, leaning towards Rachel and staring into her face in a way that she always found discomfiting. 'Let me see. How old is she now?'

'She's seven months old,' replied Rachel. 'She's doing very nicely, thank you. She's just cut her first two teeth, so that made her rather niggly for a while, but she's all smiles again now.'

'Aah . . . lovely!' cooed Judith. 'Yes, they are lovely at that age, aren't they? I don't know how you can bear to leave her, Rachel, the way you do, day after day. She is still with your mother, is she?'

'Yes, she is,' answered Rachel, knowing she sounded curt, but then she intended to. It was not the first time she and Judith had had this sort of conversation. 'She's just fine with my mother. And Mum is very pleased to be able to help; so is my dad. They think the world of little Lorna.'

'Of course they do,' said Judith, her voice as syrupy sweet as her smile. 'But little Lorna may grow up wondering who she belongs to, if you're not careful.'

'Yes, and if you don't mind me saying so, you are missing so much, my dear,' broke in Miriam. She too was smiling sweetly and looking at Rachel in a sorrowful way. 'They are not babies for long. Before you know it they are walking and talking, then they're off to school, and you feel as though you've lost them. I know I wouldn't have wanted to miss so much as a day with my two.'

'Nor me,' said Judith. 'I've only the one, of course, but I scarcely let her out of my sight until she went to school.'

'I don't feel I am missing out on anything,' Rachel said, sounding far more convincing than she was feeling. She did, in truth, wish at times that she could spend her days at home with Lorna, but she would certainly never admit it to these two busy-bodies. 'I'm home quite early in the afternoon. Lorna and I have a few hours together before Derek comes home.'

'Yes, of course. Teachers work such short hours, don't they?' remarked Judith. 'And then there are the very long holidays.'

Pauline cut in. 'Rachel is working damned hard . . . I mean extremely hard,' she corrected herself, realising from the look of horror on the faces of both Judith and Miriam that even the mildest of profanities was inexcusable in the church vestry. 'I should know because I work along with her. The children at school love her, and I believe it makes you a far more interesting person when you have a job outside the home. Anyway, I don't see why Rachel should have to justify herself to you or to anybody.'

'Why indeed?' replied Judith calmly. 'But what we say, both Miriam and I, we only say out of Christian love. Now, if you will excuse me, I must go and have a word with Norma about the hymns for Sunday. Nathan is preaching and she is deputising on the organ while Paul is on holiday. So nice to talk to you both.' She graciously inclined her head towards the two of them as she stood up, then Miriam moved with her to the other end of the room.

Rachel and Pauline looked at one another and then burst out laughing, but very quietly. 'Well, that's one Sunday morning service I shall be avoiding,' said Pauline. 'Nathan Prendergast in the pulpit breathing fire and brimstone, and Norma Shuttleworth knocking eight bells out of the organ. No, ta very much; I shall have a lie-in.'

'Honestly, Pauline, you are dreadful! It does me a power of good, though, to be with you.'

'Well, thank you. I enjoy your company as well, you know. And it's a change to get away from a husband and two kids who are telly mad! Come on, we'd best go and join the others. They'll think we're being snooty, sitting here all on our owny-own.'

When the meeting was finished, Pauline offered to run Rachel home. She had her own Morris Minor which she used for school and for generally dodging around. 'You should learn to drive, Rachel. It would save you such a lot of time and trouble.'

'We can't afford another car,' said Rachel, climbing into the front seat. 'We've only got one because Derek's been given it for his work. It's not really ours.'

After thinking for a moment Rachel continued, 'I suppose they're right in some ways, those two women. Sometimes we do set too much store by material possessions, don't we? And human relationships are so much more important.'

'Sure,' replied Pauline. 'Hey, lighten up a bit, will you? Don't let those two miseries get you down.'

'Sorry,' said Rachel. 'They make me think sometimes, that's all.'

'Well, all too soon it will be time to think about blowing the whistle in the playground,' said Pauline, stopping the car outside her friend's home. 'Oh hell! I'm on playground duty tomorrow.'

'And I'm on dinner duty. Yuck!' added Rachel. 'It's the bane of my life, dinner duty. Thanks for the lift, Pauline. See you tomorrow.'

'Yes, see you, Rachel. Goodnight, love.'

'Did your Rachel say anything last week?' asked Charlie, as he and Derek supped a Sunday pint in the Coach and Horses.

It was a mild day in early October and as Derek had walked the half-mile or so from his home to meet his pal he had felt that all was well with his world. He was, in fact, enjoying the best of both worlds. He was not normally affected by the beauties of the scene around him, but the low sun glinting through the autumn leaves, and the carpet of gold, russet and orange scrunching below his feet caused even his phlegmatic soul to stir a little. He had enjoyed his hour with Lorna whilst Rachel was at church. She smiled and chuckled for him now, and he often wondered how he had managed to father such an enchanting little girl. She had a lot of her mother in her as well, of course; she was the image of Rachel, a fact that was often commented upon. He felt a little peeved at that. She was his child, too, but no one would think so the way people cooed and gushed and said, 'Isn't she the image of her mummy? And her gran as well.'

Derek did not like that at all. He did not want the child growing up resembling that old battle-axe, Lizzie Harding. Lorna was spending far too much time with his mother-in-law for his liking. Of course he knew that that was inevitable at the moment. Rachel was always reminding him that they owed a great deal to her mother. If it wasn't for her they wouldn't be able to save up for a house of their own. He couldn't wait for that day, and if it was up to him they would move as far away as possible from the Hardings.

Life, on the whole, was not too bad though, and Rachel hadn't a clue what he was up to. He believed, in fact, that she was reaping the benefits of his friendship with Babs Ollerenshaw. He had certainly learned a trick or two from her, and Rachel, to his surprise, was proving to be a quick learner. Charlie's comment, therefore, gave him quite a turn.

'What d'you mean, did she say anything?' he queried. 'About what?' Charlie was looking steadily at him, a mite disapprovingly, he thought.

'It's obvious she didn't then. Marlene met Rachel in town – quite by accident, I mean – and Rachel said summat about the lads – that's you and me – having a good time on Coronation Day, enjoying a slap-up meal and all the rest of it. Of course Marlene had no more sense than to say that I'd come home at four o'clock and that I hadn't said owt about a meal.'

'Oh my God! Why hasn't she said anything? She didn't even tell me she'd seen Marlene. I did say, though, at the time, that there were several of us there that night. Happen she thought she'd got it wrong about you being there.'

'If you ask me, mate, you've had a lucky escape there. Are you still seeing that bird? What was she called? Babs?'

'Ollerenshaw. Aye, I'm still seeing her, Tuesday nights. I thought you knew.'

'I guessed summat o' the sort when you stopped going out wi' me on Tuesdays. But I never asked. Ask no questions and you'll be told no lies, that's my motto. It's yer own affair, I suppose, but you'd best watch out.'

'You wouldn't say anything, would you? To Marlene, I mean. You haven't told her already, have you?'

'No, I know when to keep shtoom. I won't land you in it, though I may not approve of what you're doing.'

'Aw hell! It's only a bit of fun.'

'And does she know that, this Babs Ollerenshaw?'

Derek shrugged. 'I reckon so . . .'

'She knows you're married, like?'

'Aye, I had to tell her in the end. She'd guessed anyroad.'

'You're a bloody fool, you know. Your Rachel's a grand lass, and far too trusting if you ask me. And you don't want to do anything to lose that babby of yours, do you?'

'Of course I don't! I won't. Look, mate, you keep that out of it.' He tapped the side of his nose. 'Like you say, ask no questions and you'll be told no lies. It would be a shame to spoil our friendship, wouldn't it?'

'If you say so. Same again? P'raps it'd better be a half, though. I promised Marlene I'd be back by half past one.'

'Yeah, same here. Thanks, Charlie.' But Charlie's curt nod told him that his friend's disapproval went quite deep. He didn't think for one moment that he would let him down, but he knew he would have to watch his step.

Rachel sometimes had doubts about whether or not she had done the right thing in returning to work, although she would never admit to this; not to Derek, nor to her mother, and certainly not to the nosey parkers in the Young Wives' Group. The only person she would dream of confiding in was Pauline Jeffreys.

The two of them had become firm friends despite the difference in their ages. Pauline was over ten years older than Rachel, pleasant and plumpish, with dark hair in springy sausage-like curls which complemented her round face. She presented a comfortable and motherly image, ideally suited to the reception class which she taught. She was married to Trevor who worked as an insurance agent in Melcaster and the surrounding area. They had two children, Brian aged thirteen and twelve-year-old Sarah. It was a happy marriage, although, as Pauline said, they never exactly set the Thames (or, more aptly, the Aire) on fire. Unlike Rachel, she had not returned to teaching until her children were of school age, but she would hear no criticism of her friend for the decision she had made.

They sat together in Rachel's classroom one afternoon in late October, a few weeks after the Young Wives' Group meeting at which Rachel had come under fire. They were eating sandwiches they had brought from home as neither of them was on dinner duty that day. It was a peaceful change from the din they had to endure in the dining hall.

'I don't know why you take any notice of them at all,' Pauline was saying. 'Personally, I'm sick of them and their "holier than thou" attitude towards everything and every-body. No one is suffering because you are back at work, certainly not your Lorna, and she's the most important person, isn't she? She's as happy as a sandboy, whatever that is. She's a little love, and your mother obviously adores her.'

'Yes, I know she does,' Rachel replied. 'That's what worries me, rather. And Lorna loves her gran; I can tell she does. Her little face lights up when she sets eyes on her, and she stretches out her little arms to be picked up.'

'But she does the same when she sees you, doesn't she? When you get home at teatime I'm sure she's delighted to see you, isn't she?'

'Well . . . yes, of course she is. And it's then that I hug her so close to me and I wonder sometimes how I can possibly do this, go out to work and leave her. I don't want her growing up loving my mother more than she loves me. That's what I'm really afraid of, Pauline. And listening to Judith and Miriam that night . . . well, it made me feel really guilty.'

'Then you stop feeling guilty right now! Do you hear me? That's what they want you to do. Anyway, it's half-term next week, so you'll have three whole days with your little daughter. And there are the weekends, aren't there? You have her all to yourself then. Besides, you're doing a worthwhile job here and don't you forget it.' Pauline's eyes strayed round the colourful classroom and Rachel's did the same.

'You've answered the government's plea to come back and teach the "baby boomers", so that's something to be proud of, isn't it?' These were the children born in the late forties, during the post-war bulge in the birth rate, who were now in infant schools throughout the country. Classes were large, and it was no mean feat for Rachel, and for Pauline, too, to cope with forty or more five- or six-year-olds and then go home to deal with the demands of a family.

Rachel was proud of her classroom. She loved teaching and she enjoyed – almost – every minute of it, apart from dinner duty, which she regarded as an imposition on teachers who had already been working all morning and then were forced to forgo their lunch break. A bright autumn frieze covered a section of the wall, adorned with multi-coloured leaves, squirrels, hedgehogs and shaggy chrysanthemum flowers, coloured and cut out by enthusiastic six-year-olds. There was also a composite picture of witches, black cats, cobwebs, flying bats and large golden pumpkins, in preparation for Hallowe'en. The nature table was gay with twigs bearing hips and haws, the last vestige of the early autumn, purple Michaelmas daisies, and dahlias in jewel-bright colours of red, orange and yellow. There was a pile of conkers, another of acorns, and a scattering of sycamore seeds with wings. The children of the area were very attuned to the changing of the seasons.

From her classroom window Rachel could see the hills, brown now with bracken and the dying heather which, in the summertime, had been a blaze of purple. Here and there were outcrops of rock – limestone overlaid with the darker millstone grit. A view of grandeur and awesomeness which gladdened her heart. How blessed she was, she thought, to live in such a place. When she and Derek were able to afford their own home she hoped she might be able to persuade him to live nearer to the hills. A house with such a view would be worth striving for.

The bell, signalling the end of the lunch hour, brought their little tête-à-tête to an end. 'Another day, another dollar,' remarked Pauline, standing up and throwing her sandwich papers into the waste bin. 'Half-day, I should say. Another three hours and you'll be back with your little Lorna again. That's not so bad, is it?'

Rachel smiled. She always looked forward to seeing her little daughter again at the end of the day. But in the meantime there were her other children, all forty of them, waiting in line in the yard to be summoned in by their teacher. She knew, whilst they were in school, she was in loco parentis and they deserved the very best she had to give. She would expect the same of Lorna's teacher when she was old enough to start school.

Chapter 4

It did not take as long as Rachel had expected for them to save up enough money for a deposit for their own house. She banked her salary cheque systematically each month in their joint account and it was surprising how quickly it grew. She was a thrifty young woman and had spent very little of her wages, having been encouraged by her mother, ever since she was a little girl, not to be wasteful or too extravagant.

Towards the end of 1954 she and Derek had saved a large enough sum for a deposit on a small house. They had been helped a little by Derek's parents. He was the only son, just as Rachel was the only daughter, and they wanted to do what they could to help the young people.

Mr and Mrs Watkins senior were a quiet, unassuming couple. They, too, attended St Matthew's church, but until the marriage of their respective offspring the Hardings and the Watkinses had not known one another very well, only to nod and to say hello to. They met quite regularly now, at least the two women did, at such events as Mothers' Union meetings and whist drives, but Rachel feared that her timid little mother-in-law, of whom she was quite fond, was over-shadowed by the far more dominant Lizzie.

The house that Derek and Rachel decided upon – and strangely enough, there had been little, if any, discord between them – was not a newly built one. Derek had realised that Coronation Close, on which he had formerly set his sights, was beyond their reach. They knew that their choice, ultimately, would depend on what they could afford, rather than what they would have chosen if money were no object. They visited several properties in and around Melcaster. Rachel found, to her surprise, that their house-hunting excursions, on which they were usually accompanied by eighteen-month-old Lorna, were quite pleasant outings. She and Derek seemed to be more in accord than they had been since the early days of their marriage. She did not allow herself to be too deceived, however, by his seeming change of heart. She knew that what was motivating him was his desire to be a householder, rather than a tenant of rented property, although, considering the large mortgage they were forced to agree to, they would, in effect, own only a few bricks – or stones – of the property.

But they were to own it jointly; both their names were to be on the mortgage agreement and this, in Rachel's view, was a great achievement. She had heeded her mother's constant advice that she must insist on joint ownership and Derek, albeit a trifle reluctantly, had agreed. It was made clear to them, however, that Rachel's salary, although it equalled that of her husband, was of no importance whatsoever. The husband's wage was the only one that counted when seeking a mortgage. She had found it hard to hold her tongue at this pronouncement by the building-society rep, especially when she noticed Derek's self-satisfied smirk and his 'I told you so' glance at her. But she had nodded in acquiescence. The purchase of this house was important to both of them.

Neither was she deceived by Derek's speedy decision that this little house was the one for them, even though it dated from the early years of the century, a far cry from the modern semis he had at one time admired. Rachel liked the house too – the moment she set foot inside she had a feeling that this was right – but she was aware that Derek had made a snap decision because, of all the houses they had seen, this one was the furthest away from her parents' home. The fact that it was near to Kilbeck Infant School would, she knew, cut little ice with him, but that was important to Rachel. Also

– and this was probably the deciding factor from her point of view – from the front windows of the house there was an uninterrupted view of the Pennine Hills.

It was the end one of a terrace of four greystone houses, with a small garden to the front and a larger one, with a lawn and trees, to the rear. The living area was what was some-times called a 'through room' or a 'sunshine room', which Rachel thought was preferable to two poky little rooms, one of which would never be used except at Christmastime or for special visitors. The kitchen was minute, but outside the back door there was a small wash-house and a coal shed. Upstairs there were three bedrooms, the smallest one being little more than a boxroom, but they were fortunate in having an indoor lavatory, a luxury not always found in houses of that period. Admittedly, there was very little room for manoeuvre – the bath, washbasin and toilet took up all but a few square feet of the room.

The house was, in fact, not very different from the rented house they were leaving, but Rachel did not remark on this to Derek. It was sufficient for her that, for once, they seemed to be in agreement. In perfect harmony, she might have been tempted to think, but she knew it was only the acquisition of the house that had brought them closer together. He still pursued his own interests – his nights out with the lads – twice, sometimes three times, a week, whilst she pursued hers, such as they were – church activities or PTFA functions at school. She and Derek still had not been out together for an evening, as she recalled he had once suggested.

They moved into number one, Hillview Terrace, very aptly named, in the middle of December. It was not an ideal time for Rachel as she was up to her eyes in the Christmas preparations which went on in all infant schools at that time of the year. However, her very obliging headmistress, Miss Lacey, allowed her to take a day's leave, even taking charge of the class herself, and Derek planned his travels to fit in with the removal.

Lorna, as usual, was with her maternal grandparents on moving day, but Mrs Watkins, Derek's mother, arrived in the late morning when the removal men had departed, to see if she could lend a hand. Dozens of boxes and tea chests filled the small hallway and were taking up a goodly space in the living room and bedrooms. Rachel had carefully labelled them, so it was comparatively easy to carry the contents to the correct rooms, but she had not realised, until she started to pack up, just how much stuff they had accumulated during their comparatively short marriage.

Mrs Watkins proved to be a great help, quickly and deftly putting pots and pans, cutlery, crockery, bed linen and towels away into their appropriate cupboards and drawers, often without having to be told where to place them. She had even brought sandwiches for the three of them, plus a flask of coffee, in case the gas stove was not yet working. As it happened, it was, as the previous owners, to Rachel's relief, had left the cooker as well as the bedroom carpets, such as they were, and some light fittings.

Derek had made himself useful by laying and lighting a fire in the living room, a job at which he was quite competent, having spent a year or two in the Boy Scouts before doing his National Service. There was an adequate supply of coal in the coal shed, as well as a bundle of firewood, and there was very soon a satisfying blaze in the rustic stone-built hearth. Their red and grey carpet square from their previous home had been put down at one end of the room with the G-Plan settee and two armchairs, upholstered in red moquette, and the spindly-legged light-oak sideboard, matching table and dining chairs at the other end. These items, the ultimate in contemporary design, had been wedding presents from their respective parents. The carpet was not large enough to fill the room, but the wooden floorboards had already been stained with a dark varnish, and Rachel knew this would have to suffice until such time as they could afford the luxury of a fitted carpet.

Already the room was beginning to look comfy and lived-in. When the curtains had been hung at the windows it would look lovely, thought Rachel. She nodded contentedly to herself. Their very own house; she felt a warm glow of satisfaction as she looked around at all their possessions in their new environment.

'Shall I give you a hand with these curtains, dear?' asked her mother-in-law. 'We don't want the neighbours and the passers-by all noseying, do we?'

The little terrace, though, was very quiet. On the other side of the road was a field, enclosed by a drystone wall, wherein a few cattle were grazing, and in the adjoining field a solitary horse stood under an oak tree. There would be few passers-by, as this was the outer edge of Melcaster. She had wondered if Derek might consider it too lonely, too far away from civilisation, but he had not found any fault with the location. Melcaster was not a large town by any means, and the shops and amenities – including the church and the few pubs – although they were further away than they had been in their previous home, were still very little more than a mile away.

'Yes, thanks very much, er . . . Phyllis,' said Rachel, still a trifle diffident about using her mother-in-law's first name, as she had been requested to do. 'Great minds think alike, eh? I was just thinking to myself that the curtains will add the finishing touch to the room. The previous owners left the rails, so all I'll need to do is to hook the curtains on to the rings.'

'It's a tricky job,' replied Phyllis. 'Happen I'm a bit more used to it than you are. Goodness knows I've done it often enough. Would you like me to hang them, and you can pass them up to me one at a time?'

'Er . . . no. I'd never forgive myself if you fell off a chair, and neither would Derek's dad. You do the handing up and I'll do the fixing. It's so good of you to come and help us. We do appreciate it.'

'A little help's worth a lot of pity. Righty-ho then, let's get started. Haven't you got a step-ladder rather than a chair?'

'Yes, we have actually, a pair of steps. I think Derek's put them in the wash-house.'

'Where is that lad of mine, anyroad? Derek!' Phyllis shouted, a remarkably loud shout for such a small woman. 'Derek, where are you? Go and fetch the steps for Rachel, and we'd be glad of a bit of help down here an' all.'

Derek came quickly at his mother's bidding. Rachel had noticed before that he was an obedient son who did not like to be out of his mother's good books for long.

'I'm not exactly twiddling me thumbs, Mam,' he replied, smiling at her. His blue eyes were exactly like his mother's, but that was the only resemblance that Rachel could see. He was of a stocky build with wiry, sandy-coloured hair, like his father's, whereas Phyllis was small and had once been dark-haired until she had turned prematurely grey. 'I was putting me clothes away in t' wardrobe. We want to get ship-shape as soon as poss, don't we, Rachel love?'

He smiled at her quite affectionately. He was good at putting on an act when his parents – or hers – were there, but whether they were deceived into thinking that everything in the garden was rosy she did not know. Her own mother, certainly, had Derek weighed up. To give him the benefit of the doubt, however, he did seem to have turned over a new leaf whilst they had been planning the move.

'Ne'er mind that now,' said Phyllis. 'Go and fetch them steps, there's a good lad ... You and our Derek, you're getting on OK, are you?' she asked in a quiet voice as Derek went out of the back door. 'I know he can be a bit – what shall I say? – abrupt, like. Doesn't always show his feelings. But that's a Yorkshireman for you; his dad's pretty much the same.'

'Yes, we're fine,' said Rachel promptly. 'He's thrilled to bits with the house. He doesn't enthuse overmuch, like you've just said, but I can tell he's pleased. Yes, we're ... very happy.' She was not sure whether that was true or not, but one thing she would not do was complain about her husband, not to her own mother and certainly not to Derek's.

'Good,' said Phyllis. 'I'm so pleased to hear that, dear. We've spoiled our Derek, I know we have, although I've always tried me best to make him toe the line. I'll admit we thought you were too young when you got wed, but you've made him a grand wife, you have that! He's a very lucky lad, is our Derek.'

'What's that you're saying, Mam?' Derek returned with the pair of step-ladders and opened them near to the front window. 'I thought me ears were burning.'

'I said you're a very lucky lad, having a good wife like Rachel, and I hope you realise it.'

'Of course I do.' He put an arm round Rachel's shoulders and gave her a quick hug. 'A good wife and a lovely little daughter. Yes, I'm a very lucky chap.' He glanced through the window as he spoke. 'Hey up! She's here, our little Lorna, and her gran. I thought it wouldn't be long before your mother arrived, Rachel. There's no show without Punch.'

'Derek! Don't be so rude!' exclaimed his mother.

'Only joking, Mam,' he replied, but Rachel could hear the edge to his voice which was always there whenever her mother came on to the scene. She put down the curtain she held in her hands and went to open the door.

'Mummy!' Lorna lifted her arms to be taken out of the pushchair, a sight that always warmed Rachel's heart. She looked enchanting, like a little bunny-rabbit in her all-in-one fluffy white suit with a pink lining to the hood.

Rachel picked her up and kissed her cold cheek. 'Hello, darling. Hello there, Mum. Your nana's here as well, Lorna. Isn't that exciting?'

To differentiate between the two sets of grandparents, Rachel's parents were known as Grandma and Grandad, and Derek's as Nana and Grandpa. Lorna, of necessity, spent more time with her grandma and grandad, but, as the first and very precious grandchild, she was loved and fussed over by all of them.

Work stopped for a few moments and Derek disappeared

into the kitchen to make a pot of tea. This was not something that he often volunteered to do, but Rachel knew he wanted to escape from the women's chatter. Lorna, divested of her outer clothing, played on the carpet with the few toys that Rachel had unpacked.

'We'll have to decide what we're going to do about our little pancake,' said Lizzie Harding. 'Have you made up your mind, yet, Rachel? You know that your dad and I are quite willing to come here to look after her. It's silly you having to trail to the other end of town and back again every day. I had my doubts when you chose this house,' she gave a slight shrug, 'but it's your decision, of course.'

'No,' said Rachel firmly. 'I don't think it's a good idea for you to come here, thanks all the same, Mum. It's asking too much of you and Dad.' Derek had been adamant that he did not want his mother-in-law coming and taking control of his house each day, even if she did happen to be looking after his daughter. But even he could see that Rachel could not be to-ing and fro-ing with the child, and so he had made what was for him a magnanimous offer. He would take Lorna to her grandparents' house each morning before he started on his travels. This was what Rachel now told her mother.

'Oh ... oh well, yes ... That's very good of you, Derek,' Lizzie said as he entered the room with a laden tray. She looked a mite put out, but obviously she could not refuse the offer. 'What about the other end of the day, though, when Rachel finishes work?'

'I'll pick Lorna up again,' said Derek briefly, 'on me way back. And if I know I'm going to be late ... well, we'll have to come to some other arrangement, won't we?'

'Jack and I have been wondering if we could take our turn with Lorna,' said Phyllis, somewhat tentatively. 'I know Jack's working, but I'm at home all day and I'd love to have her, say once or twice a week? What do you think, Lizzie? At the moment it's all falling on you, isn't it?'

'And we don't mind a bit, do we, my little pancake?' said

Lizzie, reaching out and stroking the little girl's wispy golden hair.

'Mum, please don't call her that,' said Rachel quietly. 'She's not a baby now.'

'Oh, pardon me. I'm sorry, I'm sure!' Lizzie sounded quite peeved. 'It seems I can't do right for doing wrong sometimes. But she'll always be my little pancake to me. I'll never forget that day she was born. Yes, Phyllis, I think that's quite a good idea, for you to look after Lorna . . . occasionally. But it isn't as if you don't see her, is it? I bring her to the whist drives and the Mothers' Union meetings, don't I, if Percy is busy? And don't the ladies make a fuss of her! You should see them, Rachel. She's getting to be quite our little mascot.'

'Yes, I can well imagine it, Mum,' said Rachel drily. 'But I don't want her spoiling.'

'She isn't,' said Lizzie, sounding quite curt. 'I can't stand spoiled children, you know that, Rachel. You were never spoiled, not like some I could mention,' her unspoken words spoke volumes, 'and neither will our Lorna be.'

'Thank you for the offer, Phyllis,' said Rachel, ignoring her mother for the moment and turning pointedly to her mother-in-law. 'I think it's a great idea for you to have Lorna a couple of times a week. It would be a nice change for her. Now, when we've had our tea we'd better get these curtains up. We were just going to do them, weren't we, Phyllis, before we were interrupted?'

'Well, I like that!' retorted Lizzie. 'Interrupted indeed! I was only bringing your daughter home. I thought you'd be pleased to see her . . . and me.'

'Of course I am,' replied Rachel. 'Don't be so touchy, Mum. Look, if you want to make yourself useful, and I'm sure you do, you can help Phyllis to put up these curtains. These two are for the front windows, and the other two for the back, OK? And I'll go and wash these pots and get things sorted out in the kitchen.'

'Very well, dear,' Lizzie sniffed in a wounded manner. 'Whatever you say.'

'What's up with her?' asked Derek, following his wife into the kitchen. 'She's got it on her today, hasn't she? Talk about po-faced; she's even worse than usual.'

'Give over, Derek. She's not usually like this.' Rachel knew, though, what was the matter with her mother. She loved to be in charge, and would not like the idea of the other grandmother taking care of Lorna, even for a short while. 'You'll have to try and be nice to her – try very hard, Derek – especially as you'll be seeing her most mornings.'

'Yeah, perish the thought. OK, OK, I'll be as nice as pie, I promise. I wish they'd go home, though, and leave us on our own.'

Rachel experienced an upsurge of real contentment after their mothers had departed and they were left alone with little Lorna. There was still quite a lot of unpacking to do, but as they had chosen to move on a Friday the whole weekend lay ahead of them.

She was astounded when Derek followed her into the kitchen to help her prepare their evening meal. Lorna had already had her tea and had then been bathed and put to bed. The little girl had stared round in surprise at her new bedroom. It was rather stark and bare at the moment, with plain blue walls which presented a chilly aspect, and a carpet that had seen better days. She was cosy enough, though, in her cot and she snuggled down happily beneath her fluffy pink blankets with Mister Ted, her favourite toy, held close to her. Rachel was looking forward to decorating that room. She had seen some attractive wallpaper with a design of nursery-rhyme characters; three pink walls, she envisaged, and one boldly patterned one which Lorna could view from her cot.

They had a quickly prepared meal that evening of bacon, sausage and eggs, which Rachel had brought with her from their previous home, with chips and thickly cut slices of bread and butter. Doorsteps, Rachel laughingly told her husband, as it was he who had cut them, inexpertly and unevenly, but at least he was helping.

She would need to go shopping the next day in Melcaster to stock up their larder and food cupboard. There was a little corner shop near to the school which was handy for every-day items; she would be able to pop in on her way home during the week. But her main shop was always done at the Co-op, where she had the added advantage of the 'divvy'. Little strips of paper were stuck into your book every time you bought something, and then you were given a percent-age of the dividend at the end of the year. That time was approaching now, and Rachel hoped there would be enough to pay for the Christmas chicken and maybe a plum pudding as well.

'Derek, do you know what we could really do with?' she said, as they tucked into their meal.

'No, tell me,' he mumbled with his mouth full of bacon and egg, which she chose to ignore.

'A refrigerator,' she replied, 'then I wouldn't need to shop nearly every day for fresh food. This bacon, for instance; it's OK, but if we'd kept it another day it would have gone off a bit.'

'Can't say I've noticed,' said Derek. 'It tastes all right to me.' He had smothered it, of course, as he always did, with a copious amount of HP sauce, traces of which now adhered to his chin and lips. 'What d'you want a fridge for, anyroad? It's real brass-monkey weather in Yorkshire, in the winter at any rate. You'll have to wait till I come up on t' pools for that, luv.'

'Yes, I know, I know. I just thought it would be a good idea. But the pantry's cold enough, I suppose.'

There was a stone slab in the pantry, as there had been in their previous house, where perishable foods, such as milk, butter and meat products, were kept, and meat was always covered with a wire mesh to keep the flies off.

'Ne'er mind yer fridge. It'd be better to get a washing machine, wouldn't it?' said Derek, to Rachel's amazement. 'Now that's what I'd call hard graft, doing the weekly wash.'

'Well, fancy that! I've never known you to have anything to

do with it. Hard graft, indeed! You usually keep well out of the way.'

'Well, yeah, happen I do. It's women's work, i'n't it? But I know how me mam used to slave away every Monday. I remember the dolly tub and t' posser and t' mangle. When I came home from school at dinner-time she'd still be at it. Then we'd have damp washing hanging all over t' show if it were raining and she couldn't peg it out.'

'And it's not so much different now,' said Rachel. 'Yes, I think I'll hold you to that, Derek. A washing machine would be grand.'

'Oh crikey!' he grinned. 'What have I started now?'

'Don't worry. We've got our house.' All they had to do was pay the mortgage each month, but she did not mention that. 'If I save up my next few salary cheques we should be able to afford a washing machine; just a small one. I think they have an electrically powered wringer attached to them.'

She smiled, contemplating how much easier washing day would be. She usually washed on a Saturday, when she was off from school, although it was, admittedly, not such a hard task to her as it had been to women a generation before. She sent her sheets to the laundry, on her mother's advice – Lizzie did the same – and she had a small boiler, instead of a dolly tub, to bring the water to the required temperature, and a smaller mangle than the great cumbersome appliances owned by her mother and mother-in-law.

'Hey, stop yer daydreaming,' quipped her husband. 'There's more to think about than bloody washing machines. Far more important things. We'll have an early night, shall we, luv?'

She smiled at him. 'Yes, that would be nice.'

He dried the pots after she had washed them and then they sat and listened to the radio for a while, both of them feeling too jaded to do any more unpacking that night.

'I'll see to t' fire,' said Derek at ten o'clock. 'You go up and warm the bed.' He winked at her and she grinned back at him. This was a vastly changed Derek, or so it seemed. She was tired, but she knew she must not say so or complain of a headache tonight. Perhaps she was being given a chance to get their marriage back on the right track, once and for all.

The fire needed to be damped down to ensure there were no remaining embers and the fireguard put round it. This was usually in place, anyway, to protect Lorna. It was chilly upstairs, but Rachel was used to that. She quickly washed her hands and face, undressed and scrambled into bed. She had had the forethought to put in a hot-water bottle so it was at least warmed.

Derek soon joined her. He was a man of few words. Hardly ever did he tell her that he loved her, but that night, as they came together, he did mutter the words, 'Love you, Rachel.'

'Love you too, Derek,' she replied softly.

They had had a few problems in that direction when they were first married, neither of them being experienced in sexual matters. She had wondered whether Derek might have had one or two relationships with girls whilst he was in the army, although he had, of course, never admitted to them. She had come to the conclusion that, most probably, he hadn't. He had seemed as naïve and inexpert as she was, and at first she had wondered what it was all about, this act of love which was supposed to start bells ringing and transport you to a seventh heaven of delight. To her it had been largely a matter of trial and error. Or maybe she was one of those women to whom it would always be a necessary evil, a part of marriage that one was forced to endure. She knew it was so to some women, but she had hoped she might be different.

And then, suddenly, things had started to improve. Derek began to show an expertise that he had not had before. She had wondered, fleetingly, where he might have learned his technique. She guessed he might have been reading a sex manual, but she was too shy to ask. Or he might have been talking to the lads, but she hoped this was not so. At all events, their lovemaking improved, although their day-to-day living and their social life remained pretty much the same.

70

Now, however, Rachel was more hopeful. Derek seemed better in every way. She realised, a few weeks later, that it must have been on that first night in their new home that their second child was conceived.

Chapter 5

Rachel handed in her notice as soon as her pregnancy was confirmed. The baby was due in mid-September, so, if all went well, she should be able to continue teaching until the middle of May. This time she did not even consider applying for maternity leave, to safeguard herself in case anything should go wrong. With two young children it would be impossible for her to work anyway, and she certainly did not wish to do so. Even if – God forbid – she were to suffer a miscarriage, she knew she would not wish to return to school. Her teaching career, for several years at least, was at an end and she did not mind at all. With a toddler and a new baby to look after, she did not envisage she'd have any time to miss her job! She wanted to be able to spend more time with Lorna, who was growing up very quickly – almost two years old already – and with the new arrival. Boy or girl, it would be very welcome, and she was glad that Derek seemed pleased as well.

He, predictably, said he hoped it would be 'a little lad'; he did not relish the prospect of a house full of women.

'But you think the world of our little Lorna, don't you?' she asked him.

'Aye, of course I do,' he said, 'but enough's enough. All men want a lad, don't they? And we don't want any more after this 'un, do we?'

'No, I suppose not,' she replied. If that was to be the case, she began to hope, for his sake, that she would not disappoint him by having a girl.

Her mother greeted the news with delight, on the face of it, though tinged with a certain restraint. Rachel guessed she was loath to lose control of Lorna, who was, understandably, growing very attached to her grandmother. Rachel would not admit it to anyone, but she was glad that she would soon be able to take her daughter away from her mother's charge and look after her on her own.

For the moment, though, Rachel continued to enjoy her time at Kilbeck Infant School. Teaching, to her, was a true vocation and she knew that, in some ways, she would be sorry to leave, especially to say goodbye to the children in her class.

One child to whom Rachel had become particularly close was a little boy called Adam Blundell. He was a bright and intelligent child, but by no means a show-off; he was popular with the other children and very active in spontaneous games of football in the school yard. He was bonny, too, with warm brown eyes, glossy dark hair and a winning smile. She had met his parents at school functions and at open evenings, when parents came, unaccompanied by their children, to talk about their progress in class. She found them to be a very likeable and charming couple who both obviously doted upon their only child, but without spoiling him. Rachel thought that Mrs Blundell leaned to her husband for support, both physically and mentally; she appeared rather frail. She knew little about them at first – it was the children in one's charge who were important, not the parents – but teachers often reached their own conclusions. Maybe the woman's frailty was the reason they had only the one child, she pondered, although it was really none of her business, she rebuked herself. She knew it was a failing of teachers, sometimes, to be dreadfully nosey.

She was concerned, one day in early April, when Adam complained in class of feeling unwell. He was listless and said he had a headache and a stiff neck, so she took the precaution of contacting his mother who, fortunately, had a telephone. Mrs Blundell came quickly and took the child home.

'I'll give him a Fenning's powder and he can go straight to bed,' she said, not appearing unduly concerned. 'Children are up and down, aren't they? He'll be right as rain tomorrow, won't you, love?'

Rachel was not surprised, though, when the boy did not return to school. It was his father who appeared a few days later, at the end of the school day, with the disturbing news that Adam had been diagnosed with polio and had been admitted into hospital.

'Goodness knows how he has contracted it,' said his father. 'We are so very protective of him, Mary and I, although we do let him play out with the other lads in the street; we don't want him to grow up to be a softie, with him being the only one, I mean.' Rachel felt so very sorry for him. The poor man looked distraught; his brown eyes, so like his son's, were full of anguish. Adam, in fact, that dear little boy, was a smaller image of his father.

'Are there any more who have been taken ill,' he asked, 'in your class or in the school?'

'No, not so far,' said Rachel. 'I haven't heard of any.'

'No, they said at the hospital that it was an isolated case,' said Mr Blundell. 'That's what we can't understand. We went to Bridlington, though, the Easter weekend – my brother lives there – and Adam was playing on the beach with his cousins. It was cold and we didn't stay long, but there may have been a sewage pipe; one never knows . . .' He shook his head. 'We try to be so careful of him.'

'So . . . how is Adam?' said Rachel, hardly daring to ask. 'I mean . . . has it affected his limbs?'

'Yes, I'm afraid so. He is paralysed from the waist down at the moment. But he's having physiotherapy every day, all kinds of exercises. He's being very brave, poor little chap.' He looked away because his eyes were misting over. After a few seconds he had recovered himself. 'I wonder . . .' he said. 'Maybe I shouldn't ask – I realise that Adam is only one

74

of forty in your class – but do you think you could find time to go and see him in hospital? I know he would love to see you. He thinks the world of you,' he added with a quiet smile.

'Of course,' said Rachel, without hesitation. 'I would love to see Adam. Saturday afternoon, perhaps? Would that be convenient? I'm sure my mother will look after my little girl.'

'Oh, I didn't realise you had a child.' Mr Blundell looked surprised.

'Yes, Lorna's two years old. She stays with my mother while I'm at school. But I'm finishing teaching soon,' she added. She did not say why. The reason might well be obvious, but you did not start telling your life story to the father of one of your pupils. He nodded, then smiled at her a little sadly.

'Saturday afternoon will be great, Mrs Watkins. Thank you so much. I'll tell Adam. I know how much he'll look forward to seeing you.'

The children in the class were sorry to hear that Adam was poorly and in hospital, although Rachel did not go into details. Some of them seemed to know already, though, that he couldn't walk.

'He's got that there polio, hasn't he, Mrs Watkins?' said one of the more forward boys. 'Me mam says so; she's dead worried about it being catching.'

Rachel did not answer, as she might have done, that there was nothing to worry about. It was true that these children of the fifties were benefiting greatly from the new Welfare State which had been introduced in 1948. The recent advances in medicine and extensive immunisation programmes had led to a steady decline in the number of infant deaths. The traditional killer diseases – whooping cough, diphtheria, scarlet fever and measles – were all on the wane. There were regular medical inspections at schools, dental check-ups and eye examinations; the children of the fifties enjoyed much better health than their parents, and particularly their grandparents, had done in their infancy. The only scourge of the present day was poliomyelitis, a viral infection for which, at the moment, there was no known cure.

She diverted the children's minds from the dreaded illness by suggesting they should make 'get-well' cards for
Adam. This they did in the afternoon activity period, using
paint, crayons, or gummed paper, whichever they chose. The
results were bright and colourful and very varied, and the
following day several of the children brought little offerings
of bars of chocolate, packets of sweets or a single orange, for
Rachel to take with her to the hospital.

She took a large bunch of grapes and a box of Smarties,
and copies of the *Dandy* and *Beano* and *Film Fun* comics;
not highly educational, but much more welcome, she was
sure, than the school reading book, for a little boy ill in bed.

Mr and Mrs Blundell disappeared for a little while so that
she could have some time on her own with Adam. He
seemed shy at first, seeing his teacher out of her normal
environment, but he soon recovered. He really did not look
too bad, all things considered. His eyes shone with interest,
although he had lost the rosiness from his cheeks.

'I have to do loads of exercises, Mrs Watkins,' he told her.
'At least, the doctors and nurses do, 'cause I can't feel
anything, y'see. They move me legs up and down, and then
they put me in a big sort of tent thing with lots of electric
light bulbs to warm me legs. And I might have to have an
operation on me feet.' He looked a little apprehensive at that.
'But I'm going to learn to walk again, and to play football!
Matron says so, and me mum and dad.'

'I'm sure you will, Adam,' she told him, with a lump in her
throat and tears pricking at her eyes. 'You are being a very
brave boy.' She was sure if perseverance had anything to do
with it, then Adam would recover.

'You'll come and see me again, won't you, Mrs Watkins?'
he asked.

'Yes, of course I will,' she replied.

And so she did, a couple of times, before he was dis-
charged to continue the physiotherapy from home and,
maybe, to attend a special school. She knew that once she

finished teaching it would be more difficult to hear news of him, but she decided she would try to keep in touch. You were warned not to become too emotionally involved with pupils, but with a child like Adam that was not always possible.

The first few weeks after Rachel gave up work were difficult.

'Want Gran. Go and see Gran!' Lorna often demanded, becoming truculent if she did not get her own way. She had a habit of stiffening herself and holding her breath until she was red in the face, and Rachel had to give her a good shaking to make her stop. Lizzie had not spoiled her; there had been a kindly discipline in her dealings with her and the little girl had certainly not been given everything she wanted, which Rachel was glad about. Nevertheless, Lorna played one off against the other.

'Gran lets me,' she would say if, for instance, Rachel would not let her have a biscuit too near to dinner-time, or, 'I shall tell me gran!' if her mother had reason to be cross with her.

Bedtimes could be very trying. There was one night when Rachel was feeling particularly weary. Lorna had wanted Mister Ted in the bath with her, and Rachel had refused. His fur would not dry, she explained, then he would be cold and wet and unable to go to bed with her.

'Want Mister Ted, want Mister Ted,' Lorna had yelled, and there had been a few tears – crocodile ones – until Rachel had managed to distract her with the bubble bath and plastic ducks. However, Mister Ted had then to be changed out of his trousers and jumper and dressed, slowly and painstakingly, in his new pyjamas, made by Grandma from the same material as Lorna's nightie. Rachel tried to keep the lid on her impatience. She knew that the child was taking as long as possible in order to annoy her mother. Even at two years old she seemed fully aware of what she was doing.

Nonetheless, she looked like a little angel when she was tucked up in her cot with her teddy bear at her side.

'Goodnight, darling. God bless,' whispered Rachel when she had kissed her.

"Night, Mummy. Say night-night to Mister Ted.' She held the bear up for Rachel to kiss.

'Night-night, Mister Ted,' said Rachel.

She gave a sigh as she went downstairs. Derek had gone out that evening, with Charlie and some of the other lads, she supposed, although she had not enquired as to his exact whereabouts. He never stayed out too late, and she appreciated that he needed a time of relaxation after his travels the length and breadth of Yorkshire. Sometimes he covered a couple of hundred miles a day, with half a dozen or more calls in the towns and suburbs.

She remembered, when they had first moved into this house, how he had seemed to turn over a new leaf. He had, for instance, been with her, more often than not, to say goodnight to Lorna. Rachel thought it was important for the child to see her mummy and daddy together before she went to sleep. But this rarely happened now, Derek often complaining that he was tired, or that she, Rachel, had all the time in the world now she was staying at home all day. She was not sure whether he resented her being at home instead of out working – earning extra money, which had been important to both of them – but she knew he would not dare to say so. After all, the fact that she was pregnant was due to him just as much as it was to her!

The last thing they had bought before Rachel had finally finished work was a television set, just a small one with a nine-inch screen which sat quite comfortably on a small table near the front window. She had been determined when they bought it that she would not become a slave to it. She knew of households – her parents-in-law's was one of them – where the curtains were drawn at seven o'clock, the furniture rearranged to face the TV set, and the rest of the evening was given over to viewing, anything and everything, whatever the BBC had to offer. There was only one channel, although it was rumoured that soon there would be a commercial channel funded by the showing of advertisements.

In spite of her good intentions, Rachel sat down thankfully now and switched on the set. There was an 'interlude' showing, a soothing image of the sails of a windmill turning. At other times there might be a revolving potter's wheel, waves crashing on the rocks, or horses ploughing a field. She waited patiently for *Music for You*, her favourite programme, presented by Eric Robinson. By the time she had watched that and *Panorama* and the late news Derek should be home again, she thought. She had used to wait up for him, but that had seemed to annoy him for some reason, and so she had started to go to bed before he came in. Whilst she was pregnant he did not attempt to make love to her. She remembered from the last time that he had found her pregnancy distasteful. This saddened her. After all, it was a perfectly normal condition and she could not understand his feelings. It would not be all that long though, now; another four months and her baby would be born.

She found herself relaxing, her troubled thoughts calmed by the music of *Swan Lake*; it was played by the BBC Concert Orchestra, whilst small black and white images of the corps de ballet drifted across the screen. The newly acquired TV set had been a boon in some ways, she pondered. Not least because there was a lovely intimate period in the afternoon which she and Lorna could share together. There was a different programme for small children each day. Lorna's favourite was *The Woodentops* – mother, father, and the twins, Willie and Jenny, who lived on a farm with their dog, Spotty.

'Spotty Dog! Look, Mummy, Spotty Dog!' Lorna would shout whenever he appeared on the screen.

Monday was the day for *Picture Book*; Tuesday, *Andy Pandy*; Wednesday, *The Flowerpot Men*; and Thursday, *Rag, Tag and Bobtail*. But Rachel knew that books were important as well; more important, in fact, than characters on the television screen. She looked forward to the time when she would be able to share her favourites – *Peter Rabbit*, *Winnie the Pooh*, *The Wind in the Willows*, or *The Magic Faraway Tree* – with her small daughter. Lorna enjoyed listening to the *Mother Goose* book of nursery rhymes, but stories, at the moment, demanded rather too much concentration. She was a restless child and was impatient if she had to sit still for too long.

Rachel fell asleep in front of the TV set that night. She had made her cup of tea and then dozed off during the news, only to wake when the screen was blank – it must have been the sudden silence that had startled her – and the tiny bright dot in the centre was disappearing. She switched off the set and went to bed.

She did not hear Derek come in at half past eleven, and she was unaware, until the next morning, that he had slept on the downstairs settee and not in their bed.

'I didn't want to disturb you,' he replied when she asked why. 'You looked so peaceful and you need your sleep.' He smiled at her and his answer seemed genuine enough. All the same, she could not help feeling hurt. Had she become so repulsive to him? she wondered.

What she did not know was that Derek had felt a pang of guilt when he had come home and, in the darkness, had watched her sleeping. How could he climb into bed with her when he had spent the last few hours in the arms of someone else? It was not the last time that he was to forsake their marital bed.

Chapter 6

Babs Ollerenshaw, the young woman whom Derek had met at the Queen's Arms on Coronation Day, was now nothing more than a pleasant memory. She had become too demanding.

She had discovered he was married, which was not really surprising. The fact that he could see her only once – or at most, twice – a week, and never on Saturdays and Sundays, was a definite giveaway. After the first few excuses, that he was away from Melcaster at weekends because of his work, he had decided to admit to his marital status; she had not believed his story about working anyway. After the revelation, she had not seemed to mind at first being his 'bit on the side', but then she had started to make impossible demands. He had to tell his wife; he had to make a choice between her, Babs, and Rachel. And so Babs had had to go.

There was really no choice at all. Derek knew he did not love Babs in the way he loved Rachel. At least, he admitted to himself, the way he had once loved her. And then there was Lorna, his dear little daughter. He could not imagine his life without Lorna.

Soon afterwards he had met Miranda Pearson, a new barmaid at the Coach and Horses, where he still met Charlie and the other lads at least once a week. Miranda was as unlike Rachel – or Babs, for that matter – in looks as could be imagined. She was tall and curvaceous with ginger hair which flowed to her shoulders in a mass of curls. The tight sweaters and short skirts she wore showed to full advantage her over-generous bust and rounded bottom. One might be inclined to dismiss her as a typical barmaid, at least as far as looks were concerned, but in spite of her obvious dress and colourful make-up, there was a certain gentility about her, a ladylike quality which Derek admired. Funnily enough, he liked his women to have an air of finesse. It was that quality that had first attracted him to Rachel.

Babs, too, was certainly not what his mother might condemn as 'common'; not that his mother had ever met Babs or known anything about her. He shuddered to think what her reaction might be if she knew he was playing away from home; she thought the world of Rachel. Babs had a stylish air about her, and he had been flattered that she had taken notice of him. But there was no point in looking back with regret. It was time for him to move on to 'fresh woods and pastures new'.

That was the phrase that had come into his head when he had first set eyes on Miranda behind the bar. He had no idea where the words came from; he had heard Rachel say them when they were moving into their new house. He reckoned they came from one of the books she continually had her nose stuck into. They seemed appropriate now. Fresh fields indeed, he pondered, gazing at her fulsome breasts straining against the thin fabric of the black and gold sweater. The thought of Rachel flitted, then, around the periphery of his mind. The guilty feelings were always there, but he had become so used to them he was able to suppress them quite quickly. If Rachel knew about his philanderings she would be horrified; she would be heartbroken, he liked to flatter himself. But Rachel did not know and she was not likely to find out. It had been a near thing, that time, with Charlie's wife, but nothing more had been said. And Charlie would never betray him, even though he might disapprove.

But would a classy bird like this Miranda even glance in his direction? Derek could tell she was classy. Her clothes, hairstyle and make-up, although they were arresting, were not what you could call cheap. And her voice, from what he could hear of it across the room, was low-pitched and faintly husky; very seductive. He decided to chance his arm. Charlie had got in the first round; now it was his shout.

'Two pints of your best bitter, luv,' he said, smiling at her in just a friendly way. It would not do to be too obvious. He had observed, in the last half-hour or so he had been watching her, that she was no push-over. 'And ... er, take one for yourself, luv.' Derek was a true Yorkshireman, not given to throwing his brass around unnecessarily, but it might be a good move to start by buying the young lady a drink.

'Thank you, sir,' she replied. 'I will have a small gin and tonic, if that's all right with you. I might as well have it now, whilst we're quiet.' She pulled the two pints, one of which he quickly took over to Charlie.

'See you in a while, mate.' He winked at his friend as he hurried back to the bar. 'Yes, enjoy your drink, luv,' he said. 'Why not? Seize the moment, that's what I always say.'

'Oh, do you? Very free with your "luvs", aren't you? To say you've only just met me.'

'Oh, sorry, luv. I mean ... sorry. It's just the way we talk round here. It doesn't mean owt ... er, anything. I wasn't trying to be forward or owt ... or anything like that,' he stumbled. He knew he must try to speak rather more correctly – or 'posh' as he termed it to himself – and cut down on the Yorkshireisms which were normally so much a part of his conversation. He could tell that this young woman, Miranda, did not come from this neck of the woods.

'It's all right; I'm only teasing,' she laughed. 'I've got used to it now, everyone calling me love. It's rather nice; nice and friendly.'

'Oh, so you're not a Yorkshire lass then?'

'No, of course not. Can't you tell?'

'Well, yes, I can actually. I know you talk a bit different, like. But I can't quite tell where you come from. South of here, is it?'

'There's a lot south of here.' She smiled. 'I can tell you

83

haven't travelled around much.'

'As a matter of fact, I have. I'm a commercial traveller, though I must admit it's mostly in Yorkshire. I cover a wide area, though.'

'I'm sure you do. I'm from Nottingham. You know, the East Midlands.'

'Oh aye . . . er, yes, I see. So they don't call folks "luv" down there? What do they say, then?'

'Oh . . . we say "me duck".' She laughed again. 'I think I prefer "luv".'

'It's a funny old world, i'n't?' Derek was feeling very pleased with himself that this initial encounter was going so well. 'I was stationed up in Catterick when I was doing me National Service. A lot of 'em were Geordies, y'know, from Northumberland way. Well, they call everybody "pet" or "bonny lad"! Or "man", even though they might be talking to a lass.'

'Yes, as you say, a funny old world.' She looked steadily at him and raised her glass. 'Here's to you. What did you say your name was?'

'I didn't. I'm Derek, Derek Watkins. And you're Miranda, aren't you? I heard somebody call you Miranda.'

'Yes, Miranda Pearson.' Rather belatedly, she held out her hand. 'Pleased to meet you, Derek.'

He felt as she smiled at him that this could be the start of something. He could be very charming when he put himself out, and he knew that his bright blue eyes, into which Miranda was now looking intently, were his best feature. He prided himself, too, on dressing nicely, usually in well-pressed grey flannel trousers and a sports jacket, always worn with a collar and tie. He had never reckoned much to the beatnik culture, condemning them as scruffy individuals with their grimy duffel coats and sandals and their unkempt beards and long hair. Derek was clean-shaven and always scrupulously clean. The Teddy boys were superseding the beatniks now, with their draped jackets with velvet collars and drainpipe trousers. The Teds, though, were renowned for getting into fights and Derek steered clear of that too. He prided himself on being a peace-loving person.

The customers waiting at the bar put an end to their chat, but Derek had approached her again when there was a lull later in the evening. She agreed that she would be pleased to meet him on Thursday, which was her night off. It couldn't be better, Derek congratulated himself. Thursday was one of his regular nights out with the lads, so Rachel would not have her suspicions aroused by him suddenly staying out an extra night of the week.

Miranda knew the score right from the start. He decided to put all his cards on the table, and she did not so much as flicker an eyelid when he told her he was married and had a little girl who was a year old. He learned, to his surprise, that she had been married, but that her husband had left her six months before for another woman.

'More fool him,' Derek remarked.

'Well, that's the way it goes.' She shrugged philosophically. 'You win some, you lose some. I have no wish to be married again, not for a long while at any rate. I don't want any ties, and you and me, we seem to get on well together, don't we, Derek? I think we understand one another.'

He had nodded. 'He's an idiot, though, that husband – ex-husband – of yours. Whatever was he thinking of? A young lass, was she, I suppose? Some little bit of fluff?'

'No, as a matter of fact she was a widow, eight years older than Bill. The motherly type, I suppose, which I certainly am not. You can't make yourself into something that you aren't. I wasn't ready to start a family. I don't know that I ever will be. But now Bill's got a ready-made family, a boy and a girl.'

'Oh, I see,' said Derek. She did not seem overly concerned about the breakdown of her marriage, nor the fact that she was now about to embark on a liaison with a married man. Tit for tat, he supposed.

Miranda was passionate, but warm and tender, too, and Derek thought she was fond of him, although they never spoke of their feelings. She was good fun, they enjoyed one another's company, and he experienced delights with her which had been unknown to him with Rachel, or even with Babs.

They usually drove out of Melcaster to country pubs where they were far enough away not to be known. Then they would return, after a drink or two, to the flat, quite near to the Coach and Horses, which Miranda shared with a friend.

He did not tell Miranda when Rachel became pregnant again. His wife was a subject they did not discuss at all. Miranda never asked about her, or about his child. His life fitted very nicely into two very separate compartments and that was the way he liked it. It wasn't as if anyone was suffering. Miranda knew the score and she certainly wasn't, and neither was Rachel, looking forward happily to the birth of their second child. He hoped it would be a boy this time. He felt very pleased and proud of himself. One of each; that was the way it ought to be.

He had forgotten, though, or he had put it to the back of his mind, what pregnancy did to a woman. As Rachel's size increased – and she seemed even larger this time than she had been when she was carrying Lorna – his feelings of repugnance returned. He could no longer make love to her, not that that mattered in the slightest. Miranda was there to satisfy his needs in that direction and Rachel did not seem bothered.

What he had not been prepared for was his feeling of remorse, which amounted almost to self-loathing, when he came home later than usual one evening and looked at his wife sleeping so peacefully in their bed. He had spent the last couple of hours in Miranda's arms, and he knew he could not, now, lie down next to Rachel, certainly not that night. He had spent the night on the settee, explaining the next morning that he had not wanted to disturb her.

His feelings of distaste increased as Rachel entered into the last months of her pregnancy, as did his feelings of guilt. It was an unusual state of affairs for him to experience such self-condemnation. He could not bring himself to make love to Rachel, but to his surprise he began to feel, also, that neither should he continue to see Miranda. Or maybe his feeling for her was not as strong as it had been at the start. At all events, he decided that their relationship had run its course and that he must tell her so. Should he tell her though, he wondered, that he was about to be a father again? He would feel awkward at confessing this, even though it was with the woman who was his wife and the night of conception had been a more or less isolated occurrence.

He decided to break the news at their next meeting. They drove out to a favourite haunt of theirs, a country inn near to the delightfully named village of Appletreewick. It was a balmy spring evening and after a couple of drinks they strolled through the village, past the pretty stone-built yeomans' cottages and along the bank of the gently flowing River Wharfe. An idyllic spot, if the circumstances had been different.

Before he had even embarked upon his confession, however, Miranda took the wind out of his sails by saying, 'Your wife's pregnant again, isn't she?'

He gave a visible start. 'How did you know? I mean . . . well, yes, she is . . . but it only happened the once, honestly, Miranda. Well, once or twice, I suppose. It was when we moved into our new house, you see and . . .' He had not previously made much of the move to their own home; it was a part of his life to which Miranda did not belong.

'You don't need to make excuses to me, lad,' she laughed. 'I can tell there's something on your mind, and I don't have to be a fortune-teller to guess what it is. You never mention your wife, and that very fact tells me there's something you're keeping from me. But I've never asked about her. We agreed at the start, didn't we, that our friendship should not be allowed to interfere with anything else.'

'I'm very fond of you, Miranda,' he began. 'I like you a lot. It's been good, what we've had together. But now . . .'

'Now it's time to call it a day?'

'I don't want to, but . . .'

'But you're beginning to feel guilty, eh? I've known for a week or two that something was amiss.' She nodded a trifle regretfully. 'She's pregnant again, that's what I thought to myself, and I was right, you see. I reckon you think more about your wife and your little daughter than you let on, maybe even more than you realise yourself. So there's no room for me any more, is there?'

'I'm sorry, Miranda. I'm really sorry.' He was amazed that she had summed up the situation so exactly.

'Then don't be. There's no room for regrets. We both knew how it was when we started seeing one another. And it was good while it lasted . . . very good. Come on, lad.' She shook his arm. 'Don't look so glum. How about another drink? One for the road, eh?'

'No, I don't think so. We'd best get back now. No point in prolonging the agony, is there?'

'Very well, then. Just as you wish.'

They drove back to Melcaster almost in silence. He did not kiss her as they said goodbye. There did not seem to be any point.

He did not sleep on the settee again, as he had taken to doing each time he had been with Miranda, unable to cope with his self-reproach. He steeled himself now to sleep next to Rachel in their double bed. He kissed her dutifully each night and then quickly turned away, not wanting to snuggle close to her as he felt that she, sometimes, would like to have done. He felt guilty about his growing distaste for his wife whilst she was in her present condition. He told himself, though, that he could not help it and that probably lots of men felt the same. Not that he had discussed it with Charlie or any of his other mates. A phrase he remembered from his church-going days often popped into his mind, the one about the Virgin Mary being 'great with child'. Rachel was certainly great with hers! He just wished September would hurry up and come and then it would all be over.

Remembering the traumas of Lorna's birth in the local hospital, Rachel had decided that she would like to give birth to her second child in her own home. Her doctor agreed that this was a reasonable request. She attended the antenatal clinic frequently during the last couple of months and the midwife also visited her regularly. She was told that her health was very good, and that there should be no problems. Her huge size was due to the fact that she was carrying an excess of water. Cutting down on salt, as she was instructed to do, did not appear to make much difference. She began to loathe her elephantine looks and longed for it to be all over.

Lorna, fortunately, was behaving herself reasonably well. She had grown accustomed now to having her mummy at home with her all the time and she had stopped pestering to see her grandma. Rachel had tried to explain to her that very soon they would be having a new baby in the house, a little sister or brother for her. That was why Mummy was so big just now, because the baby was growing inside her tummy.

But her revelations did not seem to mean very much to two-year-old Lorna. She just stared at her mother and poked at her tummy. 'Yes, you're fat, Mummy,' she said, then went on playing with her baby doll. That was far more real to her at that moment than a non-existent, as yet, baby brother or sister.

Rachel did so wish that people would not keep warning her that Lorna might well be jealous when the new baby arrived. She knew they were well meaning, but she could do without their advice. Lorna could be difficult enough at times as it was, and Rachel did not want to be told that a new baby might cause further ructions. Anyway, time would tell, but she knew she would never be guilty of neglecting Lorna.

Her pains started at around six-thirty on a Thursday morning in mid-September, right on cue according to the date the doctor had given her. And from the severity of the pains and the time lapse between them she guessed that this labour would not be as long as the previous one; her child might well be born in the next few hours. Her thoughts flew to the old rhyme about the days of the week. Always, on waking, her immediate thought was, What day is it today? Now she found herself musing that this child would be born on a Thursday. How did the rhyme go? She said it to herself inside her head.

Monday's child is fair of face,
Tuesday's child is full of grace,
Wednesday's child is full of woe,
Thursday's child has far to go . . .

That was all right then. Perhaps he – or she – would be a worldwide traveller or an explorer, or perhaps it meant that the child would reach great heights in his chosen profession. At all events, it was a better prophecy than the one handed out to Lorna – that she would be full of woe. She wasn't though, only now and again when she had one of her tantrums. Normally she was a happy enough child.

Another sharp pain took Rachel away from her silly rambling thoughts. What a time to be quoting nursery rhymes to herself! She almost laughed out loud, when the pain had ceased, at her absurdity. She nudged Derek, still fast asleep and snoring gently at her side.

'Derek. Derek, wake up. I think it's started . . . the baby.'

He gave a loud snort and blearily opened his eyes. 'What? What's up?'

'The baby. I'm in labour, Derek.'

He shot up in bed immediately. She remembered how he had wanted her out of the way as soon as possible when Lorna's arrival was imminent and this time it was no different. He had not liked the idea of the baby being born at home anyway, but this was one occasion on which she had insisted on having her own way.

'Oh! Oh dear! OK then. We'd best get moving, hadn't we? What shall I do? Shall I go and see to Lorna? Or shall I make you a cup of tea? Oh crikey!' He ran his fingers through his

nose and rounded face. She recalled how Lorna, in that split second after her birth, had looked so much like her grandmother. Now, the little girl was growing more and more like her, Rachel, in looks, with the same slight build, fairish hair and well-defined features – and more like her grandmother in temperament! Strong-willed and determined, whenever possible, to have her own way.

This little boy would be loved and cherished, whoever he resembled, just as his sister was, Rachel thought happily, leaning over him and kissing his petal-soft cheek. What a lucky young woman she was! A girl and then a boy, a nice comfortable home of their own, and a husband who, she was sure, would be just as thrilled with the new arrival as she was.

Chapter 7

Derek was thrilled to bits with his baby son and delighted that the child resembled him. Rachel had never seen him so full of beans about anything. He seemed to imagine that he and he alone had been responsible for the child's existence, until Rachel reminded him that she was the one who had had to endure the nine months' pregnancy and the labour at the end of it.

'And it's no joke, I can assure you, Derek,' she informed him, half laughing, but also half annoyed at his cavalier attitude. 'If men had to go through the experience themselves there would be far fewer children born into the world, believe me!'

'It's not been easy for me neither,' he told her, 'having to put up with you in that condition for nine months. I hope you won't want any more, 'cause I certainly don't. We've got one of each now and I reckon that's enough for anyone.'

'Yes, I'm quite satisfied, Derek,' she agreed. 'A girl and a boy. That's a nice little family.'

They decided they would call him Kevin, for no reason other than that they both liked the name.

She did not want any more children, not by design at any rate, although should one – or more – come along in the future she guessed they would be welcome. They had not really planned to have Lorna or her baby brother, but the two of them had been conceived easily and more or less haphazardly. Derek was supposed to be in charge of any birth control that they practised, but it was a very casual state of affairs. Rachel thought it might be better if she organised it herself. She decided she would visit the doctor in the near future to see if he could suggest some means by which she could be responsible for limiting the size of their family.

Derek did not seem very interested in lovemaking, however, at the moment. Rachel assumed it was because she was breast-feeding. This was another thing about which he was squeamish. He disliked seeing her with the baby suckling at her breast and would go into another room if he came across the scene, just as he had used to do when Lorna was a baby. She knew, though, that she was unlikely to be able to go on feeding baby Kevin for much longer. After a couple of months her flow of milk was diminishing. She would be relieved to get him on to a bottle.

'Then you can get up for a change in the middle of the night,' Derek's mother told him, 'instead of poor Rachel.'

He had laughed and said, 'Aye, happen I might.' But Rachel knew he was laughing at the absurdity of the idea.

In all fairness, she knew he was working very hard at the moment. He had managed to secure several new clients for Whittakers and now travelled further afield, as far as Sheffield to the south and Richmond and Barnard Castle to the north. Not that it was such a tremendous mileage, he explained to Rachel, but it did make sense for him to stay overnight now and again when there were a number of customers in the same area. And as autumn drew on the weather became more and more inclement; fog, wind and rain, and snow, too, were forecast. There was no point in driving back and forth in increasingly hazardous conditions.

By the time Kevin was three months old and Christmas was fast approaching Derek was staying away for one night, sometimes two, in the middle of the week. Rachel did not think to question his movements. He seemed contented enough with his little family when he was at home. They had fallen into the habit of making love on a Saturday night. She realised it had become more of a ritual than a spontaneous act, but she told herself that this did not matter. Derek was quite amenable these days and did not go out with Charlie and the other lads as much as he had used to. Of course, his sojourns to the border towns of Yorkshire were taking up a good deal of his time.

'We'll have to be thinking about having Kevin christened,' she told him, at the beginning of December. 'Certainly before Christmas. He's nearly three months old.'

'So what?' Derek shrugged. 'We know his name, don't we? And we've had him registered. So what's the point of having water chucked over him and folks who hardly know him promising all sorts of nonsense on his behalf? A load of rubbish I call it.'

'Derek, how can you say that?' Rachel found herself, in spite of her best intentions, getting very hurt and angry at his attitude to the things she believed in. Since the birth of Kevin her faith had grown stronger. She believed that each and every child that was born into the world was a small miracle, and that belief was intensified when she looked at her own children. She wanted Kevin to become a member of the large family of God and that was what she told Derek.

'You know what christening is all about, or at least you used to. It's baptism to be quite correct, receiving the child into the family of the Church. The christening part, giving him his name, is quite incidental.'

'Don't preach at me!' he shouted. 'I've told you before, I've had quite enough of church-going and religion to last me a lifetime. You can do what the heck you like, Rachel, but don't expect me to go along with it.'

'You mean you don't want to have Kevin baptised at all?'

'Of course I don't mean that! I reckon we'll have to have him done,' she winced a little at his expression, 'or else folks'll think it odd, especially your mother. We'd never hear the last of it. Not that I'm all that bothered about what folks think. Yes, that's OK, luv.' He seemed to have a change of heart then. He smiled at her, though she felt his smile was a trifle patronising. 'You go ahead and arrange it with your

Reverend Michael, and I'll be there along with you. You can sort out some godparents, can't you, if they insist on us having 'em? I've told you, though, it's a load of twaddle.'

She ignored his last rejoinder. It was sufficient that he had agreed to have the christening at all. She had asked Pauline and her husband, Trevor, to stand for Lorna, with another friend, Christine, from the Young Wives' Group as the extra one. She didn't want to ask Pauline and Trevor again, and Charlie, Derek's friend, and his wife, Marlene, whom she might have considered, did not attend church. So how could they be asked to make promises about the child's spiritual wellbeing?

At last she hit upon the idea of asking all four grandparents, Lizzie and Percy Harding, and Phyllis and Jack Watkins, if they would act as godparents. A little unorthodox, maybe, but they were all delighted and at least Rachel knew they would all take their obligations seriously. And if Derek didn't like it, then he could jolly well lump it! The Reverend Michael Laycock agreed that he would be delighted to baptise the baby in a little private service on the Sunday afternoon, the week before Christmas.

The christening service was a peaceful and reverent occasion and, all things considered, a very happy one. As it was the Sunday preceding Christmas, the fourth Sunday in Advent, the vicar had chosen to wear some of his magnificent regalia. The stole and hood which he wore over his cassock were of a mid-blue, embroidered with gold and silver stars, very suitable for the season. He was a good-looking man in his mid-fifties, silver-haired and regal in bearing, and he made an impressive figure as he stood at the font with baby Kevin, wrapped in a lacy shawl – crocheted by Lizzie – in his arms.

A large Christmas tree, decorated with tinsel and twinkling lights, stood at the side of the chancel, and beneath it there was a nativity scene, being built up week by week during the season of Advent. Mary and Joseph were there, three shepherds, three wise men, and the angel Gabriel, awaiting the arrival of the baby Jesus at the Christmas Eve service. There was an arrangement of holly and Christmas roses on the communion table, and the silver cross in the centre shone out radiantly in the subdued lighting of the church. Rachel thought she had never seen the place look so beautiful. A perfect setting for her precious son, now being made a member of the Church.

The vicar shook hands with Derek just as warmly as he did with the rest of the party. 'Congratulations, Derek. You have a grand little boy. I'm sure he will make you even more proud of him as he grows up. Well done! And a lovely little girl as well, of course. We mustn't forget Lorna, must we, dear?' He stooped to speak to Lorna, who was rather subdued for once in the hushed surroundings. 'I'm sure you are helping your mum and dad to look after your baby brother, aren't you, Lorna? What a lucky little boy he is to have a grown-up sister like you.'

'Yes.' Lorna smiled and nodded happily. 'He's ever such a good boy. He's my brother and he's called Kevin. And Father Christmas is going to bring him a teddy bear, isn't he, Mummy? Like my Mister Ted.'

'That's right, darling. We think so,' said Rachel, feeling a lump come into her throat. She felt her happiness was complete these days. Well, almost.

A great surprise to Rachel was how well Lorna was behaving since the arrival of her baby brother. The Job's comforters who had foretold that she would be even more troublesome and jealous had been proved wrong. Her behaviour, in fact, had improved. She adored her little brother.

'Yes, Lorna's being a great help to me,' Rachel told the vicar. 'I really don't know how I would manage without her.' She stroked the little girl's fine golden hair lovingly.

Lorna looked the picture of beauty and innocence that day. She was wearing a dress that had been specially made for her, by her grandma Lizzie, for the christening. It was bright cherry-red with white smocking on the bodice, and her grandma Phyllis, not to be outdone, had knitted her a white angora-wool cardigan.

The little girl's boasting about her brother to the vicar was by no means an isolated occurrence. She sang his praises to everyone, and not once, so far, had she shown the slightest sign of resentment that he was taking up so much of her mummy's time. What was more, she was eager to help in looking after him. Rachel would not have asked her to help in any real way; Lorna was too young for that. Besides, Rachel knew of too many instances where the elder sister in a family had become a drudge caring for her younger siblings. But right from the start Lorna had stood close to her mother and the baby, when she was feeding, bathing or dressing him. Even when she was changing his soiled nappies Lorna would stand there quietly observing every move. Occasionally she would make a comment.

'He's made a big mess, hasn't he, Mummy?'

Or, 'He's not like me there, is he, Mummy? I haven't got one of those.'

Rachel did not believe in confusing the child with details which, as yet, she could not understand, but she realised that Lorna was already learning something of the facts of life, without being aware of it, in the best possible way – by having a little brother intrinsically different from herself. Knowledge which had been denied to her, Rachel, as an only child.

She had explained to Lorna, when the little girl had watched her breast-feeding, that baby Kevin was drinking milk to make him grow big and strong, and that all babies – kittens and puppies and baby lambs as well – drank their mother's milk.

'And did I do that, Mummy, when I was a little baby like Kevin?' Lorna asked, looking puzzled.

'Yes, you did, darling. And then you had a bottle, like Kevin will have very soon.' Lorna had seemed happy at that. She smiled and nodded contentedly.

When he was three months old Kevin was weaned on to a

99

bottle and Lorna would mind him for a while while her mother went to prepare the feed. Rachel even let her hold the bottle to his mouth now and again, showing her how to tilt it so that the air didn't get into his mouth and give him a windy pain. A little later she was fascinated by the tiny jars of baby food, both savoury and sweet, that her mother bought, and she would tell Rachel which ones to buy when they were in the shop.

'He likes that carroty one, Mummy, and that choccy pudding. That's his favourite.'

Lorna was allowed to hold the spoon to his mouth sometimes, letting him suck off the gooey substance, as she had watched her mother doing. The chocolate pudding, however, made a mess, more of it seeming to end up on his bib than in his mouth. Maybe that was why Lorna said he liked it, Rachel smiled to herself, because she wanted to share a little joke with him. Already he was starting to smile and chuckle whenever he set eyes on Lorna. Rachel hoped that this happy state of affairs would continue and that the brother and sister would become good pals as they grew up.

Rachel often wondered at her contentment. She had settled down happily at home with her two children, and her teaching career seemed to belong to the dim and distant past. Her life was pretty nearly perfect.

If only she could feel that Derek was as much a part of the family unit as were the other three members. There was something – something she couldn't quite put her finger on – that seemed to be holding him back. She knew, of course, that she and Derek had very little in common and that they were, basically, unsuited to one another. They had drifted apart since their marriage, finding there were fewer and fewer interests that they shared. But that did not mean, she told herself, that they could not build a satisfactory relationship on what they had. Their two children and their home was enough, surely, to keep them together. There were countless couples, she was sure, who were in a similar situation.

As the next two years passed by, so quickly it seemed – 1955, 1956, and into 1957 – the situation did not improve. Derek was growing increasingly restless and it was clear that his mind was often elsewhere. On his job, Rachel supposed. He was certainly travelling further and further afield these days, although she could not complain about the extra money he was bringing in. One thing was certain, he was working too hard, but he would not consider leaving Whittakers – which she had suggested more than once – to find a job firmly based in Melcaster. He enjoyed travelling, he told her, and if he did not mind, then why should she?

It was true enough that Derek's travels on behalf of Whittakers took him to the very borders of the large county of Yorkshire, covering all three ridings, and into the fringes of Lancashire, Derbyshire and County Durham. But the nights he was spending away from home now were not in Hull or Nottingham or Darlington, as he would have Rachel believe, but in the much nearer town of Ripon.

He had been visiting this small cathedral city, only twenty-five miles or so from Melcaster, ever since he had started working for Whittakers. He could not have said why he liked the place so much; Ripon was not really his sort of town. There was very little of what you might call real life there; in fact, there was more in Melcaster. In some ways the little town had not yet moved into the twentieth century. For instance, an ancient custom was carried out there each night in the market square. This ritual had been in existence since God knows when; the Middle Ages, he supposed. At nine o'clock a forest horn was sounded from each of the four corners of the square by the official hornblower, the Wakeman, who then had to go and report to the mayor of the city that his duty had been fulfilled. Derek, of course, had never seen this quaint custom for himself until he started staying there overnight.

The market square was a focal point in the city, from which radiated a network of narrow winding streets. The massive cathedral, dating from the twelfth century, dominated the city. This might have been a reason for Derek, in his anti-religious frame of mind, to have disliked the place, but there was something about it that appealed to him. He knew, of course, that he had become fonder of the town since meeting Sylvia Maitland.

In one of the small streets in the shadow of the cathedral there was a small shop which was commonly called a draper's, although such establishments were gradually declining, being overtaken by larger and more affluent stores. This shop had been owned by an elderly couple, Mr and Mrs Cartwright, who were loyal customers of Whittakers. Each time Derek visited them they bought several flannelette shirts, suitable for the working man, wrap-over aprons, button-up blouses of the sort Mrs Cartwright considered suitable for middle-aged ladies, and underwear, for both men and women, which served its purpose admirably, keeping the wearer warm without any tendency towards frivolity.

It was in the winter of 1955, when Kevin was three months old, that the shop had changed hands. It was two weeks before Christmas and whereas Mrs Cartwright's only concession to the festive season had been a string or two of tinsel and a few blobs of cotton wool, resembling snow, now the whole window was a shimmering wonderland of pink, blue and gold. In the centre was a large artificial Christmas tree with shiny pink and blue baubles hanging from its golden branches, along with small items which would be suitable for gifts – babies' bootees, tiny shoes, socks, and rattles with silver bells. The shop had stocked babywear before, but it had been ordinary, everyday sort of stuff – terry towelling nappies and bibs and flannelette nighties and vests. Now there was an array of up-to-the-minute garments which any self-respecting baby would be proud to wear.

Derek stared in amazement at the dainty little nylon dresses with puffed sleeves, fur-fabric coats in both pink and blue, bonnets and bobble-hats, and jolly pyjamas patterned with teddy bears and rocking horses. Nor was the older generation forgotten. He could see no evidence of anything the men of the family might wear, but the same men could have a ball here buying gifts for their wives or girlfriends.

An almost see-through nylon nightdress in a delicate pink shade was draped enticingly in a corner and, in the other, a quilted nylon dressing-gown, pink again with a pattern of blue and white flowers. There were packets of nylon stockings on the floor of the window, lacy cami-knickers, briefs, flimsy brassieres and suspender belts.

Derek glanced up at the name above the door. A new sign announced, quite simply, 'Sylvia'. He could not wait to see the woman who had brought about such a change. He pushed open the door, hearing the comfortable clonk of the bell, one thing that had remained the same.

He might have expected the woman who had bought such frivolous lingerie to resemble his former friend, Miranda. But the woman who greeted him across the mahogany counter, holding out her hand in a welcoming gesture, was small and dark-haired, neatly dressed in a black skirt and sweater with a string of pearls at the neck.

'Good morning,' she said. 'I can guess from your case that you are a commercial traveller. How do you do? I am Sylvia Maitland. And you are?'

'How do you do, Miss Maitland. I'm Derek Watkins and I'm here on behalf of Whittakers of Melcaster. The Cartwrights, your predecessors, were loyal customers of ours, but somehow I don't think you will be requiring . . . er . . . the same sort of merchandise as before? I got quite a shock.'

'Yes, I expect you did.' The young woman smiled. 'But I thought it was time to bring the shop into the twentieth century.'

'You've certainly done that, Miss Maitland.'

'It's Mrs Maitland. I'm a widow. I moved back to Ripon after my husband died, to be near my parents, and then I saw this shop was for sale. It was something I'd always wanted, a little business of my own. And there's living accommodation above, so it couldn't be better. I've got my independence, and yet I'm quite near to my parents, just the other side of the cathedral. Just listen to me, though, nattering on about myself!' She laughed quietly. 'I'm a real chatterbox when I get going. What I should really be doing is apologising, Mr Watkins, for not having contacted you earlier.'

'The fault is just as much mine, Mrs Maitland, although I had no idea, of course, that the place had changed hands. This was meant to be just my routine visit. I do hope we will be able to continue with our business arrangement, but it seems as though you have already got some new suppliers?'

'Well, yes. My husband and I lived in Leeds and we had a few contacts there in the clothing trade. I'm sorry; it's been an oversight, Mr Watkins. I really should have got in touch with you, but better late than never, perhaps? Are you going to show me what you've brought?'

Derek opened his large suitcase, putting to one side the examples of men's long underwear and ladies' directoire knickers. 'We have a new line here in rayon-satin petticoats and some of them have matching items, er . . . briefs and bras. Lovely colours, see – pale green and lavender and peach – all very modern. I could call again next week and bring you a selection. A further selection, I mean. You can have these now if you wish.'

'Yes, thank you, Mr Watkins.' She had a little rummage through his case, choosing a few of the pretty slips trimmed with cream-coloured lace and the matching brassieres and knickers. 'I'm sure these will sell very well, and I shall look forward to meeting you again next week.'

When he called exactly a week later she welcomed him with sherry in a crystal glass and a homemade mince pie, fresh from the oven. He decided she was a very pleasant young woman, about his own age, he guessed, and that he liked her very much indeed.

She was far removed from any of the women he had flirted with previously or dallied with for longer periods. Sylvia, in fact, was not the sort of person with whom one would consider flirting. There was an innate reserve there beneath

104

her friendly and talkative manner. You knew there was a point beyond which you must not advance; so far and no further. Derek was not used to holding back and was, therefore, unsure as to why he liked this mysterious young woman so much. All he knew was that he did like her and that he would, eventually, attempt to move their relationship on to another plane.

His feelings of guilt when Rachel had been expecting Kevin had not troubled him for very long. Rachel seemed happy with their two children and had settled down nicely to the life of a full-time housewife and mother instead of being a teacher. They missed her income, of course, and he knew it was up to him now as their sole breadwinner to keep up their standard of living as much as possible. Derek did not mind working hard, so long as it was work of his choice, and his job was ideally suited to someone of his temperament. He loved the hours he spent behind the wheel, particularly driving through the lonely moorland and dales. This gave him the freedom he so much desired; on the other hand, he enjoyed meeting different people and visiting fresh towns and villages.

It had originally been the idea of Whittakers' sales manager that Derek should stay overnight occasionally in towns where he was likely to find new clients, or keep in touch with old and valued ones. As expenses were to be paid by the firm, Derek thought it was a great idea. There had been no ulterior motive at first, and then, little by little, he had started to combine business with pleasure.

There was a girl who worked in a department store in Harrogate; a pert little barmaid in Skipton – Derek, somehow, found it hard to resist barmaids; and a waitress who served him, in more ways than one, at the hotel where he stayed in York. Derek Watkins really felt he had got it made. An unsuspecting wife waiting at home for him, with his two lovely children; fun and excitement, with no strings attached, when and where he desired it; and the tantalising thought of Sylvia Maitland on the – not too distant, he hoped – horizon.

Chapter 8

To say that Sylvia Maitland was an uncaring person would
not, strictly speaking, be true. She was certainly not what
you might call immoral; she would not commit murder or
steal or do anything that would lead to her being arrested for
disorderly behaviour, nor would she ever, knowingly, do
anyone a bad turn. In fact, she seemed to be ready at all
times to do good and to help her fellow citizens. She was a
member of the Conservative Party, there was a collecting tin
on her counter for Dr Barnardo's homes, and she supported
various good causes in and around Ripon – Friends of the
Hospital, St Dunstan's Homes for the Blind, and the local
orphanage. And if by upholding these worthy causes she
should happen to bring some business her way, well then,
that was all to the good. Derek began to realise, more and
more, that here was a young woman after his own heart, a
person who endeavoured to serve, first and foremost, the
interests of number one.

Rachel's goodness got on his nerves at times, although he
could not say, in all fairness, that his wife was sanctimonious,
not like some of that Young Wives' Group crowd she hung
around with. Derek did not see much of that particular
group of people any more as he no longer went to church
with Rachel, even on special occasions. Since they had
started the crèche at St Matthew's she had been taking both
children along with her, which gave him, Derek, more free
time to do as he wished.

Strangely enough, he was feeling that these spare hours at

106

the weekends were inclined to drag. He no longer met Charlie and the other lads for their Sunday pint, and they met during the week only infrequently. This was partly because of Derek's erratic working timetable, and also because his mates, one by one, were finding themselves with other commitments. Charlie's wife, Marlene, had recently given birth to twin girls. And to Rachel's great delight she and Derek had been asked to act as godparents to the two little girls, Janice and Lynne.

One evening in the early summer of 1957, when their own two children were in bed, Derek and Rachel were having one of their increasingly rare chats.

'Can't see why you're so thrilled about this godparent lark,' said Derek, 'or surprised either. You're an obvious choice, aren't you? Who else do they know who goes to church? And they can't ask you without asking me. That's why I'm being dragged into it, I suppose.'

'Don't say that, Derek!' said Rachel. 'It's always an honour to be a godparent, and you're Charlie's friend, aren't you? That's why he's asked you.'

'Huh! If I know Charlie it'll be an excuse for a jolly good knees-up. They're having a bit of a do afterwards round at his mother's place. She was always good for a laugh, was Charlie's ma. You'll go, won't you, Rachel? And you won't go all po-faced, will you, 'cause you think they're drinking too much?'

'Of course I won't!' said Rachel, sounding very indignant. 'I'm not like that, Derek, you know I'm not. The trouble is, it's so long since we went out together that you've forgotten – haven't you? – what I'm like at a party. I used to enjoy parties and get-togethers as much as anyone, but we haven't been to one for ages.'

'Yeah, I suppose that's true. Sorry,' he mumbled. 'You're right. We haven't been out together for . . . for quite a long time.' He didn't like to think how long. He was feeling a pang of guilt, as he did from time to time when something forced him to look at himself and Rachel and their situation.

Now, as he cast his mind back, he remembered the last occasion they had been out together. They had gone to see one of those *Doctor* films, starring Dirk Bogarde, at the Gaumont, and Rachel's friend, Pauline, had baby-sat for them. They had had a jolly enough evening together, even stopping off for a drink on the way home. He recalled that Rachel had had only a small port and lemon because she was pregnant at the time with Kevin ... and now Kevin was nearly two years old. Gosh! Was it really as long ago as that? He would never have believed it, but he had, of course, been very preoccupied with other matters and the time had slipped by almost without him realising what was happening.

'Yes ... well ... I know it's been a long time,' he said now. 'And I suppose it's partly my fault ... well, entirely my fault,' he added magnanimously. 'What I mean is ... I'm working away so much, aren't I? And I can't very well turn down Whittakers' offer of all expenses paid. I'd be a fool not to take advantage of that. A touch of the high life now and again.'

'Mmm, sounds wonderful,' said Rachel. Was that a wistful tone in her voice, he wondered, or was she being just a little sarcastic? 'It's a pity I can't go with you sometime. Couldn't you wangle it, Derek? Perhaps when you next go to York. I haven't had a day in York for ages and I used to love going shopping there.'

'Oh no,' he replied quickly. Too quickly, he realised, when he saw her expression change from optimism to disappointment. 'Er, what I mean, luv, is that Whittakers book me a single room, and the meals I take – well – I'm supposed to be on my own ... which I always am, of course.' He gave a casual laugh. 'But I suppose if I was to pay the extra myself there's nowt to stop me booking a double room.'

'That's what I meant, Derek,' she replied. 'I wasn't expecting Whittakers to foot the bill. And we're doing all right now, aren't we? Your wages have gone up quite a lot since you got all those new orders. I do appreciate how hard you are working. I just wish the children and I could see a little more of you at times. But about this trip to York ...'

Derek felt his heart sink. She wasn't going to let it drop.

'I'm sure my mother would have the children for a night, and it would be such a treat for me to have a night in an hotel. The last time I stayed in one was when we were on our honeymoon in Scarborough. Just think, all those years ago. And now Lorna is four years old. I can hardly believe it.'

Rachel was in a reminiscent mood, but Derek didn't want to go along that road at the moment, not ever, if he could help it. The past was over and done with, and the future, as he tried to look ahead, was getting more and more complicated. And now he had a very difficult present situation to deal with. She seemed set on this York idea. Well, one thing was certain; he would have to arrange to stay at a different hotel. It would be out of the question to stay at the one in Low Petergate where Dora, his little waitress friend, worked. She believed he was a bachelor. The only one of his current lady friends who knew of his marital status was Sylvia. She was the only one who was important to him. Her presence in his life was becoming more and more vital to him. He had never felt like that about any woman before.

But Rachel was his wife and, at that moment, she seemed determined to remind him of the inescapable fact. And as far as his two children were concerned, well, he loved them both to bits and was very proud of them. Even people who did not care overmuch for Derek Watkins – and there were quite a few – had to admit he was fond of his children.

'I'll see what I can do about it,' he said now, in a matter-of-fact voice. Anything to try and shut her up. 'Perhaps in a few weeks' time. The trouble is that York gets so busy in the summer with tourists. You can't move for them.'

'It's not just in the summer, though, Derek. York is always busy, and I don't mind the crowds.'

'You do realise, though, don't you, that I won't be able to be with you during the day? I'll be rushed off my feet as usual, seeing clients.'

'Don't try to talk me out of it, Derek. I can manage to find my own way around York.' She smiled at him, a smile of such happiness that, for a moment, he felt a stab of something which he realised might be affection.

Just then there was a shout from upstairs. 'Mummee, Mummee . . . Come quick! It's here again.'

'Off you go,' said Derek, with a grin of relief that the subject was so conveniently changed. 'Go and calm her down.'

'No, we'll both go,' said Rachel. 'Come on, Derek. I know Lorna's got an overactive imagination, but it's very real to her, whatever it is. It's not uncommon for children of her age to have nightmares.'

Lorna was sitting up in bed, hugging Mister Ted. Her fine blonde hair was damp with perspiration, clinging to her head in curly tendrils, and her brown eyes were wide with fright. 'He's there, Mummy, behind that curtain.' She pointed in the direction of the window. 'Make him go away. Oh, please make him go.'

Rachel went across and drew back the curtains, patterned with Peter Rabbit, Benjamin Bunny and their friends. 'Look, darling, there's nothing here, nothing at all.' She made a pretence of looking in every corner and even under her bed. 'You were just having a nasty dream, that's all. There's nothing to be afraid of. Your daddy and I are here, and Kevin's fast asleep in the room next door. Everything's lovely. Now, would you like a drink of warm milk to help you to get to sleep again?'

The child nodded, but she was still glancing a little anxiously across the room. She had never been able to describe what she had seen, only something moving and then seeming to come nearer to her. Rachel realised it was a very real fear, and so she had never told her she was being silly. 'Yes please, Mummy,' Lorna said now. 'I'd like some milk.'

'I'll go and get it,' said Derek suddenly. 'How about that, eh? Then I'll read you a story before you go back to sleep. Which one do you want? "The Three Bears"?' It was the first one that had come into his head.

'No, don't be silly, Daddy! We've had "The Three Bears" millions of times, haven't we, Mummy?'

'We have indeed, love,' Rachel agreed. 'How about Daddy reading one of your new Andy Pandy books? We were watching him this afternoon, weren't we?' Yes, the exploits of the little boy in his stripey playsuit, with Teddy and Looby Loo, would be more fitting at the moment than the tales of the Brothers Grimm. 'Now, you run along to the lav, then I'll come and sponge your hands and face and make you all fresh and clean again. Feeling better now, are you?'

Lorna smiled and nodded, seemingly her old self again.

Rachel was touched by Derek's offer to make the drink and to read to Lorna, so when she had kissed her goodnight again she left him to it. There was no doubt about it, he did love his daughter and his little son as well. Lorna was behaving like a little angel at the moment, and she had looked like a cherub, too, in her white nightdress with her teddy bear in her arms.

She was 'four years and three months old', as she told anyone who asked, always being very precise about her age. In less than a year's time she would be at school and Rachel knew the day could not come fast enough for Lorna. Already she was pestering her about how soon she could start.

'Why not now?' she asked frequently. 'I can read, Mummy. And I can do sums and I can write my name, so why can't I go to school?'

And, another time, 'Why don't you ask that lady – you know, Miss Lacey – if I can go? She said I was as bright as a button. That was a funny thing to say, wasn't it, Mummy? 'Cause buttons aren't always bright, are they? The ones on my coat are black. But she had a red cardigan on, Miss Lacey, with shiny gold buttons all down the front. So I 'spect that's what she meant.'

Lorna had an answer for everything and was an uncontrollable chatterbox. Rachel had taken her into her old school, Kilbeck Infants, from time to time, where she had kept the teachers amused with her chatter. There was no doubt that Lorna was ready for school.

It was incredible the way her little family was growing up so quickly. Maybe, as the two children grew older, Derek would want to spend more time with them, and with her, too, having fun together as a family unit. Maybe this was the start of something tonight, his surprising offer to take care of Lorna after her nasty dream. But she had thought things were changing for the better several times before, only to have her hopes dashed as Derek continued to lead a virtually separate life from the rest of his family. She had almost extracted a promise from him, though, about the visit to York. She was determined that this was one chance she was not going to allow to slip through her fingers.

Derek kept his life, as much as he was able to, in separate compartments, never allowing one to infringe upon the other. None of the women with whom he philandered knew anything about any of the others, the notable exception being Sylvia Maitland. She had known right from the start that he was married with two children, although she had been kept in the dark about the casual girlfriends in York, Harrogate and Skipton. These, in Derek's view, were inconsequential anyway and could easily be dispensed with when they were no longer needed. He had no doubt that he was one of several as far as these good-time girls were concerned.

Sylvia Maitland, however, was a very different kettle of fish. He had been aware of that from the beginning and had, therefore, bided his time before venturing too close to her. It was on his second visit to the little shop in Ripon that Derek had told her of his married status. Sylvia had made the usual remark of, 'A girl and a boy? That's nice,' or some such platitude, and he had realised that she was not particularly interested in children. One might have thought that she would be, judging by the exquisite little garments for babies and toddlers which were on sale in her shop, but Sylvia, he soon learned, just liked to surround herself with beautiful merchandise and to admire the clever craftsmanship involved in creating some of the handmade dresses and little romper suits. He did not think she ever stopped to imagine a child of her own wearing one of them.

She told him that she had been married to her husband, Roger, for five years, and his sudden death from an embolism had been a great shock to her. She did, however, appear to have picked up the pieces and moved on, showing a good deal of fortitude and a resilience that some might think revealed a certain insensitivity. Derek knew she was fond of her parents. They lived quite near to her and she visited them fairly frequently, at the same time being determined to be the mistress of her own life. He wondered if there might be room in it for him, but it was some six months after they met before he plucked up courage and asked her if she would take lunch with him at a nearby pub on the corner of the town square.

The eagerness with which she agreed made Derek realise she had only been waiting for him to make the invitation. Sylvia was as keen as he was to move their friendship along a stage further. He still did not rush things for fear she should think he was wanting too much too soon. The first time he decided to stay overnight in the area he booked a room at a hotel in the town square, the one where they had lunched together on a few occasions. This time Derek invited her to take an evening meal with him, and to his delight she did not refuse when he suggested they should adjourn to his room upstairs for a nightcap.

She did not stay the night. Derek had the good sense not to ask her to do so. She was quite well known in the town as a respectable businesswoman, although people had noticed her of late in the company of Mr Watkins, the traveller from Whittakers. Little was known about him, but he was respected in the town as a man who was straightforward in his business dealings. He knew that Sylvia needed to safeguard her reputation and so she had left the hotel before eleven o'clock, Derek escorting her home along the darkened streets to her little shop, only five minutes' walk away. They had not chatted very much during the homeward stroll, both of them thinking of what had taken place between them.

It was the first time they had come together and declared their love for one another, or, rather, their feelings. The word love had not been mentioned, but their need for one another had been mutual. Derek had known, as they lay together afterwards in his large bed, that this was the woman he had waited all his life to meet. He was not sure at that moment that he actually loved her, and that was the reason he had not, glibly, uttered the words as he might so well have done. He knew there must be nothing said between them that was not strictly true and honest. But he knew that Sylvia Maitland was right for him, and he guessed, moreover, that she had the same thought, that Derek Watkins, warts and all, was just right for her. They were two of a kind. There was a certain ruthless streak in both of them, a touch of hardness and self-interest, a determination to have their own way, and if others should get hurt by their actions, then . . . that was just too bad.

These thoughts had come into Derek's mind as he had propped himself up on one elbow, gazing down at Sylvia. She was naked beneath the bedclothes and her small well-shaped breasts peeped tantalisingly over the top of the crisp white sheet. She was unashamed of her nakedness and she smiled roguishly up at him, reaching up and stroking his face.

'That was good, Mr Watkins. Very good indeed. The next time you stay overnight, how about stopping at my place? I have a nice big bed, just as comfy as this one.'

'A very tempting offer, Mrs Maitland.' Derek grinned down at her. 'And if you keep on tormenting me with that roguish smile I won't be answerable for the consequences! Come on now, you've got your reputation to consider. You'd better get yerself dressed and I'll see you home.'

He bent down and very gently kissed her small, nicely formed lips, a perfect Cupid's bow even without the aid of make-up. What he really felt like doing was pulling the bedclothes off and then watching her as she dressed herself in the provocative undergarments, which now lay strewn on the floor. The cami-knickers, brassiere, suspender belt and slip were made of red silky rayon, trimmed with black lace; not at all the sort of garments that a casual observer would expect the demure-looking Sylvia to wear. He guessed they were identical to a range on sale in her shop; not one of Whittakers' ranges, however. (The Melcaster firm was still inclined to be more conservative in outlook.) But he decided to save that delight for another time when they knew one another rather better. He congratulated himself that he was doing very well for a first time. With a show of tact and a sensitivity which did not normally come naturally to Derek, he disappeared into the next-door bathroom to dress himself and to allow Sylvia to dress in privacy.

She brought up the subject of his next overnight stay once again as they drew near to her home, a little diffidently this time, as though she were afraid of overstepping the mark.

'I did mean what I said, Derek. You know . . . about you staying the night here, with me; that is, if you would like to. There's no point in going to the expense of an hotel when I'm just round the corner.'

Derek chuckled. 'It's Whittakers what's paying, not me, luv. Come to think of it, though, happen they might get a bit suspicious like if I keep on presenting 'em with bills for overnight stays in Ripon. We could dine there first, though, at the hotel – they put on a nice meal, don't they? – and then adjourn to your place . . . that is, if you mean what I think you mean, eh, Sylvia?'

'I mean it, Derek,' she said quietly. He could see her eyes were shining with warmth and desire, and he knew that his eyes, too, were revealing the same feelings. 'And I'll cook us a meal as well, a special meal . . . the next time you come?'

'I'll come as soon as I can,' he replied, in answer to the unspoken question in her voice. 'Next week perhaps; certainly no more than two weeks.' He could tell from the momentary flicker of unease that crossed her face what she might be thinking. That he had had his way with her and that was now the end of it. He knew he must reassure her. 'Don't worry; I'll be back again, just as soon as I can manage it.' He kissed her again, briefly but warmly, on her lips. 'Goodnight Sylvia ... and thank you, for everything. It's been a wonderful evening. I'll see you soon, I promise.'

'Goodnight, Derek. Thank you too. I'll look forward to ... the next time.'

After that first slight feeling of anxiety Sylvia had known she had been wrong to doubt him. Derek from then on began to visit the shop in Ripon far more frequently than his business commitments warranted.

By the time Kevin was almost two years old, in the late summer of 1957, Derek had fallen into the habit of staying overnight in Ripon twice, or sometimes three times, a month. He always told Rachel, however, that he was elsewhere, in York, Harrogate or Skipton, or even further afield in Richmond, or Scarborough or Whitby on the east coast. She never questioned his whereabouts and, fortunately, there had never been any need to contact him when he was away. Indeed, if she had wished to do so, it would have proved difficult as he always made sure she did not know the names of the hotels where he stayed, and she did not bother to ask.

His duplicity increased as the months went by and he found himself visiting Ripon more and more frequently. In fact, he was seldom where he told Rachel he would be. Whittakers did not question where he was staying so long as the orders kept coming in, and Derek made sure that they did. Moreover, his superiors were pleased that he was continuing to increase his clientele without making too many overnight hotel bookings. They did not query the mileage on the car as he drove speedily from one town to the other, invariably ending up in Ripon.

Derek had made sure that Rachel had benefited materially from the extra customers he had gained over the last couple of years. As a family they were quite comfortably off and

Rachel, to his relief, always seemed quite satisfied with her lot. He knew, though, that this state of affairs could not continue for ever. Sylvia never asked questions about his family, and he never talked about them. It was an unspoken agreement they had. The times they spent together were set apart from the rest of their lives and they enjoyed them to the full, knowing it would be a week or more before they were able to meet again.

Despite her demure appearance and her somewhat staid way of dressing – she went in for twin sets and pearls, neat blouses and gored skirts, or full-skirted cotton dresses in the summertime – Sylvia was a passionate woman. This side of her nature showed itself in the exotic underclothes and nightdresses she chose to wear, and in her desire to please Derek when they made love. He knew that she was always as sensually aroused as he was, and he experienced delights he had not known before, certainly never with his wife.

It was not, however, solely a sexual relationship. They got on well in other ways too, having the same taste in zany films, and television programmes which Derek knew Rachel would consider to be rather inane. They liked the game shows, *Double Your Money*, and *Take Your Pick*, as well as *Opportunity Knocks* and *Hancock's Half Hour* and *The Benny Hill Show*. Sylvia would scream with laughter at the antics of her favourite comedian in a most unladylike way. She was a surprising woman and Derek was discovering many different facets of her personality as he got to know her better.

He could not help, at times, comparing her with Rachel. He knew, at the heart of him, that Sylvia was not such a good and honourable person as his wife. Rachel, for instance, would never embark upon a clandestine relationship with someone else's husband, as Sylvia was doing. It made little difference that Rachel was never mentioned between them. She still existed, and Derek guessed that Sylvia must, at times, wonder about her; it was hard to tell, though, from her complete disregard of the issue, just what went through Sylvia's mind. Rachel was a very worthy young woman, dependable, honest, and a wonderful mother to the children. And she did not nag or complain unduly. But Derek was sick and tired of worthiness. And he had always known he was not good enough for Rachel.

Now, though, he had met a woman who was exactly right for him. He knew that self-interest lay at the heart of Sylvia, as it did at his own core. He wondered, therefore, why she had not urged him to make a choice between herself and his wife. But Sylvia, like Rachel, seemed contented enough at the moment with her lot. Derek was realising, however, that there must – maybe sooner rather than later – come a day of reckoning.

But now, to add to his problems, Rachel had thrown a spanner into the works by holding him to his promise to take her to York. And, moreover, there was yet another hurdle to be faced – the christening on the coming Sunday of Charlie and Marlene's twins.

Chapter 9

Rachel, holding baby Janice in her arms, began to feel quite broody. It seemed ages since Kevin and Lorna had been this age and size, dependent upon her for everything. Kevin was now a bonny, sturdy little lad – the image of his father, people often said – already developing a will of his own, although he had never been as tiresome a child as Lorna had sometimes been. He would be two years old in a few weeks' time, but it was Lorna, his doting big sister, not his mother, who was already talking about a party for him.

Lorna was no longer the difficult child she had used to be; it was since Kevin had come on the scene that her behaviour had shown a marked improvement. The little girl was watching him tolerantly now as he knelt on the floor, piling the hymn books one on top of the other to make a tower, as he did with his building bricks. To her mother's amusement, Lorna put a finger to her lips to warn him to play quietly, and Rachel felt her heart leap with her love for them. On second thoughts, however, she decided that she would not really want to go through the trauma of pregnancy again, nor the sleepless nights and the upheaval that a new baby brought to a household. She and Derek had decided ages ago that two children was the ideal number. Not that it made any difference at the moment whatever she thought or hoped for. There was no chance at all of her having another child, considering the way things were between herself and Derek.

Her husband stood next to her as the vicar asked the godparents to repeat the promises, pledging themselves to see that these children were brought up 'in the knowledge and fear of the Lord'. Derek seemed a little ill at ease, as he always did in church, but she was sure it was not just being in a place of worship that was troubling him. There had to be something else. He had grown more and more distant towards her over the past few weeks, but she felt unable to ask him what was the matter. The days of heart-to-heart talks had gone, not that they had ever been able to confide totally in one another.

He livened up when the christening party went back to the home of Charlie's parents. When he had knocked back a couple of pints he was quite the life and soul of the party, laughing and joking with Charlie and with his pal's parents, with whom he seemed to get along famously. Rachel sat and talked to Marlene and her sister, Hazel, whilst Lorna and Kevin played contentedly with Hazel's two children, a boy and a girl of roughly the same age. We appear to be an ideal family, Rachel thought to herself, at least to a casual observer. Charlie and Marlene might well be aware, though, of the widening gulf in their friends' marriage, and surely no one could fail to notice that she and Derek had very little to say to one another.

She was beginning to wonder about the wisdom of the forthcoming visit to York. It had seemed like a good idea at the time, and Derek had given in when he had seen how keen she was for them to spend some time together on their own. Now she was having second thoughts, but she managed to convince herself that it could do no harm; in fact, it might well be just what they needed. Probably Derek was over-tired with all the travelling he was doing; maybe that was all that was wrong. She had told him to ease off a little, but he took no notice. She should be glad, she supposed, that he worked so hard. She never had any cause to complain about his attitude to his job. It was obvious that he loved it.

The day of the York visit did not get off to a good start. They called at the home of Rachel's parents to leave the children, but Derek pointedly remained in the car whilst Rachel said goodbye to them and gave instructions to her mother. She was aware of the tightness in her mother's voice as she told her to 'have a good time' and pecked her uneasily on the cheek. One would have thought she might be glad that there was a chance for her daughter to mend her failing marriage, but it seemed as though Lizzie Harding had long ago given up on Derek. She did not even wave to him as he sat waiting in the car.

He seemed a little more cheerful as they drove across the moors. They did not converse much, but Derek hummed tunelessly to himself and Rachel felt her spirits lifting a little. She loved these open stretches of moorland at all times of the year, especially now, in late summer, when they were a mass of purple heather interspersed here and there with a blaze of golden gorse.

Derek had booked a double room at a hotel close to the Minister; not his usual one, he told her, and, briefly, she wondered why. It was very comfortable, if a little old-fashioned, but it would have seemed like the height of luxury to Rachel whatever it was like, unaccustomed as she was to such surroundings. She admired the dark wooden panelling in the bar and dining room and the four-poster bed in their large bedroom.

They arrived in good time for lunch, and after a hasty snack in the bar, consisting of chicken sandwiches and a salad garnish, Derek left her to her own devices.

'No rest for the wicked,' he said jovially, rubbing his hands together. 'You'll be OK on your own, won't you? Yes, of course you will. See you back here then. I've booked us a meal for half past seven, so that'll give you plenty of time to do what you want. Cheerio then, see you later.'

Rachel felt deflated. She knew he had clients to see, but she had hoped they would be able to spend at least a little time together, visiting the Railway Museum, perhaps. She had heard him mention that he would like to go there and that, strangely enough, he had never visited the place in

121

spite of all his trips to the city. She did not feel like going there on her own, and it was more of a man's thing anyway.

However, she knew she must make the most of her day of freedom, away from the children. She decided to visit the nearby Minster, so she went up to the bedroom to get a light cardigan, then set off on her solitary sightseeing.

She found the Minster chilly and rather depressing and she was glad of her cardigan. The stained glass, of course, was magnificent, and she stood for a while admiring the Seven Sisters window before stepping out again into the brilliant sunshine. She wandered along the narrow streets and into the Shambles where the medieval houses leaned towards one another, the top storeys almost touching in places. Rachel loved York, but somehow, today, the city seemed to have lost its appeal for her. It was crowded with tourists, as well as with the local people going about their business, as Derek had warned her it would be.

She jostled her way out to the main street, then made her way to Clifford's Tower. She climbed the steps to the top, only to find when she stood looking out over the city that she was suffering from an attack of vertigo, and the view of the Minster, the rooftops and the distant hills appeared to be spinning around her. Unsteadily she stumbled away from the parapet and made her way down the steps again, glad to be back on terra firma. She did not normally suffer from acrophobia, but she was not herself today, not at all.

The day was not proving to be a great success. For the remainder of the afternoon she sat by the River Ouse, drinking a glass of refreshing lemonade and watching the pleasure boats carrying tourists through the city. She, too, was a tourist today, she reflected, but she found herself unable to enter into a holiday mood at all. The main reason was because she was already missing the children, and she could not help wondering what the evening would bring.

She was back at the hotel before Derek, and she dressed with care in a new glazed-cotton dress with a full skirt, worn over a stiffened petticoat. The turquoise colour, more green than blue, highlighted her blonde hair and brown eyes. After she had applied a little make-up she knew she was looking her best, but would Derek notice? Did he notice anything about her any more?

It was seven o'clock before he arrived back. She did not ask where he had been, although she knew the shops closed at six o'clock at the latest. She decided he may have had some calls to make out of the town. To her surprise he did tell her that she looked nice. 'Quite a bobby-dazzler,' he said, which she knew was one of his father's old-fashioned sayings.

It was a pleasant change for Rachel to have a meal away from home. At least, it would have been if the company had been more agreeable. For her part, she could not fault the meal, but Derek complained that the tomato soup was not hot enough, the beef steak was overdone, and the ice cream on the peach melba was tasteless. Not a patch on the place where he usually stayed. It was only to her, however, that he grumbled, not having the courage, seemingly, to report the failings to the waitress, probably because they did not exist.

His ill-humour continued as they sat together afterwards in the bar. He downed two pints without speaking whilst Rachel sipped at a sweet sherry. At ten o'clock they retired to bed. How Rachel wished she was at home, and how thankful she was that they were staying for only one night. She could feel tears threatening as she undressed and put on her nightdress. But when they were both in bed and the light was switched off, she decided it was up to her to make one last effort.

'Derek . . .' she said tentatively, reaching out and touching his shoulder. Already he had turned his back on her. 'What's the matter? I know there's something wrong. Can't you tell me what it is?'

'For God's sake leave me alone!' he snapped, pulling away from her. 'There's nowt wrong, at least nowt as I can do anything about. It was you as wanted to come to York. Well, you're here, and if you're not satisfied you've only got yerself to blame. I've had a hard day and I need me sleep. So stop pestering me.'

A sudden thought hit Rachel with the force of a thunderbolt. He's met somebody else! So that was what was wrong, and probably it had been so for ages. It was the only explanation. Why ever had she not thought of it before?

She lay still and silent in the gathering darkness, not even weeping. The tears did not come, although she had never felt so alone in all her life. Her only consolation was that tomorrow she would be going home again, to her children.

'Kevin'll have a cake, Mummy, won't he?' Lorna asked again, as she had been doing for the last few weeks. It was her bedtime, just a few days before her brother's birthday. 'Will you make him a chocolate one, like you made for me, with all Smarties round the edge? But he'll have two candles on it, won't he? Only two, not four like me. And next time it'll be five.'

'Yes, and just before you're five you'll be going to school,' Rachel told her. 'Of course Kevin shall have a cake. And what else do you think he would like to eat?'

'Red jelly! Not that blancmange stuff, though. I don't like it, it tastes yukky, and Kevin doesn't like it neither.'

'Very well then, no blancmange.'

'And egg sandwiches, and crisps, and sausages on little sticks and . . . and buns with icing on the top and all them little coloured things.'

'Hundreds and thousands.'

'Yes, lots of them, Mummy. Oh, I nearly forgot – ice cream, to go with the red jelly.'

'And you're sure that's all,' Rachel smiled.

'Yes, I think so . . .' Lorna's face puckered in a tiny frown. 'What about something to drink?'

'Oh yes, aren't I silly, forgetting that? Orange juice and Vimto. Kevin likes both of those.'

'It's going to be quite a feast, I can see,' said Rachel. 'And will there be anybody to help me to get it all ready, do you think?' she asked, with a teasing smile at her daughter.

'Of course there will, Mummy. I'll help,' Lorna grinned, 'and I expect Grandma will too. Grandma and Grandad will be coming to the party, won't they? And Nana and Grandpa?'

'Oh yes, you can be sure they will,' replied Rachel. There would be trouble, indeed, if they were not invited, especially from her own mother. It was far from easy, though, having both the Harding and the Watkins grandparents at the same celebration. The tension between the two older women, in particular, had increased, Lizzie becoming more and more disenchanted with her son-in-law and Phyllis very much aware of the fact, but unwilling to start a quarrel.

'And we've invited your little friend Susan from your Sunday school class, haven't we? And Carol from two doors away. And the two little boys from down the road, David and Andrew, they are coming to keep Kevin company. He's a bit young to have proper friends of his own, but he will have lots of friends when he gets older, you'll see.'

'Yes, but I'm his friend, aren't I, Mummy?'

'Yes, love, you're a very good friend to your little brother.' It never ceased to amaze Rachel the way Lorna still looked after Kevin. She might have expected by now that the little girl would have tired of the novelty of having a younger brother and be finding him irksome, but that had not happened.

'Can we invite the twins, Mummy?' she asked now. Lorna had taken quite a fancy to the baby girls, Janice and Lynne, at the christening a few weeks previously.

'Oh no, I don't think so, dear,' replied Rachel. 'They are too young to know what's going on, and we would have to ask Aunty Marlene to come as well.'

'Well, why can't we then?'

'It would be too many, Lorna, in our little house. Just be satisfied. Kevin's going to have a lovely party. Now, you snuggle down and go to sleep.' Rachel kissed her, holding her close for a moment. 'Goodnight, darling. God bless.'

'Mummy . . .' Lorna sat bolt upright again. 'Daddy will be coming to the party, won't he?'

'Oh yes, I should think so, love. Yes, of course he will. He'll be home tomorrow, so we'll ask him, but I'm sure he'll say yes.'

Rachel, however, did not feel quite so sure. On the one hand she would have said that no way would Derek dream of missing his son's birthday, but, on the other hand, he had been behaving strangely for ages now. After the disastrous visit to York they had settled down into the old routine. They occupied the same house, the same bed even, but there was no intercourse between them, either sexual or otherwise. She had considered asking him outright if he had met someone else, but she had not yet managed to pluck up the courage to do so. There was always the possibility that she might be wrong, and then she would only succeed in making matters worse than ever – if, indeed, they could be much worse than they already were.

She switched on the television set and settled down to watch one of her favourite programmes, *The Sky at Night*, one which Derek enjoyed too. But he was not here tonight and she found, to her annoyance, that she could not concentrate. Whatever was Derek up to? She supposed time would tell. There was one thought to which she clung and that was that Derek was fond of his children and surely would not want to be parted from them. As far as she, Rachel, was concerned, she felt that she would not be sorry to see the back of him. But she knew she should not ignore the marriage vows she had made some six years ago. Marriage was for life, she had always believed. She wondered whether Derek felt the same way.

It was Lorna who asked Derek, as soon as he arrived home the following day, if he would be at home for Kevin's party.

'It's next Tuesday, Daddy, so you won't be away, will you? Kevin's having a big choccy cake, an' all sorts of things, aren't you, Kevin?'

The little boy nodded, although it was doubtful that he understood all his sister was saying. He was a very bright and intelligent child, though, already talking in sentences, and he had, several months ago, dispensed with nappies.

'What!' said Derek, throwing his hands up in mock horror. 'D'you really think I'd be away when it's my little lad's birthday? Not on your life!' He picked up his son and tossed him into the air, before catching him again and whirling him madly around.

'Steady on, Derek,' warned Rachel. 'You'll have him dizzy.'

'Rubbish. You shut up, Mummy! He loves it, don't you, Kev?' The child, indeed, was chuckling and clutching at his father's sandy hair, exactly the same colour as his own. Derek put him down on the floor again and punched him playfully. 'He's my little champion, aren't you, Kevin? And don't you let your mummy make a cissy out of you. Of course I'll be at the party, with bells on! Who else is coming?'

'Oh, just the grandparents and one or two of the children's friends,' said Rachel. 'But the important thing is that you'll be able to make it, Derek. We're all pleased about that.'

'Yes . . . well, first things first,' she thought she heard him mutter as he made his way into the kitchen, sniffing audibly. 'What's for tea? I'm starving.'

Kevin's birthday was, all in all, a very happy occasion. The little boy proudly wore his badges with a figure 2 on them pinned to his new bright blue jumper, knitted by Grandma Lizzie. She had also made him a bobble hat and scarf of the same wool for wintertime. Nana Phyllis, not to be outdone, had bought him a cute little duffel coat, his first really grown-up coat. And both sets of grandparents had bought him some Dinky cars to add to his growing collection. They were lined up on his bedroom windowsill when he was not playing with them. Already he could say the names of several of the models. 'Austin, Ford – like Daddy's – Wolls Woyce . . .' Derek loved to instruct him but Rachel wondered if he encouraged the collection for his own sake, rather than the child's.

She was pleased, though, that he took time to play with

their son, when and if it suited him to do so. There was no doubt how fond he was of him. He loved Lorna, too, but his eyes lit up in a special way when he looked at his son. She knew that most fathers were proud of their sons.

Rachel also knew that both children tended to be spoiled, at least as far as material things were concerned, by both sets of doting grandparents – especially the grandmothers – who vied with one another with the gifts they gave. But she knew it was wiser not to say anything; it made them happy to indulge the children, even though there was an element of 'keeping up with the Joneses'. Today, Lorna was not forgotten, although it was Kevin's birthday and not her own. Lizzie had bought her a jigsaw puzzle as an 'unbirthday present' and Phyllis a set of little chairs for her doll's house.

But it was Kevin's day and everyone made a great fuss of him. He puffed out his cheeks, the way his mother showed him, and managed to blow out his two candles, then chuckled with delight as everyone sang, 'Happy Birthday, dear Kevin, Happy Birthday to you . . .'

After all the guests had gone he went to bed tired and very happy, cuddling his new toy panda. Even Rachel and Derek exchanged a smile as they looked down at him. For the rest of the evening, however, Derek shut himself away in the bedroom with his accounts books. He had a lot of orders to sort out, he told her, as he was off on his travels again the next day. It would be a longer trip this time; he would be away both Wednesday and Thursday nights.

'Where exactly are you going?' she asked him. 'I really ought to know where you are.' It was not just the suspicion she had that was making her ask; it seemed imperative, somehow, that she should know his whereabouts.

'I can't tell you – exactly,' he replied irritably. 'It depends on how things go. Richmond, I think, then up to Barnard Castle. That's as much as I can tell you. Anyroad, and what does it matter? I'll be back on Friday.'

★ ★ ★

Rachel felt out of sorts on Wednesday morning. Her husband had zoomed off in the car with no more than a casual wave to her and the children as they stood at the gate. They usually saw him off when he went on his travels, more for the children's sake, though, than for Rachel's. So much for the happy family time we had yesterday, she thought. It was obvious that Derek could not wait to get away.

She had a pile of ironing waiting to be tackled, and she had been telling herself for ages that she ought to clean out her kitchen cupboards. But be hanged to it! she thought. The sun was shining and a brisk walk would do her more good than moping around in the house.

'I think we'll have a walk into town,' she told Lorna, 'and do some shopping. I'll get some sausages for our dinner. How about that? And we could call and see Grandma, couldn't we?'

'Carol said I could go and play with her this morning, Mummy,' said Lorna. 'Have you forgotten?' She looked pleadingly at her mother.

Rachel had forgotten about the invitation given by Carol's mother, their next-door-but-one neighbour. The two little girls had got on so well together at Kevin's party and would eventually be starting school together. 'Oh yes, of course. Silly me!' she said. 'We'd best get ourselves sorted out then, hadn't we?'

Lorna couldn't wait to get round to her friend's house, then Rachel put Kevin in his pushchair and they set off to walk to the centre of Melcaster. The little boy usually pestered that he wanted to walk, only needing the pushchair when he got tired, but that morning he seemed contented enough to sit there. When they reached the high street Rachel was surprised to see he had dropped off to sleep. He must have been more tired than she had realised with the excitement of the previous day. She was loath to leave him outside the shops, but she was forced to do so as there was no room in the crowded butcher's or baker's or greengrocer's for a pram, even a small one. He did not wake as, keeping one eye on him, she made her purchases – sausages and bacon, a pound of apples and the same of bananas, and a crusty loaf and half a dozen of the jam tarts that the children especially liked. These were quite a luxury; she did not often buy shop cakes, but all the cakes and buns she had made had been quickly demolished at the party and she did not feel like baking again at the moment.

When they arrived at her mother's house Kevin had woken up and she lifted him out of his pushchair. 'I think he's a bit under the weather this morning, Mum,' she said. 'It isn't like him to be so sleepy and lethargic.'

'Too much excitement yesterday, young man,' said Lizzie. 'That's all that's the matter with you.' She took hold of his hand. 'Come on, let's see if Gran can find a nice chocolate biscuit and a drink of milk. That'll make you feel better, won't it? And where's your big sister today? Our little pancake girl. Didn't she want to come and see her grandma?'

'She's playing with her new friend, Carol,' said Rachel. 'I've told you before, Mum, please don't call her that. She doesn't really know what you're on about and she's growing up now. She doesn't like to be treated like a baby. And only one biscuit for Kevin. I don't want him to spoil his dinner.'

'Oh, dearie me! I think Mummy's a bit under the weather as well this morning, isn't she? We can't do right for doing wrong, can we, Kevin?'

Rachel clenched her teeth as her mother and the little boy went into the kitchen.

Percy came in from the garden when he knew his daughter and grandson were there. He had been uprooting the bedding plants that had come to the end of their summer flowering. Rachel was glad he was there. It seemed as though it was one of those occasions when mother and daughter were rubbing one another up the wrong way, and he acted as a mediator, interrupting when it looked as though there might be an argument.

Kevin drank his milk, but ate only half of his biscuit. He looked a little feverish to Rachel. His cheeks were redder than usual and when she picked him up and sat him on her knee he felt hot all over.

'I don't think he's well at all,' she said, putting her hand to his forehead. 'You're burning up, aren't you, darling? Does it hurt anywhere, Kevin?'

'Head hurts, Mummy,' he said, tentatively touching his temple.

'I'd best get him home soon, Mum,' she said, 'and put him to bed. I can tell he's not feeling well at all. He says his head hurts.'

'Only because you've put the idea into his head,' said her mother brusquely. 'Yes, happen he's a bit hot, but kiddies are up and down. You should know that by now. If I'd put you to bed every time you complained of a headache or a tummy ache you'd have turned into a proper little hypochondriac. It doesn't do to wrap 'em in cotton wool. I never did with you.'

'No, Mother. I know that only too well,' said Rachel. She remembered her mother's dictum, that 'you die in bed', and only when she, Rachel, had been quite poorly with measles or mumps had she been allowed to stay in bed, at the doctor's insistence. Even then, Lizzie had got her up as soon as she showed signs of recovering, saying she was far better off downstairs sitting by the fire than lounging in bed. Rachel, though, had tried to be more solicitous with her own children, knowing that bed-rest was essential at times. And she felt, now, that Kevin ought to be in bed.

'I know you have very little patience with illness,' she told her mother now, 'and I know there may be nothing much wrong with Kevin, but I'm not taking any chances. Come on, Kevin. Let's get you home.'

'There's no need to get all hoity-toity with me,' said Lizzie, bristling. 'Of course I know that my opinion counts for nothing round here.'

'Leave it, Lizzie,' said Percy. 'The lass is right to be worried. I'll get the car out, Rachel love, and run you home. You can't walk all that way back. The little pram'll fit in the boot.'

Lizzie's attitude softened a little then. 'Well, happen it's for the best. But I'm sure he'll be as right as rain again tomorrow. Like I've said, kiddies are down one minute and up again the next. Don't start getting yourself into a lather, Rachel. He'll be fine. Give him a Fenning's fever powder; that always did the trick for you.'

'OK, Mum,' said Rachel. 'I'll do that.' She kissed her mother's cheek, then thankfully got into the back of the car, holding Kevin on her lap. It had not been the most successful of visits.

She put her son straight to bed after persuading him to swallow a powder, as her mother had suggested. She knew they usually worked when Lorna was a little feverish, and she knew that sleep, at the moment, would be the best cure. Lorna came back at twelve o'clock as arranged, and the two of them enjoyed a meal of sausages and mash, followed by tarts oozing with raspberry jam.

'Save some for Kevin, Mummy,' said Lorna. She was worried to hear that her little brother was not well. 'What's the matter with him?' she asked. 'Has he been sick? I thought he ate too much jelly and ice cream at the party,' she added, nodding in an old-fashioned way.

Rachel smiled. 'No, love. He's got a headache and he's a bit hot, like you were that time when you were getting chicken pox. Oh dear! I wonder if that's what's the matter with him.' But she knew if it was chicken pox, then it was not too serious. 'Yes, I'll put a sausage and some potato to keep warm. I expect he'll wake up soon, then he'll enjoy it.'

Kevin slept for a couple of hours. When he awoke, the dinner that Rachel had saved for him was past its best. He could not be coaxed to eat anything, even a boiled egg with soldiers which he usually enjoyed, but he did manage to drink a cup of milk. Rachel was concerned that he was still very hot.

'It hurts, Mummy,' he said, pointing vaguely to the region of his neck, and then, without any warning, he was violently sick.

'Oh, my poor little boy!' she cried, picking him up and carrying him away from his soiled bed and into her own bedroom. 'You're really poorly, aren't you? Never mind. Mummy will ring for the doctor and we'll soon have you right again. Lorna . . .' She shouted downstairs to her daughter. 'Come up here, will you, darling, and look after Kevin? He's not very well at all and I'm going to ring the doctor.'

Dr Mason had been to the house only a few times before, to deal with Lorna's chicken pox and measles, but Kevin, until now, had been a very healthy child. He looked concerned when he had examined him. The little boy had closed his eyes again and was not responding to the voices around him, or to the ministrations of the doctor.

'I'm going to get him into hospital straight away,' Dr Mason told Rachel. 'It's far better to be safe than sorry, and I must confess I don't like the look of this little chap at all.'

'Why? What's the matter with him, Doctor?' Rachel was very frightened by this time. 'I thought he was just a bit feverish, so I put him to bed. Should I . . .? Do you think I should have called you sooner? What . . . what do you think it is?'

The doctor shook his head. 'I can't be absolutely sure, and I hope I'm wrong, but I think it could be . . . meningitis.'

Rachel gave a loud shriek. 'Oh no! I'd no idea . . .'

'Of course you hadn't, Mrs Watkins. You've done everything you could, so don't start reproaching yourself. This bacterial meningitis – if that's what it is – starts very quickly sometimes and needs treatment as soon as possible. More drastic treatment than I am able to prescribe. Now, may I use your phone?'

The next half-hour seemed like a nightmare to Rachel. Lorna started to cry when she was told that Kevin was to go into hospital, and she cried even more when the ambulance arrived. She wanted to go with her little brother and her mummy, who was accompanying him to the hospital. In a frantic phone call to her mother Rachel told her what was happening. Rachel's father said he would come at once to

133

take Lorna to be looked after by her grandparents for as long as it was necessary.

'And get in touch with that husband of yours,' said Lizzie. 'He's never there when he's needed, that fellow. Gadding off on his travels when that little lad's poorly. Tell him to get himself home.'

I will if I can, Mother, thought Rachel. The trouble was, would Derek be where he'd said he might be? She very much doubted it. She recalled that she had felt a pressing need, when he was leaving, to know his itinerary. Could it have been some sort of premonition? she wondered.

Kevin was taken speedily into the isolation ward on arrival at the hospital. Rachel could sense the urgency of the doctor and the nurses, who advised her to try not to worry. They even offered her a room for the night so that she could stay and be near to her son. She gladly accepted. She would be on her own if she went home. She felt the need to be with her precious little son and she knew that Lorna was safe with her grandparents. Dear God, please don't let anything happen to him, she prayed silently, over and over again.

It was past five o'clock in the afternoon before she had a chance to try to contact Derek. The only way she could think of doing so was through Whittakers, and she prayed that the sales manager or someone in charge would still be on the premises. She inwardly cursed her husband for not giving her the names of the hotels where he might – or might not – be staying. Fortunately, the sales manager was still at work.

'Derek Watkins? Ah yes,' he said. 'I'll see what I can do, but Derek is such a good sales rep that we often leave him to his own devices. To be quite honest, Mrs Watkins, we don't always know ourselves exactly where he is, but he brings home the bacon – so to speak – and that's all we're bothered about. Richmond he said, did he? Or Barnard Castle? I see . . . Listen, I'll ring the hotels where we know he's stayed before and just hope he's there, at one of them. No, don't worry, Mrs Watkins, I'll do it. No trouble at all. I'm only too pleased to help. I'll tell him to get back home as soon as he can, or I'll leave a message to that effect. Can you give me your number, please, and I'll get back to you.'

The nurse in charge had agreed readily that Rachel should use the phone, and she sat in a small room off the main ward anxiously awaiting a return call. But it was as she had feared. Derek was not in Richmond or in Barnard Castle.

'There is another possibility,' said the sales manager. 'We know he spends quite a lot of time in the Ripon area.'

'Ripon? But that's not all that far away,' said Rachel, surprised.

'Quite so, but he sometimes stays overnight because we have a lot of clients in that area. Come to think of it, though, he hasn't presented a bill just lately for the hotel he uses. Maybe he stays somewhere else. But it's worth a try. I'll ring them and get back to you.'

'Thank you,' said Rachel. 'It's very kind of you. You will tell them how urgent it is, won't you? Our little boy, he's very poorly . . .'

But Derek was not staying at the hotel in the town square. The hotel manager, however, remembered him from the times he had stayed there in the past. What was more, he was sure he had seen him, only that morning, calling at a shop just off the square. He promised he would try to trace him and tell him he was needed urgently at home. Yes, he would certainly impress upon Mr Watkins that it was urgent.

The message was relayed back to Rachel. Well, at least she knew he was in Ripon, but what he was up to there was anybody's guess. At that moment she couldn't have cared less about that, but it was imperative that he should get back. She knew he loved their little boy almost as much as she did.

He did not return that night, which was no great surprise to her. She spent a sleepless few hours, eventually dropping off at about three o'clock the following morning when a kindly nurse gave her a tranquilliser. When she woke the doctor allowed her to stay for a few moments at her son's bedside, but she did not need anyone to tell her that he was not responding, as yet, to the treatment. Moreover, she could see that a rash had appeared on his face, the only part of him that was visible.

And still Derek had not arrived back. Her mother came, though, in the middle of the morning, having left Lorna in the care of her husband. They were together, mother and daughter, when the doctor appeared in the small room where Rachel had been sleeping. She could see from a glance at his face that the news was not good. It was, in fact, the worst news of all.

'I'm sorry, Mrs Watkins,' said the doctor. 'We've done all we can. But it was too late to save him, I'm afraid. I'm so sorry.'

Rachel was unaware of the piercing scream she gave. But she remembered, later, that her mother's arms were around her as she collapsed sobbing on to the bed.

Chapter 10

The hotel manager did not pass the message on to Derek until the following morning. He had been told it was urgent; nevertheless, he decided it could wait until the next day. He and his wife had an important dinner engagement that evening in Harrogate and he needed to get home early to prepare himself.

He had a good idea where he would find Derek Watkins. He had seen him several times with Sylvia Maitland, the woman who owned the clothing shop not far away. Moreover, he guessed there was something going on between the pair of them, but it was not for him to tell Whittakers that their sales rep was playing away from home. Not that they would care, he supposed, so long as Mr Watkins was doing his job well. If he wasn't actually at the shop then he expected Mrs Maitland would know where he was.

As it happened, Derek was still at Sylvia's. They had breakfasted and he was packing his suitcase, ready to set off again on his travels. It was his intention to drive around to the several shops they had dealings with in the small towns in the Vale of York, and then to return for another night with Sylvia before heading home the following day, Friday. He received the news that his little son was ill and that his wife wanted him to return home with consternation. His anxiety, however, was more centred around the fact that his wife had managed to discover his whereabouts – and, possibly, the real reason for his absences from home – than the fact that Kevin was poorly. He assumed that the little boy had developed a childish ailment – chicken pox or measles, maybe. There couldn't be all that much wrong with him, he decided. He had been full of beans on Tuesday, enjoying his birthday and tucking into the party food with relish. An excess of ice cream, maybe?

'You'd better get home straightaway, Derek,' said Sylvia, who seemed to be more concerned than he was. 'Your wife wouldn't have contacted you unless there was a good reason, would she? Did you tell her you would be in Ripon?'

'No, did I heck as like!' replied Derek. 'I remember she was quizzing me about where I was going, more than she usually does, and I said I'd be in Richmond or Barnard Castle, more than likely. How the hell has she found out I'm here? She must have rung Whittakers, and they know, of course, that the bulk of our orders are in this region. Oh, bloody hell! I'll have some explaining to do.'

'But I still say it must be quite urgent,' said Sylvia. 'You go home now and see what's wrong. Your little boy will want to see you if he's poorly. And anything else . . . well, that can be sorted out in time, can't it? We've had a good run, Derek.'

'I'm not playing fast and loose with you, Sylvia.' Derek took hold of her hands. 'Please don't think that. Like you say, we've had a good run for our money, but I don't intend to let you go. If Rachel has found out . . . well, I suppose that was bound to happen sooner or later. I knew I would have to come to some decision eventually.'

'I've never put any pressure on you, Derek,' said Sylvia quietly. 'We've never talked about your wife and family, but I do know how fond you are of your children. I can tell by the things you've said now and again. I don't want it to end either. What we've shared together, it's been good. But I know we can't carry on indefinitely like this.'

Derek knew that a day of reckoning was imminent. It was the first time that he and Sylvia had discussed their relationship and where it might, or might not, be heading. 'I'll tell her,' he said decidedly. 'I'll tell Rachel about us, about you and me. I'm sure she must be a bit suspicious like, anyroad. She's not stupid.'

'And . . . the children?' asked Sylvia.

'Oh aye, the children . . . I know.' Derek scratched his head. 'That's the rub. They're grand little kids, both of 'em. But Rachel's very capable and it isn't as if I wouldn't see 'em again. I'd make sure of that.' He felt a sense of shock that he was talking this way, actually considering leaving Rachel and the children. But, for the moment, he knew he must get home and face the music. Rachel was sure to have discovered something by now. And Kevin. He mustn't forget Kevin. That was the main reason for his speedy return, although he doubted there could be very much wrong. The little lad would cheer up when his daddy arrived home. He imagined his blue eyes lighting up with pleasure and his cry of, 'Daddy!'

'I'd best be off then,' he said to Sylvia. 'Don't worry, luv. It'll all sort out in the wash, as me mam says.' He kissed her firmly on the mouth. 'I'll keep in touch. And I'll be back, just as soon as I can. Cheerio for now. Remember what I've said. I don't intend to let you go.'

As soon as he turned the key in the lock and opened the door Derek could sense there was something amiss. It was his mother-in-law, not his wife, who appeared quickly in the hallway. She looked stricken and her red eyes showed signs of recent weeping.

'Derek, thank goodness you're here.' For once her look was sympathetic, though full of sadness. She reached out and took hold of his arms. 'I'm afraid we have some dreadful news for you. It's Kevin . . . he was poorly, very poorly indeed, and I'm afraid that by the time he was taken into hospital . . .'

'Hospital!' cried Derek. 'But I didn't know that. Why didn't you say?'

Lizzie, ignoring his outburst, went on, 'By the time he went into hospital it was already too late. It was very acute meningitis, you see, Derek.'

'What are you trying to say? What do you mean?'

Frantically he pushed past Lizzie and went into the living room. His wife was sitting on the settee, all hunched up and with a handkerchief held to her eyes. His own mother, Phyllis, was at her side, with an arm around her, and he was vaguely aware of his father, too, somewhere in the room.

Rachel lifted a tragic face and looked across at him. Her eyes were swollen with tears. 'Derek,' she breathed, her voice husky and scarcely audible. 'He's gone. Our dear little Kevin. Oh, Derek . . .'

'What!' He was stunned, rooted to the spot and quite unable to move across the room to comfort his wife. 'But . . . he can't be,' he cried. 'He was fine two days ago. I don't believe it. He can't have gone so quickly.' He knew, though, that the dreadful thing they were telling him must be true, but it was so appalling, so unbelievable, that it would not sink into his consciousness.

'I'm afraid it's true, lad.' His father was at his side then, with his arm round his shoulders. 'It's been a terrible shock to us all. We can scarcely believe it. One day he was as right as rain, and the next he was . . . gone. The doctor said it happens like that sometimes. It was a particularly virulent form of meningitis. The only consolation is that the little lad didn't suffer very much, bless him.'

'And that's supposed to be a comfort, is it?' stormed Derek. He pulled away from his father's arm. 'My little lad . . . dead, just like that. And I had no idea. Why didn't you let me know how bad he was?'

'We tried, Derek,' said his wife. She looked at him sorrowfully, but not, he thought, reproachfully. He could see she was too grief-stricken at that moment to censure him for his absence. 'But we couldn't trace you in time. And then it was too late.'

Derek burst into tears, the only time he had done so since he was a small boy. Derek Watkins was normally too tough, too big a man for tears. But now he could feel uncontrollable sobs racking his body as his father led him to an armchair and made him sit down.

'A nip of brandy,' said his father. 'It's good for shock if nowt else.' His mother was there at once with a glass, the contents of which he gulped down, feeling the fiery liquid travel down to his stomach, warming him, but doing nothing to ease the pain. How could it? How could anything?

'Where's our Lorna?' he asked, glancing round the room. The little girl was missing, as was Percy Harding, her grandad.

'Percy's taken her for a walk,' said his mother. 'She doesn't know yet, poor little mite, but she senses there's summat wrong, of course. Her grandad said he'd take her to feed the ducks on t' pond, although his heart's not in it. It's taken the heart out of all of us, Derek love. Anyroad, when they come back we'd all best go and leave you on your own for a while; you and Rachel and little Lorna . . .'

Rachel, hearing the remark, realised that she was fearful of being left alone with her husband and Lorna. She had found the presence of their parents to be a bolstering support, although it had done nothing to assuage her grief. She doubted that anything would ever help to ease the pain she felt.

She and her mother had left the hospital towards midday. There was nothing they could do if they stayed and Rachel knew she must get back to Lorna. Her daughter would be wondering where she was, although Rachel was dreading breaking the news to her. Lizzie had phoned from the hospital and told Derek's parents what had happened; they had already been warned that their grandson was very poorly. Jack Watkins came to take them home and they all congregated at Rachel's house. The parents did not want to leave the young woman on her own, especially as Derek had not yet returned. It had seemed a good idea to remove Lorna from the sad scene, and so she had gone off happily enough with her grandad for a walk to the duck pond, not far from her grandparents' house.

'It's all right. You go now, Phyllis,' said Rachel, coming to an agonising decision. 'It's been good of you to stay with me, but I'll be OK. Derek's here now. Perhaps you and Jack could take my mother home in the car?' Phyllis and Jack both agreed that of course they would. 'Dad will bring Lorna back here, won't he, Mum?'

'Yes, that's right, dear,' said her mother. 'He said he'd take her back to our house and make her a sandwich for lunch, to save you the bother. I don't suppose they'll be very long now. Are you sure you'll be all right?'

'I shall have to be, won't I, Mum?' said Rachel, trying to hold back another flood of tears. 'Derek and I will have to decide how to tell Lorna, won't we?'

'You must tell her the truth, love,' said Lizzie, in an unusually gentle and understanding voice. 'She's got to be told; there's no getting away from it. And she'll need more love and comfort than ever now.'

'She will get it, I can assure you,' replied Rachel. 'But she did love her little brother so much.' She could not prevent a sob from escaping.

'We all did, my dear,' said Phyllis gently.

They said goodbye in a welter of hugs and kisses, from which Derek stood apart. His father clasped his shoulder in a gesture of support and his mother kissed his cheek, but it was clear he wanted no active part in the expressions of grief. He breathed an audible sigh of relief after they had gone. He and Rachel stood and looked at one another. She thought he might have put his arms around her at this moment of mutual sorrow, even though they were no longer in the habit of embracing, but he did not do so.

'What the hell happened, Rachel?' he asked. She could see no sign of affection or comfort in his look, only confusion and disbelief. 'And why did it happen so quickly? Didn't you realise he was ill?'

'We've told you, Derek,' she sighed, flopping down on to the settee again. Derek sat down too, not at her side, but on a chair opposite her. 'It was a very virulent form of meningitis; meningococcal meningitis – something like that – the

142

doctor said. It attacks the membranes around the brain. They did all they could; I know that.'

'Don't blind me with science,' said Derek. 'Never mind all yer long words. What happened? Just tell me.'

She explained that Kevin had seemed a little out of sorts in the morning and that she had thought he might just be over-tired after the party. 'My mother didn't think there was much wrong with him,' she said, 'and neither did I really. You know yourself how children can seem to be ill one moment, and the next they're fine again.'

'D'you mean to tell me you took the little lad to your mother's, when you knew he wasn't feeling well? And what does your blasted mother know about anything? You should start thinking for yourself, Rachel, instead of running back to Mummy all the time. You left it too late, didn't you? Admit it! You should have sent for the doctor right away at the first sign he wasn't well.' His voice was growing louder and louder and she could see the anger glazing in his steely blue eyes.

'That's not fair, Derek!' she shouted back at him, despite her grief. 'I took him out for a walk, that's all. I thought the fresh air would do him good; it was a nice sunny day. And there's no need to start blaming my mother, either. You can see how upset she is about Kevin. She loved him too, you know. My father brought us back in the car almost straight-away, then I called the doctor when I could see he wasn't getting any better. There's nothing else I could have done.' She looked at him coldly, her eyes narrowed.

'Anyway, where were you? You weren't where you said you would be. And your manager said you weren't staying at the usual hotel in Ripon either. Where were you, Derek?'

'I came as soon as I found out,' he replied. 'I wasn't told until this morning. I came straight back.'

'Don't dodge the question, Derek. I asked you where you were.'

'I was staying with a friend,' he replied, still staring at her stonily.

'A . . . friend?'

'Yes, a very good friend, as a matter of fact. Oh, for God's sake, Rachel, just leave it, can't you? Now is not the time to be talking about it. I'm back now, aren't I? And we've got to get through the next few days somehow, haven't we?'

His glance softened a little then, and the anger left her eyes, too, as she looked back at him. Not only the next few days, but the rest of our lives, she thought. She realised, though, that it was the beginning of the end of everything between herself and Derek. While his son had been fighting for his life, it seemed that Derek had been in the arms of another woman, but in her grief over the loss of Kevin, Rachel found she could barely bring herself to care.

'Lorna will be back soon,' she said. 'I'd better be thinking how I'm going to tell her. Unless . . . we tell her together?'

'No, you do it,' said Derek gruffly. 'You're far better at that sort of thing than I am. Tell her the truth, like your mother said. She was right for once. But don't go giving her any clap-trap about him being with Jesus. He's died, that's all.'

'I'll tell her the truth, Derek,' replied Rachel, as calmly as she could. 'Look, I don't understand it any more than you do, why Kevin has . . . gone. And I must admit I can't understand the ways of the Lord either, at this moment.'

'I never could,' he said abruptly.

Just then there was a knock at the door and she knew that her father had arrived, bringing Lorna back.

'She's fed the ducks and she's had a nice chicken sand-wich, haven't you, pet?' he said, trying to smile through his sadness. 'So . . . I'll leave her with you now, Rachel, love. If you want anything, anything at all, give your mother and me a ring. We're always there for you, you know.'

'Thanks, Dad,' Rachel said, feeling the tears welling up again, but she knew she must blink them back for Lorna's sake. She closed the door and bent to kiss her daughter. 'You've had a nice time then, have you, darling?'

'Yes,' said Lorna, 'but Grandad's a bit sad today. He says he's got a headache and that's why he was quiet. And

Grandma's sad too. I went into the kitchen and she was making a cup of tea, but she was crying, Mummy. What's the matter with them?' She didn't wait for an answer. 'And what about Kevin? Grandma said he was still in hospital. Can I go and see him, Mummy?' She dashed into the living room with Rachel behind her.

'Hi there, Lorna,' said Derek, smiling sadly at her. He stood up at once and, with a meaningful look at Rachel, disappeared into the kitchen.

Rachel sat down on the settee. 'Lorna, darling, come and sit next to Mummy,' she said. 'I've got something to tell you . . . about why Grandma and Grandad are so sad, and your daddy and I as well.'

The child looked up at her in puzzlement. 'Is it . . . Kevin?' she asked. 'Is he very poorly, Mummy?'

'Yes,' said Rachel. 'I'm afraid he . . . was; very poorly indeed. And sometimes the doctors and nurses can't do anything about it. They tried very hard to make him better, but . . . I'm afraid he won't be coming back to us, darling. He's gone to heaven . . . to live with Jesus.' In spite of what her husband had said she knew that was what she had to tell the little girl. It was what she, Rachel, believed, deep down, despite her anguish and her disbelief that God could be so cruel. And how could she say, bluntly, that Kevin was dead? There was a part of her, still, that found it impossible to believe, and so she could not say the word. But Lorna did.

'You mean he's dead?' she said, her eyes wide with shock and horror. 'You mean . . . I won't ever see him again?'

Rachel nodded gently. 'I'm afraid so, darling. You know what they teach you in Sunday school, that . . . one day . . . we will go to live with Jesus in heaven.'

'But Kevin's only a baby,' cried Lorna. 'He's only two. It's just old people that die.' The enormity of it suddenly struck her. She stared for an agonising moment at Rachel, then she burst into tears. Gigantic sobs shook her little body as she threw herself against her mother, her fists pummelling wildly at Rachel. 'No, no, no!' she yelled. 'He can't be dead!'

Rachel gathered her into her arms, holding her close until her sobs subsided, just a little. 'I'm afraid that's not true, dear,' she said, 'that only old people die. Sometimes children do as well ... but we don't know why. Come on now, love. We've all got to be very brave. Mummy and Daddy are upset as well, just like you.'

Her sobs stopped in a little while, but for the rest of the day she gave way now and again to bouts of weeping. Eventually she allowed herself to be persuaded to do her new jigsaw puzzle and to put her new furniture in her doll's house. Rachel hoped the little girl's pain was not as intense as her own. She remembered her fears the morning Lorna had been born, that she was destined to be a Wednesday's child, to live a life of woe. Until now, Lorna's largely happy nature had allowed her to forget such thoughts, but now she had lost her beloved little brother ... She is young, she told herself. She knew that children soon forgot their worries if they were distracted by other interests. Maybe in a few weeks' time, or less, Lorna would not be so heartbroken about her brother; the memories would fade in her young mind. But as for Rachel, she felt her heartache would go on for ever.

Lorna seemed glad to go to bed early that night, cuddling Mister Ted. She had stopped talking about Kevin, though she still looked at her mother with sad, almost reproachful, eyes. Rachel gave her a junior aspirin with her drink of milk. The child deserved to sleep well before the awful reality returned the following morning, and Rachel prayed that she would not suffer from nightmares as she sometimes did.

The next couple of days were busy with the arrangements that needed to be made for the little boy's funeral. Rachel was glad to accept her mother's offer to look after Lorna during the day, with the stipulation that the child must come home to sleep in her own bed at night. She knew Lorna's grandparents would try to distract her, despite their own grief, with little treats and outings, and Derek's parents, too, were anxious to do their share.

A sort of uneasy truce existed between Rachel and Derek as they went about the sad business of seeing the vicar and the funeral director. Now was not the time to discuss the rift in their marriage, but Rachel could not help but be apprehensive about what the future held for them as a family.

When Rachel's friends called to see her, as she knew they would, to offer their condolences, Derek pointedly disappeared into another room. Pauline Jeffreys was the first to come with a bunch of sweet-smelling roses; not funeral flowers, but a token of love for her friend. Rachel was glad of her quiet sympathy and the fact that she did not preach or try to offer any explanation for what had happened.

'I'm angry,' Rachel told her, 'as well as unbelievably sad. Why has God done this to us? I can't believe He could be so cruel.'

Pauline did not disagree. 'You have a right to be angry,' she told her. 'Don't try to stem your grief, Rachel. Let it out, cry when you want to. And remember that your friends are all here for you when you need us . . . And God is too,' she added gently, 'although it may not seem like it at the moment.'

Rachel had been dreading a visit from the stalwarts of the Young Wives' Group. She felt she could not face their platitudes. If they were to tell her that Jesus needed Kevin more than she did and that there was a purpose behind it all, she felt she would scream and rave at them. It was, however, only two of the group who came round on the Sunday afternoon following the little boy's death – Judith Prendergast and Miriam Curtis. Rachel, to her surprise, found she was heartened by their visit. They did not comment on her absence from church that morning. She could not have faced a congregation of people, however sympathetic they might be, and the two women obviously understood this.

'We are so very, very sorry,' Judith told her, with tears in her eyes, and Rachel did not doubt her sincerity. 'It is hard to understand, isn't it? God moves in mysterious ways sometimes . . .' Rachel had expected that and she waited for a well-worn cliché to follow. But all Judith said was, 'But God is there for you, Rachel, my dear. Don't forget that, though I know you must feel that He has deserted you at the moment.'

'Yes, that's exactly how I feel, Judith,' she said, amazed that the woman could be so understanding.

'We are remembering you in our prayers,' added Miriam, 'you and Derek and little Lorna.'

'Thank you, Miriam,' Rachel replied sincerely. 'I know we are going to need them.'

'How is Derek taking it?' asked Miriam.

'How do you think?' Rachel almost snapped, before adding more quietly, 'He's devastated, just as I am. He's taken Lorna out for a long walk this afternoon to try and get her away from . . . everything.'

'This may be a chance for you and Derek to draw closer together,' said Judith. Rachel nodded. She knew Judith truly believed that her prayers for their marriage would be answered, but Rachel knew, in her heart, that there was little hope of a real reconciliation. All the same, she was glad the two women had been to see her. They had amused her at times, they had made her cross, but their hearts were in the right place and she was grateful now for their friendship.

The funeral, as was only to be expected, was a very sad and poignant occasion, but Rachel found she was able to gain comfort from the Reverend Michael Laycock's words and his sympathetic and reverent ministrations. He and his wife, Kathleen, had helped her greatly in the days leading up to the funeral. They had both called to see her, together and separately, not just in their capacity as the vicar and his wife, but as personal friends. Their presence and quiet words of comfort strengthened her.

St Matthew's church was more than half full of people who had come to give their support and whatever solace they could to little Kevin's family – personal friends of Rachel and Derek, neighbours from their present and previous homes, members of the congregation and the Young Wives' Group, and several of the teaching staff from Kilbeck Infant School. Rachel could not hold back her tears as the little white coffin, bearing a wreath of late summer roses – 'To our darling Kevin, with love from Mummy, Daddy and Lorna' – was carried down the aisle by two pall-bearers. Derek, at her side, took hold of her hand, and she was glad at that moment of his nearness as they shared in their common suffering, but she knew they were, in reality, just as far apart as ever. Lorna was not with them. Rachel had decided that the sadness of the occasion would be too much for her to undergo, and so she was spending the day with her new friend, Carol, and her family.

The hymns that Rachel had chosen, however, were Lorna's favourites from Sunday school. The little girl had been teaching them to Kevin and he had started to sing them along with her in his high-pitched and sometimes piercing little voice. Rachel could hear him now in her memory as he had used to sing, 'Jesus wants me for a sunbeam, To shine for Him each day . . .'

The Reverend Michael spoke movingly of the joy the little boy had brought to them all during his all-too-short life. 'These are memories,' he said, 'that can never be taken away, and may they be a blessing and a comfort to you in the dark days that are sure to lie ahead.'

The next hymn, 'All Things Bright and Beautiful', was not a personal favourite of Rachel's, but Lorna loved it and so, she guessed, would Kevin have done as he grew older. It was beloved of all children as it told of the simple things of life which they understood – flowers, birds, cold winter winds and summer sunshine – pleasures that her dear little son had not lived long enough to appreciate.

After the heart-rending conclusion of the service at the graveside the family and a few close friends went back to the Hardings' house. Lizzie, with Phyllis's help, had prepared a simple buffet meal before they set off for church, so this was quickly assembled. Cups of tea, sandwiches and cakes were handed round in an effort to return to a semblance of normality, but it was a very sad little group of people who were gathered there. Rachel knew that the funeral meal of an older person often provided an opportunity to dispense with sadness and begin to look to the future again, but it was not so in this case. Everyone was still feeling the sorrow and piteousness of the occasion and no one spoke more than they needed to.

Rachel could see that the melancholy atmosphere was affecting Derek badly. She sensed his restlessness and irritation that he had to be there at all. She understood how he felt and it did not anger her; she knew he needed to deal with his grief in his own way. She was not surprised when he came over to her and said that he wanted to be on his own for a while.

'I'll take meself off for a walk,' he said. 'Try and clear me head a bit. You don't mind, do you? All this lot . . . it's getting to me.'

'I know how you feel, Derek,' she said. 'You go, but I'll have to stay here.' She knew he would not want her with him anyway, but he had, at least, told her what he was doing instead of storming off without a word.

He walked briskly into Melcaster, then along to the Queen's Arms on the outskirts of the town where he downed a whisky and soda. The pub was just about to close, but he did not intend to sit drinking, apart from a quick one to put some heart into him, if that were possible.

There was a phone box across the road. He entered it and dialled the Ripon number that he had called several times over the past few days, unknown to Rachel.

'Sylvia . . . Yes, love, it's me . . . Oh, I'm all right, I suppose . . . Yes, it's all over now, but it's been dreadful as I'm sure you can imagine. My poor little lad . . . I'll see you as soon as I can . . . Yes, next week, all being well . . . Yes, I love you too; you know I do . . .' It was only very recently that he had actually told her so. 'No, I don't know exactly when,

Sylvia. It's difficult . . . No, I'm not changing my mind, but I'll have to wait and see how things go, under the circumstances . . . Yes, that's right. I knew you'd understand . . . Tara, luv. See you soon.'

He left the phone box and walked along a path which led to the foothills of the Pennines. The thought of Sylvia was the only ray of hope on his horizon. He had realised, lately, that he did love her, as much as he was capable of loving anyone but himself. She was assuredly the woman with whom he wanted to share his future, eventually. He knew, though, that it would be impossible to even think of leaving Rachel at the moment, and he tried to close his mind to the effect that his leaving might have upon Lorna.

Chapter 11

'Mummy, Mummy... It's here again... Mummy, come here now! It's coming to get me!'

Rachel, sitting on her own by the fireside, dropped the book she had been trying to read and dashed upstairs to her daughter's room. She switched on the main light, although a small lamp which gave out a faint glow was always left alight at Lorna's bedside, to relieve the stark darkness and, hopefully, to help to allay her fears. The little girl was sitting bolt upright in bed, her eyes wide with fright. These night-time fears were becoming more frequent. It was the second one that week, although there had been a period after Kevin's death, surprisingly, when they had not occurred at all. Fortunately, the sight of her mother was enough to remove most of the fear from her eyes.

Rachel sat on the bed and put her arms around her. 'There's nothing there, darling. It's just a nasty old dream again. But we'll make absolutely sure, shall we? Where... where was it?'

'Behind the curtains, Mummy, like it always is. It's got Kevin, and now it's coming to get me. Make it go away, Mummy, please!'

Rachel flung back the curtains as she had done several times before, revealing the blackness of the November night outside the window. 'There, see. There's nothing there at all. There's nothing to be frightened of, but I'll stay with you for a little while, shall I?' Lorna nodded. 'Now, I'll go and get you a warm drink of milk and I'll give you a little tablet to help you to get to sleep again.'

'Tell Daddy to come up and see me,' said Lorna bossily. She had become more demanding of late, insisting that her father as well as her mother should minister to her needs.

'I'm afraid Daddy's not here, darling,' said Rachel. 'He's gone out for the evening. I don't suppose he'll be very long and I'll tell him as soon as he comes in, but you'll probably be fast asleep by then.'

'Why? Why can't I see him?' said Lorna petulantly. 'Where's he gone?'

'He's gone out with Uncle Charlie. You know he does that sometimes. Never mind, love. I'm here, aren't I? I'll go and get that drink. You have a chat to Mister Ted. See, he's fallen out of bed, poor old chap.' She picked up the beloved teddy bear and handed him to Lorna.

The little girl stared at her with accusing eyes as though she was blaming Rachel for her father's absence. 'I wanted Daddy,' she said, 'as well as you.'

'I know, dear,' said Rachel softly. 'I'm sure he won't be long. I'll be back in a minute or two.' It was almost as though she knew, thought Rachel, as she went downstairs again, that things were not right between her parents, although both Rachel and Derek tried not to let their differences and aloofness towards one another affect their dealings with Lorna.

She warmed the milk, added some sugar, then took it back upstairs with a children's aspirin tablet. She did not believe in dosing children unnecessarily, but it was important just now to calm Lorna down a little. She was overwrought and her fears were very real to her. Rachel found it even more distressing when the little girl talked about whatever it was that scared her having taken Kevin.

'Here, drink this, darling,' she said. 'It's not too hot, and there's a little tablet. It'll help you to sleep. See, I've broken it in half so it's easier to swallow.' Lorna, she was pleased to see, did as she was told. She seemed calmer now. 'Lorna,' said Rachel gently. 'You know that Kevin's in heaven, don't you? He's quite safe, and we have to believe he's happy, too.

Whatever it is that frightened you, well, it's not got Kevin, and you can be sure of that. And there's nothing here to harm you, either. It was just another nasty dream. Now, try and forget about it.'

Lorna drank the last drop of her milk and handed the cup back to her mother, but her look still held a tinge of reproach.

'There are all sorts of things to look forward to,' Rachel went on. 'It will be Christmas quite soon.' Although that was a time that Rachel, in truth, was dreading. 'And then, soon afterwards, you'll be starting school. Won't that be exciting? I know you can't wait for that.'

'Yes, and Carol as well,' said Lorna, cheering up a little. 'D'you think we'll be in the same class, Mummy?'

'Yes, of course you will, darling,' said Rachel, although she had an idea there might be too many entrants for just the one class. However, a quiet word with Miss Lacey should do the trick. 'Now, let me tuck you up again, then you can get off to sleep.' She kissed her forehead. 'Goodnight, Lorna love. God bless. There's nothing to worry about, nothing at all.'

'Goodnight, Mummy.' The child actually smiled a little, the light returning to her eyes. She seemed pacified, to Rachel's relief. But she added, 'Tell Daddy, won't you? Tell him to come up and see me, even if I'm asleep.'

She had certainly been more demanding and troublesome of late, Rachel reflected as she sat by the fireside on her own again, but it was hardly surprising. The death of her little brother had been a tremendous shock to her, as it had been to all of them. She did not mention him as much now, but whenever she did want to talk about him, Rachel did not discourage her. She had been spending more time with her grandparents, too, since Kevin was taken from them so suddenly. The older people, quite naturally, sought comfort in their one remaining grandchild, and Lorna, very cunningly, was playing on this. Grandma Lizzie, once again, was becoming very close to the child. Rachel recalled how there had been a bond between the two of them when Lizzie had looked after her as a baby, and that bond had been renewed of late.

It would be better for everyone when Lorna started school. She would have new interests, new friends, all kinds of fresh experiences to occupy her mind. Hopefully, the night-time fears would then evaporate and she would learn to be independent, not so reliant upon Rachel, or her grandmother. Rachel could not help resenting, at times, the influence her mother had on the child.

It was not only Lorna, though, who was a cause of concern to Rachel. She knew that relations between herself and Derek had reached a point of no return. There was little left now in their marriage except their affection for their daughter, and Rachel knew, whatever faults and failings he might have, that Derek loved his little girl. He had admitted to his wife, however, that he had met someone else. She had tackled him, a few weeks after Kevin's death, about his absences from home. For a while he had stayed in the Melcaster area, sleeping at home each night, but then his travels further afield and his overnight absences had started again.

'Please don't lie to me, Derek,' she had said to him. 'There's no point in trying to keep up a pretence any longer. You had told me when . . . when Kevin died that you were up in the north somewhere, but you weren't. You were in Ripon. Credit me with a bit of common sense. There's another woman, isn't there? This very good friend of yours, it's a lady friend, isn't it?'

Derek had nodded. 'I'm sorry, Rachel. I didn't mean it to happen, but it . . . well . . . it did.'

'Go on then. Tell me. Who is she?'

'She has a shop in Ripon,' Derek had replied. 'She sells . . . the sort of things we make at Whittakers. That's how I met her. And that's all you need to know . . . at the moment.'

'But it's not just a passing fancy, is it? Be honest with me, Derek. Do you intend to go and live with her, instead of with me and Lorna? I've got to know.'

'Oh, for God's sake, Rachel! I don't know!' he had cried. 'Don't pester me. I've told you, I didn't intend it to happen, but,' he had shrugged, 'well, there you are. I'm sorry, especially with – er – Kevin and everything. But you're right; it's not a passing fancy.'

Rachel had come to the conclusion that there might have been several of those. She remembered the occasion, ages ago – Coronation Day, if her memory served her correctly – when Derek had not been where he said he was, with Charlie and his mates. Marlene had let the cat out of the bag that time, and there had been other times when she had had reason to doubt him.

'You and me,' he had gone on, 'we were never right for one another, Rachel. We should never have got married.'

'Well . . . why did we then?' she had asked. 'We must have thought it would work out all right.'

'Oh, I dunno. P'raps we were too young, like yer mother said. Happen I wanted to spite her.' He had grinned weakly. 'No, I don't really mean that. I fancied you, Rachel. You were a smashing girl. I couldn't believe my luck when you said you'd go out with me. But you were always too good for me – streets ahead of me. For a start, you're much nicer and kinder.'

He had been starting to get maudlin and that was the last thing she wanted. 'Leave it, Derek,' she had said. 'You know I've never thought that I'm better than anyone else. Whatever faults I may have, I'm not a snob. And we were OK at one time.' She had looked at him keenly, half smiling. 'We managed to have two lovely children, didn't we? I know you love Lorna very much, and Kevin . . . well, he brought us a lot of joy, didn't he, in the short time we had him?'

Derek had nodded glumly. She had seen the glimmer of a tear in the corner of his eye. The only time he had ever wept, to her knowledge, was at the death of their little boy. He had been heartbroken. She had to believe there was some good in Derek – as she tried to believe there was in everyone –

and maybe this other woman, whoever she was, brought out the best in him, whereas she, Rachel, so often seemed to bring out the worst.

'I didn't mean it,' he had said. 'You know, when I said it was your fault, that you didn't call the doctor in time. I was angry, that's all. Angry with meself for not being there. It was so cruel. I couldn't believe it when I came home and found he wasn't there any more.'

'We've got our memories, Derek,' she had said quietly, 'and we've got the rest of our lives to lead. But it's best if there can be complete honesty between us from now on. I won't ask you where you are, but please . . . no more lies.'

'No more lies,' he had repeated soberly.

From that day on, he had not mentioned Ripon or the woman who lived there again. Rachel did not even know her name, but she guessed he was still seeing her, although he did not stay away from home quite as often as he had done in the past. He had, however, started seeing Charlie Fleming again, and she did not doubt that, on those occasions, he was exactly where he said he would be. Charlie was a good friend. If anyone could, he was the one to relieve Derek's low spirits, if only temporarily, whereas she and Derek had very little left to say to one another.

It might have been that the death of a beloved child would bring them closer together again. That was what her friends from the Young Wives' Group firmly believed would happen. There was only Pauline who knew the truth; that Rachel and Derek, sooner or later, would go their separate ways.

The intense pain of Kevin's death had eased a little now, and Rachel was able to think of him, and even smile at memories, without bursting into tears. She did not mind the solitude in the evenings when Derek was out. It was preferable to the tension which sometimes built up between them. It was so acute at times that she would go into another room to relieve it. The heart-to-heart chat they had had a few weeks back had been an isolated occasion. Rachel wondered why he stayed with her; she guessed it

157

was for the sake of Lorna, not herself.

She had little doubt that Derek would go his own way, possibly sooner rather than later. It was awful to think that it would not affect her overmuch, but that was the truth. Rachel no longer cared very much what he did. As far as she was concerned her marriage was at an end. It had ended the day that Kevin died, when she had discovered the truth about Derek's absences from home. She was used to his absences now and, if she were honest, she was much more contented and at ease with herself when he was away. But she knew, for Lorna's sake, that she could not 'show him the door', which was what, in truth, she felt like doing. The little girl was already showing signs of over-anxiety and trauma. She hoped, whatever Derek might have in mind, that he would wait until after Lorna had started school. When she was older and had other interests then maybe she would be better able to cope with her father leaving the family home. Because Rachel knew that, eventually, this was inevitable.

When her eyelids began to droop she knew it was time to retire to bed. Derek had not returned and he did not do so until she was dropping off to sleep. The sound of his key in the lock roused her, but he slept that night in what had been Kevin's room, as he often did. She had not been able to tell him of Lorna's request that he should go to see her, but fortunately the child did not wake up again that night.

Rachel was relieved when Christmas was over. It was a celebration she had been dreading that year. She and Derek and Lorna spent part of Christmas Day with her parents, and part of Boxing Day with Derek's. They all tried to adopt a semblance of cheerfulness for Lorna's sake, and the little girl, once again, was showered with an abundance of presents. Rachel's mother and Derek managed to be studiedly polite to one another, so the two days passed without any acrimony. Rachel's sorrow, though, increased over the holiday period, and it was the same at New Year as the thoughts of the child she had lost returned with a deeper poignancy. She was glad when, a few days into 1958, the time came for Lorna to start in the reception class at Kilbeck Infant School.

Rachel and Jenny Forrest, Carol's mother, with their two little girls, set off well before nine o'clock to walk to the school. It was a cold day with a sprinkling of snow on the ground, but Lorna and Carol, warmly wrapped in their duffel coats, woollen bonnets, scarves and gloves, and shod in shiny black wellingtons, ran ahead merrily, holding hands. Starting school was a great adventure for both of them and neither had any fears. A word with Miss Lacey, the headmistress, whom Rachel knew so well, had insured that the two little girls would be put into the same class. It would have been a disappointment to both of them if they had been separated.

Rachel found it quite a novel experience to be taking her own child to school, instead of being on the receiving end, welcoming the new entrants. Not that she had ever had charge of the reception class, but she knew that the teachers of these very young children needed to be extra patient and loving for the first few days and weeks of a new school year.

For the first day – or the first few days, depending on the temperament of the individual child – parents were allowed to take their offspring right inside the building, instead of waving goodbye at the gate, which they would be expected to do when the children became used to leaving them. Fathers were very few and far between. There were the odd one or two to be seen, but it was, by and large, a crowd of anxious-looking mothers with their children, who were making their way to the two reception classrooms. They had been informed beforehand who their child's teacher would be – Mrs Davenport or Mrs Phillips. Pauline Jeffreys, who had taken a reception class for many years, was now having a change, teaching six- to seven-year-olds. Rachel thought it was perhaps just as well that Lorna was not to be in the class of her friend, whom the little girl was used to calling Aunty Pauline. It would be better for her to be with someone whom she could regard solely as a teacher.

Rachel did not know either of the teachers. They had both started there since she had left the school. Mrs Davenport was the teacher who was to have charge of Lorna and Carol, and Rachel was surprised to see that the young woman was pregnant; several months so, she guessed. Oh dear! she thought. She hoped that looking after so many children would not be too much for her; also, with rather more self-interest, she hoped that Lorna would not have to undergo a change of teacher too soon. Still, there was nothing she could do about it. She couldn't possibly ask Miss Lacey to put her child in the other class; she had already asked a favour in requesting that Lorna might be with her friend.

Mrs Davenport, however, seemed to be a very capable person, well built and quite athletic-looking, with a smiling face and a cheerful and friendly manner. Rachel found herself warming to her. Here was a person she could trust to look after her little girl. Not that Rachel anticipated any difficulties with Lorna's first experiences of school. Several of the children were looking apprehensive, some were whimpering, and a few were crying quite loudly and clinging to their mothers' hands. She knew, though, that tears often stopped immediately once Mummy had departed, especially with a teacher who could be firm as well as kind.

Lorna smiled brightly as the teacher welcomed her. 'Hello, Lorna. You're quite used to this school, aren't you, because your mummy used to teach here, didn't she? And I know you've been looking forward to coming.'

'Yes,' the child replied, quite shyly for once, but Rachel knew she would soon find her tongue as she got to know this new person.

'Now, this is your cloakroom tag,' Mrs Davenport continued. 'See, it's got a picture of a rabbit on it. Hang it on the peg with your coat, then you will know which coat is yours. And I see you are wearing wellingtons. That's very sensible because it's snowy today, isn't it? But you've brought some

160

shoes to change into, have you?'

'Yes, they're in here,' said Lorna, displaying her shiny brown leather satchel, one of her grandma's Christmas presents.

'That's lovely,' said her teacher, 'but wellingtons do tend to get mixed up, don't they?' She smiled knowingly at Rachel, who nodded in agreement. Rachel well remembered rainy days and umpteen pairs of wellingtons all mixed up and on the wrong feet. 'So here's a clothes peg, and when you've taken your wellingtons off you can fasten them together. I'm sure you've got your name in them, haven't you?'

Rachel smiled. 'Oh yes, I've made sure of that. And what a good idea about the clothes pegs! Thank you, Mrs Davenport. Come on, Lorna, let's go and get you sorted out, then you can come back to this nice classroom. Doesn't it look lovely?'

'I've tried to make it welcoming,' said Mrs Davenport, nodding to Rachel, as one teacher to another. 'It makes all the difference, doesn't it?'

The classroom walls were arresting, with colourful pictures of fairy stories. There was a bright number frieze depicting one elephant, two tigers, three lions ... and so on. A sand tray stood in one corner with an array of coloured plastic containers, sieves, funnels and large spoons. Rachel knew it was not just intended for play, but for early experience in capacity and volume and weighing. In another corner there was a Wendy House, and in the 'Book Corner' there was a rack filled with picture books and easy reading books, including the old favourites such as *The Gingerbread Boy*, *The Three Billy Goats Gruff*, and *Tales of Milly-Molly-Mandy*, and a large edition of *Peter Rabbit*, with a comfortable carpet and child-size armchairs in which to sit.

Lorna was eager to get back and begin the first day of her school life. She hung her coat on her special peg, changed out of her wellingtons into her Clarks sandals, then waved goodbye to her mother at the classroom door with scarcely a backward glance.

'Bye, Mummy,' she said, not responding, as she usually did, to Rachel's kiss on her cheek. 'Come on, Carol.' She tugged impatiently at her friend's hand. Carol was a little less willing to leave her mother, but there were no tears and the two of them went off happily to start their new adventure.

Rachel was thoughtful on the way home and she and Jenny did not converse very much. Jenny, no doubt, was thinking of her daughter and possibly of her own loneliness now that her nest, so to speak, was empty. Carol was an only child – as Lorna now was – and her mother was a housewife. Rachel knew that she would miss Lorna. The house would seem dreadfully quiet without her. But other thoughts, besides those of her empty house, were now occupying her mind.

Going into Kilbeck Infant School at the start of a new term and seeing all the activity and excitement had awakened memories, mostly very happy ones, for Rachel. She realised that she was slightly envious of the teachers who were returning to work that day. They might pretend that the last thing they wanted, on a cold winter's day, was to return to the old routine, but she knew they would soon fall into it again, enjoying the camaraderie of their colleagues, exchanging stories about the Christmas holidays, and looking forward to a new term, whatever it might have in store for them. Kilbeck Infants had always been a happy school, both for the children and the teaching staff.

I wish I was back there, thought Rachel, saying goodbye to Jenny and re-entering her house. The thought surprised her. She had been contented as a housewife with her two children, and for long periods she had been almost able to forget her former career. It had been out of the question, anyway, to think of returning.

But now . . . Lorna was at school, Kevin had been taken from her so cruelly and unexpectedly, and there was little likelihood – in fact, none at all – of her having any more children. Perhaps, in the near future, it might be possible for her to take up her teaching career again. It might even be necessary for her to do so if Derek were to leave home. She felt as though she was balanced on a knife edge at the moment with that situation. He had not spent as many nights away from home since before Christmas, but she knew it was only a matter of time before he would go back to his old routine. Neither had he mentioned the woman in Ripon, but relations between Rachel and Derek were still as strained as ever. The only time they managed to relax and even smile together was when they were with Lorna. She acted as a buffer between the two of them.

Lorna, and Carol, too, came home for their midday meal. Many of the children stayed for school dinners, at the cost of five shillings a week, but there was no need for the two little girls to do so as they lived very near to the school and their mothers were at home all day.

Lorna was full of excitement when she came home that first lunchtime, the story of all that had happened during the morning pouring out of her. She proudly displayed her name badge, with Lorna Watkins printed in black Indian ink.

'It's so that Mrs Davenport will know who we are, Mummy, but she already knows me. And she knows Carol, too, 'cause she's my friend. Carol and me sit together at a table with two boys, Gary and Billy. Mrs Davenport called him William, but he said, "Please, teacher, they call me Billy, not William." And she said – Mrs Davenport, I mean – she said we hadn't to call her teacher, we must say Mrs Davenport.'

'Quite right, too,' smiled Rachel, remembering how she had disliked the children calling her 'teacher', as the little ones were apt to do. She guessed she might get quite weary before long of Lorna's continual, 'Mrs Davenport says this ... or that ... or the other.' But she was pleased her daughter had settled in so well.

Derek had to listen to the same tales when he came home from work in the evening. Rachel noticed that the care lines which she had observed on his face of late eased a little as he smiled at his daughter. A couple of days later, however, he spent the night away from home again. And then he continued to do so, just one night in every week.

At the beginning of March Lorna celebrated her fifth birthday. Derek was not there for the teatime party to which Lorna had invited a few friends – Susan from Sunday school, Carol and another little girl called Fiona from Kilbeck, and the two boys that Rachel had heard so much about, Gary and Billy. They were all quite well-behaved children and Rachel was able, with Jenny's assistance, to cope with the 'eats' and the games they played afterwards – Pass the Parcel, Musical Bumps, with the aid of the gramophone, and Hunt the Thimble. Lorna, wearing her golden crown as the birthday princess, was pink-cheeked with excitement. Rachel noticed she had a tendency to boss the other children around, even the two boys, and she wondered if this was a trait which would develop as she got older. It was good to see her so happy, though. Her night-time fears were now a thing of the past, or so Rachel believed and trusted; there had been no recurrence of them since she had started school.

The children were playing their last game when Derek arrived home. He acted very much 'hail fellow well met', laughing and joking with the children and pretending to box with the two boys.

'Your daddy's good fun, isn't he?' Rachel heard Billy remark to Lorna as he said goodbye and, 'Thank you for having me.' Lorna looked as pleased as a dog with two tails as her friends departed.

It was when Lorna had gone to bed that night, tired but very happy and insisting on still wearing her birthday crown, that Derek told Rachel he would soon be leaving to take up residence in Ripon. It came as a shock, although, at the heart of her, she had been expecting it.

'You mean . . . you are going to live with your . . . friend?' she asked.

'Yes,' he answered curtly. 'It's no use, is it, Rachel? It's all over between you and me. It was over a long time ago. If it

164

hadn't been for our Kevin and . . . and what happened . . .'

'Don't let's talk about that, Derek,' cried Rachel. 'Don't you think there's quite enough to consider without making things worse? Anyway, what about Lorna? We have another child, don't forget. And how is she going to feel about her daddy leaving us?'

'Oh well . . .' He gave a slight shrug. 'She'll be all right, I suppose. You mustn't think I don't care about her, Rachel, because I do, but she's a tough little customer, our Lorna. You saw her this afternoon, didn't you, bossing them kids around, even them two lads.' He smiled a little then, shaking his head fondly.

'Don't change the subject, Derek,' said Rachel. 'She's not as tough as all that, and she's already had a lot of sadness to bear, just as much as we have . . . You're going to tell her, are you, that you are leaving?'

'Er . . . well . . . I'd rather you did that, Rachel.' He looked at her pleadingly and his voice when he spoke again had a wheedling tone. 'You're so much better at that sort of thing than I am.'

She had heard that before. It was she who had had to break the news to the child that her brother had died. She stared at him coolly. 'That's right, Derek, leave the dirty work to me.'

'Aw, Rachel . . . it's not like that. I told you, ages ago, that I didn't intend it to happen.'

'But it did, didn't it?'

'Aye, so it did, and there's nowt we can do about it, except make a clean break of it, you and me. Lorna'll get over it . . . and I'll still come and see her, you know. Anyroad, she must realise that you and me don't get on all that well. She's a sharp little kid.'

Rachel, momentarily, was at a loss for words. Derek looked at her piteously for a little while before continuing.

'I'll give you grounds for divorce. You'll have no need to worry about that. An' I shan't try to contest it.'

'Oh, I see . . . and supposing I don't want a divorce?'

165

'But . . . but we'll have to, Rachel!' he pleaded. 'It'll be for the best; you know it will.'

'Why? You intend getting married again, do you?'

'Well, I dunno . . . Yeah, I suppose I do.'

'Then don't you think you might do me the courtesy of telling me her name, this . . . this other woman that you've been carrying on with?'

Derek hung his head. 'Aye, I reckon I should, really. She's called Sylvia Maitland, and she has a shop – that's called "Sylvia" an' all – near to the town square in Ripon. And that's about all, I suppose, except that we get on well and . . . and I'm no good to you, Rachel, you know that. I never have been.'

She was unable to answer that. It would be pointless to remind Derek of their courtship and their happiness in the beginning of their marriage, when they had first set up home together. But . . . had it been happiness, she wondered, or just a desire on the part of both of them to leave home? She knew that their time together was now at an end and that, fundamentally, they had never been right for one another. She nodded.

'I see,' she said calmly. 'So – when do you intend to move in with this Sylvia? I take it that that is what you will be doing?'

'Yes, for the moment anyroad. She owns the shop and the premises; she lives over the shop, you see.'

'Yes, I see,' said Rachel again. 'Very convenient for you, I'm sure. But what about your home here? This house, Derek?'

'Oh, we'll sort summat out, don't worry. I'll support you, Rachel, and Lorna an' all. I don't expect you to leave your home.'

'Well, thank you, Derek,' she replied, with a hint of sarcasm. 'At least I must be grateful for that, I suppose.'

'Aw, Rachel, give over. I'm trying to make this as easy as I can. I shall come back and see Lorna. That'll be all right, won't it? I mean . . . you wouldn't stop me seeing her?'

'I should hope you know me rather better than that! None of this is Lorna's fault, and I don't want her to be any more upset than she needs to be. Yes, you will be able to see her. But you haven't answered my question yet. When are you leaving?'

'Oh, next weekend, happen. I'll take some of me stuff and then come back for the rest.'

'And what about your job at Whittakers?'

'I don't see as there should be any problem. I'm pretty much a free agent, an' I can report to 'em every now and then, like I do now. So long as I keep getting the orders, that's all they're bothered about.'

'Yes, I'm sure it is, Derek,' she replied. 'I don't suppose you've given much thought to how I'll manage though, have you?' He opened his mouth to reply, but she went on before he could speak. 'Well, you don't need to worry. You'll have to support Lorna; that's the law, anyway. But as far as I'm concerned, you needn't trouble yourself. I shall go back to teaching. I always intended doing so eventually, and now . . . it seems as though I've no choice.'

'Aye, I know that.' Derek nodded. 'I'm sorry, Rachel, honest I am, but you enjoy teaching, don't you? And it'll give you summat to think about now that . . . well . . . you know what I mean.'

Rachel stared at him, seeing the look of relief and self-interest on his face, rather than the sympathy he was pretending to feel for her. To her annoyance, she found herself bursting into tears, the pent-up sorrow that was still at the heart of her needing to find relief.

'Now that Kevin's not here any more,' she cried. 'I know what you mean. But going back to school won't help me forget him.' She tried to hold back a sob. 'I'll never forget our little boy. You go ahead and start your new life, Derek. It's obvious there's nothing to keep you here . . . so the sooner you go, the better.'

Try as she might, she was unable to stem the flood of tears. The last thing she wanted was comfort from Derek, nor did she get it. He simply placed his hand on her shoulder.

'I loved him too,' he murmured, and when she glanced up at him she could see his eyes were moist. He walked away from her and left the room.

Chapter 12

Rachel was cross with herself afterwards for indulging in self-pity, as she felt she had done when Derek told her he was leaving. By the following day she had managed to pull herself together. She tried to behave normally with Lorna, but the little girl was so engrossed in her school activities that she scarcely noticed anything else. That was just as well, because Derek, true to his word, left that weekend to start his new life in Ripon.

He filled two large suitcases and managed to sneak them into the boot of the car, with the case containing his sales items, when Lorna was not watching. He said goodbye as he normally did, kissing Lorna and pecking Rachel on the cheek, then drove off with a cheery wave. That was what he had said he would do, leaving Rachel to tell their daughter that he would not be coming back, at least, not to live there.

'Where's Daddy?' asked Lorna on the Saturday evening, when he had not returned. 'He usually comes back on Saturday night, doesn't he?'

'Not always,' said Rachel carefully. 'He's working away this weekend. Daddy has a lot of travelling to do. You know he goes a long way sometimes, don't you, love, visiting all his shops? Well, he's got an extra-long journey this time, so he'll be away for a few days.' She hated telling even a white lie to the child, but she needed to break the news gently, and until she could pluck up the courage to do so, that would have to suffice. Lorna did not seem worried, but Rachel knew it might not be long before she started querying her daddy's absence again.

Her parents would have to be told, thought Rachel, so when Lorna had gone to school on the Monday morning, she set off for the house on the other side of Melcaster.

'Goodness me, you're bright and early on a Monday morning,' said her mother, not sounding exactly overjoyed to see her. 'I'm in the middle of doing my washing, so you can talk to your dad while I finish off.' Lizzie now had a washing machine to assist with what had used to be an arduous task, but she still stuck to the same old routine with her housework: washing on Monday, ironing on Tuesday, cleaning the bedrooms on Wednesday, and so on.

Rachel made tea for all of them, leaving her mother's to keep warm in the pot. She talked about this and that, mainly about Lorna, to her father, until her mother joined them, sighing and mopping her brow as though she had already done a hard day's labour.

'So – what's this visit in aid of?' she asked. 'I can tell by your face that you've something to tell us. No more shocks, I hope?'

'Yes, there's summat the matter, isn't there, lass?' said her father, more understandingly. 'Come on now, tell yer mother and me all about it.'

Rachel smiled weakly. 'Well, it might or might not be a shock. It depends on how you look at it . . . Derek's left me.' She spoke the words abruptly, deciding there was no point in beating about the bush with her parents.

'What! You mean he's . . . gone? Where to?' Her mother looked angry, rather than concerned.

'Oh dear! That's a bad do,' said her father, shaking his head sadly. 'Whatever has possessed him to do that?'

'Another woman, Dad,' said Rachel. 'It's as simple as that. He's met somebody else, and he's gone to live with her, in Ripon.'

'Ripon?' repeated her mother, unbelievingly, as though Rachel had announced he'd gone to Timbuktu or Outer Mongolia. 'Well, I never. Mind you, I can't say I'm surprised.

I never liked that Derek. Well, you know that, don't you, Rachel? I've never made a secret of it. He wasn't good enough for you, not by a long chalk.'

'Leave it, Mum,' said Rachel, sighing a little. 'There's no point in going into all that now.'

But Lizzie would not be stopped. 'I guessed there was something up. I knew the pair of you weren't getting on. He's got another woman, you say? Huh! Well, he's shown himself in his true colours now, hasn't he? And you're better off without him if that's the way he's carrying on. What about his parents? What do they think about it?'

'I don't know, Mum. I'm not sure whether he's told them. I thought I'd go round and see them, after I leave here.'

'I bet they know about it,' said Lizzie. 'That would be why Phyllis gave me a funny look when I saw her in church yesterday, and she didn't stop for a chat afterwards neither. Well, I wonder what they'll have to say about their precious son now?'

'What about our little Lorna?' said Rachel's father anxiously. 'Have you told her what's going on?'

'Not yet, Dad,' replied Rachel. 'She knows he's gone away – for a few days, I told her. I'll break it to her gradually, in my own time.'

'Poor little mite,' sighed Percy. 'She's had quite enough to bear for a little 'un. Well, we all have, haven't we? And now this. Eeh, Rachel, love, I am sorry.'

'Then don't be, Dad,' she replied, quite matter-of-factly. 'Actually, I've known for some time – soon after Kevin died – that he'd met somebody else. It was just a matter of time before he left. And I don't want you to worry about me, either of you. It'll all be sorted out eventually. Derek and I will get a divorce and I shall go back to teaching when—'

'Divorce?' cried her mother, seeming not to have heard the remark about teaching. 'You're surely not thinking of getting a divorce, our Rachel? I've never heard of such a thing! No, you mustn't, you can't! It's out of the question. Let him live in sin if he wants to. That's up to him but—'

'Mother, it's my life,' Rachel interrupted. 'You've just said that I'm better off without him, so why shouldn't we get a divorce? A clean break, that's what we've decided. You've said yourself that you never liked him.'

'Don't keep telling me what I've said!' retorted her mother. 'I shall say a lot more before I've finished. Divorce indeed! There's never been such a thing in our family and I don't intend to let you be the first. You don't think about the shame you're bringing on us, do you?'

'For heaven's sake, leave it, Lizzie,' said her husband. 'Like the lass says, it's her life, and personally I think she's right. She'd best be rid of him, once and for all. It's our little Lorna that I'm most concerned about. I know she's fond of her daddy.'

'Yes, I'm concerned, too,' said Rachel. 'Don't worry. I'll try to make sure she doesn't get too upset.'

'Yes, you've not thought about what this'll do to your little girl, have you?' Lizzie went on. 'Neither of you. He's gone off without a word, and as for you . . . you can't even tell her the truth.'

'Make up your mind, Mother,' said Rachel, beginning to feel very exasperated. 'One minute you're saying I don't care about her, and the next that I won't tell her the truth.'

'I've never said you don't care about her! The truth is, you've given me such a shock, Rachel, that I don't rightly know what I'm saying.' Her mother looked at her a shade more concernedly. 'Your dad and me, we've always wanted what was best for you. And Derek Watkins wasn't the best, was he? All the same . . .'

Rachel stood up before her mother could start going on again about the disgrace of divorce. 'I think we've said all we need to for now, don't you? I've got to go now because I want to see Derek's parents, and I must get back in time for Lorna. Jenny has said she'll look after her until I get back, but I don't want to be late.' She kissed her parents then made her exit as quickly as she could. She trusted her mother would come to terms with it all in time. Whether she did or not, that was the way it was going to be.

172

Derek's parents greeted her with some embarrassment.

'Eeh, lass, this is a bad do,' said her father-in-law. 'We'd no idea what was going on, his mother and me, until he told us t' other night. And we're not right pleased, are we, Phyllis? In fact, we're bloody annoyed with him. Oh dear . . . excuse my French, won't you, love?'

Rachel smiled at him. 'It's all right. I understand how you must be feeling.'

'Yes, watch yer language, Jack!' said his wife, tutting at him. 'We couldn't believe it when he told us, dear. And we told him, Jack and me – didn't we, Jack? – that it wasn't your fault whatever had gone wrong. He couldn't have a better wife than you, Rachel love.'

'Thank you,' said Rachel. 'It's just one of those things, I suppose. We hadn't been getting on all that well. You must have realised . . .'

'Well, I suppose so,' replied Phyllis. 'But it happens in a lot of marriages. You've got to take the rough with the smooth and it usually sorts out in the end. He's a bad lad. We've told him so, haven't we, Jack? But happen he'll come back when he's got it out of his system, eh?'

Rachel raised her eyebrows. And you'd expect me to have him back, would you? she thought, but she kept silent.

'I mean to say,' Phyllis continued, 'you've got to try and keep together for the sake of the children, haven't you?' She suddenly became aware of what she had said. 'For Lorna, I mean, our dear little Lorna. Oh dear! You've had enough tragedy, haven't you, without all this? But it'll happen sort out. Our Derek'll come to his senses in time.'

Rachel shook her head. 'Didn't he tell you, Phyllis, that we intend to get a divorce? I don't really think there's much chance of us getting back together.'

'Yes, dear, he did say something of the sort,' replied Phyllis, 'but I didn't take too much notice of that. Divorce! It's a big step, isn't it?'

'Yes, a final one,' said Rachel decidedly.

'That's what I mean, dear. You don't want to be too hasty. Like I say, he'll happen change his mind when he realises what he's missing – you and your little girl.'

Rachel realised there was no point in prolonging the conversation with Derek's parents any longer. Phyllis was not as condemnatory about divorce as her own mother had been, but it was clear that she didn't like the idea. And no matter how much they criticised Derek to Rachel, he was still their son. As the old saying went, blood was thicker than water, and it was only natural that they should believe that he would, in time, see the error of his ways.

How was Lorna? they asked, and Rachel explained again that the child did not know the whole truth yet, but that she would tell her when she felt it was the right time to do so. For the remainder of her short visit she steered the conversation away from the main problem, talking instead about Lorna and how she was enjoying her first term at school.

Rachel soon discovered that the idea of divorce was an anathema, not only to her mother, but to several of her associates at the Young Wives' Group. It was inevitable that the word soon got around that Derek Watkins had left his wife and had gone to live with another woman in Ripon. Rachel guessed that much of the tittle-tattling had been done by her own mother. As Lizzie had said, she had never made any secret of her disapproval of her son-in-law, and now she had a chance to show him up for what he really was.

'We were so sorry to hear your dreadful news, Rachel, dear,' Judith Prendergast said to her at the Young Wives' Group meeting, a couple of weeks after Derek's departure. Rachel did not doubt that the woman was sincere, as she always was, but the note of piety in her voice was starting to irritate her, even before she continued, 'We are praying for you, and for Derek, that he will acknowledge his wrong-doing and come back to you. And to Lorna, of course. That poor little girl! Whatever must she be thinking?'

'She knows her daddy is living somewhere else for a

while,' said Rachel curtly. 'That's all she needs to know at the moment. And please don't pray for him to come back to me, Judith. That is not what I want at all. I know you mean well,' she added, a touch less aggressively, as she saw a look of shock and disbelief appearing on the other woman's face, 'but we're going to get a divorce, you see. We've both decided it's for the best.'

'Divorce? But . . . you can't!' protested Judith. 'You were married in church, Rachel, and I know you took your vows seriously, even if Derek didn't. At least, I hope you did. Christian marriage is indissoluble. You would be going against the teaching of the Church – and of Jesus himself – if you took such a step.'

'Excuse me!' said Rachel, her best intentions not to let the woman rile her flying right out of the window. 'We are not Catholics, are we? I know they are very strict about such matters, but the same rules do not apply in the Anglican Church.'

'Oh yes, they do,' said Miriam Curtis, now joining in the conversation and nodding sagely. 'Church of England clergy are not allowed to marry divorced people. Not that you would ever consider getting married again, would you, Rachel? It would be contrary to the teaching of the Church if you did. I agree with Judith. You really should not be thinking about divorce, my dear.'

'Rubbish!' retorted Rachel, her impatience with these self-righteous do-gooders suddenly getting the better of her. 'I know of someone who got married in a church. She wasn't the guilty party in the divorce, and the vicar agreed to marry them.'

'He was going against the advice of his bishop then,' said Miriam.

'And what about Methodists?' Rachel went on. 'They are allowed to get married in church – or chapel or whatever – aren't they? Their ministers don't disapprove.'

'Oh please!' said Judith, smiling pityingly at Rachel. 'Since when did we have to take any notice of what the Methodists do? I don't regard that lot as any criterion.'

'I believe that marriage is for life,' Norma Shuttleworth suddenly declared from her perch on the piano stool. 'Till death us do part; that's what it says in the marriage service, isn't it?' The others looked at her in surprise. Norma was not married and they had never known her to show any interest in connubial matters. 'I am not married, I know.' She smiled serenely. 'But I do know that if I had been, then it would have been for life. I had a fiancé, you know – my beloved Richard – but he was killed on active service in the second world war. I have never forgotten him, and that's why I've never got married, because there is no one who could ever take his place.'

There were embarrassed murmurs of, 'Oh dear . . .' and, 'That's very sad, isn't it?' from the small group of people listening.

'Yes . . . well,' said Pauline Jeffreys. 'We guessed at something of the sort, and we do sympathise with you, Norma . . . But I really wish the lot of you would mind your own business!' she continued, raising her voice. 'Rachel is too polite to say what she thinks, but I'm not. She's my friend and it's not up to you lot to say what she must and mustn't do. She's had a rotten time recently, we all know that. So how about showing a bit of that Christian love you're so fond of spouting about?'

'But we do,' protested Judith mildly. She never seemed to show any irritation. 'Whatever we say to Rachel is out of Christian love. It is sincere and from our hearts.'

'Yes, I know that, Judith,' said Rachel. 'I do, really.' She got up suddenly from her chair. 'Sorry if I lost my rag and all that. But we'll just have to agree to disagree, won't we? OK? It's my life, isn't it? Not yours.' The three friends who had been united in their censure of her smiled and bowed their heads. 'Come on, Pauline. I'd better be getting back home. My parents are baby-sitting for me.'

Pauline, as usual, drove her home. 'My God! Those three!' she said, indulging in a mild blasphemy when she was well away from the church premises. 'Talk about interfering old busy-bodies! I felt like punching them. I'm surprised you didn't get up and walk out before now, Rachel.'

'I felt like it,' said Rachel. 'A trio of Meddlesome Matties, they are. The funny thing is, I find I can't dislike them. They're so sincere in what they say.'

'It's possible to be sincerely wrong, though, sometimes,' said Pauline. 'I say – I was having a good laugh to myself about Norma not getting married because nobody could compare with her precious Richard! Chance'd be a fine thing, I thought!'

'Oh, Pauline, you're dreadful!' exclaimed Rachel, laughing just a little. She still experienced a slight pang of guilt whenever she laughed, feeling she had no right to do so with her little son so recently cold in his grave. But she was thankful for her friend's infectious – and sometimes wicked – sense of humour, and she knew that, deep down, Pauline was full of concern for her. She was also the one friend who was backing her to the hilt in her belief that divorcing Derek was the right thing to do.

'How is Lorna?' Pauline asked now.

'She's OK, I think,' replied Rachel. 'Derek came back last Saturday and took her out. They went to see his parents and then he took her into town and bought her a book and sweets and some furniture for her doll's house. That's the trouble, of course, and I can see it getting worse. He will be the one spoiling her with treats, whilst I shall be the boring person she lives with . . . who won't be able to afford very much.'

'Oh, come on, love. Don't get downhearted,' said Pauline. 'Lorna's a sensible little girl. She'll soon sort out what's what. And she's settled in really well at school. She always looks happy when I see her.'

'She didn't ask why Derek wasn't staying at home for the night,' said Rachel. 'She knows he's working away and has found somewhere else to live. But I'm going to tell her that we've decided to live apart. It's time she knew before some other busy-body tells her. I wouldn't put it past my mother, actually.'

'The best of luck then,' said her friend as she said good-night to her. 'It'll be OK, I'm sure. Never fear.'

Rachel plucked up the courage she needed to tell her daughter, the following night, that her daddy would not be coming back home to live, but that he would still come to see her, Lorna, as often as he could.

'Why?' asked the child, frowning. 'This is where he lives, isn't it?'

'Not any more, darling,' said Rachel. 'You see . . . your daddy and I haven't been getting on very well just lately.'

'Why?' said Lorna again, still looking perplexed and cross, but thankfully not tearful.

'Well, because that's what happens to mummies and dad-dies sometimes. You know, like you fall out with your friends at school.'

'But I don't,' said Lorna. 'I don't fall out with them.'

'Oh . . . all right. Then you're very lucky, aren't you?' said Rachel. But she knew it was inevitable that the child would, sooner or later, experience quarrels, both large and small, with her school friends. At the moment, however, she was not making things any easier for her mother. 'But Daddy and I . . . we've decided to live apart, on our own, I mean. Well, not exactly on our own. I live with you, don't I? And Daddy . . . he's got somewhere else to live . . . in Ripon.' She had decided not to tell the child, at least not yet, about the woman, Sylvia. And Derek had promised he would not take Lorna to meet her until such a time as Rachel considered was right.

'Can I go and see where he lives then?' asked Lorna.

'Sometime. Yes . . . I'm sure you will be able to go some-time,' Rachel prevaricated. 'But you live here with me, don't you? This is our home and I've said, haven't I, that Daddy will come and see you, just like he did before. He was always away a lot of the time, wasn't he? Doing his travelling.'

'When is he coming again?' asked Lorna. 'I shall ask him if

I can go and see where he lives. It's the holiday from school soon. P'raps I could go and stay with him.'

'We'll see, darling,' said Rachel, sighing inwardly. 'He'll be here on Saturday, I think. Yes, I'm sure he will. But you mustn't pester him about going to stay with him.'

'Why not?' asked Lorna.

'Because . . . he's still in rather a mess. You know what it's like when you move into a new place, don't you? It takes a while to settle in.'

The child looked thoughtful, her mouth set in a stubborn, unsmiling line.

Rachel decided it would be expedient not to say any more for the moment. In some ways the disclosure had gone better than she had anticipated. At least there had been no tears. But Lorna, alas, seemed far more interested in where Derek was actually living than in the fact that he was no longer living at their home in Melcaster. And the censorious looks she was directing at her mother made Rachel realise that she, not Derek, was the one who was getting the blame for what had happened.

As Lorna had reminded her, the school holiday – the two weeks' break for the Easter period – was soon upon them. In order to make up for the further disruption in her daughter's life, Rachel planned outings for the two of them. But feeding the ducks was 'boring', the child told her after their visit to the local pond; she had done it 'millions of times'. And so Rachel tried to think of more interesting excursions – a visit to the cinema to see a rerun of *The Wizard of Oz*, and a trip to Woolworths, Lorna's favourite shop, with a whole shilling to spend on whatever she wished.

She knew she was guilty, perhaps, of indulging the child, but the surly look on Lorna's face worried her, and she felt she must try extra hard to regain her affection. It did not appear to be enough for Lorna that her mother loved her more than anything in the world, her feeling for her remaining child having deepened, if that were possible, since her little boy had died. Or maybe Lorna just did not realise how much she was loved.

'When can I see Daddy? Why? Why can't I see him?'

'Can I go and see Grandma? Grandma says I can help her to make some gingerbread men. You never make them, do you, Mummy?'

'Why? Why? Why can't I go to play with Carol?'

Rachel was beginning to grow weary of the little girl's petulance and pestering and realised she would be glad when the holiday ended and Lorna was back at school. She was hampered by having no car – she had not yet thought of learning to drive – so any excursions further afield had to be made by train. Just before the holiday came to an end she planned a special trip to York, and it turned out to be the highlight of their time together, a real turning point for mother and daughter, or so Rachel hoped.

They visited the Railway Museum, where Lorna was fascinated by the giant engines. Rachel had wondered if it might be an outing more suited to a boy – there were scores of boys in the museum – but Lorna was just as engrossed as they were and did not want to leave. But Rachel told her there were lots of other exciting things to do.

They had taken a packed lunch and they went down the steps near to the Lendal Bridge to find a form on which to dine. Feeding the ducks on the River Ouse with crusts and crumbs of cake was far more exciting to the child than the boring old ducks in Melcaster. It was a gloriously sunny day for early spring. The daffodils on the grassy banks below the city walls were in full bloom, and Lorna seemed to appreciate their golden glory just as much as she had admired the lumbering engines.

'Aren't they lovely, Mummy?' she declared, her eyes alight with wonder.

The higgledy-piggledy houses in the Shambles and the quaint cobbled streets delighted her too. My little girl has an eye for beauty, thought Rachel, wondering fleetingly what this might lead to as she grew up. She could not remember anything having captivated Lorna so much as this day in York.

Rachel managed to conquer her own fear of heights as they climbed the steps of Clifford's Tower. She recalled the unhappiness of her last visit to the city, with Derek, and her feeling of vertigo as she had stood near the parapet of the tower. She held on tightly to Lorna's hand, but the fear did not return, and Lorna, it seemed, was not suffering from the same anxiety.

'Look, Mummy – I can see that big church,' she cried excitedly. 'And the railway lines, see – and the trains. Oh, aren't we having a lovely time?'

It was, indeed, the climax of Lorna's Easter break. I've done it, thought Rachel. I've got her back again. We're going to get on fine together, Lorna and I. We're going to be good friends as well as mother and daughter. I'm going to make sure of that.

It was the Saturday before the schools were due to reopen that Rachel received a phone call from her former headmistress, Miss Lacey. Lorna had gone out with Derek, who had come back for the day to see his daughter, so Rachel was on her own.

'Mrs Watkins,' Miss Lacey began. It was very rarely that she called her Rachel. 'I believe – as a matter of fact, Mrs Jeffreys hinted to me – that you are considering going back to teaching? I've heard about your husband, of course, my dear, and I'm so sorry.'

'Well . . . yes,' replied Rachel. 'I was thinking of teaching again, but I haven't got round to doing anything about it. It's early days yet, you know.'

'Yes, I realise that, my dear,' said Miss Lacey. 'I don't want to rush you – and please say no, if it's not possible – but something has cropped up unexpectedly and I am wondering if you could help us out.'

She went on to explain that Mrs Davenport, Lorna's teacher, needed to leave the school rather sooner than expected because she had developed high blood pressure and the doctor had told her she must rest. 'She is taking maternity leave, as you did, Mrs Watkins, so we need to get a supply teacher until such a time as she returns. If, indeed, she does return; she may well change her mind.'

'And you want me?' interrupted Rachel.

Miss Lacey told her that she had been busy for the latter part of the holiday trying to arrange things with the local Education Office. A supply teacher had been detailed to start on Monday, but now she had been taken ill. 'A sudden attack of appendicitis, I believe, and so I was wondering if you could possibly see your way to coming back to us ... Rachel? I know you are not yet on the supply list, but I'll sort that out with the office. You would have been my first choice anyway, and now ... well, it seems providential. Not that the poor woman has got appendicitis; I didn't mean that. But we do know what a good teacher you are, Mrs Watkins, and how much the children have always liked you.'

Rachel smiled to herself. 'I haven't said yes yet, have I, Miss Lacey? You're right, maybe it is providential, but the snag is ... it's Lorna's class, isn't it? Do you think it would be a good idea for me to teach her, and her best friend, Carol?'

'You're a sensible woman, Mrs Watkins. I'm sure you would be able to cope with the problem. Maybe it's not ideal, but if I were to move Lorna – and Carol, too – into the other reception class – that would not be fair to them. And for the teachers to exchange classes, well, that would be even worse. Are you thinking that you might consider it, Rachel? We would love to have you back with us.'

Rachel was silent for a few seconds.

'Are you still there, dear?' asked Miss Lacey anxiously.

'Yes, I'm still here, Miss Lacey. And I've decided to say yes. I'll be with you on Monday morning, bright and early. I'll explain things to Lorna. Yes, I'm sure things will work out all right.'

Rachel managed to convince herself during the time that Derek and Lorna were away that she had made the right decision. It might, indeed, create an even closer bond between herself and Lorna. Relations between the two of them had been much more congenial since the happy day they had spent together in York.

She knew she also needed to seek an interest outside the home. It was when she was cooped up indoors that she began to feel depressed and the tortuous thoughts of her still-recent bereavement returned to haunt her. But the biggest incentive for agreeing to Miss Lacey's request was that she needed the money. She knew that Derek would be required to pay maintenance, as he was doing already, but she wanted to be financially independent.

She told Lorna the news that evening when Derek had gone back to Ripon. 'I've got a big surprise for you, Lorna,' she said.

'What?' The child looked at her suspiciously, but it was only natural that she should be a bit upset, Rachel thought, at parting from her father.

'Well . . . on Monday I'm going to teach at your school. You know, like I did before? And guess what? I'm going to teach your class! What do you think about that, eh?'

Lorna looked at her in horror. 'But you can't!' she exclaimed. 'Mrs Davenport's my teacher. Where's she gone? She's not poorly, is she?'

'No, not exactly, dear. No, she's not really poorly at all. But she's had to leave school sooner than she wanted to. She would have been leaving quite soon anyway, and then you would have had a new teacher.'

'She's having a baby, isn't she?'

'Well, yes . . . so she is, but how did you know that, Lorna?'

'Because Billy – you know, that boy who sits at my table – he told us. His mum's having a baby and Billy says that Mrs Davenport's getting fat, just like his mum. Has she had the baby, Mummy? Can I go and see it?'

'No, she hasn't had it yet,' replied Rachel, realising she had been naïve in thinking that Lorna would not have realised about her teacher's condition. After all, she had seen her, Rachel, 'getting fat' when Kevin was on the way, if she could remember so far back. 'But she has to stay at home and rest,' she went on. 'So Miss Lacey has asked me if I will teach your class. I think it will be very nice, Lorna. You know you've been saying you want to stay for school dinners, like a lot of the children do? Well, you'll be able to now, won't you, because I won't be able to get home and cook our dinner, will I?'

'So . . . will you be staying for school dinners as well, Mummy?'

'Yes, of course.'

'You'll have to do dinner duty, Mummy.'

'Yes, I daresay I will, dear.' This was one of Rachel's least favourite teaching responsibilities, but she did not say so.

Lorna was silent for a few moments, adopting what Rachel thought of as her thinking face. Then, 'Mummy, what will I have to call you?' she asked. 'Mummy, or Mrs Watkins?' The child laughed. 'That's funny, isn't it? Me calling you Mrs Watkins!'

Rachel laughed too. It seemed as though the little girl might be coming round to the idea. 'Oh, I don't know,' she said. 'We'll have to think about that, won't we? I don't really mind what you call me, so long as you don't call me teacher!'

Chapter 13

'Come along now, Lorna. Put your chair on the top of the table, like the other boys and girls are doing.'

It was the custom in all infant classrooms, at the end of each day, for the chairs to be placed on the tables to facilitate the cleaning done by the caretakers. Lorna, as had happened a few times, was the last to do this. When Rachel looked at her sternly, she grinned, then banged the chair legs on the table with unnecessary force. Rachel decided to make no comment, although a few of the children giggled.

'Now, hands together and eyes closed,' said Rachel, 'and we'll say a little prayer before we go home.' They did the same in all the infant classes. 'Lorna . . . hands together!' The child smirked at her again. 'Lorna Watkins, will you please, for once, do as you are told!'

The little girl obeyed, but with a sly glance at her mother. She screwed her eyes up tightly as she recited with the rest of the children, 'Lord keep us safe this night, Secure from all our fears . . .'

Just wait till I get you home, thought Rachel, when the other members of the class had gone. It was a warm day and they had gone straight out, not needing to go to the cloakroom for coats. Lorna, however, was as good as gold when she was left on her own, sitting quietly in the reading corner looking at a book, whilst her mother tidied her desk, cleaned the blackboard, sharpened the pencils, and did all the other end-of-the-day jobs. And Rachel knew very well that once she got her home she would say nothing at all. It would only make matters worse.

'You can't blame the child,' Pauline had said, laughing, when Rachel had reported to her that her daughter was being a 'damned nuisance' in the classroom. Not all the time, of course, but enough to cause minor disruptions and to give her mother a headache, both literally and metaphorically. 'She's rebelling, isn't she?' said Pauline. 'She doesn't like sharing her mummy with twenty-five other children. She wants you all to herself.'

'But she has me all to herself all the time at home,' Rachel had argued. 'Surely she has the sense to see that? And I have to treat her the same as all the other children when we're at school. There mustn't be any favouritism or the others would be very quick to notice. They notice her now all right, because she's such a pest.'

'She knows what she's doing,' smiled Pauline. 'The crafty little madam! Yes, she's got sense, sure enough, the sense to know she's making you cross. You know what we would say if it was any other child, don't you? That they were attention-seeking. And that's what she wants – your undivided attention. I suppose she thinks that you being cross with her is better than you ignoring her.'

'I feel like throttling her,' Rachel had declared. 'Well, giving her a good hiding, anyway.'

'Now, you know that's not true,' replied Pauline.

And, of course, it was not true. Even though she might threaten, she would never do it. Rachel did not believe in smacking children, and it was a rule of Miss Lacey, too – a very gentle and disciplined headmistress – that there must be no corporal punishment in her school.

But as the term progressed Lorna's behaviour did not improve. As Rachel had explained to Pauline, she did not misbehave continually. For much of the time she was happily engrossed in whatever she was doing. Rachel had already known she was a bright and intelligent child. She could already read a little before starting school, and had been able to write – or, more accurately, to print – her own name.

Not in block capitals, however, as so many children were taught by their parents before starting school. (And what a bugbear it was for the first teacher who had to redress the fault!) Now, well into her second term, Lorna was in the top reading group, and already on to her second book, telling of the exploits of Janet and John.

She could add and subtract in her head without the aid of counters, which many of the children still needed. Some had not yet acquired any number sense at all. And Rachel was discovering a talent in her daughter of which she had not previously been fully aware. Lorna was artistic and seemed to possess a knowledge of colour and shape and design without being taught. Infant classes, indeed, were not instructed overmuch in the skills of drawing and painting; their efforts were largely experimental and spontaneous. Lorna had always loved to draw pictures at home, but she had not been encouraged to paint. Painting was a messy occupation, and Rachel knew, to her slight remorse, that it was one she had sometimes discouraged. Such an activity could be a nuisance in the home, especially in a small house which was usually kept quite clean and tidy.

It was different at school. There was much more space, allowing freedom of movement, and the bright poster colours in their unspillable pots – at least, they were supposed to be unspillable! – appealed to all the children, both those with an artistic bent and the others who just liked to daub. They eagerly donned their little plastic aprons and stood in front of the back-to-back easels like budding Monets.

Only eight children, however, could paint at the same time, there being only four easels. So it stood to reason that Lorna could not be chosen every time. This would cause her to pout and say, 'It's not fair!' Then her play in the Wendy House or the sand tray would become more boisterous and her tendency towards bossiness – a trait Rachel had noticed before – more pronounced. Rachel knew she could not always be reprimanding her. That would be just as wrong as being over-lenient.

One of the child's most annoying tricks was pretending to forget how to address her mother during school hours. She would put up her hand, as the children knew they should do when they wanted to ask a question, but Rachel had started to groan inwardly whenever she saw her daughter's hand raised.

'Yes, Lorna. What is it?'

'Please, Mummy . . . oh dear, I mean Mrs Watkins . . . I mean, teacher. Please, teacher,' with emphasis on the title she knew her mother disliked, 'I've finished these sums. What shall I do now?'

'You already know what to do, don't you, Lorna? I've told you all to read your reading books when you've finished.'

'Oh, sorry, Mummy . . . I mean, Mrs Watkins. I forgot.'

Rachel eventually found she was at the end of her tether. She spoke to her daughter sternly at home after one such incident. 'Lorna, I wonder if it might be a good idea for you to go into Mrs Phillips' class for the rest of the term?'

'Why, Mummy?' the child asked, with an innocence which did not deceive Rachel at all. Lorna grinned. 'I like it in Mrs Watkins' class.'

Rachel found it hard to suppress the laugh that she could feel bubbling up inside her. 'Yes, maybe you do,' she replied. 'But I'm not so sure that Mrs Watkins is very happy with your behaviour. And if it continues I shall ask Miss Lacey to move you . . . Oh, come on, Lorna, stop play-acting! You're a sensible girl and you know you're behaving badly, don't you?'

Lorna shrugged. 'S'pose so. Sorry, Mummy,' she said contritely, but Rachel did not know whether her remorse was genuine or not. It was hard to tell with Lorna. 'I won't do it again, honest,' she added.

'I hope you mean that,' said her mother. 'Tell me, Lorna, what do you like doing at school, best of all?'

'I thought you knew,' said Lorna. 'I like painting and drawing, but painting's best. Those paints we have at school, though, they're for babies, aren't they?'

'Well, for small children, yes . . .'

'What I'd really like is a great big paint-box with lots and lots of colours in it,' said Lorna longingly. 'I've only ever had a titchy little one, and you never let me paint very much at home.'

'No, well, I used to think it was messy. But you're getting to be a big girl now, aren't you, and I'm sure you could cope with grown-up paints. They use them in the junior school. Now, how would it be if we were to go out on Saturday and look for a nice big paint-box, and some proper brushes, and some real artists' paper?'

The child's eyes lit up with delight. 'Ooh, Mummy, can we really? That'd be wizard!' Rachel smiled at what was becoming her daughter's pet adjective, one which Billy, her table-mate at school, favoured. 'Daddy's not coming on Saturday, is he, so I'll be able to go out with you instead. Ooh, wizard! I can't wait!'

She had not said thank you, but Rachel assumed she was too excited to have thought about that, and she did not want to keep reminding her, 'What do you say now?' She was only too pleased at the child's pleasure and the fact that she was not too disappointed at not seeing her daddy that weekend. Derek was taking a week's leave from work. He had not told her, Rachel, precisely what he was doing, but she guessed that he and his lady friend might be going away on holiday.

After Derek had been living away from home for a couple of months Rachel had relented. She had agreed that he should be allowed to show Lorna where he was living, so long as she did not stay overnight, and he used his discretion about the truth of the situation.

'I met a lady called Sylvia,' the child had told her mother. 'She said I could call her Sylvia, but her name's Mrs Maitland really, and she's got a shop. That's where Daddy's living, in the shop. Well, not really in the shop,' she giggled, 'but upstairs, I mean. He's the lodger, sort of, he says, and Sylvia makes him his tea when he's finished work, like you used to. And she serves in the shop, all by herself. There's all sorts of pretty things in the window; knickers and nighties – ladies' ones, I mean – and babies' dresses and cardigans and . . . ooh, all sorts.'

'Very nice, dear,' Rachel had replied. 'I'm glad you've had a good time.' What else was there to say? 'Daddy still loves you, and he still comes to see you, doesn't he, like I said he would?'

Lorna no longer asked difficult questions. Rachel guessed that in time she would work things out for herself. The word divorce had not been mentioned to her, although Rachel had already seen a solicitor and had started preliminary proceedings.

Nor did she mention her little brother. She had adopted his cuddly panda – which he had called Pandy – and he went to bed with her each night along with Mister Ted. Rachel had left Kevin's bedroom more or less as it had been when he was there with them, apart from the Dinky cars on the windowsill which she had cleared away; it hurt too much for her to look at them. There were still photos of him around the house, but Lorna deliberately – or so it seemed to her mother – avoided looking at them. Maybe the pain of his loss, to the little girl, was still as deep as her own. Lorna had suffered two losses, the one following quite quickly upon the other. It was, therefore, not to be wondered at if her behaviour was less than exemplary at times. And any indication that she was happy – and, consequently, forgetting to be troublesome – was seized upon by Rachel.

'It sounds suspiciously like bribery to me,' remarked Pauline, smiling, when Rachel told her about her promise to buy Lorna the painting requisites. 'I must admit, though, she's very talented in that direction. Those paintings of hers that you've put on the classroom wall, they are remarkably mature for a child of her age.'

Rachel tried to be fair and always made sure that all the children's efforts, however infantile, were displayed, but there were always one or two of her daughter's masterpieces on view. One in particular, of Mister Ted and Pandy, had been remarked upon by all the teachers who had seen it. The two toy animals were sitting with their heads close together as though they were having a chat, and Lorna had captured perfectly the soulful expression on Pandy's face.

'Yes, she takes after my mother,' said Rachel, 'as far as her artistic talent is concerned. She's like her in other ways, too. You know, bossy. Thinks she's always right!'

'Don't go blaming your mother for that,' laughed Pauline. 'It's something of a Yorkshire trait, isn't it, thinking we know better than anybody else? Don't worry about your Lorna. She's a real character, is that little lass. She'll go far.'

The thanks that Rachel had been waiting for were not long in coming when they arrived home on the Saturday afternoon and unpacked the treasures in the shopping bag. 'Ooh, Mummy, thank you,' cried Lorna. 'They're wizard!' She flung her arms around her, giving her a bear hug and a kiss, something the child did not usually instigate. 'Can I paint something now? Can I, please, Mummy? I'll be real careful.'

'Wait until after tea, darling,' said Rachel, 'then I'll spread newspaper all over the table. Isn't it exciting?'

That painting session was the first of many. Lorna spent most of her spare time painting, apart from the times during those long summer evenings when she played out with her best friend, Carol. Her behaviour at school started to improve. It was as though she didn't think of being a nuisance any more. Even Miss Lacey commented on it.

'There's a remarkable change in Lorna lately, Mrs Watkins. I wondered, at first, if we had made the right decision. Not in employing you, my dear – I don't mean that – but in leaving your little girl in the same class. I'm sorry we can't offer you the permanent position, but Mrs Davenport intends to come back, or so she says. She has an obliging mother like yours, it seems, who will look after the baby.'

A baby boy had been born a few weeks previously and Rachel had encouraged all the children to make cards of congratulations for their former teacher.

'That's all right, Miss Lacey,' she replied now. 'I think it might be as well, if I return to teaching on a full-time basis, not to teach in the same school as Lorna. It has its draw-backs.'

'Quite so.' The headmistress nodded. 'I don't know if you are aware of it, but there is a post about to come vacant in our own junior school. The teacher is leaving, quite sud-denly, because her husband has been transferred elsewhere. It hasn't been advertised yet, but I'm sure Mr Barker would be only too willing to consider you for the post if you were interested. He has heard me speak highly of you, my dear. And personal recommendation is always best.'

'Thank you, that's very kind of you,' said Rachel. 'But surely . . . that might be just as bad. Lorna will move up to the juniors in a couple of years, won't she? I don't want the same problem all over again.'

'Oh, she would be two years older and, hopefully, two years more sensible by then,' said Miss Lacey. 'And it could always be arranged that she was never in the class you were teaching. Anyway, you think about it. I know you have never taught juniors, but they always say that if you can teach infants, then you can teach anything.'

The upshot of the conversation was that Rachel applied and was duly appointed to serve on the staff of Kilbeck Junior School, starting in September 1958.

The junior and infant schools were two separate establish-ments, each with its own headteacher. They were separated by the width of two playgrounds and a brick wall, in which there was an archway leading from one to the other. Rela-tions between the two heads, Mr Barker and Miss Lacey, were cordial, and so the two staffs were on good terms as well. It was better for all concerned when this happened, but unfortunately it was not always the case between infant and junior schools.

There had been very few applicants for the position, only Rachel and a middle-aged man being short-listed. As he was really a senior-school teacher, wanting a change – 'Between

192

you and me and the gatepost, I think he's been finding secondary-modern kids too much to handle!' Mr Barker had confided to Rachel afterwards – there had been little doubt as to the outcome of the interview.

Rachel took to Mr Barker at once. Previously, she had met him only briefly at an occasional combined staff meeting. It would be hard to imagine anyone more dissimilar to Miss Lacey, she reflected; maybe that was why the two of them got on so well together. Mr Barker was quite young for a head. In his late thirties, married and with two children at the local grammar schools, he was modernistic in outlook and believed the custom of 'streaming' – categorising children according to their ability – to be outdated.

Rachel found herself in charge of a class of nine- to ten-year-olds, thirty of them, of differing intelligence and abilities. She had quailed a little at first at the thought of teaching third-year juniors – four years older than the children she had been teaching recently – but she surprised herself by how well she settled into her new job. She was helped by the fact that many of the children remembered her from her early days at the infant school. She had taught several of them before, although there were others who were unknown to her, a newly built council estate on the fringe of Melcaster having swelled the numbers.

She was delighted, on her first morning, to come across a familiar name on the register – Adam Blundell.

'Adam? Well, that's a lovely surprise,' she said, looking up from the register to see the dark-haired boy grinning a little shyly at her from his desk halfway back in the classroom. 'I remember you from – let me see – it must be more than three years since you were in my class. How nice to see you again . . . and all the rest of you, of course.' She realised she must not make too much of him, but she managed, later that morning, to have a chat with him. In fact, he stayed behind when the others had gone out to their playtime, to speak to her.

He had grown into a tall lad who showed promise of real

handsomeness, with the dark glossy hair and deep brown eyes she remembered so well. She noticed that he still walked with a slight limp, but otherwise he seemed to be fully recovered from his childhood attack of polio.

'You are looking well, Adam,' she told him. 'We seemed to lose touch for a time, didn't we? Of course, I gave up teaching for a while.'

'And we moved away, Mrs Watkins,' said the boy. 'I went to a special school – you know, 'cause of the polio – near York, but we're back in Melcaster now.'

'Ah, that must be why I hadn't seen you around then. And now, well, you're fine again, aren't you? That's very good. Your parents must be happy that you've made such a splendid recovery. Please remember me to them, won't you, Adam?'

'I'm afraid there's only Dad and me now,' said Adam, his dark eyes clouding over with sadness. 'My mum died last year.'

'Oh . . . I'm so sorry,' gasped Rachel. 'I'd no idea.'

'Well, you wouldn't have, would you, Mrs Watkins? She was never strong, you know,' he said in a grown-up manner. 'She started to be ill, last winter it was, and . . . and she didn't get better. Anyway, Dad and me, we moved back to Melcaster. We liked it best here, see, and I didn't need a special school any more. We're OK, Dad and me.' He grinned again. 'We look after one another.'

'I'm sure you do,' said Rachel. 'I'm glad about that. Off you go now and join the others. And I'll go and have my cup of tea.'

'I wish I'd known about Adam Blundell,' she remarked to Sonia Pickering, the teacher who was in charge of one of the second-year classes. 'About his mother, I mean. I felt dreadful asking about her. I'd no idea.'

'Don't worry,' said Sonia. 'I was going to tell you when I got the chance; sorry, I left it too late. But he's a very well-adjusted little lad, very mature for his age. He came into my class last year when they moved back to Melcaster.

Apparently they had moved to the York area, partly because of the special school and partly because Mrs Blundell's parents lived there. Anyway, the poor woman caught that awful Asian flu and it developed into pneumonia . . . and that was that. Robert Blundell's self-employed – he's a heating engineer I believe – so it was no problem for them to move back here. He said Adam badly wanted to get back to all his friends.'

'I see.' Rachel nodded. 'Yes, he seems to be a very popular boy. He's able to join in with them, is he, in games and everything?'

'He knows his limitations. He has a slight limp, but they have every confidence it will disappear in time. He's not the target of bullies or anything like that. I hope nobody would even think of bullying Adam. Anyway, we don't get much of that sort of thing here. Kilbeck's a happy place . . . I hope you'll like it here, Rachel, as much as you did in the infants.'

'I'm sure I will,' replied Rachel.

She did not meet Robert Blundell, Adam's father, again until the open evening which was held at the end of November, a time when parents came to the school to discuss with teachers their children's progress over the last three months. He looked very little different to when she had seen him a few years previously. His dark shining hair now showed a touch of grey at the temples, and he was, possibly, a little stockier in build. She was struck again at how like him Adam was. There was no mistaking that they were father and son, although it seemed as if Adam, in time, would grow to be taller than his father.

'So we meet again, Mrs Watkins,' he greeted her. 'I was very pleased when Adam came home and told me he was in your class. 'Guess what, Dad?' he said. 'You'll never guess who my new teacher is!'

'And . . . did you?' smiled Rachel.

'I'm afraid not.' He shook his head ruefully. 'It wasn't that I had forgotten about you – of course not – but a lot has happened in the meantime. Adam has never forgotten how you went to visit him when he was in hospital. And my wife and I, we appreciated it as well.'

'Yes, I remember,' said Rachel. 'I was so very sorry to hear about your wife, Mr Blundell. I had no idea until Adam told me.'

He nodded, smiling gravely at her. 'Yes . . . it was a bitter blow. I can't say it was a shock, because I think I had always known I might lose her. But we're managing OK, Adam and me. He's a good lad.'

'He certainly is,' replied Rachel. 'I was equally pleased, I can assure you, when I knew he was to be in my class. And he is doing really well.'

They discussed his school work, examining his exercise books and project work. He was more than competent in all subjects, but he seemed to have a particular aptitude for English, both in his understanding of the grammar and syntax and in his ability to write interesting accounts, both factual and imaginary.

'Mmm . . . very encouraging. He's taking after his mother,' said Mr Blundell. 'She was always scribbling away, was Mary. Poetry was her thing, though. And what about sporting activities? How is he coping?'

'Very well, as far as I know. We have a special teacher, of course, for PE and games. I don't take my own class for that; I must admit I'm not much of a games fanatic,' she smiled. 'But Mr Renshawe – the games teacher – tells me how hard he tries.'

'That's good. He used to talk about being a footballer when he was a little 'un, but now – well – I think he's resigned himself to just watching. He's a keen fan, though.'

'Which team does he support?'

'Leeds United! I take him sometimes on a Saturday when they're playing at home. So . . . what about you, Mrs Watkins? You decided to teach juniors for a change, did you?'

'Yes, that's right.'

'You had a little girl, didn't you?'

196

'Yes, Lorna. She's five now, nearly six.'

'And I seem to remember . . . wasn't there another?'

Rachel nodded. 'Yes . . .' she said after a few seconds' pause. 'There was another baby on the way the last time you saw me. That's what you mean, isn't it? I had a little boy, Kevin . . . but I'm afraid he died, over a year ago.'

'Oh dear! Do forgive me. I am so sorry, Mrs Watkins. And please, please convey my sympathy to your husband. I didn't mean to cause you any distress.'

Rachel looked at him sorrowfully, but she had herself well under control. 'Derek and I are separated now,' she explained. 'Don't – please don't – say you are sorry. It was for the best.' Robert Blundell, indeed, looked as though he would like to sink through the floor with embarrassment. 'Losing Kevin was dreadful – of course you will understand the feeling – but Lorna and I, we are trying to pick up the pieces again, like you and Adam are doing.'

'Life must go on,' he muttered. 'People are fond of telling you that, aren't they?'

'Yes, and it's true, I suppose. But it doesn't lessen the heartache, does it?' She looked straight into his warm brown eyes which were full of sympathy. 'It's been lovely meeting you again, Mr Blundell.' She held out her hand, not because she wished to see him go, but it was time for her next appointment. Parents were allowed fifteen minutes or so each, scarcely enough time to discuss some of the children's problems, but as much as time would allow. 'Goodbye for now. I hope we will see you at the carol service. Adam is in the choir.'

'I will be there, that's certain,' said Robert Blundell. He shook her hand firmly, smiling into her eyes. 'Goodbye, Mrs Watkins. It's been lovely meeting you again.'

Rachel was granted a decree nisi in the spring of 1959, and the decree absolute, concluding the divorce, followed three months later. They had agreed upon a settlement. Rachel was to have the house, which was now solely in her name.

Derek was paying maintenance for Lorna and would continue to do so until she was sixteen. Rachel, however, was now responsible for paying the mortgage as she earned a reasonable salary and it was considered she was well able to do so. She did not mind. She was proud of her financial independence and of the way she felt she was getting her life back together without Derek.

Her life was certainly a good deal less fraught without him. Rachel's chief concern had been that Lorna should be contented, and it did seem, indeed, that the little girl had adapted well to the situation. She hardly spoke of her father at all when he was not there, and when she returned from her Saturday or Sunday visit to Ripon she was no longer quite so communicative. At first she had been full of tales of Sylvia's wonderful shop, but now the novelty of that seemed to have palled. Occasionally she would lapse into a brooding silence, staring unseeingly into space, and at these times Rachel would resist the temptation to ask her what was the matter. She understood that the child had to come to terms with the situation in her own way, just as she, Rachel, must.

Both sets of parents, very reluctantly, had been forced to accept the reality of the divorce, realising that they had no choice. Derek's parents, in fact, were the more understanding, knowing that their son was largely to blame for the break-up of the marriage. But Rachel, who was very fond of both Phyllis and Jack, admitted magnanimously that there were faults on both sides and that it was no one's fault that she and Derek had not got on as well as they might. He might well have been a perfect husband, married to someone else, she said. She still took Lorna to see them, almost as frequently as before, but she timed her visits so that they did not coincide with Derek's.

As far as Lizzie Harding was concerned, it was as though Derek no longer existed. His name was never mentioned. But even though she had never liked him, Rachel felt that her mother would have preferred them to stay together, however unhappy they might be, rather than bring to the family the ignominy of divorce.

There was not the same closeness between Rachel and her mother as there had used to be. Rachel, although she may not have fully realised it, had finally broken away from the apron strings and was living her own life. And Lizzie resented this, especially as Lorna, her dear little pancake, was growing up as well.

Chapter 14

Rachel had little in her life apart from her home, her daughter and her job, and the occasional visit to church and the Young Wives' Group. She did not wish for anything else. She had fallen into a comfortable pattern which suited her and, more importantly, suited Lorna too.

She was a thrifty young woman. The amount left over after she had paid her mortgage and her household bills did not allow for lavish spending, but in the late spring of 1959 she decided it might be a good idea to think about central heating for her little home. A few of the other teachers on the staff had already had it installed and they spoke in glowing terms about constant hot water, about no longer having to huddle around a coal fire, and freezing bathrooms being things of the past.

'That lad in your class, Adam Blundell; his father's a heating engineer,' said Mr Renshawe. 'Why don't you ask him to give you an estimate? He's very good, I believe, and he'd probably be a lot cheaper than the Gas Board.'

But Rachel had already thought of that. She contacted Mr Blundell by phone, and was surprised at the speed he showed in coming to see her, the following Saturday morning. They discussed all the pros and cons in a businesslike manner and she agreed that his estimate was very reasonable. After she had made him a cup of coffee he left, with the promise that he would order all the requisites and start work, with his mate, during the half-term break. Early summer was a good time, he said, much better than having all the upheaval in the depths of winter. A nice man, she mused, and the memory of his smile, lighting up his kind brown eyes, stayed with her for the rest of the day.

When his van drew up a couple of weeks later Rachel was surprised to see Adam climb out from the back as well as Robert Blundell, and another young man who was introduced as Mike.

'I hope you don't mind me bringing Adam with me, Mrs Watkins,' said the boy's father. 'It's only for today. My mother usually sees to him during the holidays, but she's off on a day trip today with her Women's Institute.'

'Of course I don't mind,' said Rachel. 'But how does Adam feel?' She grinned at him. 'You thought you'd seen the back of teachers for a week, didn't you, Adam?'

'I don't mind, Mrs Watkins.' Adam smiled. 'I've brought a book to read – *Just William*, see – and a puzzle book, and Dad's made some sandwiches for us to have at lunchtime.'

'Come in then,' said Rachel, 'and make yourself at home. You can sit in that big armchair, or sprawl out on the settee, if you like.'

'Watch where you're putting your big feet, though,' said his father. 'Mrs Watkins doesn't want her nice suite all muckying up.'

'I'll take my shoes off,' the boy grinned. 'My socks are clean on today . . . Hello there.' He smiled at Lorna, who was sitting at the other end of the room, a sketch pad on her lap and a pencil poised in her hand. 'You're Lorna, aren't you? I've seen you sometimes, haven't I, waiting for your mum?'

'You might've done.' The little girl looked at him a trifle imperiously. 'I don't remember. Who are you, anyway?'

'Lorna, don't be so rude!' said Rachel. 'You know very well you've seen Adam before. He's Mr Blundell's son and he's staying here today whilst his dad puts in the central heating for us.'

'I shan't disturb you,' said Adam. 'I won't say a word if you don't want me to. I don't like people butting in when I'm trying to read.'

201

'It doesn't matter.' Lorna shrugged. 'I'm only staying in for a bit; it's raining anyway. And later I 'spect I'll go and play with my friend, Carol . . . You're in my mum's class, aren't you?' She looked at him with a little more interest.

Rachel and Mr Blundell, with a knowing look at one another, decided to leave them to it. 'I'm sorry,' Rachel whispered. 'She can be an awkward little madam, but she'll soon come round.'

'I understand.' The man nodded. 'She doesn't want her peace disturbing. Who would? Now, Mike and I will fetch all our gear in and get started. We'll try not to cause too much upheaval. You just carry on with whatever you have to do, Mrs Watkins.'

'Yes, I'm in your mum's class,' Adam replied. 'She's great, your mum. We all like her. She's a smashing teacher.'

'I was in her class once,' said Lorna, 'when she was in the infants. But I was a nuisance and she said she'd have me moved. So,' she grinned wickedly, 'I thought I'd better be good.'

Adam burst out laughing. 'You're a caution, aren't you? What's that you're drawing? D'you mind if I have a look?' He went over and stood next to her. 'Gosh! That's terrific!'

She was sketching the vase of flowers that stood on the sideboard – full-blown roses and smaller buds, even one or two of the petals that had fallen on to the polished wood.

'It'll look even better when I've painted it,' said Lorna, who was not given to false modesty. 'This is what is called a still life. I do all sorts, though. Things I can see, and things what I just make up, out of my head.'

'Imaginary things,' said Adam. 'Yes, I do that an' all. I'm no good at drawing and painting, but I make up stories – like you've just said – out of my head.'

'I'll show you my paints, shall I?' said Lorna. 'They've got a bit messed up with mixing the colours, so Mummy says the next thing I must have is a proper palette, like real artists have.' The paint-box was standing on a little table next to a child's easel, similar to the ones used in schools. 'Mummy bought me that, too,' she said, 'and a smock to wear so I don't get me clothes all mucky. I've got 'em all out ready, just in case, but I might not do any painting today. It depends . . .'

'Depends on what?'

'On my friend, Carol! I told you. We might play out if it stops raining.'

'I love the names of these colours,' said Adam, looking closely at the blocks of paint, some bright as jewels and others in more sombre hues. 'Crimson lake, ultramarine, saffron yellow, burnt umber. They sound . . . real magic, like, don't they? Better than saying just blue or brown or red.'

Lorna giggled. 'You are funny!' she said.

'And you can mix them together to make other colours, can't you?' said Adam. 'Red and blue make purple; blue and yellow make green; yellow and red make orange . . .'

'I know that!' said Lorna. 'Everyone knows that.'

'And do you know which are the three primary colours, the three most important ones?'

'Course I do . . .'

'Go on then. What are they?'

Lorna screwed up her face, as though thinking hard.

'Red . . . blue . . .' prompted Adam.

'And yellow,' said Lorna, triumphantly. 'See, I did know!'

'And all those colours together, like the rainbow, it's called a spectrum,' said Adam. 'I bet you didn't know that, did you?'

Lorna was silent.

The central heating system was installed in less than a week. Adam, to Lorna's disappointment – although she did not admit it – did not come with his father again. And Rachel, too, was aware of a feeling of anti-climax when the workmen had gone; the house felt so empty again. She did not know what she had expected . . . or half hoped for? It was, after all, a business transaction, and the heating engineer was the father of a child in her class, that was all.

There was little time, however, to brood upon what might have been, as the end of term was soon upon them, with all the extra work involved in the marking of test papers, writing reports, and the compiling of next year's class lists. And then Rachel and Lorna had a week's holiday to look forward to in the seaside resort of Scarborough.

The last time Rachel had been there was on her honeymoon. That was not a time she looked back on with particular fondness, although she and Derek, at that time, had believed themselves to be in love. She remembered the town, though, with nostalgia, and she guessed that Lorna, too, with her eye for natural scenic beauty, would love the resort.

They travelled by train and then went by taxi – an almost unheard of luxury – to their modest hotel, Rosedean, on the seafront overlooking North Bay. To their delight they had been given a front bedroom which afforded a superb view of the wide bay and the twisty paths cut into the cliff sides leading down to the sandy beach. Crowning the headland was the ruin of Scarborough Castle, the promenade path becoming steeper as it rose to the precincts of the twelfth-century relic. And below, against the towering cliffs, the gulls were wheeling and screaming.

'Listen, Mummy. What a row they're making,' said Lorna. 'And what a lot of them! Millions!'

'It seems like it, love,' said Rachel. 'They nest on the cliffs, you see. If we walk round that path that goes right round the headland – that's the part that sticks out into the sea – we'll be able to see them all. I only hope they go to sleep at night, don't you?' But Rachel guessed that the two of them would be too tired after days in the bracing sea air to be disturbed by gulls.

When they had unpacked they went outside and walked upwards towards the castle, not going into the grounds, however, but taking the road which led past St Mary's church. Rachel had remembered that from there, there was a wonderful vantage point. You could look down through the trees, now verdant in their late summer foliage, to the South Bay and the harbour and the Grand Hotel, glorying in its importance as it overlooked the Spa Bridge.

'See the fishing boats, way, way below in the harbour?' said Rachel, pointing.

'It's a long way down. We must be very high up, Mummy.'

'So we are, but there's a steep path and some steps leading down to the promenade and the harbour. We can't go now, there isn't time before our evening meal, but we'll go another day. There are lots of exciting things to do.'

Centuries-old graves, almost black with age and with the inscriptions almost totally obscured, abounded in St Mary's churchyard. Some were tumble-down and overgrown, some were covered with lichen, but there were others more carefully tended. The graveyard, however, was not a sombre place. The sight of the gravestones did not bring Rachel the anguish that it might once have done. The sun was shining in a cloudless sky, and standing there with her remaining child, looking down on the roofs of the old fishermen's cottages, she felt a sense of wellbeing and of hope for the future. She was able to think of Kevin now without the feeling that she was being torn apart. She felt blessed by her precious memories of him, and she knew that she and Lorna were going to have a wonderfully happy holiday.

In a smaller graveyard, set aside from the main one, there was a grave which stood apart from many of the others, inasmuch as it was always well tended and the vase by the simple headstone filled with fresh flowers. This was the grave of Anne Brontë, the youngest daughter of the ill-fated family, who had spent her last days in the resort, and had then died, in 1849, at the age of twenty-nine, in the little guest house on the cliff, where the Grand Hotel now stood.

How sad, thought Rachel. But there was such poignancy and romance in the story as well, and the tragic young woman could not have chosen a more peaceful spot in which to lie. Lorna was dancing a little jig of impatience. It could not mean anything to her, staring at some old grave of somebody she had never heard of. The next words the child uttered were very apt, bringing Rachel back to the present.

'What a lot of dead people, Mummy. Come on, let's go back now. I'm starving.'

Rachel smiled. 'Come to think of it, so am I!'

'I wonder what it'll be for tea?'

'It might be fish and chips, seeing as we're in Scarborough. Freshly caught fish in crispy batter, and golden-brown chips. How about that?'

'Yummy!' said Lorna.

They were not disappointed. The high tea was, indeed, fish and chips. Grilled plaice, though, coated in tasty breadcrumbs, not the battered cod Rachel had expected, with homemade apple pie to follow.

There was little to do in the evenings, but darkness did not fall until about ten o'clock so they were able to enjoy another walk along the promenade. It was common practice for the more modest hotels and boarding houses to serve three meals a day – a cooked breakfast, midday dinner, and what was known as a high tea. As this was served at five-thirty, the evenings were long. There was a television set in the visitors' lounge, but Rachel did not intend to spend her precious holiday time goggling at that; you could watch the telly any time. She and Lorna would walk and talk and read, she decided, and Lorna could draw. And she had also brought along a variety of puzzles and games to occupy them until it was bedtime.

Rachel knew that Lorna, like any other child on a rare seaside holiday, would want to spend quite a lot of time on the beach. And so they set off the following morning armed with bucket and spade, towel and rubber sandshoes, Lorna wearing her bathing costume beneath her dress. The weather, however, had changed slightly. The sun was still shining, though fitfully, but there was a sneaking little wind which made it necessary to wear a cardigan.

Rachel hired a deckchair and settled down in the lee of a windbreak to read and to keep a watchful eye on her daughter. Lorna made a few sand pies, but having no one to talk to she soon got tired of that.

'Make a sand castle then,' said Rachel, 'like that little girl over there is doing. Or, better still, go and ask her if you can help her.'

'No, I don't want to,' said Lorna. 'Why should I? She won't want me anyway. Look, she's got her little brother with her.'

'So she has,' said Rachel, sighing. Her euphoria of the previous day seemed to be rapidly disappearing. 'Well then . . . see if you can find some pretty shells and pebbles. There, where the tide's going out, there's sure to be a lot of nice shells.'

'OK, then.' Lorna went off with her bucket, but returned a few moments later. 'There's only a few cockle shells, nothing exciting. Anyway, I'm cold, Mummy.'

'Yes, so am I,' agreed Rachel. 'It is rather chilly, isn't it, darling? Let's pack our things up and go for a walk. We could go to the harbour and see the fishing boats. There might be some fishermen unloading their catches.'

This seemed to be of far more interest to the child than her solitary sand-pie making. Rachel had not stopped to think that she might be bored or lonely.

'What a fishy smell, Mummy,' Lorna said, wrinkling up her nose. 'It's nice, though, isn't it? I like it . . . and look at all those things they're selling.' Cockles, mussels, shrimps, crabs, lobsters and freshly caught silvery fish in abundance were on display on the myriad stalls near to the harbour wall. 'And look at those seagulls. Aren't they greedy? Look! Look at that one swooping down for the fish.'

One or two passers-by smiled at the little girl who was so entranced by her surroundings.

'Yes . . . See, he's got it in his beak,' said Rachel. 'When we get back you'll be able to draw a picture of him, won't you?'

Lorna nodded contentedly. She was silent for a few moments, leaning on the promenade railings, looking down on the harbour. 'Mummy . . .' she said. 'Look at that boy over there. It looks like . . . yes, it is. It's that boy – you know, the one who came to our house with his dad – Adam . . . something or other.'

Rachel looked and realised, with an unaccountable surge in the region of her heart, that it certainly was Adam Blundell. And standing next to him, watching a fisherman mending his net, was Robert Blundell, too, casually dressed in light cotton trousers and a chunky sweater.

'Oh yes,' she said casually. 'So it is. Adam Blundell and his father. That's very strange. We were talking about the holidays, at school, about where everybody was going, but Adam didn't say he was coming here.'

'P'raps he didn't know then. Did you tell them – your class – that you were coming to Scarborough?'

'Yes, as a matter of fact, I did,' said Rachel.

'Come on, Mummy.' Lorna pulled at her hand. 'Let's go and talk to them, shall we? Quick, before they go.'

'Why?' Rachel grinned at her daughter, although she did start to walk quickly in the direction of the harbour. 'I thought you told me he was a big-head? He's a real clever clogs, that Adam; that's what you said.'

'Yes, I know I did . . . but he's OK really. Wouldn't it be funny if they were staying at our hotel, Mummy?'

The Blundells, however, as they were to discover, were not staying in the North Bay area, but at a more prestigious hotel situated on the cliffs overlooking South Bay.

They chatted for a while near the harbour. 'Well, this is a lovely surprise, Mrs Watkins,' Robert Blundell remarked, 'and Lorna, too. This has quite made our day, hasn't it, Adam?' The boy smiled and nodded, but seemed a little embarrassed, too, at seeing his teacher away from her usual environment.

'It was me that saw you first,' said Lorna excitedly. 'We were up there, by the fish stalls, and I said, "Look, there's Adam."'

'You didn't tell me you were coming here, Adam,' said Rachel. 'You know – when we were talking about holidays?' Adam looked nonplussed, but his father answered quickly.

'It was very much a last-minute decision, Mrs Watkins. We couldn't make up our minds where to go, but Scarborough's an old favourite for both of us, so we decided to come here again.'

'We'd been talking about going to Blackpool,' said Adam. 'But then Dad changed his mind . . . didn't you, Dad?'

'Yes, well, I can change my mind if I want to.' His father grinned, at the same time giving his son a glance – a warning 'Shut up!' glance. 'A woman's prerogative, they say but . . . Anyway, here we are.'

'Have you been making sand pies, Lorna?' asked Adam, looking at the bucket and spade she was carrying.

She shook her head. "Course not! That's what babies do. Well . . . I might have made one or two, then I was going to make a castle, but I got a bit fed up on my own. So we went to look at the boats instead. Will you help me to make a castle, Adam?'

'Yes, I'd love to,' replied the boy.

'Oh, don't pester him, love,' said Rachel. 'I expect Adam and his dad have all sorts of things planned . . . haven't you?'

'Nothing at all,' said Robert Blundell, smiling and looking very contented. 'Our time's our own. We're free as birds on the wing, you might say. And what a lovely feeling it is, too. You must appreciate it, Mrs Watkins, after a hectic end of term.'

'You can say that again!' she replied wholeheartedly. 'You are sure Adam won't mind having a little girl as a companion? She's four years younger than him.'

'No, he'll be delighted. You heard him say so.'

'I thought he might just have said so to be polite.'

'Adam doesn't say things he doesn't mean. Come on . . . let's catch up with them.'

Adam and Lorna were already on the beach, staking a claim to a patch of sand and getting stuck in with the digging. Rachel, for the second time that morning, sat down on a deckchair and Robert joined her.

'Do you think we could dispense with the formalities?' he said, leaning forward and looking at her intently. 'My name is Robert, as I'm sure you know, and I would be so pleased if 'that is what you would call me.'

'Of course,' she replied. 'I would love to. And I'm Rachel.'

He nodded. 'As I already know. I'm so pleased we've met you here, Rachel – what a coincidence, isn't it? – and I know Adam is pleased as well.'

The children made a magnificent castle with a moat leading to a nearby rock pool, from which the water flowed, complete with battlements and a bridge. Building had to come to an end, however, when Rachel said they must get back to Rosedean for lunch.

'Must we, Mummy?' said Lorna. 'It's not fair! If we leave our castle somebody'll go and jump on it. I know they will.' She was eyeing two boys of around Adam's age who were playing nearby.

'Never mind. We can make another one sometime,' said Adam. 'Anyway, it'll all disappear when the tide comes in.'

'You've cut it a bit fine,' said Robert, glancing at his watch, 'if you've to get back to North Bay for twelve-thirty. Our hotel's only five minutes' walk away, over the Spa Bridge, so we'll go and get the car and I'll run you back.'

'That's very good of you,' said Rachel. She had quite lost track of the time whilst talking to Robert, and she agreed with him as they made their way up the steps to the promenade that, in some ways, it was rather restricting to have to return to the boarding house for a midday meal. On the other hand, it was good value for money, something which, to a born and bred Yorkshire lass like Rachel, was not to be ignored. The hotel where Robert and Adam were staying provided bed and breakfast and an evening meal, leaving the clients free to take their lunch elsewhere.

'Gosh! Isn't it posh?' said Lorna, when she first set eyes on the palatial expanse of the aptly named Ocean View Hotel. 'It's a lot bigger'n ours, isn't it, Mummy? Why can't we come and stay here?'

'Because ours is nice and cosy and it suits us very well,' replied Rachel, a mite embarrassed. It certainly was, as her daughter had said, posh. She was a little surprised that

210

Robert could afford such luxury, but he was a businessman with his own small company, and the central-heating trade was booming at the moment.

'There's nothing to stop you coming to have a meal here, though, is there?' said Robert, winking at Lorna. 'How would you like that, eh? Will you and your mum do us the honour of being our guests for dinner tonight?'

'How very kind of you. Yes . . . thank you. We would be delighted,' said Rachel. She knew it would be churlish to refuse; besides, she had no intention of doing so. She was enjoying Robert Blundell's company and she knew he had invited them because it was what he wanted, and not out of politeness or protocol.

'The quickest way back to your hotel is over the Valley Bridge and through the town,' said Robert, as all four of them climbed into the Ford Anglia parked in the grounds of the hotel. They arrived back at Rosedean with ten minutes to spare before their midday meal would be served.

'Till tonight then,' said Robert. 'I'll come and pick you up at seven o'clock, in time for the meal at seven-thirty. Be sure to tell them you won't be in for tea, won't you?'

'Of course,' said Rachel. 'We can walk to your hotel, though. You don't need to come and fetch us.'

But Robert quashed her protestations. 'I wouldn't dream of letting you walk. I'll see you later. And you too, young lady.' He grinned at Lorna. 'Late night for you tonight, eh?'

It was a rare pleasure for Rachel to spend some time – and money, too – in the high-street shops. She hardly ever had time to do so at home, and nor did the shops in Melcaster provide such choice or style as the ones in Scarborough. Feeling in an expansive mood, she treated herself to a new dress from a shop on Newborough. It was up to the minute in style. Semi-fitting, with a shorter and slimmer skirt than the dresses she had previously worn, it was in her favourite shade of sea-green silky rayon, flecked with tiny black and white flowers.

Lorna, too, was treated to a new dress, and an added surprise was that she was allowed to choose it entirely on her own. She chose a bright red dress with large white polka dots and a white collar and edging to the cap sleeves. Rachel reflected that it was a good job she had packed Lorna's black patent-leather shoes, and her own best shoes, cream leather with medium stiletto heels and bar straps across the instep. She had doubted that there would be an opportunity to wear them, unaware of what Fate had in store for her.

How wonderful it was to be going on what amounted to a real date, she thought. Although she told herself not to attach too much importance to it; they just happened to have met in the same place at the same time, that was all.

Lorna's eyes were wide with wonder as she stared at her surroundings in the huge dining room of the Ocean View Hotel, at the lightness and brightness of it all, the crystal chandeliers, the dazzlingly white tablecloths, the frescoed ceiling and the gilt-edged mirrors which made the room seem twice as long as it really was.

'Isn't it posh, Mummy?' she said again, as she had said when she had seen the outside of the hotel. She spoke in a hushed voice, seeming to realise it was not a place in which you would shout.

'You look posh, too, and so does your mum,' Robert told her. 'And Adam and I have got dressed up too, in your honour.'

Rachel knew it was not the sort of establishment where gentlemen would be allowed to appear in the dining room without ties, and holiday gear – sports shirts and shorts – such as was permitted at their own humble guest house, would be strictly taboo here. It was a warm evening, however, and several of the gentlemen were seen divesting themselves of their jackets. Robert and Adam did the same, revealing crisp shirts, almost identical in pale blue cotton, with which Robert wore a striped and Adam a jaunty red bow tie.

Lorna giggled a little when the black-suited waiter shook out her napkin, almost as big as a tablecloth, and placed it with a flourish on to her knees. There was a choice of menu here, not the set meal which was standard fare at their own boarding house. Rachel helped Lorna with her choice, as the child was quite bewildered by the variety of food on offer.

'Mummy, why are we having fruit before our dinner?' the little girl asked, in a loud whisper, when their starters arrived – melon and grapefruit cocktail in little silver dishes. 'We usually have it at the end, don't we, for pudding?'

'It's what they call a starter,' Rachel explained. 'You'll be having a pudding later.' It was her daughter's first taste of the high life, and almost Rachel's first as well, although she knew she could soon get used to it!

Adam was tucking into tomato soup, which Rachel felt she would have been afraid to order lest a drop should be spilled on the pristine whiteness of the tablecloth, but the boy seemed to have no such fears. And Robert's prawn cocktail, well, that was the height of luxury.

Robert ordered a bottle of wine; red, he suggested, a Cabernet, as that would go well with the Steak Diane they had both chosen for their main course. Wine, indeed, was a very rare indulgence for Rachel, and she knew she hadn't a clue about the different varieties and which went with what. Adam and Lorna had lemonade with their roast chicken, then they all had lemon meringue pie, the speciality of the chef, as a dessert.

Both children were inclined to be quiet. Rachel guessed that not only was Lorna slightly overawed – an unusual state of affairs – but she was also enjoying the sumptuous food too much to allow for wasted time in conversation. And as for Adam . . . Rachel was not sure how he was feeling. She was aware of his eyes upon herself and his father as they laughed and talked together, so easy in each other's company. When she met his glance he looked away as though he were discomfited.

After he had addressed her once or twice as Mrs Watkins

she told him, 'I'm Rachel tonight, Adam.' She laughed. 'Well, I'm always Rachel, aren't I, not just tonight? But that's what I would like you to call me.'

'And me too?' said Lorna. 'Can I call you Rachel as well?' They all laughed, Adam more than anyone, Rachel was pleased to see.

'No, you can't!' he said. 'She's your mum, and you're a cheeky monkey! But perhaps my dad will let you call him Robert. Will you, Dad?' Rachel was not sure that she approved of that. She thought Uncle Robert, as a courtesy title, might be more fitting, but then again, that would be presuming too much. The matter was taken out of her hands, however.

'Certainly,' said Robert, beaming at Lorna, who went pink-cheeked with pleasure. 'That would be just fine.'

After the grown-ups had had coffee they all went for a walk along the cliff-top path. The fitful weather of the morning had improved as the day went on and now it was a mild, balmy evening. Dusk was just beginning to fall and the lights around the bay shone like necklace of jewels. Rachel felt contented and utterly at peace. It had been a lovely evening, a happy time for all of them, she hoped, but now it was time to bring it to a close. Lorna was unable to suppress her yawns. Her mother did not say, 'Bedtime, young lady!' knowing that the little girl would not want to seem like a baby in front of the much more grown-up boy; besides, Rachel, too, was loath to say goodnight.

'I'll run you back when you're ready,' Robert said quietly, nodding towards Lorna, yawning again. 'Not because I want the evening to end,' he added, turning to look at her. 'I don't . . .' His eyes glowed, more black than brown in the gathering twilight. They had stopped for a moment on the Spa Bridge, looking out across the wide expanse of ocean. 'But there's always tomorrow. May we see you again, Rachel . . . you and Lorna?'

'Well . . . yes, that would be lovely,' she answered. 'If you're sure . . . I mean, there's Adam to consider, isn't there?

He might want to – oh, I don't know – go fishing, go swimming, kick a ball around, whatever boys do.'

'We've a whole week, haven't we?' said Robert. 'You did say you were staying for the week? Well then, there's lots of time to do everything.' Briefly, he placed his hand over hers as it lay on the railing. Then, 'Come on,' he said. 'They'll be wondering what we're up to.'

Adam and Lorna were at the other end of the bridge, Lorna beckoning impatiently. 'I need the lav, actually,' she said, doing a jig on one foot, then the other. 'Come on, I'm dying to go.'

They all burst out laughing, but Lorna did not seem to mind. What a let-down, Rachel smiled to herself, after what had shown promise of being a romantic moment. Trust children to bring you back down to earth! They hurried back to Ocean View where Lorna had another surprise, because Adam and his father had their own bathroom and toilet attached to their room, not at the end of the corridor, as it was at Rosedean.

'Wasn't it nice tonight, Mummy?' said Lorna, as Rachel tucked her up in the single bed only a couple of feet away from her own. 'Where d'you think we'll go tomorrow?'

'Oh, I don't know. I think we'll have to wait and see what Mr Blundell suggests. We'll be going in his car, won't we?'

'Mmm . . . I'm glad we've met them, Mr Blundell and Adam, aren't you?'

Rachel smiled. 'So Adam's not a big-head any more?'

'Well, I s'pose he is sometimes. But I think it's because he knows all sorts of things. He's real clever, Mummy, isn't he? But I don't think I should call his dad Robert, do you, not really?'

'No, perhaps not just yet, dear. Let's wait and see how things go. Now . . . off you go to sleep.'

They drove over the moors to Whitby the next day. The town resembled Scarborough in some ways, with the sound of gulls, the smell of fish, and the ruined abbey and the parish church, again called after St Mary, perched on the cliff top above the town. But it was much more of a port and a fishing town than its more select neighbour. It was impossible to get anywhere without a stiff climb, either up cobbled streets or steep steps – 199 of them, so Adam said, up to the ruined abbey and the church. The boy had stopped a few times to rest, but it was an achievement, his father told Rachel, for him to have managed it at all. Lorna, skipping ahead of all of them, did not notice his slight tardiness.

'Captain Cook used to live here, in Whitby,' Adam told them as they stood, getting their breath back and enjoying a gull's eye view of the town below – the red roofs and the steep winding alleys of the old port of the town, and the busy harbour on the other side of the River Esk. 'You know, the explorer, and they built his ship, the *Endeavour*, here ... didn't they, Mrs Watkins ... er, Rachel?'

'Yes, that's true, Adam,' she replied. Captain Cook had been mentioned briefly in a class lesson about famous Yorkshiremen, but she guessed that Adam would have read up about him and probably knew far more, now, than she did. What pupils did not realise was that a teacher needed to be only one step ahead of her class! The sign of a good teacher was the ability to impart the knowledge in an interesting way.

'I've read about him, see,' Adam told them now. 'And I know that whaling fleets used to go out from here two hundred years ago.'

'You're a mine of useless information, aren't you?' chaffed his father, punching him gently on the arm.

Adam grinned. 'Not really useless, Dad ... I say, you don't think I'm showing off, do you? It's just that I like to find out about things.'

'And we're very impressed, Adam,' replied Rachel.

Lorna gave a deep sigh.

Later in the week they visited Robin Hood's Bay. There, the narrow main street plunged down a ravine to the sea and the old fishing village far below. A tangle of houses, inns, shops and cafés perched precariously on rocky ledges, connected by winding passages or steep flights of steps. An artist's paradise. Rachel watched her daughter as she stopped from time to time on the way down, gazing intently at the view of red-roofed cottages and miniature gardens full of late summer flowers. There had been little time for the child to draw or paint that week, but Rachel knew Lorna would store up the pictures in her mind to recapture later on paper, just as she, Rachel, would draw on her fund of memories when she was home again in Melcaster.

'Now, Adam, what can you tell us about this place?' asked Robert as they stood on the pebbled beach. 'Robin Hood's Bay. I doubt that Robin Hood ever came anywhere near here.'

'Ah, but he did,' replied Adam. 'Apparently he came here to get boats ready to escape to the continent . . . and there used to be a lot of smuggling here in the olden days.'

'Oh, trust you to know everything as usual!' said Lorna, sticking her tongue out at him. 'Real clever clogs, you are! Come on, I'll race you back to the top.'

'Lorna, don't be so cheeky!' shouted her mother, but the child was way ahead of them all, scrambling up the steps and slopes like a mountain goat. Most of the time the two youngsters had got along well enough. Only now and again had this streak of resentment shown itself, as if Lorna was jealous of the attention that Adam, as the elder, seemed to be receiving.

'Let her be,' said Robert quietly. 'She'll be as right as rain again when we catch up with her.'

Adam did not intend to race; he couldn't if he tried. He needed a few stops to catch his breath, as did Robert and Rachel, before they reached the top.

'Ha, ha! I won!' said Lorna gleefully.

'So you did,' said Robert. 'Good for you! Now, back to Scarborough, and fish and chips for lunch. How about that?'

They did not spend all their time together as a foursome. Adam and his father went out in a fishing boat one day, and

217

another time they went swimming in the open-air pool. Rachel and Lorna explored the ruined castle, enjoyed the pleasures of Peasholm Park and spent several happy hours in the shops. The weather was not fine and fair all the time, but a mixture of sunshine and showers. They dined at their own guest house in the evening, but occasionally they met the other two for a midday meal.

And on the last evening they all dined once more at Ocean View, walking again, as dusk was falling, along the path which led to the Spa Bridge. They stopped there as they had done before, looking out at the now familiar scene of the harbour and the sweep of the bay.

'I have a confession to make,' said Robert, closing his hand over hers.

'Oh, and what is that?' She turned to see him looking smilingly at her, his eyes full of the warmth and friendship they had enjoyed that past week.

'I knew you were coming to Scarborough . . . Adam told me. And that's why I decided we would come as well.'

She smiled. She had guessed as much, but then she had told herself that she was reading too much into what was just a coincidence. 'But . . . how did you know when we would be here? We have five weeks' holiday.'

'Adam mentioned the Bank Holiday weekend, that you would be here then. Of course, we may not have found you. But I'm very glad we did.'

'So am I,' said Rachel.

'And . . . may I see you when we get back home? I wanted to ask you before, but I thought it was best not to, not whilst Adam was in your class.'

'Yes, I would love to see you again,' said Rachel.

'Without the children?'

'Yes . . . if that is possible,' said Rachel. 'Without the children.'

Adam and Lorna had run ahead and were looking in the other direction. Robert seized his moment and, for the first time, leaned towards Rachel and gently kissed her on the lips.

218

'Thank you for making this a perfect week,' he said.

'Thank you, too,' said Rachel. 'I thought it all might be coming to an end . . .'

'But it isn't,' said Robert. 'I hope this is just the beginning, Rachel.' He kissed her again. 'Till next week . . .'

Chapter 15

'You couldn't fool me, Dad,' said Adam, laughing, as they unpacked their suitcases after the week's holiday. 'You planned it, didn't you? We went to Scarborough because you knew Mrs Watkins would be there?'

'I can't deny it, son,' said Robert. 'Why? Was it so obvious?'

Adam nodded. 'Well . . . I guessed anyway.'

'Actually, I told Rachel, on the last night,' Robert admitted, 'that I had been hoping we would meet, that I wanted to get to know her better. She didn't seem surprised.'

'You fancy her then, Dad?' Adam was grinning knowingly.

'I don't know that I would put it quite like that. I admire her greatly. I think she is an extremely nice woman and, as I've said, I want to get to know her better. We do intend to start . . . seeing one another. You wouldn't have any problem with that, would you, Adam?' Robert asked the question quite sincerely. He wanted his son to be happy about his friendship with Rachel Watkins. If there were to be any animosity it might be better not to start down that road at all.

'Of course not, Dad. Why should I?' asked Adam. 'You mean . . . because of Mum?'

'Well . . . yes. It's less than two years since your mother died. I thought you might think it was . . . too soon?'

'Well, I don't, Dad. You did everything you could for Mum. I know how much you cared about her.'

'Yes, I did indeed. I knew she was never a strong person. I knew that when we were married. She seemed to catch every illness that was going. It wasn't always easy . . . but I loved her.' Yes, he had loved her, Robert reflected, right to the end, although the more intimate side of their marriage had suffered because of Mary's fragility and, at times, her unwillingness to be a partner to him in every sense. There were certain things he could not and would not dream of sharing with his son. He realised, now, how Adam had grown, not only in stature, but in confidence and understanding as well. He was a very mature boy for his ten years.

'I like Mrs Watkins,' Adam said now. 'Well, you know I do. She's been a fantastic teacher, and she's a lovely person as well, isn't she? Ever such good fun and friendly and just . . . nice. Are you going to marry her then, Dad?'

Robert laughed. 'It's a bit soon to be thinking about that, isn't it? But let me put it like this: I would never start seeing Rachel – or anyone for that matter – if I wasn't serious about her. I'm not what you might call a lady's man.' He smiled. 'I don't know that I ever was, but we're getting on fine at the moment, Rachel and me, enjoying one another's company. But there is one slight snag . . .'

'And I can guess what it is,' said Adam. 'Or who it is. Lorna. Am I right?'

'Yes . . . Lorna,' Robert sighed. 'Don't get me wrong. She's a delightful little girl. And so funny and quick-witted, too, for a little 'un. But she's been on her own with her mother for quite a while now. She still sees her dad, of course. From what Rachel says I get the impression that Lorna's very fond of him, and she admits that Derek – that was her husband – always thought the world of Lorna.'

'Yeah . . . She liked you, though, Dad – Lorna, I mean – when we were on holiday. I could tell she did.'

'It might be different if I was there all the time. And then, of course, there is the tragedy of the little boy that died. You know about that, don't you?'

Adam nodded. 'Yes, I know about it. And Lorna told me she once had a little brother, Kevin, but she didn't say very much about him.'

'I wouldn't want the little girl to feel that everyone was

deserting her. Her dad, her brother . . . and now her mum.'

'Rachel's not going anywhere.'

'No, but there will be times when the two of us – Rachel and I – will want to be on our own.'

'Dad, I think you're making problems where there aren't any,' said Adam. 'Lorna's a little scallywag! I've told her so a few times, but she's only a kid. She'll grow up, and if she's anything like her mother, she'll turn out to be a great girl, won't she?'

Robert smiled wryly. 'I have a feeling that Lorna will be nothing like her mother. She looks like her – she's such a pretty little thing – but as far as temperament goes . . . Wow! I can see sparks flying if anyone crosses Lorna.'

'I've told you, Dad, she's only a kid. And I like her! If you're going to spend more time with Rachel, then perhaps I can look after Lorna sometimes, if Rachel will let me.'

'OK, let's see how it goes,' replied his father.

Everything went well for a while. Lorna seemed to accept that her mother was still seeing Robert, after getting to know him during the Scarborough holiday. Sometimes they went out together as a foursome at the weekend, and at other times they would dine together, either at Rachel's home or at Robert's.

Robert and Adam lived in a semi-detached house which was much more modern than Rachel's, with a larger kitchen and bathroom and more mod cons. It had been newly built when they moved into it after their return from the York area. It did not have the same view of the moors as Rachel's, but she liked the individuality of the houses where Robert lived. Though built in pairs of semis, each pair was slightly different from the others in design, some with gable ends, others with a built-out porch, and with variations in the styles of the doors and the windows, and each house had a garage at the end of a shared driveway. The quiet cul-de-sac was called Sycamore Close, and trees of the same name had been planted along the grass verges, saplings as yet, but promising shade and colour in years to come. This new development was on the outer fringe of Melcaster, not as near to Kilbeck School as Rachel's home, but not too far away either.

There were times, though, when Rachel and Robert wanted to be on their own. If they wished to see a film or to drive out of Melcaster to a country inn, then that would involve baby-sitters for both Lorna and Adam. Both children disliked the term, especially Lorna, who had been known to stamp her feet and shout that she was not a baby, but Adam realised that 'baby-sitter' was a new phrase that everyone was using now, and that, even at ten years of age, he was still not old enough to be left alone in the house.

Robert's next-door neighbour, a middle-aged widow who was very fond of Adam, agreed to see to him when his father was out. And Rachel's mother, of course, was only too pleased to look after Lorna. She was delighted at the idea of a new man in her daughter's life. Rachel had wondered how she would react after kicking up such a fuss about the divorce, but she seemed to have put that right out of her mind. Lizzie took to Robert straight away, and to Adam as well. Adam was the sort of boy to whom grown-ups, as well as his own peer group, responded easily.

'We're just friends, Mum,' Rachel warned her as they washed up after a huge Christmas dinner. She was fearful lest her mother should speak out of turn and cause embarrassment to Robert. They had spent most of that festive day, all together, at the Hardings' home, Lizzie in her element showing off her cooking and homemaking skills.

'Oh, don't you try to pull the wool over my eyes!' laughed her mother. 'The way that fellow looks at you, he wants to be more than friends. And we're very pleased for you, Rachel, your dad and me. He's a lovely man, a vast improvement on that other one you had! He'll make you a wonderful husband.'

'But he hasn't said anything yet, Mum!' hissed Rachel. She and Robert both knew, though, what was in the other's mind.

There were times, especially in the cold winter evenings, when they wanted to stay in – not go out – together. Sometimes Adam went along with his father to Rachel's house, and he and Lorna would occupy themselves playing ludo, snakes and ladders, or dominoes. Adam had even started to teach her the rudiments of chess and was proud of the speed at which she was picking it up. He was remarkably patient, especially as the child was several years younger than himself.

Rachel and Robert would snatch what little time they could to be alone. They had kissed and held hands, but they both knew that further intimacies would have to wait. And at nine o'clock – or ten at the latest – Robert and Adam would have to return home. It would have been more convenient for them all to spend the night under one roof, but this was impossible. Rachel's house had only three bedrooms, as had Robert's, and it went without saying that it was out of the question for the two of them to share a room.

'Marry me, Rachel,' said Robert, one evening in the January of 1960. 'It's what we both want, isn't it?' They were at Robert's house, the two children upstairs looking at Adam's large collection of comics, and both of the grown-ups aware that soon it would be time for them to say goodnight and for Robert to drive Rachel and Lorna back to their own little house.

'We can't go on like this,' he went on, 'each of us in separate houses, when all we want is to be together. You want it as much as I do, don't you, darling?'

'Of course I do, Robert,' Rachel replied. 'I've been waiting and hoping . . . but you hadn't said anything. I was beginning to wonder . . .'

'I love you, Rachel,' he said, kissing her gently on the forehead, stroking her pale golden hair which flowed in soft waves back from her temples. 'I've loved you for ages. You must know that . . . but I knew I had to wait, to see how things would work out. There are others to consider as well as ourselves, aren't there?'

'Yes,' she nodded. 'Adam and Lorna . . . I can't see that Adam will be any problem at all, not now he's got used to me as a family friend and not just his teacher.' She laughed. 'That must have been rather off-putting at first.'

'I think Adam is only waiting for me to ask you,' smiled Robert. 'He's growing up fast. And later this year he won't even be at your school, will he? He'll be at the senior school; the grammar school, we hope.'

'And Lorna?' said Rachel, taking hold of Robert's squarish hand, idly stroking each finger in turn. 'How would you feel about having charge of Lorna? She can be a little terror for me at times.'

'I know, I've seen her at work! There is a rebellious streak there, I must admit, but so long as she knows she is loved and cared for, just as much as ever, I'm sure she will adapt to a new situation. She's a sensible little girl. Children like to feel that they're safe and secure; that's the important thing.'

'She's gone through some traumas though, already. Losing our Kevin – she adored her little brother, you know – and then her daddy leaving us . . . We must try to make sure that nothing else happens to upset her. As you say, so long as she's safe and secure, and she knows that we love her . . .'

'You will marry me then, Rachel? Please say yes!'

'Yes, I will marry you, Robert.' They came together in a loving kiss and embrace that sealed their promise.

'I love you so much,' said Robert. 'I will never, ever, let you down.'

'I know that,' said Rachel. 'And I love you too. I've never been more sure of anything.'

'When shall we tell the children?' asked Robert, when they had kissed several more times.

'Let's see. It's Saturday tomorrow,' said Rachel. 'Lorna will be with her father. What about Sunday? Come for lunch on Sunday and we'll tell them together.'

'Congratulations, Dad! And you too, Rachel,' said Adam on hearing the news. 'That's what I've been waiting to hear.

Great news, isn't it, Lorna? Your mum and my dad getting married!'

'I s'pose so.' Lorna did not look exactly overjoyed. 'I hadn't really thought much about it. Where will we live? Will we stay here, Mummy?'

Rachel and Robert had talked about the question of whose house, and come to the conclusion that it might be better for her and Lorna to move into Robert's house. Here, in Hillview, there were memories of Kevin and Derek, whereas in Sycamore Close they could make a fresh start in new surroundings.

'No . . . I don't think we'll be staying here,' said Rachel, but not too decidedly. She was aware of the closed look that had appeared on her daughter's face. 'There's more room at Robert's place, isn't there? Well, slightly more room,' she added truthfully. There was, in fact, not much difference in the size. 'And it's more modern. You can have a nice big bedroom all to yourself.'

'I've got a nice bedroom here, Mummy . . . and this is where Kevin used to live with us, isn't it?'

'Yes, I know that, dear.' Rachel felt a tug, then, at her heartstrings. She could not tell Lorna that this was a very good reason for moving, that if they stayed here, then Adam would move into the bedroom which had once been Kevin's. 'But we won't forget Kevin,' she continued, 'even though we leave this house.'

'I shan't ever forget him,' said Lorna. She set her mouth in a stubborn line before she went on. 'There's only three bedrooms, though, at . . . Uncle Robert's.' She had agreed that this was the best way to address him. 'And there are four of us, aren't there?'

'There are only three bedrooms here as well, silly!' said Adam with a good-natured laugh.

'Yes, I know that! And don't you call me silly! I can count, can't I? One, two, three, four; there are four of us. So there's not enough room.'

Rachel raised her eyes heavenwards as she glanced at

226

Robert. She guessed her daughter was being deliberately obtuse.

'But people who are married sleep in the same room, don't they?' said Adam. 'And that's what your mum and my dad will be doing.'

'Oh . . . right,' said Lorna. 'I hadn't thought of that.' But Rachel knew perfectly well that she had. 'Like you and Daddy used to share a room, Mummy?' she asked, with an air of innocence.

'Yes . . . something like that, love,' said Rachel. 'But we want you to be happy about . . . everything.'

'Oh, I am,' said Lorna nonchalantly. She thought for a moment. Then, 'Can I be a bridesmaid?' she asked.

Once they had decided they were to marry there did not seem to be much point in waiting too long. It seemed a very long time until the summer holiday, so they decided they would get married during the Easter break – on Easter Saturday, in fact – and then they would have time for a week's honeymoon before Rachel had to return to work.

The Reverend Michael Laycock surprised Rachel by refusing to marry her in St Matthew's church. He explained how he was bound by the directives laid down by his bishop. He could, however, hold a service of blessing for her and her new husband after they had gone through a civil ceremony with the registrar.

Rachel was disappointed. She had thought, after her family's long association with the church, that the vicar might have been a little more lenient. She disliked the idea of a civil marriage, and her mother, as might have been expected, was adamant that 'no daughter of mine will get married in a register office!'

'I'm sorry she's so difficult, Robert,' Rachel said to her fiancé. 'Goodness knows what you must think of her! She can't seem to help interfering.'

Robert, though, was very tolerant of Lizzie Harding. 'She's a very warm-hearted person underneath all the bluster,' he

227

said. 'And her world revolves round you and Lorna. All she wants is what is best for you, and I'm delighted that she seems to think I fit the bill! You know, when I go anywhere, I go to the Methodist church. They are a lively, friendly crowd. We could get married there if you're agreeable.'

Lizzie did not object too strongly to the idea of the Methodist church – although it would not have made any difference to Rachel if she had – and arrangements were made for the service to be held on Easter Saturday at the red-brick chapel on Melcaster High Street. Rachel had attended one or two services there with Robert, to familiarise herself with the surroundings.

She missed the awesomeness and the 'beauty of holiness' which pervaded the atmosphere at St Matthew's. The climate of this place was very different. For a start, Rachel had always been brought up to show reverence in a place of worship, and she was amazed, therefore, at the amount of chattering that went on before the service. They were respectful enough, however, once the minister, the Rev George Black, appeared, not dressed in fancy regalia, but in an ordinary grey suit with the addition of a clerical collar. The singing was hearty, the preaching sincere, and the congregation – who did not know Rachel, and only knew Robert a little – welcoming. She felt she had made a good choice for her marriage service.

For the wedding Rachel wore an elegant cream-coloured silk suit with the new-style narrow knee-length skirt. Her cream straw hat had a large brim, the crown trimmed with a pink velvet rose. Pauline, her matron-of-honour, and Lorna were both dressed in blue. Pauline's outfit was a simple suit, similar in style to Rachel's, with a neat matching pill-box hat, and Lorna's a dress of cornflower-blue silky rayon in a rather more grown-up style than the full-skirted cotton dresses she had previously worn. The twenty guests, all close family or friends, met together afterwards at the Co-op café, on the top floor of the Emporium in Melcaster High Street.

Robert's parents, who lived in Leeds, were there, as was

his brother, Kenneth, and his wife and family, who lived in Bridlington on the east coast. Rachel had no close relations apart from her parents, but she had several loving friends and close neighbours who had been invited along to share in her joy. And all who saw her radiant smile as she cut into the wedding cake with her new husband wished her all the happiness in the world. She deserved it.

'To Rachel and Robert...' They lifted their glasses of champagne and toasted the newly-weds, confident that, this time, Rachel would find true love and contentment.

In the middle of the afternoon the couple left in Robert's Ford Anglia to spend their honeymoon in the Cotswolds.

Deciding on a venue for the week they were to spend away from home had proved to be more of a problem than Rachel and Robert had anticipated.

'Where are we going on our holiday, then?' Lorna had asked, aware from what she had heard her mother and Robert discussing that holiday plans were in the air. 'Can we go to Scarborough again? Adam and me, we'd both like that, wouldn't we, Adam?'

'Don't be silly! We're not going,' Adam had said. 'It's just my dad and Rachel... your mum, I mean. That's what people do when they get married, they go away together on their own. It's called a honeymoon.'

Lorna had stuck out her lower lip in a pout, which Rachel had tried to ignore; she usually came round. It was Robert who had said, 'Never mind, Lorna. It's only for a week, and we'll take you and Adam to Scarborough – or somewhere else just as nice – in the long summer holiday. How about that, eh?'

Lorna had shrugged. ''S all right, I s'pose...' She had not made too much fuss after that, realising it would not make any difference if she did, and she had begun to look forward to the wedding. Her father, very recently, had married Sylvia, in a quiet little ceremony in Ripon. She had only found out about it afterwards and that had annoyed her. Why couldn't everything have stayed the way it used to be? she thought crossly to herself. Everything was upside-down. But at least she had a new dress to wear, a very grown-up one, and before the wedding it would be her seventh birthday. Mummy had promised to buy her some oil paints, real grown-up ones with a special palette.

In the end they had decided on the Cotswolds area for their honeymoon as it was not too far away and they could keep in contact with the family at home. They were to spend the first three nights in Cheltenham, which they had booked in advance, it being the Easter weekend, and then they would go wherever their fancy took them.

Adam was to spend the time with his grandparents in Leeds, and Lorna with hers in Melcaster.

'We're going to have a lovely time together, you and me,' Lizzie told the little girl as they drove home after the wedding. Rachel and Robert had left about an hour before, so it was not surprising that the child was looking a little downcast.

'And Grandad, too,' said Lorna, nodding towards her grandfather at the wheel.

'Yes, me an' all,' he laughed. 'It's yer grandma, though, that's doing all the planning. Me, I just do the driving, but we'll have a good time this week, sure enough.'

Lizzie was delighted to have her dear little granddaughter staying with them for the week. Poor little girl! It wasn't to be wondered at if she felt somewhat left out in the cold, what with her father remarrying – although that was good riddance to bad rubbish as far as Lizzie was concerned – and now her mother. Rachel deserved some happiness, though, and Lizzie was sure she would find it with that nice fellow, Robert Blundell. Her concern, though, at the moment, was that dear little Lorna should not feel neglected.

'You've always been my special little girl, do you know that, Lorna?' Lizzie told her as she got the child ready for bed that evening. Then they sat together in a big armchair whilst Lorna had her hot chocolate and a homemade short-bread biscuit. 'My little pancake baby, that's what I used to call you,' she laughed, 'but I think your mummy used to get cross when I called you that.'

'Why did you, Grandma?' asked Lorna. 'I 'member that's what you said.'

Lizzie explained that they had all been eating pancakes, because it was Shrove Tuesday, when Lorna was about to be born. 'And then, the next day, you arrived. Our little pancake baby. That's why you've always been special.'

'And there was Kevin as well,' said Lorna. 'Wasn't he special, too, Grandma?'

'Of course he was, darling,' said Lizzie, tears coming into her eyes for a moment. 'But you were the first, weren't you? Our very first grandchild . . . Come on, now, let's get you into bed. We've got an exciting week ahead.'

Easter Sunday, of course, meant church. A special service with the vicar togged up in his finery of white and gold; spring flowers – daffodils, narcissi and deep-red tulips – in shining silver vases on the communion table; and a rousing anthem from the choir declaring that 'Christ is arisen . . .'

There were Easter eggs for Lorna from her grandma and grandad, her mother and Robert, and one from the couple that Lizzie thought of as 'her other grandparents'.

On Monday Percy drove them to Bolton Abbey where they wandered round the priory ruins, then had a picnic by the banks of the River Wharfe.

Lizzie felt tired when they returned home, more tired than she would admit. Nor did she want to confess to her hus-band, or even to herself, that looking after her grandchild was harder work than she had anticipated. When she had cared for her as a baby she had been several years younger. Now, in her late sixties, the extra years were beginning to take their toll. And then there was that niggling pain in her chest which, so far, she had tried to ignore.

She decided that a comparative rest would be in order for

the next day. So on the Tuesday morning Lizzie and Lorna set out all the ingredients to make some more of the shortbread biscuits that Lorna liked so much. Percy, noting that the womenfolk were busy, said a cheery goodbye and set off to take what he called his daily constitutional around the streets of Melcaster.

Lizzie used only the best butter for her very special shortbread. But it did make the mixture rather rich and crumbly and it kept cracking and breaking as she rolled it out with her rolling pin. Lorna, at her side, dressed in a brightly coloured apron, was longing to help, but this was a tricky business. Lizzie was beginning to wish she had not embarked upon this chore at all, especially as she was not feeling too well this morning. She had not wanted to ask Percy to stay in that morning, but she hoped he would not be too long.

She managed to roll out sufficient dough for the first batch of biscuits, then she handed the fluted cutter to Lorna. 'Here you are, love. Now, see how many biscuits you can get out of this mixture. Keep them close together, the way you've seen Grandma do it. That's it; clever girl. You're doing splendidly . . . Now, we'll lay them on this baking tray and I'll put them in the oven.'

Lizzie did not get as far as the oven. As she turned away from the table a massive pain grabbed at her, like a vice, squeezing at her chest, her upper arm, the region around her heart. She gave a cry. 'Oh . . . oh, help! Oh . . . oh, Lorna, whatever is happening to me? Oh, please God . . .'

The tin fell out of her hands and crashed to the floor, surrounded by all the crumbling biscuit shapes, as she clasped at her ribcage, then fell with a sickening thud on to the floor. Lorna stared in horror at the scene. Her grandma was lying motionless on the blue and yellow tiles, her glasses that she wore for close work all askew on her nose. Lorna thought she had bumped her head on the corner of the table as she fell. There had been an awful bang which was probably why she was not moving. Grandma must have knocked herself out.

'Grandma, Grandma . . .' She knelt on the floor beside her, taking hold of her shoulders and shaking her gently. 'Wake up! Come on, you'll be all right. I'm here . . . it's Lorna. Oh, Grandma, please wake up!' But her grandmother was not responding. Lorna took hold of her hand and squeezed it, but she did not seem to notice. A terrible thought struck her and she bent down closer, putting her ear to the place where she guessed her gran's heart might be. There was no sound. Lorna gave a loud shout, more of a scream. 'Grandma! Oh, somebody . . . please help!'

She ran out of the back door, up the next path and hammered on the door. She knew the lady who lived there. She was called Mrs Penswick and she and her gran were quite good friends. To her relief the door opened almost at once.

'Hello there . . . It's Lorna, isn't it? You look as though you're very busy. Doing some baking, are you, dear?'

Lorna grabbed at her hand. 'Oh, Mrs Penswick, please come, quick! It's me gran. She might be . . . dead.'

Mrs Penswick, also, could evoke no response from the motionless figure. She stood up again looking very serious and her face had gone white. 'Where is your grandad, darling?' she asked Lorna.

'He's gone for a walk. He said he wouldn't be long. Why? Is Grandma . . .?' She did not want to say the word again. Surely it could not be true. Grandma could not be dead, not so quickly.

'We need to get a doctor to see to your gran,' Mrs Penswick said, not answering Lorna's unspoken query, but the woman knew it was already too late. 'Just come next door with me, dear – it's all right, your gran will come to no harm – and I'll ask my husband to go and find your grandad. I don't think he'll be far away. And we'll ring for the doctor . . .'

Percy Harding arrived back home with Mr Penswick just as the doctor was getting out of his car. He shook his head when he had examined Lizzie. 'I am sorry. It's too late. There's nothing I can do. I can arrange for . . . your wife to

233

be taken away, though. It would be for the best. I believe you have your little granddaughter staying with you?'

'Yes, apparently our little Lorna was alone with her when it happened,' said Percy. 'If only I'd known . . . I would never have gone out. She didn't say . . . Whatever must you think of me, doctor, going out and leaving her?'

'Knowing Mrs Harding, she probably didn't want to make a fuss,' said the doctor. 'She might have been feeling unwell for a while, or it might have been a massive heart attack that just happened out of the blue. That's my guess, although there will have to be a post mortem, with it being a sudden death.'

'We'd best get in touch with my daughter,' said Percy dazedly. 'She's away on holiday. In fact, she's on her honeymoon, poor lass. I'm not rightly sure just where they are. But she said she'd ring. I hope to goodness she does. And our Lorna, poor little mite.' He shook his head sadly. 'She thought the world of her gran.'

'I know you'll take good care of her, Percy,' said the doctor reassuringly, 'and she'll feel better when her mother gets back. Look after yourself, now; that's the important thing.'

'We'll see to him,' said Mr Penswick, 'the wife and me. They can have a bite of dinner wi' us, Percy and t' little lass. What are neighbours for, eh, if not to do one another a good turn?'

Lorna stayed at the Penswicks' house with her grandad for the next few hours. Mrs Penswick went next door and cleared up the mess on the floor and turned off the oven which had been lit to bake the biscuits.

The little girl was told what she had already guessed, that her grandmother, sadly, had died. She had gone to heaven to live with Jesus, her grandad said, which was what her mother had said when Kevin died. She could not be persuaded to eat or drink anything, apart from the merest morsel of chicken, a spoonful of potato and a few sips of orange juice. She sat still and silent, only speaking in a quiet little voice when she was spoken to. They went back home at teatime as Percy was hoping he would get a phone call from Rachel. If she did not ring, then he did not know what he would do. Ask the police to find them maybe, or put out an SOS call on the radio or television.

But Rachel did call, sounding very cheerful and light-hearted. Her father hated having to spoil her new-found happiness. After a cry of anguish, a shocked silence and then a hurried conversation with her husband, she said they would come home at once.

Lorna cheered up a little when she heard that her mother would be back later that evening. Percy knew it would be pointless to put her to bed, and so they sat quietly together with the television playing away in the background, but neither of them were really aware of what they were watching.

It was after ten o'clock when Rachel and Robert arrived back. Rachel rushed into the house and embraced her father, then she turned to Lorna who was standing in the middle of the room looking helpless and alone.

'Lorna, my darling, what a dreadful thing to happen,' she cried. She put her arms round her daughter, holding her close. The tears that had refused to flow for the last few hours now broke forth from Lorna. She sobbed and yelled, a paroxysm of rage as well as grief shaking her small body.

'I want my grandma!' she cried. 'You went and left me . . . you don't care about me. But Grandma did . . . She said I was her special little girl . . . and now she's gone and died . . . and I want her back!' She pushed roughly at her mother. 'Go away, you! I want my gran . . .'

Chapter 16

'I can't wait to leave school,' said Lorna to her friend, Carol Forrest. 'Actually, I want to leave home as well. That's why I want to get a job and start work, then I can save up for a flat of my own. Or I might get somebody to share with me . . .'

Lorna could see the look of tolerant amusement on Carol's face. She had told her this same thing several times before and she knew that Carol thought she was mad, that it was all pie in the sky. Well, maybe it was, but there was no harm in wishing and hoping. Her friend was a very well-behaved, well-disciplined young lady who would not dream of disobeying her parents or doing anything that might displease them.

The two girls had been in the same class since they were five years old, firstly at Kilbeck Infant and Junior Schools, and then at the Melcaster Grammar School for Girls. They had recently sat for their O-level exams and Carol intended to go into the sixth form and, eventually, take a nursing course at a hospital. The only sign that she was sticking up for herself, as far as Lorna could see, was that she had said she would prefer a hospital away from her home town – Leeds, for instance – rather than Melcaster, which was the one her parents would prefer.

The friends no longer lived in the same locality. Lorna had moved when her mother had remarried, to Sycamore Close, but she still spent a good deal of her time at Hillview. That was where she was on that June afternoon in 1969, in Carol's bedroom listening to *Sergeant Pepper's Lonely Hearts Club Band*. They had both loved The Beatles ever since the fab four had burst on to the pop scene some five or six years before. But this album was more experimental, more in keeping with the hippie movement which had taken off in Britain a couple of years before during the 'Summer of Love'.

'I wish you'd change your mind and come into the sixth form with me,' said Carol now. 'Why won't you? It won't be like real school. Not so many rules and regulations and you can drop the subjects that you don't like or are not very good at. You could concentrate on your art.'

'You sound like my mum,' sighed Lorna. 'She wants me to take my A-levels and then go to art college. She'd really like me to be a boring old teacher, like she is, but I think even she has realised there's no chance of that.'

'Your mum's not a boring old teacher,' retorted Carol. 'From what I can remember when you and I were in her class, she was a jolly good teacher and everybody loved her. You were a damned nuisance for her, though; I remember that.'

'So do I,' Lorna giggled. 'I was a terror, wasn't I?'

'And it seems to me that you're not much different now!' said her friend. 'I expect you were jealous, though, weren't you? Seeing your mother with all those other children.'

'I might have been,' agreed Lorna. 'I suppose I wanted my mum all to myself. I always seemed to be having to share her with something or somebody. Well, I still am . . .'

'You mean . . . Robert? I thought you got on OK with him?'

'I do. I must admit he's a great guy and he's been really patient with me. But he and my mum, they're still so wrapped up in one another, all lovey-dovey; it makes me sick at times. That's one of the reasons I want to get away and live on my own.'

'And what does your mum say about that?'

'Well, I haven't told her, have I? I've got a hard enough job convincing her that I want to leave school. I've had to more or less promise that I'll go to night school and take my A-level in art. As a matter of fact, Robert has backed me up. You see, he left school at fifteen and started work as an apprentice heating engineer and now he's got his own business and I reckon he makes a bomb.'

'So they must be rolling in it, he and your mum, now she's a headteacher?'

'They don't go short of anything. But then, neither do I. They're pretty generous with me, I know that, but I'd rather be earning my own money and doing my own thing.'

'You're still thinking of applying for a job at Paige's, are you?'

'Not just any old job. A post as a designer, if you don't mind! I'm going to wait until we've finished school and then I shall go round to the factory in person, with my portfolio, and show them what I can do.'

'Portfolio, eh? That sounds posh! I'm sure they'll be impressed, Lorna. Your paintings and drawings are just super.'

Lorna gave a confident smile. 'I'm telling you, Carol, I shall be chief designer at Paige's before I'm done, you'll see.'

'Well, there's nothing like aiming high. And your mum's certainly got to the top of her profession, hasn't she?'

'As far as she wants to go, yes. I suppose it's not an easy job, but she seems to cope all right. And of course dear old Robert is always there to do his share of the chores.'

'And what about you? Do you do your share?'

'Oh, I lend a hand now and again,' she answered airily. 'From what I remember of my dad – my real dad, I mean, Derek – he never lifted a finger to help my mother when he was living with us. She used to wait on him hand and foot like somebody demented. But you should see him now helping Sylvia in the kitchen.'

'Do you still go to see him?'

'Yes, but not as much as I used to. They're wrapped up in one another an' all, my dad and Sylvia. They don't have time for anyone outside their own little circle.'

'Oh, I'm sure that's not true, Lorna. I'm sure your dad still cares about you, just as your mum does.'

'Yes, maybe . . . But it's the way it seems to me sometimes.

My mum and Robert, my dad and Sylvia; I feel as though I'm on the outside looking in. I wish there was somebody who put me first . . .' She stopped and looked at Carol, who was frowning a little and regarding her strangely. 'What's up? Does that sound selfish?'

'No . . . not really. But people do care about you, Lorna. You have loads of friends. And I like to think you're my special friend . . . aren't you?'

'Yes, of course I am. I suppose I'm just feeling a bit sorry for myself. I do, sometimes. I remember my gran – you know, Grandma Lizzie, my mum's mum – she used to tell me I was her special little girl. She told me so that last day, and then she went and died on me!'

'Yes, I remember. That was awful.'

'Yes, it was . . . And then I was awful to my mother. I don't think she's ever quite forgotten it. I feel we've never got back to being as close as we were before . . . Oh dear! I'm getting all soppy and sentimental, aren't I? I'd best be off. Mum'll probably have the tea ready by the time I get back.'

'Yeah. See you tomorrow then,' said Carol, rising to her feet. 'Oh, one more thing before you go. How's Adam going on? I haven't heard you mention him much recently.'

'He's OK as far as I know.'

'Is he still working for that newspaper in Halifax?'

'No, he's moved to Leeds. He managed to get a job as sports reporter for an evening paper there, which suits him down to the ground.'

'Oh, that's interesting,' said Carol. 'Leeds, eh? That's where I fancy going to do my training.'

'Oh, you do, do you?' Lorna grinned. 'You've always had a thing about Adam, haven't you?'

'Not really. He's a good-looking lad and . . . well, yes, I suppose I might have fancied him a bit. Lots of girls did. But he never looked in my direction. Anyway, he always seemed so much older. I expect he thought of us as silly kids.'

'That's certainly how he thought of me! We used to fall out something dreadful before he moved to Halifax. Mum and

Robert were jolly glad when we were living apart, although they probably wished it was me that had gone, not Adam.'

'There you go again! I'm sure they didn't.'

'Well, let's say that Adam and I get on better now, but we don't see all that much of him.'

'Has he got a girlfriend, do you know?'

'I don't know. He's been out with one or two, I believe, but nothing serious. I'll make enquiries! I can put in a good word for you if you like, tell him you might be going to live in Leeds.'

'Don't you dare! I'm just . . . interested, that's all.'

'Yeah . . . Anything you say,' laughed Lorna. 'See you tomorrow, kid.'

Rachel Blundell had been appointed as headmistress of Kilbeck Infant School on Miss Lacey's retirement two years previously. She had taught in the junior school for a few years after her marriage and then she had been deputy head of an infant school on the other side of Melcaster, finally returning, as it were, to her roots, to the school where she had started her teaching career getting on for twenty years ago.

Now, as she approached her fortieth birthday, Rachel pondered, as she often did, on how happy and fulfilled she was in all aspects of her life. She enjoyed her career, although she did not live for it, as many infant heads were known to do. She had continued with her teaching because Robert had encouraged her to do so. They both believed that doing a satisfying job added an extra dimension to what was already a very happy marriage.

Rachel was busy. Life, indeed, was hectic at times, but never too exhausting. She now had her own car, a red Mini of which she was very proud – and equally proud of her ability to drive – and a cleaning lady to do the rough work for her once a week; Robert had insisted on that. The other household tasks, cooking and washing-up and the day-to-day tidying, the three of them shared, although rather unequally.

Rachel knew she should insist on Lorna helping more around the house, but she had told herself that the girl was busy studying . . . and she was sure she was no better and no worse than thousands of other teenage girls.

Lorna could, of course, be here now, she thought as she dashed around the kitchen, helping her to prepare the meal or, at least, setting the table. Exams were finished so there was no longer the excuse to fall back on that she had homework or 'swotting' to do. Instead of which she was round at Carol's house and would only put in an appearance when everything was done.

Carol Forrest, though, was a very nice, sensible girl and Rachel hoped that she was having a good influence on her daughter. She, Rachel, had not seen much of Jenny, Carol's mother, since they had moved away from Hillview, but she was pleased that the two girls had remained friends. Carol was contemplating a career in nursing, a very worthwhile choice, unlike Lorna's, whose only idea at the moment seemed to be to leave school and start work at that factory that made greetings cards and suchlike. Rachel appreciated that Lorna was artistic – it was she who had helped, years ago, to foster the talent in the child – but the girl did not seem to realise that she could not hope to walk into a plum job straight away. She would most likely be stuck in an office as the tea girl or employed in the processing or packing department. If only she would agree to go to art college, or, at least, to go into the sixth form and obtain her A-levels.

The subject came up again during the evening meal, and Rachel could not help feeling a little exasperated because it was Robert who started it.

'There's an advert in tonight's paper,' he said, addressing his remark to Lorna, 'that you might be interested in. Paige's Paper Products are advertising vacancies in all departments. Phone or write for an interview; that's what it says.'

'Gosh! That's great!' said Lorna. 'That's what I was waiting for. Well, no – I wasn't actually waiting for them to advertise.

I intended going round there anyway when school's finished, to show them what I can do.'

'That's the spirit!' said Robert. 'You show 'em, girl!' He turned to his wife who was on the verge of protesting. 'Listen, love, she can but try. We know our Lorna's a jolly good artist, but if she has to start at the bottom – well, so be it. Look at Adam. He started as little more than a tea boy, didn't he? And look at him now.'

'At least he spent some time in the sixth form, didn't he?'

'Yes, so he did, but what does that matter? Lots of lads, and lasses, too, start work at sixteen – or even fifteen.'

'And I'll take my A-level in art, I promise, Mum,' said Lorna. 'I can go to night school when I've finished work.'

'They've not taken you on yet,' replied Rachel. 'Let's just wait and see what happens . . .'

'I can't understand her,' Rachel said to her husband later that evening. Lorna, as she often did, was listening to records in the solitude of her bedroom. 'So she wants to start work – to show her independence, I suppose – fair enough. But why does she want to stay in Melcaster? You'd think she'd be hankering to get away. To go to an art college, for instance. That would be an adventure, wouldn't it? Why stick around here? She's let us see often enough that she thinks her life here is boring!' That was one of Lorna's favourite adjectives.

'She's only sixteen, love. Starting work would be the first step she could take on her own. And don't be so sure that she wants to get away. Her roots are here, in this town and this environment. And maybe she's not as self-reliant as she would like us to think. She's taken a lot of knocks, you know.'

'Yes, I realise that, Robert. And so did I . . . but you helped me to forget, didn't you?' She turned to her husband, sitting at her side on the settee. 'Well, not to forget, but to start again. Oh, my darling, I am so very, very glad that I met you.' She took hold of his hands in hers, then leaned forward and kissed him gently on the lips. 'You've made such a difference to my life.'

In marrying Robert she had not only gained a loving husband, but a son as well. She had come to love Adam almost, if not quite, as much as she would have loved her own son, Kevin, had he grown to maturity. Adam had been by far the more biddable and considerate of the two adolescent children growing up in the home together. He had had his moments, of course, of awkwardness and ill-humour, but they had usually occurred when he was provoked by Lorna. When he had left home two years ago, to live firstly in Halifax and then in Leeds, Rachel had missed him very much.

'As you have to my life,' replied Robert, returning her kiss. 'I love you so very much . . . But, as I've said to you before, we must be careful not to exclude Lorna. She knows we are all in all to one another. I've seen her watching us sometimes and you can't be sure what is going through her mind. It's important for her to know that we still care about her very much.'

'I'm sure she knows that,' said Rachel, but not too convincingly. 'But I can't forget how she's turned against me, more than once . . . When Kevin died, and then when Derek left us, as though it was all my fault . . . And when my mother died, that was the worst of all . . . And we're still not all that close, not the way some mothers and daughters are. I know she's had a lot to cope with – so much that I wonder if that old rhyme was right. You know, about Wednesday's child being full of woe – and I can't help but feel she blames me.'

'You seem OK to me,' said Robert. 'As I've just said, she's only sixteen. You ask any mother with a sixteen-year-old daughter, and you'll find that they're not much different.'

'Yes, maybe you're right,' said Rachel.

Paige's Paper Products was an old woollen mill which had been taken over during the decline of the Yorkshire woollen trade and converted to its present function some five years before. As its name suggested, the factory produced paper products of all kinds, the main line being greetings cards of myriad varieties. Christmas cards, birthday cards, as well as those for wedding anniversaries, engagements and christenings, to wish the recipient good luck in a new job or a new house, congratulations on the birth of a baby, or commiseration in times of sickness or bereavement. Whatever the occasion, Paige's had an appropriate card. Many of them were quite exclusive in design and – more to the point for Yorkshire folk who liked to get good value for their 'brass' – were retailed at a reasonable price. They also produced wrapping papers, note books, stationery and sundry office items.

Lorna wrote for an interview, giving details of her scholastic endeavours. She had sat for eight O-levels and was hopeful that she would get good grades in all of them. One of the subjects was art. She had emphasised this, but the reply she received informed her that, at the present time, they had no vacancies in the design department. They would, however, subject to interview, consider her for a post in the accounts office, having noted that maths was one of her subjects.

She grimaced when she read this. Yes, she could do maths OK, but it was not something she enjoyed. It was boring, boring . . . Still, they had asked her to go for an interview and, undaunted, she intended to take her portfolio of art work along with her.

'Oh dear . . . Do you really think you should be wearing that dress for your interview?' asked her mother, eyeing her up and down. 'I mean to say,' she went on, as Lorna gave a sigh of exasperation, 'you look very nice, love, but . . . it's rather short, isn't it?'

'It's the style, Mum! It's a mini-dress. Hadn't you noticed that everybody's wearing them? Well, perhaps not everybody. I don't suppose you would; you're a bit past it, aren't you? But all my friends have got them.' She stopped, seeing the injured look that had appeared on her mother's face. She hadn't meant to hurt her, but it was not hard to do; she took offence very easily, usually about something and nothing.

They seemed to be continually rubbing one another up the wrong way.

'I don't consider I'm past it, Lorna!' her mother retorted. 'I should hope I'm not past anything, not just yet. But you'd hardly expect me to turn up at school dressed as you are, would you?'

'I'm sorry, Mum. I didn't mean to be rude. But you're always going on at me.'

'No, I'm not.' Her mother sighed. 'It's you who thinks I am. I've told you, you look very nice, and I suppose the other girls who are there will be wearing them.' She smiled. 'Don't bend down, that's all.'

'It's all right, my knickers are clean on,' said Lorna.

'Lorna, honestly.'

'Well, I can't put a coat on, can I? It's a boiling-hot day.'

'So it is. Well, good luck, darling. Show them your work if you get a chance, but try not to be too disappointed if they're not interested. They did say it was office work.'

'They'll be interested, believe me. I shall make them sit up and take notice. Tara then. See you later.'

The factory was only ten minutes' walk away and Lorna, glad to be out of doors, almost skipped along the sunlit streets. Her shining golden hair which she wore in a shoulder-length page-boy style bounced gently in time with the spring in her step. Her carefree demeanour and the bright yellow dress she was wearing caught the eye of several passers-by. They smiled at her, feeling that she was adding a little more sunshine to their day, and she smiled back. Lorna was happy. School was over for good and all. No more exams or homework; she had agreed to do her A-level art, but that would be a doddle. And no more school uniform! For the last few months the girls had been turning the waistbands of their skirts over a few times to make them into the new mini length. Now she could put the boring navy-blue thing into the dustbin! She felt sorry for Carol who would have to wear hers for another year at least.

Paige's was in the same street, on the fringe of Melcaster,

as Whittakers Mill where her father was still employed. There was only one woollen mill now remaining in the town, where tweed cloth of a high quality was produced. All the other mills had been turned over to other light industries, such as the manufacture of clothing, plastics, or kitchen equipment. Not that Melcaster had ever been a forerunner in the woollen trade, but the older inhabitants regretted the decline of what had once been the area's staple industry.

Lorna was on her best behaviour that afternoon. She knew she could be charming and could give the right impression when it was expedient to do so. It was Brian Paige himself who conducted the interview, together with one of his assistant managers, Miss Adelaide Bertram. She was the person in charge of the accounts office so she asked a good number of questions. She seemed satisfied that Lorna would gain the maths O-level, which would be to her credit, but not essential. Mr Paige explained that they liked their new employees to have a working knowledge of all the departments and he hoped that Lorna would become acquainted with the processes of paper production and printing as well as the office work. She guessed he was looking to bright young applicants, such as herself, for his future managerial posts, and the idea pleased her. But that was not her main objective in coming here.

'I am pleased to say we can offer you a job here, Miss Watkins,' he said eventually, 'in our accounts office. You will be working along with Miss Bertram, and I am sure you will get on very well. Now, if you have any questions you would like to ask us?'

'Yes, I have,' replied Lorna. 'Thanks for saying you'll take me on – and I accept the offer – but I did say, didn't I, in my letter, that I really want to be a designer? I've brought some of my work to show you.'

'Yes, I had noticed,' said Mr Paige, who had glanced, once or twice, at the brightly coloured folder at the side of Lorna's chair. One could hardly miss it with its swirls of psychedelic colour, especially as it was one of Paige's own products. 'But we did explain in our letter that we have our own team of designers, and also a few trainees. There is no vacancy there at the moment.'

'And you have just been employed to work with me,' added Miss Bertram.

'Lots of young people who come for interview bring samples of their work along; you'd be surprised. It's very rarely what we're looking for.' Mr Paige's eyes, behind the horn-rimmed spectacles, softened a little as he looked at Lorna. He smiled. 'However . . . seeing as you've put your drawings in one of our own folders . . . Let me take a look, Miss Watkins.'

Eagerly she picked up the folder and handed it to him.

Lorna's artistic bent had led her in all sorts of directions, and the samples of work contained in the folder showed her talent at work in many styles and in different media. Painting in watercolours, from a rough pencil sketch, was still her favourite form of art work, but instead of vast landscapes taking in a bold sweep of scenery, she liked to concentrate on just one aspect of the scene. A study of two seagulls, for instance, sitting on the sea railing at Scarborough, the backdrop of the bay and the harbour being secondary to the foreground. Or a clump of golden daffodils highlighted against the greystone walls of the city of York.

She had experimented over the years with oil colours as well, and the present trend towards the psychedelic movement, in art as well as in music, was made for such a medium. Swirls of shocking pink, vivid orange, acid yellow and vibrant green which, at one time, would have been said to clash, were now found in juxtaposition with one another, illustrating record sleeves, posters and book jackets. Lorna had tried her hand at zany animals – tigers with pink stripes and leopards with green spots in a jungle background, and an underwater seascape with exotic fishes and marine creatures which were out of this world.

She watched as Brian Paige flicked through the top few papers. From the look on his face, one of tolerant but cursory interest, she could see that he expected to find that the samples would be like hundreds of others he had seen, very run-of-the-mill and not worthy of further inspection. But his glance altered as he continued to study the paintings and drawings in front of him, showing more and more interest as he worked his way through the score or more of examples.

He stopped and laughed out loud at one of them, holding it up to show Lorna, and Miss Bertram as well. 'This is your teddy bear, I suppose, Miss Watkins? And your toy panda? What a delightful study! I love the expression on the animal's face, so pensive.'

Lorna smiled. 'Yes, Mister Ted – that's what I called the teddy bear – and Pandy. I did that one – well, the original one – when I was about five or six years old, but I've perfected it since then. It was very sad really. You see, my little brother had died – he was only two – and that was his toy panda. So I suppose Pandy would look . . . sad.'

'That's a lovely story,' said Brian Paige, smiling at her. 'And this would make a charming birthday card for a child. In fact, I can visualise a whole set of these, different poses with the teddy bear and the panda, at Christmas, at Easter-time, on holiday . . . You have a real talent, Miss Watkins. I'm sorry if I was dismissive at first. I've seen so many young hopefuls with their work and they are usually . . . well, just amateurish, on the whole.' He glanced towards Miss Bertram who was looking a little put out. 'This puts a different complexion on things, Miss Bertram. A talent like this, we can't afford to ignore it.'

'Yes, they look . . . very nice,' said Miss Bertram, a trifle grudgingly. 'Of course, you know far more about that side of things than I do. But I still need a good competent girl to work with me, and I thought we had found her.'

'So we have,' said Mr Paige. He smiled across at Lorna. 'Please forgive us talking about you like this, my dear. So very rude, but I'm beginning to get quite excited!'

It was agreed that Lorna should start work in the office, under Miss Bertram's supervision, on the following Monday, but that Mr Paige should ease her, gradually, into the design department on a part-time basis. Reading between the lines, she gained the impression that the team of designers and artists guarded their positions jealously, and she guessed they would not be too pleased at the arrival of a wet behind the ears sixteen-year-old, such as herself. But I'll show them, she determined, when I get the chance.

And, in the meantime, Mr Paige wanted her to work, at home, on her illustrations of the toys – the teddy bear and the panda. This thrilled her more than anything. Her very first assignment! How exciting!

Her mother and Robert, particularly her mother, seemed flabbergasted at the news. 'That's wonderful!' exclaimed Robert.

But her mother was much more guarded. 'He's not just humouring you, is he?' she asked. 'Because it's a job in the office he's given you, isn't it, not one as an artist? Don't build your hopes up too much . . . and I still think you should get some more qualifications.'

'Well, thanks very much, Mum!' Lorna could feel herself bristling like a porcupine. 'I might have known—'

'We're very pleased for you, Lorna,' interrupted Robert. 'We always knew you could do it, didn't we, Rachel? I think this calls for a celebration. Adam is coming home this weekend, so how about us all going out for a meal on Saturday night? What about that new Italian place, Bellini's, near the market place? I've heard it's very good.'

'That sounds lovely,' said Rachel. 'Don't you think so, Lorna?'

'Yeah . . . it's fine by me,' said Lorna, but not with a great deal of enthusiasm. Her mother always managed, somehow, to put a damper on things. She was trying though, it seemed, from her next remark, to set things right again.

'I'm so pleased your new boss liked that picture of Mister Ted,' she said. 'Just fancy that! I remember putting it up on the classroom wall all those years ago, the original one, I mean. What is he like, this Brian Paige? I don't think I've ever come across him.'

'What do you mean; what is he like?' Her mother asked such daft questions at times.

'Well, how old is he? Is he short or tall, fat or thin? Is he nice-looking? You know perfectly well what I mean, Lorna.'

The girl shrugged. 'I s'pose he's not bad-looking for an old fellow. It depends what you want. He wears glasses with black frames, and he's still got all his hair, dark hair. And I've just said . . . he's old.'

'How old?' It was Robert who asked the question, and Lorna could see the twinkle in his eye.

'Forty-something . . . same as you,' she said, grinning at her step-dad.

But her mother was not amused. 'Well, thanks very much, Lorna,' she said in a tight voice. 'That's just what we wanted to hear.'

'I was only joking, Mum . . .' But once again she had managed to put her foot in it. The trouble was, her mother had no sense of humour.

It was good to see Adam again. Lorna realised that the two of them got along better when they saw one another only occasionally. He worked for an independent newspaper in Leeds, covering the sports fixtures, and he had just started reporting on other incidents of interest in the West Riding as well. It was this step up the ladder of promotion that the family was celebrating as well as Lorna's new job.

Adam had, by now, almost completely recovered from the polio which had attacked him so suddenly when he was a youngster. He had been left with a slight limp, which did not inconvenience him too greatly, but he knew his limitations. His love of football had continued, although his dream of becoming a professional footballer had long since been abandoned. He was capable of a friendly knock-about game, but nothing more. He found it a great privilege, however, to follow the fortunes of his favourite team, Leeds United, and others of the same calibre in the First Division, and to write about their successes or failures each week in the Saturday *Courier*.

He was an active young man; he drove a BSA motorbike and also enjoyed fell walking on the lower slopes of the Yorkshire moors and dales. Lorna, studying her step-brother appraisingly when he was not aware of it, came to the conclusion that he had grown into a very handsome chap. He wore his straight and glossy brown hair rather long, as was the fashion, and his warm brown eyes which, she recalled, had used to twinkle mischievously when he was a boy were always alert and alight with interest and enthusiasm for whatever he was doing. He was taller than his father now, almost six feet in height, and neither too plump nor too thin. Yes, all in all a very good catch for some lucky girl, one of these days, mused Lorna.

'The parents are becoming very with it in their old age, aren't they?' Adam whispered to Lorna on the Saturday evening, as the four of them sat around a table in Bellini's. It was covered with a red and white checked cloth, and in the centre there was a candle stuck into the neck of a Chianti bottle and a small pottery jug containing a posy of fresh marigolds. 'I mean to say – an Italian restaurant, for goodness' sake! Things are looking up.'

'Shh . . .' warned Lorna, although Robert and Rachel were not listening. Their heads were close together as they perused the giant-sized menu written in spidery writing on a sheet of imitation parchment. 'I got into trouble the other day for saying they were old. Mum was really hurt, I can tell you.'

'Then you should watch what you're saying, shouldn't you, little sis?' He half smiled, half frowned at her. She knew he was teasing her. 'Not always the soul of tact, are you?'

'No, not always,' she grinned. 'Like you were saying though, things are looking up. We actually have proper spaghetti now, long strands of it cooked in a pan. We'd only ever had it from a tin before, the Heinz sort.' She looked across the table, raising her voice. 'Mum, I'm just telling Adam that you made some spag bol the other week, didn't you?'

'So I did, dear,' said Rachel. 'Spaghetti bolognese! Very adventurous for me. We're just trying to decide what to have now. I'll have veal escalopes, I think, with Parma ham.'

'And spaghetti alla carbonara for me,' said Robert.

'Careful, Dad,' laughed Adam. 'Are you sure you know what you're ordering?'

'Oh, I think so. I know it has smoked ham in it. Anyway, what does it matter? It all adds to the fun, doesn't it?'

It was a very pleasant evening, and weekend, too. Lorna felt proud to be seen with her handsome step-brother as they zoomed around the outskirts of Melcaster on Sunday afternoon, on his BSA motorbike, with Lorna on the pillion at the back, clinging tightly to his waist.

'Don't worry, I'll take great care of her,' Adam had told Rachel. 'I don't go fast.'

'Don't you? Oh dear! You are a spoilsport, aren't you?' said Lorna. 'I thought we'd be doing a ton-up when we got away from here.'

'Take no notice of her, Rachel,' said Adam. 'She's safe as houses with me. And I've got an extra crash-helmet, see. Better to be safe than sorry.'

It was her first experience on the back of a motorbike and, in spite of her bravado, Lorna found that the speed they got up to as they whizzed around the country lanes – no more than 60 mph – was hair-raising enough. Adam slowed down a lot as they drove along Hillview where she had once lived.

'Adam – there's Carol in the garden,' she shouted. 'Wave to her . . .' Adam could not hear, but Lorna waved frantically. Her friend just stared in puzzlement. 'Adam, Adam . . .' Lorna poked him in the back and yelled at him. 'Stop a minute! Let's say hello to Carol.'

He finally twigged what she was saying and brought the bike to a halt.

'Oh, so it's you!' laughed Carol, as her friend took off the crash-helmet. 'And . . . Adam. Hello there, Adam. Long time no see.' Lorna noticed that Carol blushed a little as she spoke to him.

'Hi there, Carol. Yes, it's been a long time.'

'I'm just helping Mum with a spot of gardening, but it's hot work.' Carol recovered her composure by taking a handkerchief from her trouser pocket and wiping her face.

'Too hot by far,' agreed her mother, Jenny, coming to join them. 'Hello, Lorna, and you too, Adam. I suggest we all go inside and have a nice cooling drink of homemade lemonade.'

Adam watched the two friends as they laughed and talked together. How they had grown up, and it seemed to have happened all in an instant. One minute they had been little girls, and now, suddenly, they were young women. And very attractive young women, too, both of them; one blonde and one brunette.

He had been struck the previous evening by how pretty Lorna had looked in her sunshine-yellow dress. It had complemented perfectly her golden hair, and the touch of green eye-shadow – the first time he had noticed her wearing any – had highlighted her lovely hazel-brown eyes. She looked just as attractive today, more casually dressed in trousers and a jumper. Carol, too, was wearing trousers and a blue and white striped top which matched the colour of her eyes.

He was interested to hear that she was considering doing her nurse's training at a Leeds hospital. 'I'll look out for you, then,' he said, noticing that she lowered her eyes and looked coy.

'Oh, it won't be for ages yet,' she replied, 'but . . . that would be very nice.'

Adam was not sure what to say in reply, so he said nothing. He was still pretty inexperienced when it came to the opposite sex. Going to an all-boys grammar school had not helped matters, and during his early teenage years he had felt self-conscious because of his limp, although it was scarcely noticeable to anyone but himself. It had almost gone now, though it was still evident if he got overtired.

Anyway, he had a girlfriend now, of sorts. He had been out with Janet, one of the junior reporters, a few times, and he enjoyed her company. And those two girls, Lorna and Carol, no doubt they would have boyfriends before long. The idea of this – of Lorna, at any rate – disturbed him a little. It was the first time he had thought about his young step-sister being old enough to go out with boys. In fact, it was the first time he had thought of Lorna as anything other than a sister.

Chapter 17

By the time Lorna was seventeen years of age, in March 1970, she was well established at Paige's, both as a wages clerk and as a part-time designer. As she had anticipated, there had been a little animosity at first when Brian Paige had introduced her in the design room. Marion Grundy was in charge of the team. She was tall and dark with an arresting appearance and manner, but Lorna was not one to be intimidated. She resigned herself to being more or less ignored for the first few days, until the word got around that this new kid had talent, real talent.

Marion, to her credit, had been one of the first to acknowledge this. 'Not half bad!' she had commented, when she saw the designs that Lorna had been working on for the set of children's cards, with Mister Ted and Pandy in a variety of poses. Dressed in sailor suits for a day at the seaside, blowing out the candles on a cake for a five-year-old, staring up at Guy Fawkes atop a bonfire, and sitting beneath a Christmas tree, both of them wearing red bobble-hats. 'Very charming . . . though a little bit chocolate-boxish for my taste.'

Marion's inclination was towards a more dramatic, avant-garde scene. She loved strong colours and bizarre patterns. The late sixties had been a flamboyant, multi-coloured period, culminating in the flower-power summer of 1967, and now, into a new decade, the trend was still continuing for extravagance and boldness in colour and design. Marion was soon to learn that Lorna had her own ideas in this medium, too. At the present time they were working on new patterns for wrapping paper, both traditional and contemporary. Lorna's zany jungle animals and her exotic marine creatures had been considered and – somewhat half-heartedly – accepted, but Lorna guessed that the reluctance the other designers were pretending to show was to stop her from getting too big for her boots. She was good and she knew it, and she knew that they knew it, too!

Lorna was contented. She was even enjoying living at home and, at the moment, had no thoughts of leaving, because her mother, recognising that she had settled down well at Paige's, had stopped nagging at her. She attended night school twice a week, both for art and accountancy, and that seemed to satisfy Rachel.

The year had opened with a triumph for the youth of Britain. The age of majority had been lowered from twenty-one to eighteen, with effect from the first day of January. Lorna could not see that it would affect her very much personally, although it would be rather fun, she supposed, to vote in a general election, should Harold Wilson decide to call one. It would be next year, though, before she could vote. At the moment she was only seventeen. When she was eighteen it meant she would be able to marry without her parents' consent.

Then, soon after her seventeenth birthday, she met the man of her dreams.

Lorna first set eyes on Craig Boothroyd at a Young Farmers' Ball which was held in the civil hall in the April of 1970.

She had been reluctant at first when invited along by her friend, Carol. One of the few boys that Carol had met since entering the sixth form was Neil Monkton who was a son of a farming family; they owned a small mixed farm on the outskirts of Melcaster. Neil had asked Carol if she would accompany him to the Young Farmers' Ball which, so he told her, was the highlight of the social calendar for the farming community. Also, he asked, could she bring along a friend to be a partner for his pal, Billy Redman, who did not know many girls.

'Who's this Neil, then?' asked Lorna. 'I've not heard you mention him before. Is he a new boyfriend?'

'No, of course not,' said Carol. 'Well, I've an idea he might like to be a boyfriend, but he's rather shy and he's not got round to asking me out till now. We don't see the sixth-form boys all that much, just now and again when we have a joint school disco – all very proper, you know, and chaperoned by the teachers.'

'So who's this Billy? Is he in the sixth form too?'

'No, I don't really know who he is. Just a friend of Neil's. I think he works on his father's farm.'

'Billy Redman! What a name!'

'Why? What's wrong with it?'

'Well, they sound like a couple of clod-hopping farmers' boys to me.' Lorna giggled. 'Billy Redman who doesn't know many girls. And this Neil, who's too shy to ask you to be his girlfriend. No, I don't think so.'

'Aw, go on, Lorna. I'd like to go, and I don't want to go without you. If you don't like this Billy person it won't matter. It's only for one night, and I believe they put on a terrific spread. My mum told me; she went once, years ago. You've got the wrong impression – about Neil at any rate. He's not a country bumpkin. When he's finished in the sixth form he's going to college to study new farming methods.'

'OK, you don't need to sell him to me. I'm sure he's very nice.' Lorna pretended to think for a moment before answering, but she had already changed her mind and decided she would go with her friend. It sounded as though it might be a good do, if only for the eats. 'All right then, you've twisted my arm. What sort of a do is it, though? Casual, or do you have to get dressed up?'

'Oh, best bib and tucker, I think, as my mum might say. Mum says she'll treat me to a new dress, and I'm sure you can afford to splash out, can't you? You're a working woman now.'

257

'Yes, it has its advantages, I must agree,' said Lorna. 'How d'you fancy a shopping trip to York, then?'

'It sounds fab! You'll go then, to this ball? Shall I tell Neil to go ahead?'

'Yes, why not! Young farmers, here we come!'

They did not shop at the most exclusive of the York shops. Both girls had been brought up to count their pennies, and so they went to C & A – to the most expensive department, though – and found just the dresses they wanted. They went for ankle-length, though, rather than the mini-dresses they both preferred, as they felt they would be more in keeping with the occasion. The contemporary pattern on Lorna's dress, interlocking large and small circles in vivid green, yellow and orange, was highlighted by a black cummerbund around the waist, whilst the red and black flowers on Carol's more floaty dress complemented her dark hair. And as they had not spent a fortune on the dresses they were able to afford shoes to match, sling-backs with the fashionable thick heels, Lorna's in emerald green and Carol's in red.

Robert drove Lorna to Carol's home where the two girls were to be picked up by Neil, in his father's car. Lorna was impressed that Neil, at only seventeen years of age, could already drive and often had the use of his father's Ford Estate. She was not overimpressed by Neil himself, however, or by his friend, Billy Redman, on first appearances at least.

Neil was tall with lanky arms and legs and dark straight hair which was continually flopping over his forehead. Billy was just the opposite, much shorter than his friend and thick-set, with a mop of almost white-blond hair which stuck up in spikes from his pink scalp. Lorna had wondered if he would have a red face, as his name suggested, and she could not help giggling to herself as they were introduced. His face was not red, but very pink and shiny like a newly bathed baby. She was not surprised that he had never had a proper girlfriend, or so Carol told her.

'He's harmless, though, don't you think?' whispered her friend as they all sat together around a table at the side of the polished floor, which had been cleared for dancing. The civil hall was used for a variety of purposes, for meetings, conferences, concerts, dances and parties. 'He's Mr Monkton's chief farm-hand, apparently. Neil says he's got a real way with animals, especially the cows. He treats them like they're his best friends.'

'Thank you very much! I'm sure that's what I really wanted to hear right now,' said Lorna. 'Billy Redman, best friend to all the cows. Yes, I'm sure he's harmless. But what use is harmless, eh? I want to have a good time. When is the fun going to start?'

The name of the function, 'Young Farmers' Ball', was not strictly correct as there were many middle-aged and even elderly people there as well. The organisation had been taken in hand by the younger element, but their parents and some grandparents had come along as well. Several of the elderly farmers looked a little ill at ease in their lounge suits or, in a few cases, evening suits, which had been taken out of mothballs, whereas the younger men were quite accustomed to dressing up in their mod gear after a hard day's toil on the land. The ticket had stated 'Dress Optional', but protocol assured that there was nothing too outlandish to be seen there that evening. No mini-skirts – Lorna and Carol were glad they had dressed appropriately – and all the men were wearing ties.

The dancing was a mixture of the old and the new. A local band, consisting of two guitarists, a drummer and a pianist, provided the music, alternating with a man who was a wizard on the Hammond organ. Lorna and Carol had learned the elementary steps of ballroom dances such as the waltz and the quickstep at school – although dancing with another girl was never much fun – and at youth club, so they were able to stumble around the floor with Neil and Billy who, for politeness' sake, they guessed, invited them to dance. More to their taste was the twist and rock 'n' roll, when you could just

259

jive around on your own without the need of a partner.

'The March of the Mods' got everybody going, even some of the older folk, and the wooden floor resounded with the stamping of hundreds of feet. After that dance everyone sat down again, many going to replenish their glasses from the bar which had been set up at the side of the room. Lorna and Carol, and Neil, too, were not supposed to drink as they were not yet eighteen, and Mr Monkton, Neil's father, who had appointed himself as chaperone for the evening, insisted that they should stick to the rules. Maybe, when it came to suppertime, they might be allowed a glass of white wine, he promised, as it was a special occasion.

'Big deal!' whispered Lorna to Carol, but she was, in truth, quite enjoying herself. The spirited dancing had brought a glow to her cheeks and a sparkle to her eyes. It was not what you might call a swinging occasion, not with so many older folk there, but this crowd of people, mainly from the farming community, did know how to let their hair down and have a good time. And Lorna had a feeling that real excitement might be just round the corner.

Neil had sat down next to Carol and was trying to engage her in conversation – he certainly seemed keen on her – but Billy, after excusing himself to Lorna, had moved away to sit with a group of lads who were quaffing pints of ale. She watched him down two pints in rapid succession and decided that beer and the company of the lads were of more interest to Billy than the pursuit of girls.

They were on their feet again before long, however, as the MC announced that they were to have a 'Paul Jones', and, following that, the supper would be served. The girls had no idea what a Paul Jones was until Mrs Monkton explained that the men formed one circle and the ladies another, then everyone marched round, in opposite directions, to the tune of 'Here We Go Round the Mulberry Bush'. When the music stopped, you were to dance with the person opposite you. Then, at the end of that dance, the circles were formed again, and so on.

The first time the music stopped Lorna found herself opposite a middle-aged man who, she soon discovered, was an expert at the quickstep. She tried manfully to follow his lead, but only succeeded in falling over his feet. 'They don't learn you young 'uns to dance these days, do they?' he said, and she knew he was glad when the quickstep came to an end. She would have loved to have told him it was teach, not learn, but she knew it would be rather rude, and he was, most likely, a friend of Mr Monkton.

She joined the circle again, wishing she could escape and sit down, but opting out was not encouraged. When the 'Mulberry Bush' music stopped the next time she found herself looking up into a pair of the bluest eyes she had ever seen. Blue eyes in a weather-beaten face, more brown than red, a leanly handsome face with thin lips which were curved upwards in a smile, and mid-brown hair with just a suggestion of a russet hue. She noticed all these features in an instant before the man spoke.

'Hello there. I've struck lucky this time, it seems. I've spent the last few minutes clutched to the bosom of a middle-aged matron. Whew! I was glad to come up for air.'

Lorna laughed. 'Same here! Well, what I mean is, my partner wasn't to my liking either. Or I to his, to be honest. He criticised my dancing. I'm not very good at ballroom dancing, you see, but I can just about manage a waltz. This is a waltz, isn't it?'

'Yes, one of the oldies.' The organist had struck up with the three-four rhythm of 'When I Grow Too Old to Dream'. 'Don't worry. I'm not much of a dancer, either. Motown music, that's more my scene.'

'Yes, me too.'

'I'm Craig, by the way. Craig Boothroyd. I noticed you earlier on this evening, you and your friend. You're with the Monktons, aren't you?'

'Yes. At least my friend, Carol, came with Neil, and I came as a partner – sort of – to his mate, Billy. Do you know them, then?'

261

'Yes, of course. We all know one another. That's why there's such a good atmosphere. All pals together, sort of thing. My father's farm adjoins the Monktons' place, as a matter of fact. They're our nearest neighbours.'

'Oh . . . so you're a farmer, too?'

'Yes, afraid so.' He grinned. 'What about you?'

'What do you mean, what about me?'

'Well, first of all, what's your name? That's the most important thing, isn't it?'

'I'm Lorna. Lorna Watkins. And I've got nothing to do with farming, but you probably realised that. I work at Paige's – you know, the paper place in Melcaster. I'm . . . I'm an artist. I design their birthday cards and wrapping paper and all that.'

'Wow! Clever stuff, eh? An artist! And will you invite me round to see your etchings?'

She was not sure whether he was joking or not, so she did not laugh. 'There's not just me,' she said. 'I mean, I'm one of a team of designers . . . and I work in the office as well, part-time.'

'And what do you do in your spare time, if you have any? It sounds as though you're quite a busy young lady.'

'Oh, this and that. I go out with a crowd from work sometimes. To discos, or to one of the local pubs, but I don't let on to my mum where I'm going, see, because I'm only seventeen, and I'm not supposed to drink, not officially.'

'Oh, I see. I thought you might be older than that . . .' There was a humorous glint in his eye and, again, she could not tell whether he was joking or not.

'No, I'm only just turned seventeen, last month, actually. And I go to night school twice a week, and I've always spent a lot of my time on my art work.'

'You go out sketching, you mean?'

'Yes, in the countryside round here, and further afield sometimes.'

'I've never seen you. You hide yourself away, do you?'

'No, not really. Usually I just do the sketching out of doors

262

and I do the painting later. I've just got a colour camera. My parents bought it for my birthday, so I can take a snap of the view I want and then reproduce the exact colours.'

'Great! You're certainly into this art scene, aren't you? I suppose you still live with your parents, do you?'

'Yes . . . for the moment,' she said, hoping his comment did not mean that he thought of her as a little girl. 'With my mum and Robert; he's my step-dad. My real dad lives in Ripon. He got married again, you see. Well, so did my mother.'

She hadn't intended to ramble on so much, but her partner didn't seem to mind and she was finding him very easy to talk to. As the waltz music was drawing to a close he said, 'Come on, let's get away, shall we, before this "Mulberry Bush" nonsense starts again? I don't want to lose you now I've found you. We'll go and get a drink, then we'll sit together at suppertime. That is, if you would like to?' He smiled at her, sensing her slight hesitation. 'What's the matter?'

'Nothing. I'd love to have supper with you, but I don't want Mr and Mrs Monkton to think I'm being rude, and I was really supposed to be with Billy.'

'Oh, Billy's not much of a one for the girls, you take it from me! And I'll go and have a word with Bert and Mavis. Even better, I'll ask them if I can join your party. Come on, let's go and see them.'

Mr and Mrs Monkton – Bert and Mavis – were sitting out the rest of the Paul Jones. 'We'd be delighted for you to join us,' said Bert. 'So you've met our charming little guest, have you? Well, that's very nice. Isn't she lovely? And you'll be in safe hands with Craig here, Lorna. He knows how to treat a young lady, and he's not a Romeo or owt like that.'

'Thanks for the vote of confidence, Bert,' laughed Craig. 'We'll go and get a drink. Lorna can have a glass of wine, I take it? And then we'll come and sit at your table.'

The supper was a help-yourself buffet arrangement, and when everyone's plate was filled – to overflowing in some cases – they could sit where they wished. There was no formal seating plan, but a good deal of waving and 'yoo-hooing' and saving of seats. There were eight of them seated around the table – Mr and Mrs Monkton, Neil and Carol, Billy Redman and one of his drinking companions, and Lorna and Craig. Billy looked across and grinned at Lorna, giving her a 'thumbs-up' sign. She guessed he was relieved that she had let him off the hook for the evening by finding another partner. She began to feel more kindly disposed towards him. He seemed a very genial, uncomplicated fellow who preferred to be with people he was familiar with rather than strangers, especially girls. If it hadn't been for Billy she would not have been here this evening and would not have met this personable young man who was sitting next to her.

Carol's mum had been right about the spread that the farmers provided. Supper was served in a separate room, and the table at the side positively groaned with the weight and abundance of the foodstuffs displayed there. Chicken legs, slices of turkey, pork, beef and home-cured ham; all the meat, in fact, had been home-cooked in the various ovens of the farmers' wives. Sausages, various salads and garnishes, quiches and hand-raised pork pies. And, if you were still not replete – or filled to bursting, as many of the guests claimed to be – there was a selection of delectable desserts to follow. Custard tarts, Yorkshire curd tarts, apple pie, chocolate gateau, or, for those more conscious of their waistlines, fresh fruit salad. Lorna had never seen such a spread, although she came from a home where food had always been regarded as one of life's pleasures as well as essentials.

She learned more of Craig as they ate their meal, and when supper was over he stayed with the Monktons' party. They danced now and again, but spent most of the time talking. She discovered he was twenty-two years old, the only son of Jim Boothroyd who owned Sheepscar House, a very prosperous farm, she deduced from what he was telling her. She realised she knew the farm by sight, when he told her the locality. She had often passed it on bike rides or in

264

her parents' car, and had admired the long, low, greystone building with the mullioned windows and tall chimneys. It stood in a fold of the hills, surrounded by tall trees, and on a rise of land facing the main road. But far enough away, Craig said, for the noise of the traffic to be dulled.

'What sort of animals do you have?' asked Lorna, aware that she was very ignorant about farming, even though she had lived, virtually, in the country all her life. 'Sheep, obviously . . .'

'Yes, sheep, of course; cattle, mainly for milk, although we do keep a beef herd; poultry; pigs; and a little arable land. What is known as a mixed farm.'

'And you've always worked on the land, ever since you left school?'

'And before,' laughed Craig. 'When I was a little lad my dad had me working, only during the holidays, of course, because I was away at boarding school.'

'Were you? Where was that?' Lorna was impressed. She had never met anyone who had been to boarding school.

'Oh, a minor public school near Sedbergh,' he told her. 'And then I went on to an agricultural college in Lancashire, so I'm pretty well attuned to what I'm doing. Dad relies on me a lot with me being the only son; well, the only child, in fact.'

'So you live with your parents, too?'

'No, as a matter of fact, I've got my own little place, a cottage on the edge of the farm. It belongs to my father and I moved into it about six months ago.'

'On your own?'

'Er . . . yes.' He hesitated a moment. 'On my own. The farm-hands used to live there, years ago. It made sense at one time for farm workers to live on the premises, but nowadays they've all got their own motorbikes or cars and they all live not too far away. I'm making my little place more habitable. It was quite primitive when I moved in, but I'll get there in time, mod cons and all that. I think a bathroom is the next thing on the agenda, and an indoor loo, of course.'

'You mean you haven't got an indoor toilet?'

'No, just a privy at the end of the garden, at the moment.' He laughed. 'You're not used to that, I take it?'

'Well . . . no. Our house is quite modern. And in the last one, we had a bathroom.'

'You've been lucky then. A lot of the old stonebuilt houses in this area still don't have bathrooms. Anyway, when I've got the place all ship-shape you must come and visit me.'

'Thank you, that would be lovely,' replied Lorna, not altogether sure that he meant it. This was too good to be true. He was such a handsome young man, in a lean, almost gaunt way, and so very friendly and entertaining. He reminded her of Diggory Venn from Thomas Hardy's *The Return of the Native*, even to the corduroy jacket he was wearing – a very well-cut dark brown one – with fawn trousers and a striped tie which she guessed might be his old school colours.

'Actually, I'd like you to come to the farm before that, if you would,' Craig went on. 'I wonder . . . would you consider doing a painting of Sheepscar House? I know my parents would be thrilled to bits, and you've said already what a striking picture it makes against the background of the trees and hills. I would pay you, of course.'

'Oh, I'd love to,' said Lorna. So he really did want to see her again! 'I'm not bothered about any payment, but I'd really love to paint the farmhouse. I'll have to find a good vantage point.'

'We'll look for one together, shall we?' said Craig. 'Listen, Lorna . . . I'd like to see you again, soon. But I want it to be all above board. I'm a few years older than you, so, if I take you out, I would like it to be with your parents' permission.'

'I'm old enough to please myself,' said Lorna, with a touch of resentment that he should be regarding her as a child. 'And my mum and Robert wouldn't mind. I've been out with boys before, you know.' And so she had, but only the lads from the youth club and usually in the company of others. She guessed that this, though, was rather different. Craig was a man, not a callow youth, but she did not want him to think he was her first boyfriend.

'Nevertheless,' said Craig, smiling at her, 'I would like to come and meet your parents. What about Saturday? I know we've only just met, but I would like to see you again . . .'

Before the evening ended it had been arranged that he would call for her on Saturday evening for their first date. They would go to the cinema, maybe, and then to a country inn; a very respectable one, he assured her, bearing in mind that she was, officially, under the age for drinking. He left before the end of the evening, holding on to her hand as he said goodbye to her. Lorna did not concern herself with why he had gone early or why he had come on his own that evening. She was so happy that the thought did not occur to her.

'I can't believe it,' she said to Carol in an excited whisper as the evening was drawing to a close. 'Craig's asked me to go out with him, and he wants me to do a painting of his parents' farm. He's really nice, Carol, and he's so handsome, isn't he?'

Carol shook her head. 'You've got it bad! Come down to earth, love.'

'I'm so excited! What about you? Are you going to see Neil again?'

'I might . . . He's not bad when you get to know him. Look, they're coming over here now, Neil and Billy. It's the last waltz, so I suppose they think they'd better dance it with us. You're having more than your fair share of men tonight, aren't you?'

Lorna laughed, then smiled happily at Billy as they took to the floor to the strains of the 'Anniversary Waltz'. She wished that Craig had stayed to dance the last waltz with her, but in only three days' time she would be seeing him again.

Chapter 18

'So . . . what do you think of Craig, then? Do you like him?'

Lorna was certainly 'high' after her first date with Craig Boothroyd, but her mother knew it was not from drink, and certainly not from drugs, but just from excitement and happiness. Rachel was glad to see her that way. She could so easily have been secretive and uncommunicative about this new boyfriend, but, to give him his due, Craig had insisted that he should meet her parents before taking her out.

'Yes, we like him very much,' Rachel replied. 'Don't we, Robert?'

Her husband smiled and nodded his agreement. 'Yes, so we do. And it's good to see you looking so happy, Lorna.'

'Don't start getting carried away though, love,' said Rachel. 'After all, he's the first real boyfriend you've had, isn't he? And it's early days yet. You've only been out together once, and you can't be sure he will want to go on seeing you.'

'Oh, trust you to go and spoil it all!' Lorna's joyous expression had changed, as it was apt to do so quickly, to one of annoyance. 'I sometimes think you don't want me to be happy at all!'

'Lorna! That's a dreadful thing to say!' exclaimed her mother. 'Robert has just said he's pleased to see you looking so happy, and that goes for me as well. But I don't want you to get hurt, darling. You're only seventeen, and Craig's several years older than you, isn't he?'

'He's twenty-two, that's all.'

'Well, that's five years. And the difference is quite important when you're only seventeen.'

'So what?' retorted Lorna. 'Adam's twenty-one, isn't he, and he and I get on OK. Craig's not much older than Adam.'

'But Adam's your brother, so there's no comparison.'

'Step-brother, actually.'

'Yes, all right. Step-brother if you want to be precise,' Rachel sighed. 'But you've grown up together for the last ten years or so, haven't you, so he's just like a brother. The way you used to fall out was just like a real brother and sister.'

'We don't fall out now.'

'All right, all right! But it's not Adam we're talking about, is it? This Craig . . . he seems so much more mature. I want you to be . . . to be very sure before you commit yourself to . . . anything.'

'Good heavens! She's only been out with the young man once,' said Robert, trying to lighten the conversation. 'Aren't we getting a bit heavy? So . . . tell us about it, Lorna. If you want to, that is. I'm sure he looked after you very well. He seems a very caring sort of young man.'

'Yes, he is. Thank you, Robert,' said Lorna, pointedly excluding her mother for the moment. 'We went for a drive up towards Malham Tarn. But it was getting dark by then, so we found a nice little country inn and we chatted all evening. We get on very well. I didn't have anything to drink – only an orange and a lemonade – and Craig only had one pint because he was driving.'

'Yes, I can see he's very sensible,' said Robert. 'And . . . you're seeing him again?'

'Of course! You know I am. I told you, didn't I, that he wants me to do a painting of the farmhouse? So he's coming for me tomorrow after lunch and we're going to do a recce of the place, find the best spot for me to do my sketch and take a few photos.'

'That's lovely, dear,' said Rachel, in an effort to put things right. 'You're doing so well with your art work, aren't you? I can see now that you were quite right to go to Paige's.

Another commission! I can see you'll be famous before long!'

'It's not a commission,' replied Lorna, rather frostily. 'I'm doing it because I want to. Anyway, I'm going to bed now. Goodnight Robert . . . Goodnight, Mum . . .'

'Goodnight, darling . . .' Rachel looked after her, a little regretfully. It was years since Lorna had given her a goodnight kiss. That had probably come to an end, of course, because the girl had not wanted to look silly or babyish in front of Adam. And now, they had got out of the habit.

'Oh dear!' she said, when she was sure her daughter was out of earshot and not eavesdropping. 'I do seem to put my foot in it, don't I? Whatever I say to Lorna, it turns out to be wrong, or she takes it the wrong way. I do like that young man, and I don't want her to think otherwise.'

'Darling, there are times when you take things far too seriously. In fact, you take yourself too seriously.' Robert came to sit next to her and put his arm around her. 'It's one of the things I love about you, your earnestness and the way you feel strongly about things . . . but you really must try to lighten up a bit at times. I've told you so before, haven't I? I think that's why you rub Lorna up the wrong way. She's all happy and feeling on top of the world, and then she's brought crashing down again.'

'You mean . . . I do that to her?'

'You don't intend to, I'm sure . . .'

'But you think I spoil things for her? That's what she said . . .'

Robert was silent for a moment. 'I know how much you love her,' he said, 'and I have grown to love her, too, just as you love Adam. We have been a very happy little family, Rachel, but there are sure to be ups and downs, especially in families where second marriages are involved. I know you have Lorna's best interests at heart and that's why you say the things you do . . . but not always too wisely.'

'Oh, I do, Robert. That's just it. I'm concerned about her, and what I'm afraid of, now, is that she is going to make exactly the same mistake as I did. She'll rush headlong into marriage with the first man that comes along, and I can just see it all going wrong. And that Craig – he reminds me a little bit of Derek.'

'What do you mean? He's nothing like Derek, not in looks or personality or anything. You used to tell me, though, that Derek was rough and ready, that his manners left a lot to be desired, although he never seemed all that bad to me.'

'He's mellowed, Robert. I've got to admit that Derek's changed. He's a nicer person than he used to be. That must be Sylvia's influence.'

The two men, Robert and Derek, had met from time to time when Derek had called for or brought Lorna home. Rachel and Sylvia had met occasionally as well. As the years had gone by there was less and less animosity between the two couples, although they could not be said to be friendly.

'It's his eyes,' Rachel went on. 'That's what I meant. Craig's bright blue eyes; they were the first thing I noticed about him, just as they were the first thing I noticed about Derek. And I wondered if that was why Lorna had been attracted to him. Subconsciously, I mean. She's still very fond of her father, you know.'

'Which is just as it should be,' replied Robert. 'You know I've never tried to exclude him. That's why Lorna's kept her own name and not changed it to Blundell.'

'But I fear she'll be wanting to change it to Boothroyd before long.'

'There you go again! You're looking too far ahead, Rachel love. Let's just wait and see how things go, shall we?'

'That's all we can do, I know that. But they have nothing in common, nothing at all. He's a farmer, born and bred; it's in his blood. But as for our Lorna . . . well, she can hardly tell one end of a cow from the other. I bet she wouldn't know the difference between a cow and a bull.'

'She would if one started chasing her!'

'That's what I mean. Oh dear! She's not cut out for life as a farmer's wife. And if I can read the signs correctly, that young man is looking for a wife. He's even got his own little

271

cottage and he's living there on his own. Just think what a temptation that might be for Lorna. You know she's restless here sometimes, although I must admit she hasn't been too bad recently. That's exactly what I wanted to do, though, to get away from home and have a place of my own . . . Oh, Robert, I'm worried, I really am.'

'And the more you worry, the worse you will feel. Just stop it, Rachel! Pull yourself together.' Robert, for once, sounded quite cross. 'You really must get things into perspective. You know what Lorna's like. If we try to stop her from seeing him – which we can't do; we've already told Craig he can take her out – then she will only go and defy us. Try and relax, just be glad she's met a nice young man. There are a lot of pluses. We think he's quite wealthy, and he's got a good steady occupation, he's educated and he talks nicely – and I know you think that's important – and I'm sure he'll look after Lorna. Anyhow, what will be, will be . . . and if he decides that she's not the girl for him after all, then I'm sure he will let her down lightly.'

'But I don't want her to get hurt . . .'

'You can't have it all ways, Rachel, my love. She's sure to suffer a few knocks along the way. Don't we all?'

Yes . . . my Wednesday's child, thought Rachel. But, please God, don't let her make the same mistake as I did.

The courtship of Lorna and Craig – for it was soon obvious that that was what it was – went on apace as the summer advanced. But they could not meet as frequently as they might have done if Craig had had a normal nine-to-five job. He was subject to the farming times and seasons – lambing time which went on well into May, and, following that, the summer rituals of hay-making and sheep-shearing. His father had a good team of men, however, with extra labour engaged at hay time and shearing time, and so Craig was able to delegate a good deal of the work.

When they had been seeing one another for four months Craig asked Lorna if she would marry him. She agreed at once – it was what she had been waiting for – but, to her mind, he spoiled things by saying he must talk to her parents before giving her a ring. And her mother and Robert – although Lorna was convinced it was her mother who was to blame – went and spoiled things even more by saying that they would prefer them to wait until March to get engaged, when Lorna would be eighteen.

'That's fine,' said Craig, smiling. He never seemed to lose his cool. 'So long as you don't expect us to have a long engagement. Lorna and I are very sure about what we are doing. And I promise I will take very great care of her.'

'It's not fair!' Lorna complained afterwards, when they had returned to Craig's little cottage. 'My mother always manages to mess things up. Why should we have to wait? What difference does it make?'

'It doesn't,' said Craig, 'not to you and me. We are engaged, aren't we, as near as makes no difference, and if it will make your parents happier for us to wait till March before you start wearing a ring, then . . . so be it. But we are going to get married next year, come what may.' He put his arms around her and drew her towards him, stroking her blonde hair, then gently fondling the soft skin of her neck and the curve of her breasts, before lowering his mouth on to hers in a passionate kiss. 'There . . .' he said, drawing away and smiling down lovingly at her. 'Doesn't that show you how much I love you?'

'Yes, of course it does. And I love you, too,' said Lorna, lifting her face up to his for some more kisses.

Craig had been attracted to the lively girl the moment he had met her at the Farmers' Ball in the spring, and it wasn't long before he had convinced himself that she was, in fact, the very girl he had been waiting for since his fiancée, Sheila Barrow, had deserted him. Sheila, he supposed, all things considered, had been a more suitable choice. He had known her for ages. She was the daughter of a farmer who lived a few miles away and everyone had taken it for granted that the two of them would marry. They had even got engaged and, although she had not moved into the cottage with him, she had stayed the night on several occasions. And then she had had the audacity to walk out on him. She had met a man who was – of all things – a solicitor, and she had decided she had never really wanted to be a farmer's wife at all.

That had happened a few weeks before the spring ball, and it was only at the last moment that Craig had decided to attend. He would, normally, have been accompanied by Sheila, and he had felt so downcast at first at her betrayal that he had found himself indulging in self-pity. How could he go along to this event and have everyone feeling sorry for him? Then his common sense had prevailed. There were far better fish in the sea than ever came out of it . . . although he had not been expecting to meet such a delightful one as Lorna Watkins, and certainly not so soon.

He had known at once that he wanted to go on seeing her, but he also knew that he must proceed with caution. She seemed to be still a child in some ways, although she tried to put on a 'woman of the world' façade, and he admired her verve and determination to make a go of her chosen career. She was certainly a very talented artist. He was aware of her mother's slight wariness on meeting him, although both Rachel and Robert Blundell had made him welcome in their home and he liked them very much.

Lorna was very young, though. It was only natural that her mother should be protective towards her. Craig's own view, at the beginning, was that maybe she *was* too young and inexperienced to be thinking of marriage, especially marriage to a farmer. But that didn't stop him wanting to carry on seeing her. And then, almost before he realised it, it was too late. He had fallen in love with her, he knew that his love was returned, and he knew that he wanted to marry her and take her to live with him in his little home, Lilac Cottage.

As the weeks went by he knew that, as far as feelings and emotions were concerned, Lorna was far from being a child. She responded eagerly to his kisses and his ever more

274

ardent embraces, but he remained conscious of the fact that she was a young and unspoiled girl, and he felt, also, that Rachel Blundell was trusting him with her precious daughter and that he must not do anything to harm her.

On the night that her parents had advised him to wait until she was eighteen before becoming engaged, they still had not made love in the fullest sense. Lorna was annoyed with her mother – he gathered that this was quite a regular occurrence – and he wanted to comfort her, to make up to her for her disappointment.

'We are engaged really, aren't we, Craig?' she said, as if trying to convince herself. 'I mean, we don't need a ring, do we, to show we belong to one another?'

'No, of course not, darling,' he said, kissing her again.

'Craig . . . I do want to belong to you, in every way.' She looked up at him longingly, but so very trustingly. 'You know what I mean, don't you? But you've never asked me to . . . you know . . . so I wondered if you were not sure?'

'Of course I'm sure,' he replied. 'I'm sure I want to marry you and sure I want to make love to you. But I know it would be the first time, for you, wouldn't it? I'm so afraid of doing anything to hurt you, my darling.'

'You won't. You couldn't hurt me. I love you, Craig.'

And so they came together in the bedroom up in the eaves with the sloping roof, on the bed with brass rails, which had been in the family for generations. He was gentle with her, as he would have been with any woman. He had never wanted to be rough or demanding in the act of love, although he was a passionate man and he knew that Lorna was responding to the ardour he aroused in her. He sensed she was a little nervous, as was only natural, but he would help her to overcome that. He had every confidence that in this area of their life they would be compatible.

Lorna sighed contentedly, but she had become very quiet. Craig knew there was something troubling her and he could guess what it was. He had suspected that, sooner or later, she might begin to ask questions about his past.

275

Lorna stared up at the pattern of cracks in the whitewashed ceiling between the rafters. She felt safe and secure in Craig's arms. That was where she wanted to be, and now she really and truly belonged to him. She pushed away the slight feeling of disappointment and anti-climax, knowing that their lovemaking could only get better and better. And she told herself she should have realised that, for Craig, it would not be the first time. It was silly of her to have supposed that it could be so.

'Is something troubling you, darling?' he asked, as though he could read her mind. 'I didn't hurt you, did I? I tried to be gentle, but—'

'No, you didn't hurt me. Well . . . not very much, but it will be better next time, won't it? But . . . er . . . you've done this before, haven't you, Craig?'

'Oh dear! Is that what's worrying you?'

'Not exactly worrying me, but I suppose I would have liked it to be the first time for you, like it was for me. Am I being silly?'

'Well . . . I think you are really.' He stroked her hair back from her brow and kissed her tenderly. 'I'm older than you, and it stands to reason, doesn't it, that there have been others?'

'How many others? Were there a lot?'

He laughed good-humouredly. 'No, of course not. But you knew I'd been engaged, didn't you?'

Lorna nodded, a little petulantly. Carol had informed her, soon after she had met Craig, that he had been engaged to a girl called Sheila. Neil had known all about it. 'Yes, I knew, but I tried not to think about it. I don't like thinking about you with anyone else.'

'And you don't need to, my darling. They are all history now. They have been ever since I met you. It's you that I love and you that I want to spend the rest of my life with.' He drew her into his arms and kissed her again. 'Now, are you convinced?'

'Yes, of course I am. We will be happy, won't we, Craig?'

'Yes, we will. For ever and ever.'

Lorna was dismayed that the ever and ever could not start straight away. But, because of her mother's intransigence, it would be a year, possibly longer, before they could get married. She decided to spend the intervening time getting acquainted with the farm and the animals and looking forward to being a farmer's wife.

She liked Craig's parents very much, and if they treated her more as a granddaughter or favourite niece than as their son's future wife, she supposed she could not blame them. For that was how she would seem to them. They were quite old – approaching their sixties – far older than her own parents. They were delighted with the painting she had done for them of Sheepscar House, and Lorna knew that it was, indeed, one of her best pieces of work. Soon after they had met she and Craig had chosen a good vantage point for her preliminary sketches and photos – an outcrop of rock from which the land dipped then rose again to where the house itself overlooked the shallow valley. There was a gorse bush in the foreground, and she had highlighted this to add a splash of golden colour and to lead the viewer's eye into the picture. The painting, which Craig had had framed for his mother's birthday, had now been given the place of honour over the fireplace in the Boothroyds' cosy living room.

Lorna had been surprised at the vastness of the farm which seemed to stretch for miles. Not only were there countless sheep grazing on the slopes of the hills, but a large herd of cows munching contentedly in the nearer pastures. She had always thought of cows as being placid, gentle creatures. She loved the descriptions of Tess, as a milkmaid, in Hardy's novel, her affinity with the animals and her feeling of contentment when sitting on her three-legged stool in the barton, with her cheek resting against the cow's flank. Craig had laughed at her when she told him of that.

'I think we have progressed a bit further than that, love,'

he said. 'No three-legged stools in our milking parlour; no winsome milkmaids either. Anyway, it's all done by machine nowadays. I think you've got a very idealised view of it all, but you'll learn!'

Yes, she supposed she would learn, but she could not imagine that she would have all that much to do with the farm itself. Craig had agreed that she should keep on with her job at Paige's after they were married, but only if she wished to do so. She had a bicycle and it was not all that far away, not much more than a mile. She hoped that she would, eventually, learn to drive a car. If her mother could do it, then so could she. Perhaps she would have her own little Mini.

The cottage itself was a dream. It was stone-built with a slated roof, a tall chimney at each end and leaded windows which caused the sun's rays to glint at an angle into the rooms. She could not believe how romantic it all was, just like something out of a story. It was not exactly roses round the door, but there was a lilac bush beneath the front window. This had given the cottage its name many years ago, and it had grown now into a large and beautiful bush with purple blossom which scented the air throughout the summer months. There was a buddleia bush, too, which attracted a variety of butterflies, some of which Lorna had never seen before; a laburnum bush, shedding its golden flowerets on to the crazy-paved path leading to the front door; a small patch of lawn; and a flowerbed which was a riot of colour and perfume. There were tall lupins in variegated shades, marigolds, marguerites, sweet williams and night-scented stock, all growing together haphazardly as nature had intended. Lorna took it upon herself to do the weeding of the patch whenever she visited the cottage. She appreciated a nice garden. Her father and Robert both had quite attractive ones, but she had never become involved in any of the chores. It was different here, though. This little garden, very soon, would be hers – well, hers and Craig's – and it was something she could do to show him she intended to pull her weight.

The cottage was charming inside as well as outside. There was a living room – in the olden days known as a parlour – in which the red-tiled floor sloped, imperceptibly, from back to front. There was a fireplace with a side oven, and the old-fashioned furniture was in keeping with the surroundings – a three-piece cottage-style suite with chintz covers and a huge oak dresser which reached to the ceiling, filled with blue and white crockery and an assortment of patterned meat platters. There was also a grandfather clock and a plant-stand holding an aspidistra, and with those items the smallish room was quite full.

The kitchen was larger, because it was in here that the family – or whoever – in times past had cooked and eaten, even washed at the large sink, sat at the fireside and generally congregated. The cooking range in this room – a huge black one – was a much more complicated affair, but Lorna had been pleased to see that there was a modern gas stove as well. And Craig had plans, too, to annexe part of this kitchen space for his new bathroom and indoor toilet, which he promised would be ready long before Lorna was due to move in. The cottage was heated solely by the fire in the range, but Robert had said he would install central heating for them as a wedding present.

From the kitchen a winding staircase led upstairs to two bedrooms, of roughly the same size, with rafters and sloping ceilings. At the moment there was a double bed in each room, one with a modern mattress, the other with an old flock one. Lorna wondered, fleetingly, about the sleeping arrangements of the farm-hands who had used to live here. Two or three to a bed, she supposed, or maybe some of them had slept at the main farmhouse. (Sheepscar House was similar in construction, but much larger and with more rooms both upstairs and down.) Comfort and privacy, she guessed, would have been unimportant, so long as the workers had a space in which to lie down for the night.

There was no suggestion that Lorna should go to live at Lilac Cottage until after the two of them were married; Craig did not even hint that he wished her to do so. She shocked him a little at one point by telling him that, if she were pregnant, then her parents would be forced to agree to them getting married.

'You're not, are you?' he asked, sounding quite alarmed.

'No, of course I'm not, silly,' she said. 'But I'm only saying, if I was . . .'

'If you were, then your parents would be disappointed, wouldn't they, both in you and in me? And I value their good opinion. I feel I'm letting them down sometimes when we make love, but . . . You're so lovely, Lorna. It's hard for me as well. I wish we could get married sooner, but we've promised them we'll wait.'

'Perhaps they're hoping we'll split up in the meantime,' said Lorna. She knew her mother liked Craig, no one could help but like him, but she knew he was not the man she might have chosen for her daughter.

'Well, we won't split up,' said Craig. 'We'll show them! Your mother will be able to have the lovely wedding she's dreamed of for her daughter. We're only humouring them, you know, by waiting. But it will be worth waiting for, darling.'

It was not only Rachel who had doubts about the wisdom of the match, but Jim and Millie Boothroyd as well.

'Are you sure you're not rushing into this on the rebound, son?' asked Jim, after they had met Lorna several times. 'She's a lovely little lass, I'll grant you, but that's all she is – a little lass. You want a help-mate, you know, somebody that'll be able to muck in with you on t' farm.'

'That's what I thought when I was engaged to Sheila,' retorted Craig. 'Ideal farmer's wife, I thought, apart from the fact that . . . well, I was very fond of her. But it turned out that it wasn't what she wanted, even though she was a farmer's daughter herself. Girls want to choose their own careers today, Dad. You can't force them into a mould where they don't belong.'

'But you want a family, don't you?' asked his mother. 'You want at least a couple of sons – I've heard you say so – so what's the use of a lass who wants a career, eh? Sheila, now, she was good farming stock. This little Lorna – oh aye, she's a pretty, dainty little lass, but she looks as though a puff of wind would blow her over.'

'Don't keep going on about Sheila, Mum. She's history now. And who's to say that Lorna can't have children just as well as any other girl? I know she's only small, but she's sturdy and healthy. And – don't you worry – I won't want her to carry on with her job for ever. I want to start a family as soon as we can.'

'And she knows that, does she?' asked Millie.

'We haven't talked about it yet, but most girls want a family, don't they?'

'I should hope so. I could do with a lass who would help me in t' dairy. And perhaps take a turn on the stall on market day, every now and again.'

'Well, you never know your luck, Mum,' laughed Craig. 'Although I should imagine Lorna will have her hands full at first, looking after the cottage and going out to work as well.'

'Going out to work?' questioned his father.

'Yes, that's the intention,' replied Craig. 'I said so, didn't I? Just for a while, at any rate.'

'Huh! Girls can't make up their minds what they want these days. When yer mother and me got wed there was no question of her carrying on working. She stayed here and helped me.'

'But times have changed, Dad. Sometimes a girl needs to carry on working to help with the cost of running a home.'

'That doesn't apply with you. Don't talk so daft! We've never been badly off, and you've got your own little place, rent free an' all. Your lass won't need to work. If she wants to carry on with her painting and drawing, though, there's nowt stopping her, is there? I must admit she's a grand little artist.'

'That's true,' said Craig. 'Actually, I'm hoping that she will,

281

eventually, decide to work from home. But I hope you'll be happy for us, Dad, and you too, Mum. I really do love Lorna and I'm sure we can make it work.'

'Of course we're happy for you, lad,' said Millie. 'We've no daughter of our own to make plans for, so we'd best start thinking about our only son's wedding. You're going to have a nice big do, aren't you? Eeh, she'll make a lovely bride, won't she?'

In September Carol Forrest went to Leeds to start her training at a hospital there. She had done only one year in the sixth form, but as she would be eighteen in only a few weeks' time, it had been agreed that she could start straight away. Her parents had agreed, but reluctantly, not wanting to part with their only daughter, but they knew she would receive a good training in a city hospital, and that even if she had opted to stay in Melcaster she would still, most likely, have been living in a nurses' home.

She was living in nurses' accommodation at a hospital in Meanwood. It was a couple of miles away from the noise and grime and the rows and rows of terraced houses and high-rise flats in the city centre. It was a pleasant area with parklands and open stretches of green, almost like being in the countryside. The hospital itself was in a largish park, an ideal place for Carol, a country girl, to live for her first experience of being away from home.

When she had been there for a few weeks she decided to invite Lorna to come and visit her. She was still going out with Craig Boothroyd, very seriously from all accounts, but surely she would be able to spare one weekend away from him? If Carol had any ulterior motive in issuing the invitation, then she tried to convince herself otherwise, although she had an inkling that if Lorna did come, she would stay with her step-brother, Adam. Carol had not seen him whilst she had been in Leeds, although she had kept her eyes open whenever she was in the city centre. But Leeds was a big place, and no doubt Adam would have forgotten the remark he had made about looking out for her when she came to live there. She could, of course, have asked Lorna for his address, but this would have been much too forward. She had been brought up to believe it was always the man who made the first move.

She was over the moon when Lorna agreed to come on the second weekend in October. She would be staying overnight at the home of Adam's grandparents, where he had been living for the last eighteen months. What was more, Carol had been invited to stay there as well as she had been granted a weekend pass from the nurses' home.

The two friends met at City Station just before lunchtime on the Saturday morning. Lorna had caught an early train in order to make the most of the weekend. Carol was due back at the hospital on Sunday afternoon, so time was very precious. They exchanged hugs and told one another how well they were looking, then deposited their overnight bags in the left-luggage office before going out into City Square.

'Now, where are you taking me?' asked Lorna. 'I'm in your hands.' She had visited the city several times in the past, but she did not know it as well as Carol, who could now be considered a resident of the place.

'We'll go and have some lunch first,' said Carol, as they set off walking along Boar Lane. 'I say, it was really kind of your grandparents to invite me to stay as well. No, they're not really your grandparents, are they? Adam's, I mean.'

'That was my mother's idea,' said Lorna. 'She thought the pair of us would be safe there, and of course we'll have Adam to look after us, won't we?' She cast a sidelong glance at her friend.

'Yes. It will be nice to see him again,' said Carol in a casual-sounding voice, not looking at Lorna. 'Actually ... I thought he might be meeting you off the train as well.'

Lorna laughed. 'Sorry to disappoint you. Don't worry; we'll be seeing him later. He's taking us out tonight. As a matter of fact, he's working this afternoon, but I told him we wanted some time on our own anyway; we've a lot to catch up on. Now . . . lunch. Where do you suggest?'

Carol chose Schofield's department store where, on the top floor, they served delicious sandwiches, savouries and tempting desserts. They found a secluded corner and settled down with their prawn sandwiches and salad, two huge chocolate eclairs and a pot of tea for two.

Lorna was pleased to hear that Carol was enjoying her nursing course. At the moment she was on the children's ward, which was breaking her in gently, but she knew that during her training she would experience the more unpleasant aspects as well – the viewing of operations, coping with bedpans and sickness, not to mention terminal illnesses and the sometimes unavoidable deaths. Fortunately she was not squeamish, but Lorna knew that she would not have lasted five minutes on such a course.

'And what about Neil?' asked Lorna. 'Are you still seeing him? Well, writing to him, I mean. Obviously you can't see him very much.'

'I wrote to him,' said Carol, not very enthusiastically. 'And he wrote back, of course . . . but it was never serious, you know, like it is with you and Craig. He was just somebody to go out with.'

'Until somebody better came along?'

'I didn't say that.'

'You didn't need to,' laughed Lorna. 'It's written all over your face.'

'I don't know what you mean,' said Carol, a trifle distantly. 'I don't need to ask if you're still seeing Craig, do I? You've still got that starry-eyed look. Goodness, that was love at first sight, wasn't it? Are you any nearer getting married?'

'No, worse luck! They're still saying we've got to wait till I'm eighteen before we even get officially engaged. But we'll probably get married soon after that.'

'Has Adam met Craig? Does he like him?'

'They've met a time or two,' replied Lorna. 'They seem to get on well enough. I was hoping Adam would stick up for me and tell our parents there was no point in making Craig

284

and me wait. But he didn't; he seemed to agree with them . . . Actually, he's not said very much about Craig at all.'

They finished their meal, then spent a very pleasant couple of hours in the department stores – Schofield's, Marshall and Snelgrove (purely for window shopping), Lewis's, and Marks and Spencer. Lorna bought tights and underwear and a stripey sweater in blues and greens which she intended to wear when they went out that evening. Carol followed suit, but her sweater was in coral pink, patterned with a black scrollwork design, which went well with her dark hair. Lorna did not know where Adam would be taking them, but she knew that Carol would want to look her very best. And as for her, Lorna, she was always glad of an excuse to buy something new.

They collected their luggage from the station, then caught a bus to Headingley. Adam's grandparents lived just off Otley Road in a quiet residential area. Both girls received a warm welcome. Charlie and Eva Blundell, Robert's parents, had always treated Lorna as though she were their own grand-child, and they were very pleased to accommodate her friend, too. They were a delightful couple in their early seventies, although neither of them looked their age. Charlie was an older version of Robert, Lorna always thought, and Eva was a very hospitable woman – like Grandma Lizzie had been but with a much quieter and gentler nature. She had obviously made an effort with the guest room. On the twin beds there were fluffy pink towels and rose-scented soap for the girls to use, and a vase of late summer roses on the dressing-table. The whole aspect, overlooking the nearby Beckett's Park, was very pleasing. The semi-detached house was a large one, and as well as having a bedroom upstairs, Adam also had his own den downstairs, a study cum sitting room where he could do his writing and entertain friends if he wished.

He arrived home at five-thirty after reporting on a Leeds United fixture. He kissed both girls lightly on the cheek, which, Lorna noticed, caused her friend to turn quite pink and lose her power of speech. But Lorna chattered enough for both of them, so it was doubtful that Adam noticed.

'So you're taking us out, Adam?' said Lorna. 'We're looking forward to that, aren't we, Carol?'

Her friend nodded. 'Yes, very much. It's . . . it's very kind of you, Adam.'

'Not at all. It isn't often that a chap has not just one, but two beautiful girls to entertain. Where do you fancy going?'

It was Carol that he was looking at, and she blushed slightly again and shook her head. 'I don't mind. Anywhere . . . Where do you suggest?'

'Well, there's a very nice Indian restaurant opened not long ago on Briggate. As a matter of fact, I've taken the liberty of making a reservation because they get very busy on Saturday night, but I knew that if you didn't fancy it, I could always cancel.'

'No, that sounds lovely,' said Carol, suddenly finding her voice and seeming to forget her embarrassment. 'Actually, I went to an Indian restaurant not long ago with some of the nurses. Not that one; it was in Meanwood, but it was very good.'

'That's great then,' said Adam. 'What about you, Lorna? Do you like Indian food?'

'Don't know.' Lorna shrugged. 'I've never had any, but I'm sure it'll be OK.' If she were honest she felt a little dubious. Her taste in food was pretty conservative and she disliked curry, but she did not want to be a spoilsport.

She was won over when she saw the restaurant and made up her mind she was going to enjoy the evening. It was called, not very originally, Star of India and the outside was painted in bright but not garish colours – red and green with touches of black. Everything inside was sparkling and clean: the cutlery, the starched white tablecloths and napkins, the red-shaded lamps on each table, the Indian artefacts – the bells, gongs, daggers, and small elephants made out of brass – which decorated the walls and shelves, and the Indian waiters were immaculate in their native dress. Asian music was being played softly in the background and the whole ambience made one think of the East.

'Now, what are you eating?' asked Adam, handing them each a giant-sized menu. Both girls chose chicken tikka masala, Lorna deciding that you couldn't go far wrong with chicken, and Carol persuading her that she would enjoy it, which she did. Adam had a very hot and spicy curry. He told them it was something he would not get at home as his grandparents were strictly 'roast meat and two veg' sort of people. They drank a red wine of Adam's choice, and then ended the meal with a traditional Yorkshire curd tart; the chef was clearly paying tribute to the country – and county – which he had now adopted as his own. The coffee was far more bitter and strong than Lorna was used to, served in minute cups, but the whole meal had been a unique and enjoyable experience.

Lorna noticed that Carol had overcome her shyness and she became more talkative as the evening advanced. Adam seemed to be giving her the most attention, and Lorna felt a little peeved at this, but she reminded herself that Adam could talk to her, Lorna, any old time, whereas Carol was something of a novelty. Moreover, she knew that her friend fancied Adam. She had done so for ages and it looked as though she was about to attain her objective. Now, why did that not please her as much as it ought to do? Lorna asked herself.

They moved on to a disco that Adam knew of, when they left the Star of India. Lorna and Carol were used to discos, which had even come to sleepy Melcaster now, but they all soon decided that the sound of the music at this one was too cacophonous and the place too crowded, as was only to be expected on a Saturday night. Also, Adam suspected that there was drug-dealing going on, and he knew it was down to him to protect these young women who were in his charge.

They readily fell in with his suggestion that they should go home, and a taxi which he hailed on the Headrow soon whizzed them back to Headingley. Adam owned a car now – he had exchanged his motorbike for a Morris Minor – but had not driven that evening because he guessed he might be drinking more than usual.

His grandparents had gone to bed, as they often did before he arrived home. He made coffee and the three of them chatted and listened to records until the early hours of the morning. Adam had recently bought a stereo system and the girls scrutinised his wide-ranging collection of records. The Beatles, inevitably – everyone had at least a few Beatles records – The Who, The Rolling Stones, Simon and Garfunkel, Cilla Black, Cliff Richard, as well as a selection of classics, chiefly Wagner, Prokofiev and Sibelius. The girls opted for Cliff Richard who was easy to listen to – and less likely to wake up the grandparents – and so Cliff sang away in the background, about going on a summer holiday and being a bachelor boy, whilst they chatted.

Lorna sat and listened, bemused, as Carol and Adam seemed to be finding more and more things that they had in common – their shared taste in music, food and literature. Lorna enjoyed the same books as well – Thomas Hardy, Jane Austen and the Yorkshire writers, Phyllis Bentley and Winifred Holtby. They had been well taught at Melcaster Grammar School and so had developed a love of reading – but she kept quiet on the whole, letting the other two talk together. She was not surprised when Adam suggested that Carol should meet him again – if she wished to, which, of course, she did. The hospital at Meanwood was only a mile or so away from Headingley; it could not be more convenient.

The two girls said very little to one another when they finally went to bed at two a.m. They were far too tired, but Lorna could see that Carol was walking on air.

They had a very lazy Sunday morning whilst Eva Blundell cooked a massive Sunday dinner. She was determined that her guests should enjoy at least one meal under her roof, as she had been foiled the night before by them eating out. The

Yorkshire pudding, with lashings of gravy, was served before the meal in true Yorkshire tradition. Then came the roast beef, roast potatoes, carrots, sprouts, peas with horseradish sauce, followed by homemade rhubarb tart and custard. But this, Adam told them, was the standard Sunday fare at the Blundell home.

He drove Carol back to the hospital, from where he would go on to Leeds city centre to see Lorna on to her train. The two girls hugged one another and promised to write or phone, then Lorna watched as Adam kissed Carol circumspectly on the cheek, saying he would see her on Tuesday night. They had already made a date.

Lorna and Adam hugged one another, too, as she boarded her train. 'Look after yourself,' he said as he kissed her cheek. 'Give my love to the parents . . . and my regards to Craig. Tell him to take good care of you.'

'Oh, he does, don't you worry,' said Lorna. 'Thanks for a lovely weekend, Adam. And . . . I'm glad you're going to see Carol again.'

'Yes . . . well . . . so am I,' he replied. He gave her an unfathomable look before he turned and quickly walked away.

She flopped down in the corner of the compartment. Now why on earth, she wondered, should she feel so deflated? It was great, simply great, that her step-brother had got friendly with Carol, and Carol would be overjoyed. She stared out of the window at the passing scenery. By the time they had left the urban sprawl behind and were heading for the Vale of York and then the Pennine Hills she had managed to put Adam and Carol to the back of her mind and she was looking forward to seeing Craig again.

Chapter 19

It was almost exactly a year later that Lorna and Craig were married, at the Methodist chapel in Melcaster. It was the one where Rachel and Robert had married some eleven years earlier and where they had worshipped fairly regularly ever since. Lorna was far less consistent in her attendance, but she had been there occasionally, and as Craig and his family were not attached to any particular place of worship, they regarded it as the bride's privilege to make the choice.

Jim and Millie Boothroyd, however, had conferred with Rachel and Robert about the venue for the reception and had expressed a desire to help with the cost.

'Craig's our only son – well, our only child,' Millie explained, 'and we want to do what we can to make it a special day for both of 'em. So we'd be pleased if you'd let us go halves with the cost. And I shall look forward to seeing your little lass in all her bridal finery, just as much as if she were my own daughter. We've really taken to her, Jim and I, haven't we, dear?'

'Aye, so we have,' replied Jim. 'We wondered at first, with her being so young, like, just as you must have done. It was sensible of you to make 'em wait. But I think they've proved to us that they love one another, haven't they? So let's make it a right good do, eh?'

Rachel and Robert got along very well with the older couple and were pleased to fall in with their ideas. They decided, with Lorna and Craig's agreement, that the reception would be held at a popular country lodge, The

Wayfarer's Rest, about a mile out of Melcaster.

It was a mellow sunlit day in early October. The harvest was safely gathered in and the farming community had turned out almost in its entirety to see Craig and his young bride tie the knot. The chapel was almost full with Craig and Lorna's friends and relations, Rachel's colleagues from school, plus neighbours and others who just loved a nice wedding. And a goodly number of them had been invited to the reception which was to consist of a sit-down meal, then a disco in the evening for the young folk and any older ones who wished to attend.

Rachel was glad that Lorna had gone along with her suggestion that she should have a traditional wedding dress; she had feared the girl might insist on her usual mini style, which a lot of girls were choosing for their bridal outfits. But she had seemed only too pleased to bow to tradition and her mother's wishes. Her stylish dress was of ivory silk in a princess line, with long, closely fitting sleeves and the panel seams embroidered with pearls and tiny silken flowerets. Her long silk-tulle veil was held in place with a small beaded headdress and she carried a bouquet of roses in autumn shades of gold and apricot.

Lorna had insisted that she wanted only one bridesmaid, Carol, not a horde of tiny – and unruly – attendants, and she wore a similarly styled dress in a warm golden colour, her small posy of white and pale yellow roses.

Rachel felt a lump in her throat as she watched her daughter walk down the aisle on Derek's arm – it had been Robert, not Lorna, who had decided that that was how it should be. Her real father must give her away – and tears sprang to her eyes.

'Be happy for her, darling,' whispered Robert at her side, aware, as always, of his wife's slightest movement and every doubt she might be feeling.

'I am,' she replied, sniffing a little. 'Truly I am.' She knew that Craig was a good man and that he loved Lorna very much. Lorna looked radiant with happiness as she turned and smiled at her bridegroom on reaching the chancel steps, and later, when the ring was placed on her finger, no one in the chapel could fail to be aware of the love which flowed from one to the other.

Rachel just hoped and prayed that her daughter had some idea of what lay ahead. The life of a farmer was a hard one, with long and tiring days. It would not always be romantic and glamorous in the country cottage with the lilac bush in the garden and the idyllic bedroom under the eaves. She had tried, tactfully, to tell her daughter this, but Lorna persisted that she knew exactly what she was doing. She would love Craig for ever and ever, and her mother had just heard her make a promise to that effect.

Lorna felt the joy bubbling up inside her as she walked back down the aisle on the arm of her new husband, Carol following behind with Tony, the best man, Craig's friend from the agricultural college who farmed with his father in the Skipton area. She smiled proudly and confidently at members of the congregation who were smiling back at her. The whole chapel seemed to be filled with smiles. Adam, who was acting as an usher, grinned affectionately at her, closing one eye in a friendly wink.

She had not seen much of Adam recently; he had been back to Melcaster only four times this year. She had assumed he was busy, not only with his reporting, but with his new girlfriend, Carol. She knew they had been out several times since that meeting last autumn and seemed to be getting on really well. Then she had heard, from Carol, that they had split up. It had not been right after all, for either of them. A mutual decision, Carol had said, but she had been unwilling to say more. And now she was back with Neil, the farmer's son.

Neil was also at the wedding, acting as an usher, because the Monkton and Boothroyd families were friendly. Neil and Carol could not sit together at the reception. The seating arrangements were complicated with the bride's mother and father both having remarried, so the ushers had been placed at a different table with some of the other guests. Carol was relieved to see that Adam and Neil were not sitting next to one another, although she knew they must have spoken together earlier in the day when the guests were arriving at the church.

Carol had not told Lorna the real reason for her splitting up with Adam. How could she? Lorna was blissfully happy in her engagement to Craig and her friend did not want to disturb her. She knew that Lorna was unaware of her step-brother's feelings for her. Carol had soon worked out that Adam was very, very fond of Lorna and that it went far beyond brotherly love. It wasn't so much what he said about her, but Carol felt that she was always there, like a spectre between the two of them. She never raised the matter with Adam as she knew he would deny it, probably laugh it off. She wasn't even sure that he realised how deep his feelings for Lorna went. She had thought it somewhat incestuous, until she reminded herself that Adam was not, in fact, Lorna's brother, although she sometimes referred to him as such. They were, in actuality, not related by blood at all. But Carol had grown tired, in the end, of trying to compete with a paragon, and so she had broken it off with Adam, and they had parted quite amicably.

She had enjoyed going out with Adam, but he was much more intense than Carol had imagined, serious-minded and given to contemplative – although not in any way sullen – silences. She had still been writing, spasmodically, to Neil, and when she encountered him on a weekend visit home she had agreed to go out with him again. He had visited her in Leeds, staying at a bed-and-breakfast place near to the hospital. She was finding him good fun now she knew him well; far less earnest than Adam Blundell. Neil was now at agricultural college, but as it was not too far away, in the Vale of York, they managed to meet fairly often. Not that Carol had any thoughts of getting married or even engaged just yet. Secretly, she thought her friend was barmy, tying herself down at eighteen years of age, but there had been no way that Lorna would be dissuaded. And she did, indeed, look very, very happy.

Lorna and Craig honeymooned in London for a few days. Lorna had been to the capital only once before. Their parents had taken them there on a holiday when she was ten and Adam was fourteen, and they had done the usual sightseeing: Buckingham Palace, the changing of the guard, the Tower of London and Madame Tussauds. They had stayed at a modest little hotel in Bloomsbury, but this time they were staying at the Strand Palace Hotel, which Lorna thought was the height of luxury and extravagance. Craig told her it was nothing like as grand as the Savoy Hotel, further along the Strand, and one day they took a peek inside at its gilded opulence, treading on the deep-piled carpets as though they had every right to be there. Craig promised her that one day, when they were wealthy, they would stay there, but the Strand Palace was more than grand enough for Lorna.

It was wonderful that they could now give free rein to their feelings without any sense of guilt. They made love night and morning, passionately but tenderly, and Lorna rejoiced that it was getting better and better every day, and every day she was falling more and more in love with her husband, and he with her.

But when they could tear themselves away from the bedroom there was the whole of London to explore: the sightseeing, shopping and theatre-going. They sailed down the river to Greenwich and viewed the *Cutty Sark* and the Maritime Museum, visited St Paul's cathedral and Westminster Abbey, and walked in the parks – Hyde Park, Kensington Gardens, Green Park and St James's – where the trees were in their autumn splendour. The sun glinted through the bowers of russet, gold, vermilion and orange, formed by the wide-spreading branches, and the fallen leaves lay in a thick carpet on the grass and scrunched beneath their feet.

'You should have your sketch book and your paints with you,' Craig told her. But Lorna had her camera with her at all times. She took photos from interesting angles and vantage points, not only because she wanted to paint the scenes later, but because they would be a permanent record of their honeymoon. It was a week which she knew would remain in her memory for ever; some of the most precious moments, indeed, could not be recorded on film, but were locked away in her heart and mind.

The hotel was very near to the West End theatres. They watched a performance of *Twelfth Night* at the nearby Aldwych Theatre, the first time either of them had seen a professional Shakespearean production. Lorna had once played Peaseblossom in a shortened and simplified school version of *A Midsummer Night's Dream*, she told her husband, and he, not to be outdone, informed her that he had played a forester in *As You Like It*, but it was only a non-speaking part.

The next night, though, when they watched *The Mikado* at the Savoy Theatre, he was able to boast that he had played the title role in his school production.

'But it was an all-boys school, wasn't it?' asked Lorna. 'Who played the three little maids, then?'

'Oh, they were boys as well,' he said, 'in the best Shakespearean tradition. His female characters were always played by men, you know.'

'Yes, I did know,' replied Lorna. Her new husband liked to air his knowledge at times.

'I was too tall to play Yum-Yum,' he went on. 'But I made a pretty impressive Mikado, though I say it myself.'

'You amaze me,' said Lorna. 'Is there no end to your talents? I had no idea you could sing.'

'I can make a reasonable sound, that's all,' he said, 'and they put me in the school choir. Don't worry, darling. You haven't married a genius; I'm a fairly average sort of bloke really.'

But she had learned during their courtship that he could play the piano and the clarinet (after a fashion), having had lessons in both these instruments whilst he was away at boarding school. The piano he had had at home at Sheepscar House had now been moved to Lilac Cottage. There was scarcely room for it in their living room, but they would eat all their meals in the now fully modernised kitchen. She had also discovered that he was well read and enjoyed a wide range of literature, both classical and contemporary, and he could tackle with ease any odd jobs that needed doing around the house – putting up a shelf, mending a fuse or papering a room.

'You're a pretty remarkable girl yourself,' he told her as they strolled along the Embankment. The cloudless night sky was sprinkled with stars and there was a waning moon shining over the Royal Festival Hall on the opposite bank of the river. 'You could have gone a long way with your painting if you hadn't decided to marry me . . . but I'm very glad you did.'

He stopped and kissed her, and she responded to him as she always did. But his remark had alerted her.

'Who's to say I won't still go a long way with my painting?' she retorted. 'You know I'm going back to work.'

'For the moment . . . yes,' said Craig.

But she knew she would, most probably, not be working at Paige's for very long. They had talked about starting a family and she guessed that Craig would not want to wait indefinitely. Well, that was fine by her, but . . .

'But I shall still be able to work at home, Craig,' she said, 'even if I have a baby. That was what we agreed, didn't we? My designs are becoming very popular, and I know Mr Paige will want me to keep coming up with new ideas.'

'Yes, of course. I've just said, you're a very clever girl, aren't you?'

And if his tone was just a teeny pit patronising she soon forgot about it as he enclosed her again in his arms. They stood by the Embankment wall and embraced. Then they watched the shimmers of gold in the murky waters of the Thames, reflected from the overhead strings of lights, and gazed across to Westminster Bridge and the awesome and majestic sight of Big Ben and the Houses of Parliament silhouetted against the dark sky.

'"Earth has not anything to show more fair ..."' quoted Craig.

'Except that Wordsworth was writing of the beauty of the morning, and this is night-time,' Lorna reminded him.

'It's an amazing sight, even so, isn't it?' he said. 'I'm a country boy through and through, but this scene never fails to impress me.'

'You've seen it before, then?'

'Yes, a few times. London has always had an appeal for me ... but 'ah'd best not forget ah'm a Yorksheer lad an' all.' He exaggerated an accent that he had almost lost. 'And the day after tomorrow I'll be back home being a farmer again. And you, my darling, will be a farmer's wife.'

'Yes ... so I will,' replied Lorna.

She had known her life would be very different, without her mother continually reminding her of the fact, as she had done before her marriage, but she had convinced herself that she would adjust and cope very well with all that being a farmer's wife entailed. Several weeks into the marriage she had begun to realise that her life was, indeed, very different. It was very tiring, too, coping with a home as well as a job, but she was managing to do so, and the minor disagreements that had arisen between herself and Craig had soon been ironed out, because they loved one another so much.

He had never expected her to get up with him and make his early breakfast, as he rose as soon as the alarm went off at five-thirty. He then made himself a slice of toast and a cup of tea before going out to start work in the fields or milking parlour. But he did like to have a cooked breakfast later, at around half past seven. Lorna had agreed that she could manage this, although she had, formerly, rolled out of bed at eight-fifteen in order to be at work by nine.

She could cook bacon and eggs, plus the sausages, tomatoes or mushrooms that Craig liked to have with his fry-up, and he seemed satisfied with her efforts. She did not eat any of it, however. She was accustomed to eating only a bowl of cereal or a piece of toast in the morning, which was all she had had time for. She did not always manage to have his breakfast on the table by seven-thirty. She was gradually getting to be a few minutes later each day, which had Craig drumming his fingers with impatience, although he did not say anything. He must have told his mother, though, because Millie soon suggested that Craig should have his breakfast with them, as he had used to do. It was hardly fair to expect Lorna to cook his fry-up when she did not eat any herself.

Lorna was relieved. She could concentrate on the evening meal which she made when she came home from work and which they ate around seven in the evening. She had not helped her mother very much in the kitchen, she recalled now, to her shame ... and to her regret as well, because, if she had been willing to listen, Rachel would have given her good advice. But she taught herself, with a basic cookery book when necessary, and managed to rustle up quite palatable meals: sausage and mash, toad-in-the-hole, and simple casseroles and stews. At least Craig never complained. Their desserts were often custard tarts or fruit flans bought from the bakery near to her place of work, but she promised herself she would master the skill of baking in due course.

Their first minor altercation took place when Craig came home one evening and almost tripped over one of the farm cats which had come into the cottage and was sitting by the fire.

'What the hell's he doing here?' he said. 'Shoo! Off you go, Tiger. Scram! You know you're not allowed in here.'

'Oh, he's not doing any harm,' said Lorna. 'He was meowing outside the back door so I brought him in and gave him some scraps of chicken. Then he went and sat by the fire. It's cold outside.' She had grown fond of the farm cats, especially Tiger, a tabby with brown and fawn stripes in a perfectly symmetrical pattern which appealed to her very much. Blackie, a sleek black tom, always on the prowl, was not quite as friendly.

'But they're not house cats,' said Craig. 'You mustn't encourage them to come inside. Sitting by the fire, indeed!' Tiger had been slung out unceremoniously by the scruff of his neck.

'Aw, Craig, you're cruel!' she said. 'Poor Tiger. He's just like the cat Adam and me had at home, but he got run over and they said we couldn't have another one, because I got so upset.'

'I'm sorry, darling,' said Craig, a little more sympathetically. 'But they are working cats, Tiger and Blackie. They are well looked after, but they live in the barn. They have a job to do, keeping down the vermin. You wouldn't be very pleased if he brought home his booty for you to admire, would you? A nice plump mouse, or even a rat!'

'Ugh, Craig! Give over!'

'Well, that's what cats do,' he laughed. 'If you want a pampered house pet . . . well, I suppose you could have one. But it would soon pick up wild ways, living on a farm. You've a lot to learn yet, my darling.'

She hated it when he said that, that she had a lot to learn. She considered she was doing jolly well. And she managed to sort out, eventually, the problem of her getting to and from the factory.

When she had lived at home – which, strangely enough, was how she still thought of her mother and Robert's house – she had walked to work, or, if it was raining, Robert had sometimes taken her. She had decided, on coming to live at the farm, that she would cycle there; she had sometimes cycled to school in the fine weather. But that was the problem – the weather was not always fine.

She had come out of the cottage one morning to find that

the rain was sheeting down and her husband was nowhere in sight. He had driven her to work, once, on a similarly inclement day, in the farm Land Rover.

'What's up, luv?' called Bill, one of the farm-hands who was just walking past the cottage. 'Oh aye, pissing it down, ain't it? Oh dear! Sorry, luv ... excuse my language.'

'That's OK,' Lorna laughed. 'But I've to get to work, and I don't know where Craig is. Do you think ...?'

'You want a lift?' said Bill. 'No problem, luv. I was just going to suggest it. I'll take you meself. Hang on a minute; I'll just go and get the Land Rover.'

But Craig, when he found out, was far from pleased. Whether it was because Bill had not asked permission, or because Lorna had not tried to find him, she did not know.

'Lorna, you must not appropriate the farm Land Rover for your own use,' he told her. 'It might have been needed elsewhere.'

She had never heard him speak so high-handedly and it upset her. 'Oh, so it doesn't matter then, if I get soaked going to work?' she retorted.

'Of course it does, darling ... I'm sorry.' She had to admit that he was almost immediately contrite. 'Look, we'll try to come to some arrangement. If it's raining I'll come back to the cottage at eight-thirty and take you. OK? But it might be better if you could arrange a lift with somebody at Paige's.'

She had asked around and discovered that a man who worked in the packing department – a middle-aged married man with two children – passed the farm entrance every day on his way to work. He said he would be only too pleased to give Lorna a lift to and from Paige's, and they came to an arrangement about a payment to help with the cost of his petrol.

As Christmastime approached Lorna felt she was really getting into the swing of everything. She was glad she no longer had to battle against the elements cycling to work – because, as December arrived, so did the first snow – and she was getting to grips with cooking more appetising meals.

She had even made a few tentative attempts at baking at the weekends, aware that her mother-in-law never put on to the table any cakes, pies or puddings that were shop bought. And she was extremely proud of the fact that she had made her own Christmas cake and stored it away in an airtight tin, as she had seen her mother do, although she was not adventurous enough, yet, to tackle Christmas puddings.

Lorna's first Christmas at Sheepscar Farm was one she looked back on later as a magical time. On Christmas Eve Rachel and Robert had decided they would go to the midnight service at St Matthew's, the church Rachel had used to attend before her marriage to Robert. The holier-than-thou attitude of some of the women there had annoyed her, especially their reaction to her second marriage. But Rachel missed the reverence and the solemn beauty of the worship there – the Methodist chapel was a little too 'happy-clappy' for her taste at times – and she felt it was time she returned, if only for an occasional service. Adam, who was at home for two days, went with them, and so did Lorna and Craig, and Craig's parents.

It was a while since Lorna had attended any church service, apart from her marriage, and she found herself strangely moved by the reverent atmosphere, and yet one could sense the joy there, too, as they all met together to celebrate the birth of the Lord Jesus. The whole ambience of the place lifted her spirits – the shining Christmas tree, the crib scene by the font, the melodious singing of the choir, and the Reverend Michael, resplendent in his robes of midnight blue embroidered with silver stars. She slipped her hand into Craig's as they sang, 'O come let us adore Him . . .', then she said a silent prayer, something, she realised to her slight guilt, that she had not done recently. 'Thank you, God, for my husband, Craig . . . and please let us always be as happy as we are now.'

When they went out of the church a light fall of snow had added the finishing touch to a true Christmas card scene.

The glow from the lighted windows made pools of gold on the pristine white ground, and every tree and bush sparkled silver in the moonlight. It was good to meet with old friends, who all greeted her, congratulating her and Craig on their marriage and wishing them well. Pauline, her mum's old friend, was there with her husband, and the trio of women from the Young Wives' Group who, for some reason, her mother had fallen out with all seemed very jolly and matey now as they chatted away with her mum and Robert. More like an Old Wives' Group now, thought Lorna, wondering if they still met under their former name. Adam was standing a little apart, and Lorna realised he probably did not know any of these people.

'Adam's on his own,' she said. 'Let's go and have a word with him, Craig . . . You look lost and lonesome,' she told him. 'We've come to rescue you.'

He smiled when he saw them. 'Thank you, but I can assure you I am neither lost nor lonely. I'm just standing here looking and listening, as I always do. It's part of my job; you never know when there might be a story to report! Thanks for inviting me along tomorrow to the merry-making. I'm looking forward to it.'

Christmastime at Sheepscar House was celebrated in the traditional way. Year after year the old decorations came out of the loft – the paper streamers and fold-up bells, the Christmas tree lights, the fragile glass baubles, with every year another one broken – and every year Jim cut down a small pine tree from a coppice on the farmland. Millie always cooked pork, though, from one of their own pigs, rather than turkey; this was the tradition at Sheepscar. Everyone agreed that the succulently tender meat with the crispy crackling, served with sage-and-onion stuffing and apple sauce was a banquet fit for a king – or queen. Even Queen Elizabeth, at Sandringham or wherever she was, could not be enjoying a better Christmas dinner, Jim proudly told his wife.

There was plum pudding with brandy sauce to follow, mince pies, then the inevitable cup of tea without which no northern meal would be complete. Then they all settled down to watch the Queen's televised Christmas speech. All of them being Millie and Jim, Craig and Lorna, Rachel, Robert and Adam, and Rachel's father, Percy, who, eleven years after his wife's death, was still living alone and managing to look after himself very well. Millie and Jim were hospitable people who had welcomed their new daughter-in-law's family into their fold, and they had insisted that Percy Harding should come along as well. The Boothroyds had very few relations of their own nearby, having only the one son, and their brothers and sisters were scattered the length and breadth of the country – in Shropshire, Gloucestershire, Devon and Northumberland – mainly involved in farming.

The next day, Boxing Day, it was the turn of Lorna to do the catering, but she was let off lightly by only having to prepare a tea – there was cold pork, sufficient for all of them, to be eaten up for lunch. The same group of people gathered together in Lilac Cottage for the meal she had prepared: sandwiches, quiches, and a selection of homemade cakes, amongst which her Christmas cake took pride of place.

Only Adam was missing. Lorna felt disappointed that he could not be there; he had not yet shared a meal with her and Craig in their little home. He had told them he must be back at work by Boxing Day. There would be a lot of news to catch up with and there was always an important football fixture the day after Christmas Day.

Robert wondered if his son had a girlfriend back in Leeds. He hadn't said so, but he seemed rather quiet and secretive. It had looked, for a time, as though he might start to think seriously about Carol, that friend of Lorna's, but nothing had come of it. Still, Adam was only young, Robert told himself, still only twenty-three, and there was all the time in the world before he needed to think of settling down. As for Lorna, she had burned her bridges all right, but she seemed happy enough, radiant, in fact.

'That was a reight good spread,' said Jim, after they had demolished almost everything Lorna had prepared. 'Your

Lorna's making you a grand little wife, our Craig. You should be really proud of her, shouldn't he, Millie?'

'I'll say!' replied his wife. 'She's shaping up really well. Those almond tarts; I couldn't have made 'em any better meself.'

'Yes, I am proud of her,' said Craig quietly.

Lorna knew that that was praise indeed from her in-laws. She knew they liked her, but she did wish they would not treat her as a child. Or as a farmer's wife in the making. She was married to a farmer, but she was certainly not out of the same mould as Millie, nor could she ever be.

Early in the New Year of 1972 Lorna realised she was pregnant. She was not surprised; she knew that Craig had stopped taking any precautions, and they made love frequently. He was overjoyed when she told him what she suspected, but she urged him not to say anything to his parents until she was quite, quite sure. A visit to the doctor soon confirmed what she had already guessed. She was expecting a baby towards the end of August. She told her mother and Robert who were pleased, but seemed a little surprised that she should be pregnant so soon, and her father, Derek, expressed his delight, over the phone, at the idea of a grandchild. She knew that her dad, for all his faults, was fond of children.

It was then time to tell Millie and Jim Boothroyd, and they were ecstatic with happiness at the news.

'Eeh, that's grand!' exclaimed Jim. 'Especially if it's a little lad, eh, Craig? A farmer's son to carry on the good work.'

'Don't say that, Dad,' Craig quickly rebuked him. 'You know as well as I do that it might be a girl, and whatever it is it'll be welcome.'

'Well, of course I know that, lad,' said his father. 'I was only saying, like, that it would be nice—'

'But you've years and years ahead of you, haven't you?' said Millie. 'How lovely! Our first grandchild.'

Lorna had been a little upset and worried, too, at her father-in-law's remark. Secretly, she thought she would like a

304

little girl, but she didn't dare to say so. As Craig had said, either a boy or a girl would be very welcome. But she couldn't help feeling that Craig, deep down, agreed with his father.

'Of course I don't,' he insisted, when she asked him. 'All I'm concerned about is that you will be all right, and the baby. So I don't really want you to carry on working much longer, darling.'

As it happened, Lorna was glad to concur with his request because the first few months of her pregnancy were ghastly; she suffered from morning sickness, heartburn and a general feeling of lassitude. She finished work in April and soon began to feel much better.

Brian Paige, who had come to like her very much as a person and to admire the work she produced, was sorry to lose her, both from the design room and the accounts office. It would be simple enough to get another office worker, but designers of Lorna's calibre were few and far between. She agreed to continue submitting her designs to Paige's on a freelance basis. She was already working on a set of farm-animal greeting cards, and on the London scenes, from snapshots taken on her honeymoon.

She found she enjoyed working at home. She had always done so before, of course, but to a lesser degree. Now the whole of the day was hers to draw and paint to her heart's content. She could not understand why Craig should be annoyed, on coming home in the middle of the day, to find the kitchen table spread with painting paraphernalia and his wife sitting by her easel at the side of it.

'For goodness' sake, Lorna!' he exclaimed. 'What the hell do you think you're doing, messing about with paints in the middle of the day? I thought lunch would be ready.'

She stared at him in shocked surprise. 'But . . . you have your lunch at the farmhouse. You always do. I wasn't expecting you.'

'Yes, maybe I always have in the past,' he replied. 'But not any more – at least, not every day. My wife is not at work now – are you? – and when I come home at midday I think it's only reasonable that I should have a bite to eat with her, don't you? What about your lunch, anyway?'

'Oh, I don't always bother much for myself,' said Lorna. 'After all, I cook a big meal at night, don't I? I was going to have something when I finished this.' She was adding the finishing touches to an idealised painting of a cock and hens in the farmyard, which Craig glanced at with what, she thought, was a scathing eye.

'Well, I'd be pleased if you would put that away for the moment and make your husband a spot of lunch. Bread and cheese will do, with some pickles...' He stopped when he saw her mutinous face. 'That's not asking too much, is it?' But then, at the sight of her tight lips and the glimmer of a tear in the corner of her eye, he put his arm round her.

'Oh, come on, darling. I didn't mean to get cross, but it's half past twelve, and this is the kitchen table, for goodness' sake!'

'I'll have it cleared in a jiffy,' she said, freeing herself from his arms and angrily starting to push the palettes and water pots and papers to one side. 'Heaven forbid that anything should interfere with my husband's lunch.'

'I'll help you,' said Craig, more placidly now, 'and I'll help to make the sandwiches too, though that doesn't require a great deal of effort, does it? Oh, darling, we mustn't quarrel, must we?'

She shook her head sadly, before flinging herself into his arms. 'Oh, Craig, I'm sorry. But I get so engrossed in what I'm doing. And I must get this assignment finished.'

'I know, I know. It's important to you, isn't it? But we mustn't let little things like this come between us.'

To Lorna, her painting was not a little thing, but she did not say so. They quickly cleared away and made a snack lunch which they both enjoyed. Freshly baked bread – another of Millie's accomplishments, which she made from time to time – with crumbly cheese from their own dairy and home-pickled onions. Lorna was a little less indignant by the time Craig had drunk a strong cup of tea and was ready to start work again.

'Just let me know when you intend coming home for lunch,' she said, 'and I'll be ready for you. I was really surprised to see you.'

'OK, it's a deal,' he replied. 'You can carry on with your painting now, although I think a breath of fresh air would do you more good. And – don't forget – you won't have as much time for this sort of thing once the baby arrives.'

'I know that, Craig,' she answered, quite sharply. 'You don't need to remind me.'

Their next disagreement took place when Craig came across his wife standing by the gate of the pig-sty, her sketch book in her hand, making rough sketches of the mother pig and her piglets, recently weaned, with their snouts in the trough, noisily and greedily feeding.

'Mind out of the way, Lorna!' he shouted. 'I want to come in there.'

She moved quickly to one side as he strode past her, emptying a bucket of pig swill into the trough.

She had not moved quite quickly enough. 'Look out!' she yelled. 'That splashed me!' Only slightly, to be sure – a globule of the revolting-looking mess had landed on her face and another on her hand – but she disliked his high-handed manner and his implication that she had no right to be there.

Indeed, that was what he now told her. 'Stop fussing! It hardly touched you. I don't know what you're doing here anyway.'

'You do, Craig. I'm sketching. Something I get paid for doing, remember.'

'I've told you before, Lorna, these animals are not nursery-rhyme characters to be put into pretty pictures. They're working animals, or else they're ones that we have killed for food. Yes, food, Lorna,' he continued, seeing her expression of disgust. 'You enjoy roast pork as much as anyone, don't you? Well, this is where it comes from, distasteful as it may seem when you look at these cute little piggy-wiggies. But they'll grow up . . . and it's time you did as well.'

He apologised later, but he had hurt her feelings quite badly this time. They did not often fall out, though, and they were both looking forward, as the summer advanced, to the birth of their child.

At Craig's persuasion, Lorna tried her hand at helping in the dairy, where their own butter and cheese were made. Not in any great quantities, but for home use and to sell at the market in Melcaster. But it soon became clear that Lorna could not master the skills or the dexterity of hand involved in these arts, which had been handed down through the generations. Millie and her elderly dairymaid, Ellen, were able to manage much better without her.

Determined to prove herself, though, in some direction, Lorna discovered she was quite useful in the farm kitchen where Millie, when she was not cooking for the family, made her own jams, marmalades and chutneys, again for home use and to sell at the market. Lorna loved the huge farm kitchen with the stone floor, the early-Victorian tiles on the walls, the hooks on the ceiling from which the sides of bacon and pork used to hang, and the high north-facing windows, the idea being that not much heat should be allowed to enter, in an attempt to keep the place cool. It had, of course, been modernised to a degree. It now contained more modern cooking appliances as well as the range, it was centrally heated, and various rugs and carpet pieces took the chill away from the stone floor. The massive dressers were the homes for an impressive number of stewpans, saucepans, jampans, fish kettles, steamers, colanders, moulds and funnels, mainly fashioned from gleaming copper and brass. They added a pleasing touch of colour and brightness to an otherwise dingy working place.

Lorna's fingers became stained and sore with topping and tailing blackcurrants and gooseberries, hulling strawberries, and taking the stones out of plums and damsons. These were the varieties of jams that Millie made, and Lorna stuck the labels on to the glistening jewel-bright jars, pleased that she had had a hand, however small, in the making of them. She cut up oranges and lemons and grapefruits for marmalades, both green and red tomatoes for chutneys, and took her turn at shredding red cabbage, and peeling onions and shallots for Millie and Ellen to pickle or to make into bright yellow piccalilli. Her eyes watered, but she was pleased to be of assistance to her mother-in-law and to earn her praise.

Millie was not unappreciative. She was growing fond of her daughter-in-law and did not forget to tell her son, quite frequently, that, 'the lass is shaping up well'.

Something that Lorna really enjoyed was taking a turn on the market stall. There was an old market hall in Melcaster which was open from Monday to Saturday. There the more permanent traders had their stands, selling crockery, pots and pans, second-hand books, cut-price perfumes and cosmetics, toys, cheap jewellery and haberdashery. Inside the hall, too, were the butchers' stalls and a fishmonger's. But the proper market days were Tuesdays and Saturdays when the farmers and market gardeners came from the Melcaster area and further afield to set up their stalls in the small cobbled square outside the market hall. It was a colourful sight, with gay striped awnings over the stalls, which overflowed with fruit, vegetables, flowers and farm produce.

Lorna had loved to go there with her mother when she was a little girl. She used to spend some of her Saturday pocket money at the sweet stall, taking an age to choose between the pear drops, sherbet lemons, Yorkshire mixture, aniseed balls, peppermint drops – myriad varieties – in their glass bottles, or the penny chews and twists and small bars of chocolate. Her mother, she recalled, had bought the homemade fudge, or the butter and treacle toffee which the lady had cracked with a little silver hammer. Amazingly, the same stall was still there, with the same rosy-cheeked lady, more grey-haired now, though, and a good deal plumper.

She had wrinkled her nose as a child at the various smells: the ripe fruit and, towards the end of the day, the slightly decaying vegetables; the perfume of sweet williams, stocks and carnations from the cottage gardens; and, overriding all the other smells, the odour of cheese from the farmers' stalls.

It was her task, now, to cut the cheese for the customers with a wire cutter and wrap it in greaseproof paper. They sold two varieties, creamy and crumbly, both emitting a pungent, but pleasant, aroma. The golden butter was pre-packed in half-pound packets, and the brown eggs already placed in their egg boxes, in dozens and half-dozens. Making a colourful display of red, orange, yellow and green, at one end of the stall, were Millie's preserves: her jams, marmalades, chutneys and pickled onions.

By the end of the day the stall would be almost empty, and Lorna would go home with Craig, satisfied that she had played her part in the life of the farm. She enjoyed serving the customers and chatting with them. She knew many of them – neighbours and friends of her parents from way back, and her own school friends – and, especially for the older folk, this pretty golden-haired girl with the cheerful smile brightened up their day. Towards the end of July, however, she was growing heavy with the child and could no longer stand for long periods. She knew, now, that the time had come for her to stay at home and wait for the baby to put in his – or her – appearance.

Chapter 20

Her labour pains started early in the morning of the twenty-fifth of August. Craig quickly drove her to Melcaster Hospital, the very place where she had been born nineteen years earlier.

A revolutionary idea, frowned upon in some hospitals, but tolerated, if not encouraged, at Melcaster, was for the father to be present at the birth. Many men were squeamish and preferred not to be there, but Craig was well used to the experience of birth, and Lorna was glad to have him there to hold her hand and give her moral support.

Her labour was comparatively short and easy for a young woman of such slender build, but she had youth on her side. She had ceased to worry about or even to give a thought as to the sex of the child as she laboured and wrestled with the gas-and-air machine. Then, just after midday, she was urged to give one almighty push . . . and she heard, almost immediately, the cry of a child.

'It's a girl!' cried the midwife. 'Congratulations, Lorna, and you too, Mr Boothroyd. You've got a lovely little girl.'

'A girl?' said Lorna. She felt a surge of joy, followed by the remembrance that her husband had wanted a boy; or at least she had assumed he did.

'Yes, we have a lovely little daughter,' said Craig, stooping to kiss her. 'Well done, darling.'

'You're not . . . disappointed, then?'

'Of course I'm not,' he replied, smiling at her, but she thought his voice sounded a shade too hearty. 'You're OK and so is the baby; that's all that matters.'

He moved quickly out of the ward, as the midwife still had important jobs to do. A few moments later Lorna was sitting up with the child in her arms, her tiny baby weighing six and a half pounds, with an abundance of brown hair, slightly tinged with a russet tone – Craig's hair – and, from what she could see of her little face, an overall resemblance to her husband. Well, that should please him, she thought, if he felt let down at her giving birth to a girl.

Her mother and Robert came later in the day, full of congratulations and delight in their granddaughter. 'I can say she's my granddaughter, can't I?' said Robert. 'She's absolutely delightful.'

'Yes, she's beautiful, darling,' said Rachel. 'Not much like our side of the family, but beautiful for all that.'

Millie and Jim Boothroyd arrived soon after the Blundells had departed. The rules on visiting were quite strict. The new mothers must not be allowed to get overexcited or tired. Jim appeared a little embarrassed, as men often did in a maternity ward. He peeped in the cot at the foot of the bed.

'Oh aye, she's lovely, isn't she?' he said. Rather awkwardly he stooped and kissed his daughter-in-law's cheek. 'Well done, lass,' he murmured.

And then Lorna saw him turn towards Craig. 'Never mind, lad,' he said, in what he imagined to be a quiet voice. 'Better luck next time, eh?'

Lorna could not forget her father-in-law's remark. She felt she had failed to come up to scratch, despite the affection they all had for her baby girl. They called her Karen Louise, and in due course she was christened at St Matthew's church. This was Lorna's choice. She recalled the feeling of true joy and hopefulness she had experienced there at the Christmas Eve service, and remembered, too, that she had been happy as a child at the Sunday school there.

It was Craig's idea that they should ask Adam to be godfather, and her friends Carol and Brenda, whom she had worked with at Paige's, were godmothers. There did not appear to be any embarrassment between Adam and Carol. She was still seeing Neil when she could spare time from her nurse's training, and it was believed that Adam had a girlfriend, although he was still cagey and largely uncommunicative about such matters.

Karen soon developed into a bonny, sturdy child. She had Craig's clear blue eyes and russet-brown hair, although hers showed a tendency to curl. She had a chubby face and her cheeks were always rosy as she spent a good deal of her time out of doors, in her pram or pushchair at first, and then toddling around in her mother's wake.

She started to talk and to walk before she was a year old, and as she grew her resemblance to her father became more marked. As for Craig, he did not once so much as hint that he was disappointed at her being a girl. Indeed, it seemed as though the child might become a Daddy's girl. Their affection for one another was noticeable; the little girl would lift up her arms and cry, 'Dada!' – the very first word she uttered – whenever he appeared through the cottage door. Lorna, trying not to be jealous, realised that this was because Karen was with her all day, whereas her daddy, out at work most of the time in the fields, was more of a novelty.

She loved her baby girl with an intensity she had not felt before, not even for her husband whom she still loved deeply. But this love of a mother for her child was something quite different. She found it hard to believe, and yet wonderful, that she should feel such a bond with the tiny, helpless baby she held in her arms, and as the child grew, so did her love for her. What a difference she had made to all their lives. Lorna found it difficult to recall a time when Karen had not been there, an integral part of the family.

She remembered how, when she herself was a baby, her mother had left her in the care of Grandma Lizzie whilst she resumed her teaching career. She couldn't recall her baby days, of course, but she could vaguely remember that as a toddler she had spent a lot of time with her gran, and then

Kevin had come along, her dear little baby brother whom they had lost so tragically. She did not often think of Kevin now, but when she did all the anguish of that awful time would return to her. How dreadful it must have been for her mother to lose her little boy. Lorna, now, with the fervent love she had for her own little girl, could not imagine anything more tragic or heartbreaking.

She could not imagine, either, going back to her job at Paige's and leaving Karen in the care of her mother. Such a thing was not possible, of course, because Rachel was working herself, still very much a career woman, the headmistress of Kilbeck Infant School. And yet that was what Rachel had done; she had left her, Lorna, with her gran. No doubt she had had her reasons and Lorna did not feel she had suffered from it. Her grandma, she recalled, had been kind, but quite firm, and Lorna had loved her very much. But was this the reason, she asked herself, why there was still a certain restraint between herself and her mother, Rachel? A resentment, maybe only half recognised or acknowledged on her part, that she had been handed over to someone else as a child, and a feeling of guilt, even now, on Rachel's part, that she had done this?

Maybe she, Lorna was being too introspective. But she felt, somehow, that the time had come when she should, if it were possible, try to draw closer to her mother, not be so critical of her or take offence at things she did, which she knew, oftentimes, she was guilty of. She started, therefore, going round to see her mother regularly, every Saturday afternoon, wheeling Karen the mile or so in her pushchair, or begging a lift from Craig if the weather was inclement. Robert usually drove her home again, stowing the pushchair away in the boot of the car. Rachel and Lorna did, indeed, begin to develop a new closeness, strengthened by their mutual love for little Karen.

Lorna, though, unavoidably, was bound to spend the greater part of her time in the cottage or surrounding area alone with her child. She found, by the time Karen was one year old, that she was growing increasingly restless. She felt she could understand, now, why her mother had wanted to return to work, especially, she recalled, as her parents' relations with one another had been far from perfect. Not that Lorna could complain about her own relationship with her husband. They still loved one another very much, although she had to admit there were times when he was impatient and inclined to be irritable with her.

When Karen was a small baby, asleep in her cot or pram for long periods during the day, Lorna had occupied herself with her painting. She was still producing designs and illustrations for Paige's, not as regularly as she had done before the baby was born, but she was determined not to let go of her work altogether. It was vital to her innermost self and to her existence as a person in her own right. When the little girl was one year old, however, she was into everything, touching and reaching out for things and following her mother wherever she went. It was impossible for Lorna to paint or even draw, and she did not believe in imprisoning a child in a play-pen. On the one or two occasions when she had tried to do her work Karen had upset a jar of water, scattered pencils on to the floor and had been more than usually demanding. And so Lorna had started to work in the evenings when the child had gone to bed.

Craig resented this. He wanted his wife to be with him in the evenings, in their sitting room, watching television or just chatting together or quietly reading, not painting away in the kitchen, oblivious to him and to everything around her, as she tended to be when engrossed in her art. Neither was he as admiring of her artistic efforts as he had used to be.

The two of them were slowly beginning to grow apart, although it was barely perceptible at the moment. It was possible that only Lorna and Craig themselves were aware of it, but it saddened Lorna very much. Their marriage had been a wonderful, magical thing, and she had thought the rapture would last for ever and ever.

Then, towards the end of 1973, Lorna discovered she was pregnant again. She was rather surprised that this had not happened before because, in spite of their slight disagreements, they still made love regularly and with the same fervour and feeling for one another. Their second child was due to be born in July the following year, and the two of them drew closer together again, their former irritability forgotten as they looked forward to another child coming into their family.

Lorna found herself hoping desperately for a boy, not because that was particularly what she wanted, but because, this time, Craig was quite open about wanting a son. So were his parents, particularly his father. Lorna started to worry about what they would say if she were to let them down again, the fact that Karen had turned out to be such a little treasure and that they all loved her very much notwithstanding.

Her pregnancy, this time, was not an easy one. As well as the usual morning sickness in the early stages, she developed swollen ankles and high blood pressure. She put on too much weight for such a small person and she was forced to go into hospital two weeks before the baby was due in order to rest and to keep her blood pressure down. She was worried about leaving Karen, but she was assured that the little girl was being well looked after and was happy with Grandma Millie.

'She's looking forward to seeing her baby brother,' Millie told Lorna when she visited her in hospital, '. . . or sister,' she added, seeing the worried look on Lorna's face.

It was discovered, when her labour pains started, that it was to be a breech birth. She struggled for a while, Craig anxiously holding her hand and giving her encouragement, but the doctor decided, eventually, that she had suffered for long enough and that he would perform a Caesarean section. Lorna was only too pleased to be able to drift away into oblivion.

She awoke, a couple of hours later, to see the white-coated doctor and her husband at the side of her bed. The nurse at the other side was holding a blanketed bundle in her arms. Lorna blinked confusedly, then, remembering what had happened, she struggled to a sitting position. 'What did I have?' she asked. 'Is it . . . a boy?'

'No, Lorna,' replied the midwife, placing the bundle into her arms. 'You've had another little girl. Just look at her; she's beautiful.'

Lorna glanced at her husband, even before she looked down at the baby. 'Yes, Lorna,' he said. 'It's a little girl.' He smiled at her, sadly, she thought, and then he stooped and kissed her. 'Never mind, darling,' he said.

The baby certainly was beautiful. She was all pink and white, not having had to go through the whole trauma of birth, which made some babies red and wrinkled. Her head had a covering of golden hair like chicken down, and her features were delicate and finely drawn.

'Oh, this little one's a real Harding!' exclaimed Rachel when she first set eyes on her second granddaughter. 'She's lovely, darling. So is Karen, of course, but this one is just the opposite of her sister. Small and fair and dainty; yes, a real Harding.'

'Well, I hope I'm going to be allowed a little share in her as well,' said Robert, laughing. 'I've got two lovely grand-daughters by proxy now. It doesn't look as though that son of mine is going to present me with any grandchildren, not yet awhile.'

'Craig wanted a boy,' said Lorna, rather despondently. Only her mother and Robert were at the bedside at that moment and she felt she had to give voice to her fears and foreboding. 'I think he's disappointed, and I know his parents are. They were here earlier, and I know they feel I've let them down.'

'They didn't say so, surely?' said Rachel, sounding quite horrified.

'No, not really,' said Lorna. 'But I can tell; it's more what they don't say than what they do. And the minute I came round after the operation Craig said, "Never mind, darling." He didn't need to have said that, did he? No matter how disappointed he felt. But I suppose all men want a boy sometime, don't they?'

'So they say,' replied Rachel, 'but I don't know whether it's true or not. I think most men are happy with whatever God sends, boys or girls, even if they end up with three or four of one sort and none of the other. I'm sure Craig will be happy with this little one. How could he not be? What are you going to call her? Have you decided?'

'No, we've not talked about it yet.' Lorna sounded tired and her parents decided it was time they left.

'Don't get disheartened, love,' said her mother, kissing her. 'It'll all be fine, you'll see.'

Robert kissed her too. 'Thank you, Lorna,' he said. 'You've certainly made us very happy anyway. Well done!' He squeezed her hand. 'Chin up, now. We'll see you again soon.'

'Oh dear!' said Rachel as they made their way out of the ward. 'I do hope Craig comes round. He did want a boy; I know that. I do so want their marriage to work. I was dubious at first as you know, but I thought things were going well.'

'So they are,' said Robert. 'Stop worrying! This will be just a minor set-back. They'll be OK, you'll see.'

Craig was cheerful when he visited her the next day. He brought flowers and magazines and good wishes from all the work force at the farm. They had all signed a big card which pleased Lorna very much.

'How's the baby doing?' he asked, taking a peep at the sleeping child in the cot. 'She's not very big, is she? And she looks rather pale, probably because she's got such fair hair.'

'She's quite big enough,' said Lorna feelingly. She had not forgotten her struggles in the early stages of labour. It had been much worse than the first time. 'She's got my hair and she looks like me.' And then, because she could not help herself, 'I'm sorry if you're annoyed that she's not a boy, but that's the way it goes. She doesn't look like you either, but I'm afraid I can't do anything about that.'

'Hey, come on, darling,' said Craig. 'What's all this about? Of course I'm not annoyed. Why should I be? We've got two lovely little girls. I admit it would have been nice to have a boy . . . but the odds are that the next one will be. Now, it's time we started to think of a name for our second daughter, isn't it? Have you had any ideas?'

Lorna liked the name Joanne, and Craig, who thought she should have two names like her sister had, suggested Emily.

'Joanne Emily Boothroyd,' said Lorna, feeling a shade happier now that her husband had, at least, shown an interest in naming the child. 'Yes, that sounds very nice.'

She had not been pleased, however, to hear Craig's remark about the 'next one'. As far as she was concerned two children were quite enough, for the moment at any rate, perhaps for ever. She broached the subject with the doctor when he came round to the ward the next day, asking whether the problems with her pregnancy and childbirth had made it difficult or unwise for her to have any more children. She was hoping he might say that this was so.

'No, there is no reason why you should not go on having healthy children, Mrs Boothroyd,' he told her. 'The chances are that the next pregnancy and birth would be quite normal. After all, your first child was born without any problems, wasn't she? I told your husband the same thing when he asked me yesterday . . . What's the matter? You look worried.'

'Yes, I am, rather,' said Lorna. So Craig had already been checking up on his chances of more children? 'I've had two girls, you see, and my husband is desperate for me to have a boy. I know he is, and I know he's blaming me. He thinks it's all my fault.'

'Then he couldn't be more wrong,' replied the doctor. 'If anybody is to blame for your children being girls, then it's him, not you.'

Lorna looked puzzled. 'How is that?'

'Because it's the male chromosome that determines the sex of the child,' he explained. 'I don't want to get too technical, but I can assure you that that is the way it works. And you can tell him so if he starts to put the blame on you.'

'Yes, maybe I will,' smiled Lorna.

'I hope you are wrong, though, Mrs Boothroyd, about him blaming you. I think you will find, as time goes on, that he will be thrilled to bits with his little girls and it just won't matter any more. I should know, I have three girls of my own, and I just accept that that is the way it has to be . . . If you don't want any more children just yet, though – and I think it might be advisable to wait a little while – then you could always try the contraceptive pill. Have you thought about it?'

'No, I haven't . . . but I might,' she said. 'Thank you very much, Doctor. You've been very helpful.'

Lorna knew, however, that Craig would not approve of the pill and so she did not tell him what the doctor had said. He liked to be the one in charge of such matters. She was able to leave hospital after ten days, and the following week she made an appointment with her own family doctor in Melcaster. He agreed that it would be a good idea for her to start taking the pill as soon as her cycle returned to normal, although he did not think it would be advisable for her to do so for ever. But 'sufficient unto the day', thought Lorna as she took the packets home and hid them away in her dressing-table drawer.

By the time Karen was approaching her third birthday she was a robust girl, tall for her age and well built, too, without being plump. She was developing into what might be called a tomboy. Craig had not got his longed-for son, but he did have a daughter who, it seemed, might well grow up to be as good as any farmer's boy. She loved the animals and was not afraid of them. She accompanied her daddy occasionally when he was doing jobs that would not be too dangerous for a child to be around. She wore red wellingtons and blue dungarees and she had her own little spade and hoe which Craig was teaching her to use in a careful manner.

She helped her mother in the cottage garden, but she much preferred to be with her daddy in the fields or orchard, digging potatoes out of the ground or picking plums and apples from the low branches of the trees. She had even had a ride with Craig on the tractor, wearing a hard hat which was now obligatory for all farm workers. He took very great care of her, and Lorna knew that Karen would be safe with him. She had worried at first about such a small child running about the farmyard, but Craig assured her that he never took his eyes off the child.

Lorna was busy, with two children to look after. All the same, there was only a certain amount of work to be done in the small cottage. She found she was still able to continue with her art assignments for Paige's. The farmyard scenes she had done, using the animals of Sheepscar as models, had been very popular as birthday cards. These were in a set of six portraying the cows, sheep, pigs, cock and hens, horses, and the sheepdog, Harvey, who was allowed to live in the farmhouse with Jim and Millie.

Lorna had included the farm cats, Tiger and Blackie, in the dog picture. She had always preferred cats to dogs, and she still encouraged the two cats to come into the cottage for scraps of meat and to warm themselves by the fire when she saw them lurking nearby. Especially Tiger, as Blackie remained somewhat aloof, but the little girls were growing fond of both of them. Lorna had to make sure, though, that they visited only when Craig was nowhere around, and that no wind of it should reach her husband's ears. She tried to explain to Karen that it was their secret, that Daddy did not like cats very much so she must not let on to him. She hated being deceitful, but there were times when she got a little tired of his dictatorial manner, and this was a way of exerting her independence.

Brian Paige had been impressed with the animal cards,

and they had sold so well that he had now asked her to design a set of Christmas cards using the same animals. Lorna knew that her husband would not approve. He had accused her before of prettifying the animals and making them into nursery-rhyme characters. She drew the line at giving them human characteristics, or making them into humorous figures by dressing them up in little jackets or dresses. She had too much respect for them to do that, although she couldn't help thinking that it had worked very well for Beatrix Potter, and Kenneth Grahame, of course.

But she had to put them into a Christmassy setting and she racked her brains trying to come up with original ideas. There could be nothing too original, though, about the Christmas story; it had all been done so many times before. The barn was essential for a setting for some of the pictures. Jesus had been born in a barn of sorts, although she guessed it would have been more like an earthen cave than the large wooden structure at Sheepscar.

There were no animals in the barn on the day Lorna went in with the two little girls, only piles of hay. The farming implements were at the other end, so she knew that Karen would be quite safe playing in the hay whilst she made some preliminary sketches of the high rafters and the old hay-wagon in the corner. She could envisage an almost black midnight sky and a solitary star shining through the barn door. She sketched away whilst Karen gathered the hay in her arms and threw it around – Lorna would make sure it was tidy again before they left – and Joanne sat in her pushchair, placidly smiling and watching her big sister.

Suddenly Karen gave a shriek, and Lorna looked up from her drawing to see the farmyard gander which had waddled into the barn and was advancing on the little girl. He was the only creature of which Karen was the slightest bit afraid. He was a sort of farmyard watchdog to keep the hens in order and possessed an aggressive streak.

'Shoo! Shoo! Go away, Gandy!' cried the child, waving her arms at him. The hay she was holding scattered and some of

322

it fell on to Gandy. He did not like that at all. He lurched forward and pecked Karen on the leg.

'Ow! Ow!' she yelled, screaming and running to her mother. 'Mummy, Mummy . . . he's bit me, that horrid Gandy!'

Lorna was a little afraid of him, too, but she managed to shoo the large bird away and out of the door. She gave her daughter a cuddle and inspected the damage. Karen was not hurt very much. It had only been the slightest nip. If she had been wearing her usual dungarees it wouldn't have made a mark at all, but Lorna had dressed her in a cotton frock that morning because the June weather was warm. She was a tough little girl who did not cry very often. Her tears, more of fright than hurt, soon stopped, and Lorna pacified her when they got back to the cottage by tying a bandage around her leg, although it was not really necessary. Her sketching, of course, had come to an end for that day.

She knew that Craig would notice the bandage, but Karen insisted on keeping it on for the rest of the day. Lorna did not want to argue with her. She could be wilful at times. Like I used to be, Lorna thought ruefully, remembering the battles she had had with her mother at times. Not any more, though; she and Rachel were the best of friends at the moment. It was futile to hope that Karen would keep quiet. It was the first thing she told her father when he came through the door on finishing his work.

'Daddy, Daddy, look! That horrid Gandy, he bit me.'

'It's nothing much,' said Lorna. 'Only a little nip, but she insisted on having a big bandage. It's better now, isn't it, Karen?'

But Craig, of course, demanded to know how it had happened. Lorna kept silent, listening resignedly to Karen's tale of how Mummy had been drawing and naughty Gandy had come into the barn and she hadn't noticed, and then to Craig's recriminations.

'Really, Lorna, I thought I could trust you to take better care of her than that. You questioned it when I took her into the fields with me, but she came to no harm in my care, did she? You get so wrapped up in your blasted drawing that you can't see what's happening under your nose. Just keep your eye on her in future. It had better not happen again!'

'It won't . . . I'm sorry,' said Lorna meekly, realising that she was at fault.

It was sheer bad luck, the following week, that Craig should appear round the corner of the pig-sty when Lorna was engaged in sketching the latest litter of piglets. She had visualised two children in this scene, possibly with holly in their arms and bright red bobble-hats on their heads, leaning over the wall to look at the piglets, just as Karen was doing now.

'Lorna, what the hell do you think you're playing at?' he yelled. 'Don't you know there's a slurry pit round that corner? Take your eyes off Karen for one minute and she'd be off round there, and the next thing you know she'd be drowning.'

'She's nowhere near the slurry pit,' retorted Lorna. 'She's here with me, and I never do take my eyes off her.'

'Then how can you draw if you're watching her all the time?' He snatched the sketch pad out of her hands, something he had never done before, glancing at the drawing with a look of disdain. 'You're determined, aren't you, to carry on with this nonsense in spite of what I say? Well, it's got to stop, Lorna. Your place is in the home with your two children. Come on, Karen, you can come with Daddy for a while.' He thrust the sketch book back into Lorna's hands. 'And just you remember what I've said.'

Lorna was furious, too angry to give way to tears as she wheeled Joanne in her pushchair back to the cottage. How dare he speak to her like that? And she was damned if she was going to give up her art work. Why should she? Anyway, Craig had said, when they got married, that she could keep on working, at home, if not at the factory.

He had calmed down somewhat by the evening when both children were in bed. But it was not Craig's way to go back on his word when he had made a statement; Lorna had come to realise that.

'I am sorry I shouted at you,' he said, 'but there are times when you still don't see the dangers, Lorna. I shouldn't get cross in front of the children, I know that.' Although he often did. 'But I mean what I say. I don't want you to carry on with this work for Paige's. It's taking you away from the girls ... and from me. It isn't as if we need the money. My mother never needed to work, except to help my father on the farm, so I don't see why you should work either.' Listening to him, Lorna realised he was turning into a carbon copy of his father. More refined, of course, and more well spoken than Jim, but just as dictatorial. 'Anyway, I'm hoping you will have another little one to look after before long. And then you certainly won't have time to play about with your drawing. A little brother for Karen and Joanne. That's what we want, isn't it, darling?' He smiled at her, but she felt that underlying the affection she knew he still had for her, there was a patronising tone – which she had noticed before – and more than a hint of dominance.

She ignored the reference to another child, knowing, at the moment, that it was impossible for her to conceive; Craig was still in ignorance of her contraceptive practices. But she was determined she was not going to be treated as the little woman at home, as Millie had always been content to be. Nor was she going to relinquish her career.

'No, Craig,' she replied, in as calm a voice as she could manage, knowing that to shout or get angry would serve no purpose. 'I will not give up my work for Paige's, and there is no way you can make me do so. I don't neglect our children. I'm sorry about what happened today, but I still say that Karen was in no danger.'

His eyes narrowed. She had never seen him look so annoyed with her. 'Are you defying me, Lorna?' he said. 'I am telling you that I don't want you to go on working for Paige's. If you are short of something to do, then my mother can find you some work, although, from what I remember, you

325

'weren't much help in the dairy.'

'I am not a blasted dairymaid!' she yelled, forgetting her intention to keep calm. 'I'm not a farmer's wife, either.'

'Oh yes you are. You became one when you married me.'

'Well, I'm not a proper one . . .'

'Huh! You can say that again!' His sarcastic sneer made her shout all the louder.

'If you're not satisfied with me, Craig, then it's just too bad. I look after the children and the house, and I cook the meals and do the washing and God knows what else. And – yes – I am defying you. I will not give up my art work. Do you hear? It's the only thing that keeps me sane sometimes in this God-forsaken place.'

Craig turned pale with anger, and his eyes, usually so warm and friendly, were lifeless stones, more grey than blue. His fists were tightly clenched as though he was trying to keep himself under control, but Lorna had no fear that he would strike her. He never had, that was not his way, but his scathing words could hurt just as much. 'Well, if that's the way you feel, then there is no point in me trying to keep you here, is there? You are a disappointment to me, Lorna. You have never tried to fit in with our ways, not once since the moment you came here. You knew this was a working farm, but you seem to think it's some sort of . . . Disneyland.'

'That's a lie,' she retaliated, 'and you know it. I've tried as hard as I can. I've helped at the market, and I've worn my fingers to the bone – literally – helping your mother with her blasted jams and pickles. What more do you want? Whatever it is, I'm afraid I can't give it to you. I hate it here!'

For once Craig seemed to be at a loss for words. He looked at her impassively for several moments, still unsmiling. 'I'm sorry it's come to this,' he said at last. 'You don't fit in and that's the top and bottom of it. But for the moment there's little we can do about it . . . Yes, you're right.' Well, that was a brave admission at any rate, thought Lorna. She was actually right about something? 'I can't stop you from painting and drawing, but perhaps it might dawn on you, eventually, that I don't approve. And I always thought that a wife was supposed to fall in with her husband's wishes.'

'Good grief! This is not the Victorian age,' yelled Lorna. 'This is nineteen seventy-five, for God's sake! Times have changed a little bit, Craig.'

'And not always for the best,' he retorted. 'Anyway, I've said my final word, Lorna.' He stalked out of the room, then out of the cottage door. She heard it close behind him. She did not know where he was going; to say goodnight to his precious animals, maybe. They obviously meant more to him than she did, or their daughters. He was fond of them both, but she knew he badly wanted a son.

She sat by the window as the light gradually faded – it did not get dark until after ten o'clock on these midsummer evenings – looking out on the garden she loved so much. She felt more in control of herself now, but with her calmer mood came the realisation that this was their first really bitter quarrel. What on earth was happening to them? Why were they saying such dreadful, hurtful things to one another? Surely Craig didn't mean that he wanted her to leave? That was what he had said, though, or words to that effect. And neither did she mean it when she had said she hated the farm. On the whole she had been happy there, if only he would see that he could not force her into the image he had in mind for her, that of a passive farmer's wife. She did mean it, however, when she said she intended to carry on with her art work. And she also meant it when she vowed to herself that she would have no more children, but Craig did not know that yet.

He was not exactly contrite when he came back at eleven o'clock, but she could see he was ready to go some way towards making up their hurtful quarrel. He put his arms around her.

'I think we both said things that we didn't really mean,' he said, stroking her hair and kissing her forehead. 'We must try to put this behind us, Lorna.' He did not say he was sorry, but she supposed that was too much to hope for.

They did not make love that night. Possibly they were both still too sore about the angry words they had exchanged. Very soon though, before a week had passed, they came together again in a full expression of their love for one another.

Maybe this time we will have been lucky, thought Craig. He could not understand why his wife did not conceive. If only she could, and soon, he thought, it would be the answer to all their problems.

Chapter 21

Lorna knew that her husband was sure to discover her deception sooner or later. He was growing increasingly curious as to why she did not conceive. At times she was almost tempted to tell him what she had been doing for the past year, but always changed her mind, fearing his wrath. She even wondered if she should stop taking the pill and fall in with Craig's wishes. She had little doubt, if she were to stop taking precautions, that she would soon become pregnant. But Lorna had a stubborn streak, and she knew it. Her husband was still inclined to be high-handed in his dealings with her, and this was a small way in which she could cock a snook at him without him knowing it.

The climax came a week before Christmas. Both little girls were in bed and Craig had gone upstairs. She guessed he wanted to choose a book to read from the selection he had on their bedroom shelves, and also to take a peep at their two children, fast asleep in bed. He often did that at night, and she knew, despite his hankering for a boy, that he was very fond of his two little girls, especially of Karen. Their elder child, of course, was more like him in looks and it seemed, as time went by, that she would take after him in other ways as well.

'Lorna, Lorna ... Come up here at once!' Suddenly she heard him shouting from the top of the stairs. She jumped up quickly. His loud voice would wake the children if he wasn't careful.

'Hush, Craig!' she cried, but in a quieter voice than his, as she bounded up the stairs. 'You'll wake the girls. What's the matter, anyway?'

Oh no . . . She might have guessed. She knew as soon as she entered the bedroom just what was the matter. He was standing by her dressing-table, the bottom drawer where she kept her underwear was open, and he was holding a tell-tale packet in his hand. Her immediate reaction was one of apprehension, almost amounting to fear, but she was angry as well.

'What are you doing in my drawer?' she rebuked him, knowing, though, that her misdemeanour was greater than his and that she did not have a leg to stand on, as the saying went. 'You know my dressing-table is private to me, just as yours is to you. I would never dream of—'

'Yes, I'm not surprised you try to keep it private, you . . . you deceitful little madam! How dare you, Lorna? How dare you do this,' he flung the packet on to the bed, 'without telling me? Because you daren't tell me, that's why. Because you knew I wouldn't approve.'

'Shut up, Craig!' she retorted. 'You'll have the girls waking up. If you want to scream and yell at me then at least make sure they can't hear. But you have no right to be prying into my personal belongings.'

'I've every right!' he snarled. 'But I agree that we don't want the children overhearing what I have to say to you. Go on, get off downstairs.' He gave her a push, only a slight one, to be sure, but it was the first time he had ever done so much as lay a finger on her in anger, and she was shocked.

'Don't you push me!' She backed away as though he had actually struck her. 'Don't you ever do that again, Craig Boothroyd, or I'll—'

'OK, OK.' He put up his hands in a gesture of compliance. 'I shouldn't have done that, I know, but you make me so angry, Lorna . . . Go on; I'll be down in a minute.'

'Why, Lorna? Why?' he asked, when he had calmed down a little. 'The worst thing about all this is that you have been so secretive. Although I don't approve of the pill, anyway. I

330

would never want you to take it because I don't consider that it's safe; there could be all sorts of complications. But . . . why did you have to take such measures?'

'Because I don't want any more children, I suppose,' she answered, sounding quite meek, although she was still churning up inside.

'What? Not ever?'

'Well, certainly not yet. Maybe not for ages. I've got two little girls to look after, and I can assure you that that is quite enough. You're not with them all day and every day like I am.'

'I notice you still have time for your painting, though, haven't you?'

'Oh, for heaven's sake, Craig! Let's not start on that again. I've told you before, I don't neglect the children, and I don't neglect you.'

'Ah, but you are neglecting me, aren't you? You are well aware that I would like another child – yes, a boy, I'll admit it – and yet you have deliberately tried to prevent it.'

'Yes, because I am sick to death of hearing you – and your parents – going on about wanting "a little lad", as your father puts it. And how do you know, if I do want you want, that I won't go on having girls? I might end up with a dozen girls. And d'you know what? It would be down to you; it would be your fault. It's the male . . . er, seed, or whatever, that determines the sex.'

'You're talking nonsense, Lorna.'

'Oh no, I'm not! It's what the doctor told me when Joanne was born. I thought you would have known the facts of life, Craig. There's not much you don't know, is there?'

'I'm sure I don't know what you are talking about,' he answered airily, 'except to tell me that you don't want any more children. Very well then, Lorna, if that is the way you feel then there is no more to be said.' He turned away from her, burying his head in his book.

There was silence for a while – it seemed like hours, although the clock told her it was only twenty minutes –

331

whilst she flicked through the pages of a magazine, unable to settle to reading an article or even to concentrate on the pictures. She doubted that Craig was reading either. She saw him look across, fleetingly, at her once or twice, before returning to his book.

Lorna was beginning to feel, maybe, that she was at fault, and that it was she who must make the first move towards putting an end to this dreadful quarrel. They couldn't carry on like this. They had never harboured grievances for long or gone for days without speaking, as she knew some couples did.

'Craig . . .' she began cautiously, when she could bear the oppressive silence no longer. 'I'm sorry . . . I realise I was wrong. I should have told you how I felt.'

He closed his book and put it on the arm of his chair, looking at her steadily. 'It makes me sad, Lorna, to think that you don't want any more children. But you know, don't you, that I won't force you? I'm not that sort of a man. That's why it has upset me so much, to think that you had to hoodwink me like that. You should have told me. I would have carried on – you know – taking care of that side of things.'

'I just wanted a breathing space. Joanne's just started walking – and about time too! – so I'm going to have my hands full. But . . . if it's really what you want . . . another baby . . .'

'I've told you, I won't make you do anything you don't want to do. And if you'd rather wait a little while . . . so be it. But you stop taking that blasted pill, do you hear? It's you I'm concerned about. I've heard there are nasty side effects, and I don't want you to be in any danger.'

'I wasn't,' she answered, although the severe headaches she had suffered from time to time whilst talking it had worried her. 'All right; I won't take any more.'

'I do love you, you know, Lorna,' he said, 'and we mustn't quarrel like this . . . Friends again?'

'Yes . . . Friends again.' She smiled at him rather sadly. She felt that this quarrel and the others they had had recently had left a scar upon their marriage. Some of the magic they had used to know had disappeared. A thought struck her. 'Craig, what were you doing in my drawer anyway?' she asked. 'It gave me a shock. It's not like you to snoop around.'

'I wasn't snooping, darling,' he replied. 'As a matter of fact, I was looking for some wrapping paper, and I thought that was where you might keep it, in your bottom drawer. Men are hopeless at shopping for things like that, and I do have one or two surprises to wrap up . . . for a certain person.' It would be Christmas in a few days' time.

'Oh yes, I see.' She nodded. 'I'll find you some paper. It's in the kitchen drawer. You weren't looking in the right place.'

'Lorna . . . we won't let this spoil our Christmas, will we?'

'No, of course not,' she replied. 'We'll put it behind us. I'll think about what you've said.'

But they didn't make love that night, and Lorna guessed that the first move in that direction would have to come from her. Craig, also, could be stubborn.

Rachel had now broken up from school for the Christmas holiday. She was glad to see an end to the Christmas carols, nativity plays, the parties, the decorations and the making of cards, crackers and calendars; all the excited buzz which had permeated the school for the last few weeks. It was great fun while it lasted, but exhausting, although she was forced to admit that she could escape from time to time into her private little room, whereas the class teachers got no respite at all.

She was pleased when her daughter rang and said she would call that afternoon with the two little girls. Rachel's granddaughters were a source of great joy to her. She was only sorry she could not see them more often, but she was busy and so was Lorna. She was pleased, though, that Lorna's marriage was working out well. She had had doubts at first, but Lorna seemed happy, and Craig was a grand fellow.

As soon as she saw Lorna that afternoon, however, her

maternal instinct told her that there was something amiss. There was a worried look in Lorna's eyes, behind the smiling face. Robert was at home, too; he occasionally allowed himself a half-day away from his work. They all chatted together for a while and then, after a whispered word with his wife, he offered to take the girls to the nearby children's playground, just for a little while, before the light faded. He could sense there might be 'woman's' talk' in the offing. Robert departed with Joanne in the pushchair and Karen trotting along excitedly at the side; they were both very fond of Grandad Rob, as they called him.

'Now, what's the matter?' asked Rachel. 'I can see there's something troubling you. Of course, you don't have to tell me if you don't want to, love . . .' she continued, as Lorna was not answering.

'Of course I want to tell you, Mum,' she said, after a few seconds' silence, 'but I don't want to be disloyal to Craig, and I suppose I don't want you saying I told you so.'

'Lorna, love, I would never say that,' replied Rachel. 'To my mind it's a pointless remark, and I will never say it.' She looked fondly at her daughter. 'Why? What's happened? Have you and Craig fallen out?'

'Sort of . . . You always thought it wasn't right, didn't you, Mum? That I was too young to get married.'

'I had my doubts at first, darling, but that was because I didn't want you to make a big mistake . . .' Like I did, she added silently to herself. 'But when we got to know Craig we liked him very much. I thought things were going so well for you both. I was only saying to Robert the other day that you both seem very happy, with your two lovely little girls.'

'That's the problem, though. He wants a boy – you know that, don't you? He's always on about it – and I'm not sure that I want any more children, not now, maybe not ever.' She told Rachel about the pill, and Craig finding out, and their bitter quarrel. 'And now, I just don't know what to do.'

'Would it be such an awful thing to have another baby?' asked Rachel gently. 'I know it was pretty bad last time, but the doctors know about that. They would take great care of you.'

'You think I should then? That I should do as Craig wants?'

'Only if you want it as well. You're young, Lorna, and it's best to have your children while you're young. And ... it might be rather nice to have a little boy in the family again,' she added wistfully.

'You sound like Craig's dad!' said Lorna. 'Supposing it was another girl? Supposing I went on and on having girls and no boys?'

'It's worth, perhaps, one more try?' said Rachel tentatively. 'And if it's another girl, so what? At least Craig would know you had made the effort. It's worth it, isn't it, for the sake of your marriage?'

'Maybe,' said Lorna. She was silent for a moment, then, 'Do you ever think about Kevin, Mum?' she asked. 'Is that why you would like me to have a little boy?'

'It might be ...' Rachel smiled. 'I don't think there's a day goes by when I don't think of Kevin, darling. He was a little treasure, wasn't he? We all loved him so much, your dad as well. Derek thought the world of that little boy. But my thoughts are not sad any more. I remember him, and I feel glad for the joy he brought us while he was here. I can't be sad, Lorna. I have you and your girls, and Robert. We have had such a happy marriage. I'm really a very lucky person.'

'And Adam as well,' said Lorna. 'Is he coming home this Christmas?'

'Yes, Adam,' said Rachel, smiling again. 'He's been like a son to me, and a big brother to you. Yes, he'll be home for a day or two ... What I'm trying to say is that I want you to be as happy in your marriage as I am in mine. But there must be give and take on both sides. It's worth a little compromising sometimes, for the sake of peace and harmony ... Oh, here's Robert back with the girls. We'll have to be quiet. Little pigs have big ears, as they say.'

Lorna laughed. 'Oh dear, don't mention pigs, Mum! They were the cause of another row between Craig and me ... I'll remember what you've said. I'll go home and think about it all. Thanks for listening, anyway. I feel a lot better now.'

'That's what I'm here for, to listen,' said Rachel, feeling very close to her daughter. 'You must do as you think best, of course ... but what you have – you and Craig – is worth clinging on to. Just remember that.'

Lorna found herself thinking about her mother's words over the next couple of days. Her thoughts drifted to her little brother, Kevin. She had been only four years old when he died, yet she remembered him well – his resemblance to her father, Derek, his bright blue eyes, his engaging smile and his happy chatter, for he had just started to talk in an intelligible way. Lorna had two little girls and had decided she was satisfied at that. But she was beginning to realise that her decision might have been due to her stubbornness and unwillingness to give in to Craig's wishes. They had had a few battles of will and this had been her way of getting back at him.

Now, although it went against the grain, somewhat, to admit she might have been wrong and to have a complete change of heart, she came to a new decision. She would go ahead and have the baby her husband wanted so much; at least, she would go ahead and have another baby, the sex of which would be up to Fate to decide.

It had saddened her that Craig had kept his distance from her in bed, apart for the casual goodnight kiss, since their argument a few nights ago. They had behaved quite normally to one another during the day, and this day, Christmas Eve, had been particularly hectic with the final preparations for the festive season, culminating in hanging up the stockings and getting two excited little girls off to bed. When they finally went to bed themselves she drew close to him, putting her arm over his chest.

'Craig ...' she began. 'I don't want us to be like this, all distant and ... and not making love.' She took a deep breath. 'I've changed my mind. I've decided you were right. We should have another baby . . . and I think it would be lovely if it was a little boy.'

As he turned towards her she could see, in the faint light shining through the curtains, that his eyes were aglow with eagerness and with a warmth she had not seen there for quite a while. 'I'm so glad, darling,' he said, drawing her very close to him. 'Actually . . . I've been reading up about what you said. You were quite right. The sex of the child is down to me; I hadn't realised that. So I suppose it is my fault, in a way, that we've got two daughters.'

'And there's no telling we won't have another . . .'

'Never mind, darling.' He stopped her words with a passionate kiss. 'It's worth a try, isn't it?'

She did not conceive straight away. She had three more periods, and then, in April, when the expected event did not arrive, she began to be hopeful. It was soon evident that her hopes were to be fulfilled. The usual morning sickness began and the general feeling of being unwell that she had experienced with her first two children. A visit to the doctor confirmed what she already knew. And she had worked out for herself that the baby would be born on or around the twenty-fifth of December. A Christmas baby.

The early lassitude and sickness passed and she began to feel well again. Summer started early that year and the hours she spent in the sunshine with her two little girls brought a healthy tan to their faces and arms. Both Lorna and Joanne were fair-skinned, however, and had to be extra careful to protect themselves from the sun's severe rays. For it was being said, as the days grew hotter and there seemed to be no likelihood of the heat-wave ending, that this summer of 1976 was the hottest in Britain for two hundred and fifty years. All over the country reservoirs began to dry up and water rationing was enforced.

On the farm the cows seemed more lethargic than ever and loath to leave the coolness of the milking shed. The hens were crotchety and flapped around making a good deal of noise. The two cats, Tiger and Blackie, and the sheepdog, Harvey, sought patches of shade in which to rest, the dog's long pink tongue hanging out as he panted and drank thirstily from his water bowl. Lorna was sure the sheep must have been relieved when shearing time arrived; she watched them skipping and frisking around merrily in the fields, happy to be rid of their hot and bulky fleeces. Imagine wearing your thickest winter coat in this weather!

Eventually the heat was too much for Lorna. She was putting on excess weight again, as she had when she was expecting Joanne, and she was forced to rest to east her swollen ankles and her cumbersome body. And then, suddenly, without any warning, she awoke in the early hours of a morning in mid-August with severe pains. She lay still for a moment, unable to grasp what was happening. Maybe she had imagined it; a bad dream, perhaps, in which she had thought she was giving birth. But there it was again, unmistakable that time, an agonising pain clutching at her abdomen. She flung back the bedclothes and as she sat up she realised that something else was wrong. She looked down to see there was blood on her nightdress and on the sheets.

'Craig, Craig!' she cried, shaking him furiously. He was a heavy sleeper, but always woke up immediately at the sound of the alarm or if an emergency occurred. 'Wake up; there's something wrong. It's the baby! Oh, Craig, I think we're going to lose it.'

He was wide awake at once. 'Oh, God, no . . .' He was fearful when he saw what was happening, but he acted swiftly. 'Come along, darling, carefully now. Put your dressing-gown on, and I'll ring for an ambulance.' At first he had thought of calling the doctor, or running her to the hospital himself in the car, but he realised there was no time to be lost; this looked very serious.

Mercifully, the ambulance arrived in ten minutes' time and the orderlies carefully lifted Lorna on to a stretcher and into the vehicle. Craig was unable to accompany her because he could not leave the little girls, but he assured her he would be along as soon as possible when he had handed them over to his parents' care.

Lorna was bleeding quite badly by the time she arrived at Melcaster Hospital and was suffering the severest pains she had ever known. The doctor quickly put her out of her agony with an injection and then tried his hardest to save both the mother and her child. But it was too late. When Craig arrived at the hospital an hour or so later he was met by a sombre-faced doctor.

'I'm very sorry, Mr Boothroyd,' he said. 'I am afraid your wife has lost the baby.'

'But what about Lorna?' cried Craig. His thoughts at that moment were all for his wife. 'Is she all right? She's not ...'

'Your wife will be fine eventually,' said the doctor. 'But she has had a difficult time; two difficult pregnancies, in fact.' He was the doctor who had delivered Joanne. 'I was hoping everything would be normal this time, but it was not to be. I would strongly advise you to wait a while before you increase your family.'

Craig nodded soberly. 'And ... the baby? What was it? Could you tell?'

'Yes, indeed we could, Mr Boothroyd. It was a boy.'

Craig felt a stab of anguish and despair. 'But why? Why did it happen?' he asked.

'We don't really know,' replied the doctor. 'But sometimes, if there is something wrong with the child, Nature decides to abort it. Maybe it is for the best, in the long run.'

Lorna was still drowsy when Craig saw her, but she was aware of what had happened. 'I've let you down,' she said tearfully, '... again.'

'No, you haven't, darling,' he tried to assure her, holding her close. 'So long as you are all right, then that is all that matters to me. You mustn't brood on it, Lorna love. Just think about yourself and concentrate on getting well again ... I love you so much,' he added.

339

★ ★ ★

But it was from that time onwards that the sparkle irrevers-
ibly began to disappear from their marriage. They both
knew it would be unwise for her to conceive again, for a
while at least, and this brought a certain wariness to their
relationship. At Craig's insistence she had stopping taking
the pill, and they knew that other methods were not entirely
foolproof. Their lovemaking, which had once been such a joy
to both of them, became mechanical and even half-hearted at
times.

Whatever is happening to us? thought Lorna. She could
not believe that their marriage, which had been so wonderful at first, was showing signs of going the same way as so
many other marriages did, with the couple going through
the motions and staying together 'for the sake of the children'. She recalled that her own parents may have done just
that, until Sylvia had come on to the scene.

The words of a song kept running through her mind,
something about the flame of love dying. She could not
remember the title or many of the words, but it seemed so
apt, so heartbreakingly fitting. She knew she should try to
rekindle the fading embers of their love into a flame again,
but Lorna was beginning to lose heart. She feared that Craig
no longer loved her. Especially as he had begun to stay away
from home on some nights. Only occasionally, to be sure,
but she was fearful of what the future might hold.

Craig had always enjoyed attending animal auctions. There
was a monthly one in Melcaster and others further afield, in
Skipton and Settle. Neither of these places were very far
away and normally he had gone back home the same day,
once any business transactions had been completed. But
things at home were not normal at the moment. He was well
aware that the cracks that were gradually appearing in the
fabric of their marriage were not entirely Lorna's fault; he
was to blame as well. But for whatever reason, they were
there, and he felt he needed a break occasionally from the

tensions that built up when he and his wife were together. And so he had put up at a modest bed-and-breakfast place, now and again, when he had attended the auctions away from home, spending the evening in the pub with the locals, many of them farmers whom he knew, and returning home the next day feeling somewhat refreshed.

This habit he had fallen into, of being away for a night every fortnight or so, came in very handy when, in the summer of 1978, he met Avril Shaw at the Skipton auction. She bought a couple of heifers he had for sale and so they had started talking. She was a chatty person, easy to get on with, and he felt immediately that they were on the same wavelength. As it was still only just past midday he invited her to go with him for a drink and a sandwich at a public house he knew of, just behind the main street.

He learned that she was the owner of a farm near Grassington, which was only a few miles away from the market town of Skipton. He realised he may have looked surprised on hearing that she owned a farm, because she quickly went on to tell him that her husband, the joint owner, had died in a tragic accident eighteen months previously.

'The tractor skidded and overturned on an icy stretch of road,' she told him. 'A freak accident, really. No other vehicle was involved. Harry was thrown clear, but he broke his neck in the fall. There was nothing anyone could do.'

'I'm so sorry,' he said. 'How terrible for you. You don't need to tell me any more ... I'm sure it must bring back painful memories.'

'From time to time, yes, it does. But I had to pick myself up and carry on for the sake of our little boy. Simon was three and a half at the time. He's five now and he's recently started school. Have you any children, Mr Boothroyd?'

'Yes ... two little girls. Karen's six – she started school last year – and Joanne is four.'

'Two little girls! That's lovely! I was hoping Harry and I would have a little girl eventually, but ...' she gave a slight shrug, 'it was not to be. Never mind, Simon's a grand little lad, though I say it myself. He's been a real comfort to me, Mr Boothroyd.'

'I'm sure he has . . . My name's Craig,' he said, smiling at her. 'Do you think we could dispense with the formalities . . . Mrs Shaw?'

She laughed. 'Yes, of course. My name is Avril.'

'Yes, I know. You wrote it on the cheque, didn't you? I'm sure you must be pleased you have a son to follow in the tradition, aren't you? My two daughters are very dear to me, of course, but I badly wanted a son. The tragedy was that my wife was expecting again two years ago, and she had a miscarriage. It was a boy . . . and since then . . . well, it's not been too good. Tell me about yourself, though. How do you manage to run the farm on your own? I suppose you have some good farm-hands?'

He learned that she had a farm manager, Tom Jackson, who would be driving down to Skipton shortly to pick up the heifers in the cattle truck. Avril came from a farming family, she told him, one that reached back several generations, as did his own. Her husband, Harry Shaw, had taken over Whitegates Farm from his father, and on his marriage to Avril he had had the property put into joint names. There had been no problem, therefore, about inheritance when he died so suddenly, nor about the management of the farm. Craig gathered that the farm was a prosperous one; a mixed farm, rather like Sheepscar, he imagined. And he guessed, also, that Avril, with the help of her manager and farm-hands, would be more than capable of running it.

He found himself watching her intently as she talked. She was not what one might call a beautiful or even a pretty woman; her looks were too robust and distinctive to be dismissed as mere prettiness. But she was very attractive, with dark hair cut short, silvery-grey eyes, and strong features on a face which was tanned brown by the sun, although her rosy cheeks suggested she always had a healthy colour. Craig guessed her to be roughly the same age as himself, and he later learned that this was so. They were both thirty years of age.

To his consternation, he realised he was comparing her with Lorna. What an ideal wife Avril would have been for him, he thought. Two like-minded people with the same ambitions and the same view of life and of how it should be lived. He had always known that Lorna was not cut out to be a farmer's wife, and yet he had gone ahead and married her, believing and hoping that she would adapt and might even grow to like the life. He had loved her, of course, he reminded himself, passionately and – he had imagined – deeply. But had there not, also, been a certain fascination attached to Lorna because she was so unpredictable, so different from the kind of girl he had always supposed he would marry? It was too late, of course. They were married, Lorna and he, for better or for worse, and must remain so . . . for the sake of the children, he told himself.

He said goodbye to Avril later that day, telling her how pleasant it had been to meet and talk with her. The pleasure, it appeared, was mutual, and as they smiled at each other neither of them had any doubt that they would meet again.

That was how it had started. Neither of them, in the beginning, had intended to fall in love, but there was an inevitability about it. They were so right for one another, and it was not long before Craig had convinced himself that his marriage to Lorna had been a mistake.

He had lost little time in contacting Avril again; he had her address and telephone number. They had started meeting regularly, and in due course Craig began to stay overnight at Whitegates Farm. Avril, as well as Craig, felt guilty when she thought about his wife and the two little girls (whom, of course, she had not met). But it was comparatively easy to persuade herself, as Craig did, that his children would get used to the idea of their parents not living together, so long as they had their mother there to love and care for them. Simon had soon become very attached to Craig and was beginning to regard him as a father figure. But Lorna was still in ignorance of what was happening.

It was in 1980, two years after their first meeting, that Avril issued an ultimatum. 'You really must tell your wife what is going on, Craig. You are not being fair to her, or to me. I can't carry on like this, and I don't intend to either. You tell her now, or else . . . it's all over between us.'

He knew it was unlikely she would carry out her threat; she had said similar things before, but he knew that this time he really must do as she asked. He gathered her into his arms, delighted in the softness of her rounded figure and the healthy scent of her sunburned skin. 'Don't worry, my darling,' he said. 'I will tell Lorna this weekend . . . and my parents too. I give you my word.'

He dreaded telling his parents, even more than his wife, that he intended leaving Sheepscar Farm and taking over the managership of Whitegates for Avril Shaw. Tom, Avril's old manager, had now reached retiring age, so it had seemed opportune for Craig to replace him. Lorna, he suspected, might not be too surprised that the time had come for them to part. But what would Jim and Millie Boothroyd say?

He spoke to them first, before telling Lorna. They were shocked, as he had expected them to be.

'What! I can't believe I'm hearing this!' Jim took hold of his own rather prominent ears and waggled them to and fro. 'What the bloody hell are you talking about, lad? You're saying you've got friendly with some woman or other, and you're going to shack up with her and manage a farm for her? Over my dead body! What about this 'ere farm? You were going to take over from me, weren't you, when the time came? And what about your wife, and your kiddies? Do they know about this?'

'No, not yet, Dad,' replied Craig, a trifle uneasily. 'I've come to tell you first. About this farm . . . I daresay we could still come to some arrangement when the time comes. I know you wanted me to take it over.'

'Aye, well, that was the intention. But this 'ere puts a different complexion on things. It seems as though you've got other ideas. Well, I might change me mind an' all.'

'You've got plenty of excellent farm-hands, even if I'm not here,' Craig went on. 'Those two new lads, Percy and Ron, they're getting the hang of things, and Jack could easily take over as manager; he's very capable.'

'Oh aye, you've got it all worked out, haven't you? I can see now what you were up to.' Jim nodded knowingly. 'Persuading me as we needed some more hands, and that yer mother needed a new dairymaid.'

'So I did, Jim,' said Millie. 'Ellen was getting past it, and this new lass is shaping up really well. Just listen to the lad, now, instead of going off the deep end. I'd guessed, even if you hadn't, that there was summat wrong between our Craig and Lorna. Much as we love the lass she's not really got used to being a farmer's wife, has she?'

'No, I'll grant you that,' said Jim. 'But she's a grand little woman is Lorna, even though she can't tell one end of a cow from t'other. And in my day fellows stuck by their wives and didn't go off with some other wench as took their fancy. What do you intend to do about Lorna and the little girls, anyroad? Have you thought about that, eh? Lilac Cottage is their home.'

'Yes, I realise that,' replied Craig. 'That's why I've come to see you first, you and Mum.' He sighed deeply. 'I didn't want this to happen, believe me, but Lorna and me . . . it's all washed up. She knows it as well as I do. The cottage is mine, isn't it? You gave it to us as a wedding present. So I intend to put it into Lorna's name, and it'll be hers for as long as she wants it. That's if you agree, of course?'

'That's the first sensible thing you've said so far,' replied his father. 'Of course we agree, don't we, Millie? Lorna's got to have a home, and our two little granddaughters. Nay, lad . . .' Jim shook his head despairingly, 'I can't understand what the hell you think you're playing at.'

'I'm sorry; I knew you'd feel like this,' said Craig. 'But there's no turning back. I've made up my mind. Lorna will manage all right; there's no rent and no mortgage for her to see to. She'll be OK.'

'Aye, apart from the fact that her husband's walking out on her,' said Jim, giving him a look of disgust. 'I don't like it and I never will. But you'd best get off now and tell your wife before somebody else does. And make sure you tell her that her home is still here, on t' farm with us, whether you're here or not.'

He told Lorna that evening when the girls had gone to bed. She accepted his news, at first, more calmly than his father had done; his mother, to his surprise, had been more understanding.

'Why didn't you tell me before?' asked Lorna, quite matter-of-factly. 'I'm not entirely stupid, Craig. I knew you had met someone else. I just didn't know who it was.'

'I'm really sorry, Lorna.' She could tell he was finding it difficult to meet her eye. 'I did love you so much, I still do . . . care about you. But it's not right, is it? It's never really been right. I shouldn't have married you; it was not fair to you. But it's been worse since you lost the baby. Everything seemed to fall apart then. You'll be better off without me . . .' His soliloquy petered out as he became aware of her staring coldly at him.

'It fell apart when you met this Avril person,' she said bitterly. 'What I find so unbelievable is that you have been carrying on with her for so long. Two years, you say?'

'I kept meaning to tell you, Lorna, but I didn't want to hurt you. And I thought it would be better if I waited till the children were older. Old enough to understand, perhaps. Karen's eight now, isn't she, and Joanne's six . . .'

'Oh, so you think that's old enough, do you, Craig? Let me tell you that children never really understand when their parents split up.' Lorna was remembering her own heartache when her father left. 'Their parents may pretend they do to make themselves feel better, but they don't. Anyway, I shall leave you to tell Karen and Joanne. For the moment I have nothing more to say to you.'

She left the room, unable to hold back her tears any

longer, and she did not want him to see her crying. In the solitude of her bedroom under the eaves she flung herself on to the bed, weeping silently. Her wonderful marriage had gone all to dust. A quotation – Shakespeare, she thought – flashed into her mind.

'Golden lads and girls all must, as chimney sweepers, come to dust . . .'

Their marriage had been a golden one, full of promise and hope and love. And now . . . it was nothing but dust and ashes . . .

Chapter 22

'Oh, Lorna, I'm sorry, so terribly sorry. I can't believe this is happening,' said Rachel when Lorna broke the news to her the following week.

She had waited until Craig had departed for his new abode in Grassington, which he did quite quickly once he had made up his mind. The girls had been more puzzled than upset. He had promised he would come and see them often. He also told them that they must come and see him at the farm where he was working, 'if it's all right with Mummy'. She realised he was giving the impression that he was simply working elsewhere, and not admitting that he had a new lady friend and that he and Mummy were living apart. Lorna remembered that that was exactly what her own father had implied when he had gone to live with Sylvia, but she, Lorna, had not been fooled, and neither would Karen and Joanne be, she suspected.

'You mustn't worry about me, Mum,' said Lorna. 'I'll be fine, honestly I will. I've got the cottage – at least Craig has acted honourably there, and his parents, too – and, thankfully, I've learned to drive, so there will be no problem about the girls getting to school.' She had been driving for about six months, passing her test the first time, and Craig had bought her a Mini Shooting Brake of her own. Was it a guilt present? she had wondered at the time, and now she was sure of it.

'I may even go back to Paige's, part-time,' she said. 'Brian keeps telling me there's a job for me there if ever I want one.' She had kept up with her assignments, working from home,

348

but she realised she would have time on her hands – too much time – now that Craig had left and it might be an opportune moment to take up Brian Paige's offer.

'Yes, I think that's a good idea,' said Rachel. 'It would stop you sitting around and brooding. I found my teaching was a godsend when your father and I parted. Of course, teaching is convenient when you have a family, because your holidays coincide with your children's. It's rather more difficult with other jobs. But I would always be here to help during the holidays. You go for it, darling, if it's what you want.'

Lorna nodded. 'Yes, I'm considering it. It will be the long summer holiday soon, so come September I'll see what I can do.'

'You're very calm about it all, dear,' said Rachel, 'but then, I suppose . . . you might have had some idea what was going on?'

'You should have seen me a few days ago,' said Lorna. 'I was OK when Craig first told me, and then I went to pieces. I felt like tearing him to shreds at times. And at other times I was just . . . sad. So sad that it should all come to nothing. But you were always doubtful, weren't you, Mum?'

'I have wondered recently,' replied Rachel, 'about the two of you. I could see things were not right. But before that – after my first misgivings – I thought you had a lot going for you. Far more than your dad and I ever had. You were so happy and seemed to love one another so much . . . Oh dear! It's like history repeating itself. I'm so sorry, darling; I didn't want you to have to go through the same traumas as I did. But you know that Robert and I are always there for you. You must let us know if there is anything we can do to help. I suppose . . . you will be getting a divorce?'

'We might,' said Lorna, in a casual tone. 'On the other hand, I might refuse, or make him wait a long time. I certainly don't want to get married again.'

Adam looked shocked when his father told him that his step-sister's marriage had come to grief.

'That's despicable,' he said, 'going off and leaving her with two little girls. How low can he stoop? I feel like going and giving him a piece of my mind; in fact, I'd like to punch his head in, treating Lorna like that.'

Adam was back in Melcaster for what was a very rare weekend at home. He now had his own flat in Leeds, quite near to the city centre, which he had bought, rather than renting. At the age of thirty-one he was doing very well. He was now the chief sports reporter for his newspaper, and as well as reporting other hot topics of news and doing the book reviews he had his own column, which came out once a week on a Friday evening.

In this column he was permitted to write whatsoever he chose, be it about world events, or more local events, or he could air his views on things which were of interest or importance to him. The first woman prime minister, Margaret Thatcher, who had come into office the previous year, gave him a lot of scope with her hardline policies and her 'lady's not for turning' speech. And across the Atlantic Ocean in the USA the Republicans had chosen the former actor, Ronald Reagan, as their presidential candidate. Adam was inclined to agree with cynics who declared that Mr Reagan had never read a book, apart from the Bible, in his life, and that his mind, therefore, was free of any intellectual clutter, but he was prepared to give him a chance in his resolution to bring back the glory days to the USA.

Often though, Adam wrote about simpler issues: the rebuilding and modernisation that was going on in nearby Bradford, in the name of progress, and which he deplored; or the visit of a well-known pop group to the Leeds town hall, once the undisputed province of the Yorkshire Symphony Orchestra; or the upsurge in the use of home video recorders, with which you could, miraculously, record even when the TV set was switched off.

All other matters paled into insignificance, however, when Adam heard about Lorna and Craig's marriage. 'I'd like to kill him,' he said, but more broodingly than viciously.

Robert knew he was not at all likely to carry out his threat, either to kill Craig or to give him a good thumping; Adam was not that sort of guy. But his father was watching him very carefully; his reaction had certainly been extreme.

'I don't think we should condemn Craig too harshly,' Robert said cautiously. 'I know what he has done is wrong. Obviously we can't condone it, but Rachel and I have known for some time that things were not right between them. Maybe it was never right; we've never been able to see Lorna as a farmer's wife. She didn't fit in, you know, and I'm sorry to say that I don't think she always tried to.'

'Then he shouldn't have asked her to marry him, should he? It's certainly not Lorna's fault, any of it. She was only a girl. Only eighteen, wasn't she? Far too young to be married.' Adam sounded indignant, unwilling to believe that Lorna was in any way to blame.

'Well, they loved one another very much at the time, or so we believed,' said Robert. 'Rachel and I grew quite fond of Craig. We found him to be a very pleasant and helpful young man. Rather self-opinionated, of course, but that's public school for you. You didn't know him as well as we did, though, did you?'

'No, I don't suppose I did,' said Adam, sounding preoccupied.

'And what about you?' asked his father. 'What about your love life? Is it working out all right with . . . Sally? That was the name of your latest one, wasn't it?'

'Don't say it like that, Dad, as though I've got a different girl every week. I'm not a Casanova, you know. Some of them are just good friends, that's all. But – no – it didn't work out with Sally. I'm too choosy, I suppose. The trouble is I can't find anybody to compare with . . . well, the sort of girl I have in mind.'

Robert looked at him curiously for a moment before saying, 'It's Lorna, isn't it? You're comparing every girl you meet with Lorna. I'm right, aren't I?'

351

'Yes . . . I'm afraid so, Dad.' Adam gave a long shuddering sigh. 'It's a relief to tell you, really, but you won't say anything to Rachel, will you? She would think it wasn't quite right. She might even think it was shocking. She always refers to Lorna as my sister, but she isn't, is she, not really? Well, not at all.'

'No, she's not your sister. She's no relation to you,' said Robert thoughtfully. 'So there's no reason at all . . . How long have you felt like this about Lorna?'

'Oh, ages and ages. I'm not sure how long, but it's a good while since I stopping thinking of her as my kid sister. I love her, Dad, I really do, but I've never been able to tell her. She doesn't feel the same way about me. I know she doesn't.'

'But I don't suppose you've tried to find out, have you?'

'No, I haven't. I went away when she was in her early teens, and then, suddenly, she'd grown up, and I realised what she meant to me. And then, almost before I knew it, she'd gone and married Craig Boothroyd. I tried to like him – I did like him – and I tried to get over my feelings for her . . . but I can't.' He stared broodingly across the room, with unseeing eyes.

Robert was at a loss as to what to say, but he knew that Lorna was in too vulnerable a state at the moment to cope with such revelations.

'Keep it to yourself, Dad,' said Adam, seeming to come to his senses again. 'Just for now, at any rate. Rachel will be in soon, won't she, so we'd better act normally.' It was four-thirty on a Friday afternoon and Rachel would soon be back from school.

'No, your secret's safe with me,' said Robert. 'And I think . . . well, I think it would be great, eventually, if things were to work out the way you want them to. But Lorna's in a highly sensitive state of mind at the moment. She can be very touchy and unpredictable; well, you know what she's like, don't you? So it might be advisable not to say anything yet awhile.'

'Don't worry, Dad. I don't intend to,' said Adam. 'But I'll

call round and see her and the girls as I would have done in any case. I'll go tomorrow.'

He found Lorna in a bright and brittle mood the following day.

'I don't want to talk about Craig,' she said. 'I'm sure my mum and your dad will have told you all you need to know. We can't talk anyway, while the girls are here. I've made a picnic tea, Adam, and I thought we could have a drive out somewhere. Bolton Abbey, maybe; the girls like it by the river there.'

Karen and Joanne both loved Uncle Adam and looked forward to his visits. They spent a happy, carefree afternoon together on the banks of the River Wharfe.

'Are you and Craig going to get a divorce?' Adam asked tentatively, when the girls were out of earshot. 'I suppose you will have to, won't you?'

'I don't see why,' replied Lorna. 'It wasn't my idea for us to separate. No. Why should I? I'll make him wait, the two-timing bastard! Anyway, I've told you, Adam, I don't want to talk about it.'

'OK,' said Adam resignedly. 'Just as you wish . . . Tell me about your art work. Have you anything new in mind?' He felt his spirits plummet. Lorna's overconfident voice told him she was still in love with her husband.

Lorna settled into a routine with her two daughters, more because she knew she must, than because she was happy about it. Craig had gone and that was that, but there was one thing about which she was determined. She was not going to give way and let him have an easy divorce, even though he was prepared to admit to being the guilty party – which, indeed, he was – and provide her with sufficient grounds. This was her way of punishing him; she could think of no other. She would not refuse to let him see the girls; that would be petty and spiteful. Besides the fact that he had the right to see them, according to the law, which he did almost every week, she would never let her girls suffer any more than they had to as a result of the marriage break-up.

Lorna well remembered her own visits to see her father in Ripon, and how it had gradually dawned on her that the woman whose premises he was occupying was, in fact, not just his landlady, but his mistress. Not that the word 'mistress' would have come into her thinking as a child, but she knew that Sylvia had taken her mother's place in Derek's affections. Quite soon, of course, the two of them were married, and her mother had married Robert.

She did not doubt that Karen and Joanne would draw their own conclusions about what was happening without her having to explain too much. Karen, always the more forward of the two sisters, had already asked, quite a while ago, why she had three grandads when most other children had only two: Grandad Jim at the farm, Grandad Derek in Ripon – whose wife, for some reason, was known as Aunty Sylvia – and Grandad Rob who was married to Grandma Rachel. Lorna had explained, very truthfully, that their grandma had once been married to Grandad Derek, and they had seemed to understand. So maybe the complexity of this present situation would not be too much of a trauma for them.

The two girls were both happy at the school they attended, so Lorna had no worries in that direction; she knew it was important that they should be contented at school. They did not attend Kilbeck Primary, where their grandma was the head of the infant school, but North Road School, the one nearest to Sheepscar Farm, on the road which led northwards out of Melcaster.

Lorna started work again at Paige's factory towards the end of 1980. It wasn't so much that she wanted or needed a job – she had been contented enough to work at home on her artistic commissions, and she had been very satisfied with the remunerative rewards – but she knew that the countryside surrounding Lilac Cottage, though lovely in spring and summer, could appear gloomy and oppressive in wintertime. She needed to get out for a part of each day for a change of environment, to meet different people and to stop herself becoming depressed and too introspective. Brian Paige offered her a part-time position in the accounts office, doing roughly the same job as she had done before. She was satisfied with this. Lorna knew, and Brian Paige knew, too, that she would have been capable of leading the team in the design department, but Marion Grundy still held that position. All Lorna required was a job that would fill a few hours of each day, where she was amongst people with whom she could share companionship and feel she was at home.

She laughed and chatted with them during the break-times, and went out occasionally in the evening with some of her former associates who still worked there; her mother and Robert were always willing to baby-sit, as were Jim and Millie, who still did not hold with the way their son was behaving. No one would imagine, watching Lorna joking with her pals as though she didn't have a care in the world, that her heart was still very sore. She would not say it was breaking – she was made of sterner stuff than that – but she still loved Craig, and part of her, although she realised it might be foolish and futile, still longed for him to come to his senses and return to her. And she knew this was the reason why she was still refusing to grant him a divorce.

Two years were to pass before Lorna finally realised that what she was still hoping and praying for was not going to happen. The year of 1981 brought a collective sigh of heartfelt relief to the inhabitants of the West Riding of Yorkshire when, in May of that year, Peter Sutcliffe was jailed for life after committing the Yorkshire Ripper murders. Adam, working in Leeds, was particularly relieved; his young woman colleagues in the office had been too terrified to venture out in the dark, and he had worried, too, for his beloved Lorna in Melcaster, which was not too far distant. He still wanted to be near her, to take care of her always, but, alas, she was still officially married to that bounder, Craig Boothroyd.

In July, Prince Charles married Lady Diana Spencer in St Paul's Cathedral, watched live on television by 700 million people. Lorna, watching the beautiful young bride smiling and waving to the cheering crowds, sensed, somehow, her underlying apprehension. She had been even younger than Diana when she had married Craig. She had been so in love with her husband, so full of optimism, and yet a little fearful, too. I hope they will be happy, thought Lorna. I hope that they will still be as happy in ten years' time as they are today, not lamenting that their marriage is all in ruins, as mine is . . .

1982 was a year filled with war and violence: the Falklands conflict, the escalation in the Middle East of the war between Iraq and Iran, and the bombing by the IRA of the Horse Guards in Regent's Park. On a happier note, Princess Diana gave birth to a son, William, on June twenty-first.

And it was the news, coming at the end of 1982, that Avril, Craig's new lady love, was pregnant that finally made Lorna agree to a divorce. She knew that any hopes she might have had for a reconciliation with her husband were finally dashed. It would be pointless now, as well as small-minded, to behave in anything less than a civilised manner.

She even agreed to a meeting with Avril, early in 1983, and was surprised to find that she did not dislike the woman. She found her to be honest and straightforward, as well as pleasant, not making any attempt to dissemble or to show remorse at stealing another woman's husband. At least, that was how Lorna had viewed the situation before the meeting, but she now realised that Avril was far more suitable to be a wife to Craig than she had ever been. Karen and Joanne appeared to like her too, and they got on well with her son, Simon. He was a friendly little lad, who was now nine years old, a year younger than Karen and a year older than Joanne.

Lorna could not help feeling a pang of regret and sadness at the thought of the five of them playing at happy families together, and she felt convinced, too, that the child Avril would give birth to later that year would be a boy. Craig would get the son he longed for; two boys, in fact, because he seemed to get along extremely well with Simon.

It was not that Karen and Joanne went to visit their father and his new family all that often, but that situation, quite soon, was about to change. The main reason for Avril coming to visit Sheepscar Farm early in 1983 was because, in a few months' time, she would be living there. Jim and Millie Boothroyd had decided it was time they retired. Jim suffered with lumbago, and Millie's hands were becoming knotted with arthritis; her work in the dairy, often in freezing temperatures in the winter, was finally taking its toll. They were buying a small bungalow, not too far from the farm, on the road leading to Melcaster, and Sheepscar Farm was to be handed over to Craig. They had made threats when Craig had taken up with Avril – particularly Jim – that they might well change their minds about their son inheriting the property. But he was, after all, their only son, blood was thicker than water, and their anger had diminished as the years had passed. Craig would be the new owner and he would live at Sheepscar House with his new wife and family. Avril's farm, Whitegates, would be sold and the profits used, in part, to restock and to make improvements to Sheepscar.

All three of them, however – Jim, Millie and Craig – were agreed that this would make no difference at all to Lorna. Lilac Cottage was her home; it belonged to her unreservedly, to do with as she wished. This was part of the divorce settlement, along with maintenance for Karen and Joanne. Lorna loved her home. She was happy there, at least as happy as she could be in view of all that had happened. She did not want to leave it, but she could foresee that having her former husband and his new wife living only ten minutes' walk away was too close for comfort.

Lorna was now thirty years old and newly divorced. She had thought it would not make much difference to her – after all, she and Craig had been living apart for three years – but she was surprised to feel that a part of her was missing. She felt incomplete, sort of hollow inside, and she knew she had reached a turning point in her life. It would be better, she decided, for both her and the girls, if she were to get right away from the farm. As she had feared, it was too claustrophobic living close to the new Boothroyd family. Craig had married Avril in June, and in July she had given birth to a boy, Timothy James. Craig had tried to act in a matter-of-fact way – Lorna appreciated his attempt not to upset her too much – but she could tell he was jubilant. She had found it hard to keep her emotions under control as she admired the baby, and gave way to tears when she was alone.

'Why don't you go away for a holiday?' her mother suggested, towards the end of the long summer holiday from school. 'You look tired, darling, and I know you've been through a trying time just lately.'

'We've had a holiday, Mum,' she replied. 'I took the girls to Butlins for a week, didn't I?'

'Which was fine for them, but not much in your line, was it, love?'

'No, not really . . . but they're going back to school in a week or two so there isn't time. Especially Karen starting at the grammar school.'

'Actually, I was thinking you could have a few days – or longer if you wish – on your own. Robert and I would look after the girls. You think about it, love. You deserve it, and it would do you the world of good.'

'On my own? I don't know that I fancy that . . . Anyway, I'm putting the cottage up for sale. I've decided; we can't stay there, Mum. It's driving me mad, never knowing when I'm going to bump into Craig or Avril, and the girls are continually running round to the farmhouse. It's not right, we're too much on top of one another.'

'Well, I must say I agree with that. I think it would be wise to move from there, but you can think about that later. There's no rush, is there? Look, I've got a travel brochure here. Take it and have a look at it. Robert and I have had some lovely holidays with Galaxy Tours, you know. Italy and Austria . . .'

To satisfy her mother Lorna took the brochure home. She idly flicked through the pages, but soon found herself mesmerised by the tempting holidays that were on offer. She had been abroad only a few times, to Brittany, Holland, and Belgium, with her mother and Robert, and Adam, of course. She and Craig and the girls had holidayed much nearer home, in Scarborough, Filey or – once – in the Isle of Man.

Would she dare to go? she wondered. Could she pluck up the courage to go on one of these tours on her own? Why not? She was not a young girl any more, she had never been what you might call shy, and her mother assured her that people on coach holidays were always very friendly; you need never feel that you were on your own. When she went into the travel agent's on the high street she felt sure she had left it too late; they would be booked up for mid-September. But, to her surprise, there were several vacancies. She came away scarcely believing that she had booked for an eight-day holiday – she did not want to leave the girls for any longer – by coach and air to Italy. She would be staying on the shores of Lake Maggiore and Lake Garda.

Adam's sabbatical had been arranged for quite some time. His newspaper had granted him three months' leave and he had been saving up like mad to take himself off to the USA, to travel, of course, and to see the sights that interested him the most, but also to give himself time to get on with the writing of his novel which, at the moment, was at the planning stage. It was to be a murder mystery, set in Yorkshire, for which he would draw upon his knowledge of the crimes he had reported, the villains he had encountered in court, and the police officers he had met. All purely fictional, of course, but the more he thought about the hero-detective of his novel, DI Guy Summersby, the closer he became to him, almost as though he were a friend or relation.

Adam knew he needed a change, not just of environment, but to clear his head. He had been dwelling on his feelings for Lorna for far too long. He believed it would be wrong to tell her how he felt until she was divorced, and she had dragged her heels about that, which only convinced him the more that she still loved her husband. By the time she had made up her mind – or had had it made up for her – Adam had already planned his sabbatical. The only person, still, in whom he had confided was his father.

'Off you go to the States, lad,' said Robert, 'and have a damn good time. It'll help you to sort your feelings out, if you get right away from everything.'

'I won't change my mind about Lorna,' said Adam. 'I love her, Dad, and I know I always will. I've waited long enough, but I think she needs time to adjust right now; she's still hurting. But at least she knows now that it's all over between her and Craig. When I come back I shall tell her how I feel . . .'

Galaxy Tours were becoming very well known, particularly in the north of England, for their coach tours, both at home and abroad, especially as they managed to combine comfortable hotels, appetising food and interesting locations without being too pricey. It was only last year that they had started using air travel as an alternative to the cross-channel ferry and the long drive across parts of Europe. Lorna had flown only twice before, once to the Isle of Man when the children were small, and before that, on a family holiday to Brittany, soon after her mother had married Robert. She had chosen to fly this time as she wanted to make the most of their precious time in Italy without too much coach travelling.

She felt all of a flutter inside on the morning of her departure, although she managed to hide her nervousness in front of Robert, who was driving her to the pick-up point in Melcaster, and the girls, who did not mind at all that she was having a holiday on her own – they were looking forward to spending a week with their gran and Grandad Rob.

Lorna was the only one to be picked up at the bus stop near the market square at eight-thirty on a sunny September morning. A cheery driver loaded her case into the boot, she kissed the girls and Robert, who would now be driving them to their schools, and then, with a slight lump in her throat, she boarded the coach, carrying her travel bag and a light raincoat. There were a few people on the coach already; it had started its journey in York and after various pick-up points en route would arrive eventually at Manchester airport.

She sat on her own as there was plenty of room, looking out at the familiar scenery which she was leaving behind and hoping she had made the right decision. It had seemed like a good idea at the time to have a holiday on her own, but now she was not too sure. The next pick-up point was in Leeds, where a chatty middle-aged woman came and sat next to her for the rest of the journey. Lorna reminded herself that this was only what they called the 'feeder' coach. They were to board their holiday coach on arrival in Milan. It was doubtful that this woman would have the seat next to her then; she might not even be on the same tour.

'Where are you going, dear?' asked the woman. 'It would be nice if we were on the same tour, wouldn't it? I'm on my own as well, so we could pal up, couldn't we? I'm going to Tuscany and Florence.'

'Sorry, I'm going to the Italian Lakes,' said Lorna, trying to sound regretful, but in truth experiencing a feeling of relief.

'Oh dear, what a pity!' said the woman. 'Never mind; I usually find somebody else who's travelling on their own. Another woman, of course.' She nudged Lorna's elbow. 'I've had enough of men to last me a lifetime.' She glanced surreptitiously at Lorna's left hand. She still wore her wedding ring; after all, she was still called Mrs Boothroyd, even though it no longer meant anything. But Lorna would not be drawn into divulging details of her private life, and the woman was not quite bold enough to ask. Before they got off the coach at Manchester airport, however, Lorna had learned that her companion had been married twice and divorced twice. She felt rather sorry for her; all the same, she was not sorry to say goodbye.

361

She was relieved when she had located the correct departure desk, had her luggage checked in and, finally, found the gate through which to go to board the plane. She followed the herd, staying close to the ones who had the Galaxy label on their travel bags. By the time she boarded the aircraft she no longer felt nervous; in fact, she was rather proud of herself for coping so well with the initial stages of the journey.

The flight was not what one might call the height of luxury, but she found it an interesting experience. A late luncheon was served – breast of chicken in a white wine sauce, followed by a piece of chocolate gateau and strong coffee. She was amazed at the speed with which the meal was cleared away afterwards, but there was little time to spare as it was a short flight to Milan. Lorna still had not met any of the travellers who would be on her tour. The two men next to her on the plane were obviously Italian businessmen, who had smiled at her, but then had talked solely to one another during the journey.

She stepped off the aeroplane into brilliant sunshine. The weather in England, though still sunny at times, had turned chilly now in the mornings and evenings, and this was something else. A hot sun blazed down out of a cloudless azure-blue sky, although the lengthening shadows across the tarmac showed that it would soon be evening. Lorna was relieved that the Galaxy tour company had organised everything so well. When they had reclaimed their luggage and had their passports checked, the various tour guides were there to escort them to their coaches, waiting outside the airport.

The courier of the Italian Lakes tour was a jolly young woman of about Lorna's age who introduced herself as Gina. The driver was called Mario, and he smiled and waved at the company although he spoke hardly any English. The seats on the coach were pre-booked. Lorna's was about halfway back, seat number twenty-two, and it seemed for a few moments as though seat number twenty-one might be left vacant. Then a man boarded the coach, scrutinising the numbers on the sides of the seats, as everyone did when searching for their rightful place. He stopped at number twenty-one.

'This is me, I think,' he said, smiling at Lorna. 'Well, well; it seems as though I've struck lucky, doesn't it?'

Oh crikey! she thought, suddenly feeling very shy and unsure of herself. She didn't think she could cope with flirtatious remarks or a man who might try to 'get off' with her. Not knowing how to answer, she simply smiled back at him, cautiously, and said, 'Yes . . . it's your seat.'

She had noticed him before. He had already been on the feeder coach when she boarded it and she presumed he had got on at York. He was, as the old cliché went, tall, dark and handsome! She took him to be older than herself; early forties, maybe. His hair was greying slightly at the temples and when he smiled he revealed gleaming white and even teeth. His own? she wondered in passing, thinking he was altogether too good to be true, but she was certainly not ready for a flirtation.

'We'd best introduce ourselves,' he said, 'seeing that we're to be travelling companions. My name's Benedict Frazer, or Ben – that's what folks usually call me. How do you do?' He held out his hand and she felt hers enclosed in a firm grasp.

'How do you do?' she replied. 'I'm Lorna. Lorna Boothroyd. I'm . . . pleased to meet you.' She knew that that was not considered correct, but she felt she must say something. This was not what she had anticipated; in fact, she had not given any thought as to who might be sitting next to her.

'Have you been to Italy before?' he asked, the sort of question fellow travellers invariably asked one another. She replied that she hadn't, and she learned that he was quite a seasoned traveller, having visited Rome, Florence, Venice and Milan, but this, he said, was to be more of a relaxing holiday.

He was easy to talk to and his soft-spoken voice with more

than a trace of the familiar Yorkshire accent was pleasant to the ears. She soon discovered that she might have misjudged him. He did not make any further attempts to faze her with teasing remarks, but just seemed pleased to chat to her. He told her that he was a dealer in antiques; he had a shop in York on one of the little cobbled streets near the Minster. His trustworthy assistant, Alec, who lived in the flat above the shop, was in charge this week. Ben himself lived on the outskirts of York on the road leading to Knaresborough. He was divorced, but he had custody of his son, Nick, who was nearly sixteen and in his O-level year at school. He also had a daughter, Chloe, who was eighteen and shared a flat with her boyfriend. His former wife was now living in Canada with her new husband.

He told her all this in quite a matter-of-fact manner, neither playing for sympathy nor being blasé about his circumstances. In the face of such openness, Lorna felt she must be equally open and honest with him. She told him she was recently divorced and that she had two daughters. She also told him that she had chosen this particular holiday because she wanted to do some sketching. She hoped to find inspiration for her work as a commercial artist in what she had been told was the magnificent scenery of northern Italy.

By the time they had arrived at their destination, the little town of Stresa on the shore of Lake Maggiore, Lorna felt as though she had known Benedict Frazer for years.

Chapter 23

It was an idyllic week for Lorna, and she believed it was for Ben, too. By mutual agreement they sat together for meals, although neither had asked the other if they should; it was just assumed that they would stay together. Several of their fellow travellers thought that they were already a couple – even on their arrival in Stresa it had seemed so – and were surprised to discover that they had only just met.

The hotel was quite a modest one, but with a homely and friendly ambience. They enjoyed a variety of well-cooked and typically Italian dishes, as well as roast beef and roast pork, served for the benefit of the English guests! But Lorna and Ben much preferred the pizzas and pasta dishes prepared in the way only real Italians were capable of. The hotel was situated on Stresa's tree-lined promenade, across the road from Lake Maggiore. Lorna was fortunate enough to have a front bedroom which overlooked the lake and the lovely Borromean Islands.

The only fault she could find with the room – apart from its size; all single rooms were pitifully small – was that it was very noisy. It was on the main road which encircled the lake, and until the early hours of the morning traffic could be heard zooming by – cars and motorbikes with blaring horns (the Italian police seemed to have little control of either the speed or the noise), as well as the sound of strident Italian voices. They stayed there for three nights, but it was only on the first night that Lorna was kept awake. She was overtired by the journey and the events of the day, but unable to sleep because of the tumult of thoughts in her mind.

Be careful, she told herself that first night. She had met a very personable man, and she was attracted to him as she believed he was to her. But they were both on holiday, far removed from the reality of life and work back home in Yorkshire. She was determined to enjoy herself, but to remember that this would be just a holiday friendship and could never be anything more.

She was to discover that a holiday in Italy was by no means a peaceful or a quiet one. Maybe in the small villages of the Dolomites, which they visited on an excursion later in the week, peace and tranquillity could be found, but the lake resorts were filled with noise and laughter and the sound of music from the many cafés and bars. As they sat, on the second evening, drinking their lagers and martinis at a lakeside bar, they were serenaded by a swarthy musician with black curly hair and black twinkling eyes, playing his violin and singing the melodious Italian airs, so much more poignant when heard in the magical setting of a moonlight night, in the country of their origin and with a pleasant companion at one's side. It was then that Ben held Lorna's hand for the first time, and when they returned to the hotel he kissed her very gently on the cheek; nothing more. As she lay in bed that night she could hear the strains of 'Santa Lucia' drifting through the partially open window, now and again drowned out by the sound of the traffic.

During the day the lakeside resorts were a blaze of colour, late summer flowers blooming in the gardens and the flower-erbeds and hanging baskets on the promenade. The waters of the lake were a clear, bright blue, and as they sailed across to the Borromean Islands the sun shone down from a cloudless sky. Isola Bella, the largest island, was the site of a magnificent palace and beautifully laid-out gardens, but Lorna preferred the more peaceful Isola dei Pescatori on which there was a small fishing village.

It was here that she wandered away to be on her own for a while. Ben understood that she needed solitude – if it were possible to find any on an island besieged by tourists – to sketch and to take her photographs which would help her with her paintings when she returned home. The little island was overrun by cats, black, ginger, tabby and tortoiseshell, living happily amongst the fish and the certainty of regular meals. One large stripey one reminded Lorna of Tiger, back home on the farm. He sat still long enough to allow her to do a drawing of him, against a background of colourful fishing boats. She took a photo, too, to remind her of the bright red and yellow hulls against the vivid blue of the lake. Then the cat got up and stretched lazily, before giving her an arrogant stare and prowling away again.

They left Stresa behind on the fourth day of the holiday, travelling through rugged alpine scenery to their second resort, the town of Garda, situated at the southern end of the lake with the same name. Here, the stretch of water was so wide that you could imagine you were at the seaside, and the other side of the lake was way out of sight. The hotel was more peaceful, situated in a quiet street away from the town. Garda was an ancient town of narrow cobbled streets, stone archways, ochre-tinted houses with crumbling plaster, and fascinating shops selling all manner of merchandise to attract the tourists – silk scarves in vibrant colours, leather handbags and purses, ceramics, silverware, ash-trays and dishes made from onyx or marble, Venetian glassware – as well as the butcher's, baker's and general stores where the local folk bought their speckled sausages and salami, their myriad varieties of pasta, and their exotic fruit and vegetables – glossy purple aubergines, gigantic yellow and green striped marrows, velvety peaches and apricots, and oranges the size of which Lorna had never seen before.

She spent time on her own there, buying gifts for the family and some little treats for herself, whilst Ben wandered off in search of antiques shops. He was sure he would find a few hidden away in the backstreets. He had a nose, he told her, for sniffing them out. When Lorna had done her shopping she found a quiet, shaded square away from the

367

clamour and the crowds. She made a sketch of one of the lovely old houses where washing hung from the balcony and a window box overflowed with scarlet geraniums and begonias. There did not seem to be any sign of life, apart from the washing, in the yellow stuccoed building with the closed shutters, but she kept her eyes open lest an irate Italian *donna* should appear and send her about her business. But this did not happen. Lorna concluded that whoever lived there might be having a siesta, something English visitors were disinclined to do.

Their last evening was spent in Milan, as it was from there that they were to fly home the next day. Ben and Lorna sat at a café in the square which housed the massive cathedral, Lorna savouring the taste of the strong Italian vermouth that she had learned to appreciate this last week. It had been a truly magical time. She knew the sights and sounds and the smells of this happy and bewitching country would remain with her for ever. The aroma of roasted coffee beans and that unique fragrance of foreign tobacco was all around her now. She wished that this moment might never end . . . All the same, she knew she was looking forward to seeing her family again, especially her two dear little girls. They seemed a lifetime and a million miles away.

'What are you thinking about?' asked Ben, placing his hand over hers. 'Come back to earth, Lorna love; you're miles away.'

'So I am,' she smiled back at him. 'You know what I'm thinking about, don't you? Going back home tomorrow. It has been a wonderful week, Ben, and I have enjoyed being with you so much, but . . . well, we have to return to reality now, don't we?'

He squeezed her hand. 'You're making it sound as though it's all coming to an end. It doesn't need to, you know. I don't want our friendship to end, Lorna.' She could see from the warmth and the look of fondness in his eyes that he was sincere in what he was saying.

'I don't know, Ben,' she replied. 'I've been telling myself all week that this is a holiday friendship, and that I will go back to my family, and you will go back to yours . . . and that is that.'

'But it doesn't need to be like that, surely? Of course we have to go back home. We both have our responsibilities, haven't we? But I suppose I was taking it for granted that we would carry on seeing one another. I have become very fond of you, Lorna. In fact . . . I love you. I know it is very soon to be saying this. We have only known one another a week, but I really do.' He regarded her solemnly, as she did not answer. 'What have you to say?' he asked quietly.

'I say . . . that I'm very touched,' she replied. 'I've grown fond of you too, Ben. And I would like to go on seeing you . . .'

Be careful, said a voice inside her head. You have been here before. She had fallen in love with Craig in an instant, believing it to be the love of a lifetime. They had truly loved one another, she and Craig, but obviously not enough. She had not dared to think, this time, that she might be falling in love again. She liked Ben very much and she believed him to be a good and genuine sort of man, but she could not tell him, yet, that she loved him. She did not even dare to admit it to herself.

'So you will meet me, will you, when we get back to Yorkshire? We don't live all that far away from one another, do we? But it wouldn't make any difference if you lived at Land's End or John O' Groats; I would still want to see you.'

'That's nice, Ben,' she said. 'So would I . . . But there's not just ourselves to consider, is there? We both have families and we can't just ignore them. We can't please ourselves entirely in what we do.'

Ben nodded. 'That's true, but as far as I'm concerned there's only myself and my son, Nick. I gave up on Chloe long ago. She's a very difficult and wilful girl. She's always been determined to have her own way. She and I didn't see eye to eye at all. We had some blazing rows, I can tell you. So . . . when she announced that she was going to live with her latest boyfriend – Jason, he's called – I must admit I was glad to see the back of her.'

Lorna was surprised. She could not imagine, from what she knew of him, that Ben was capable of having a blazing row with anyone. 'She's your daughter, Ben,' she replied, cautiously. 'I'm sure you must have some feelings for her?'

'Yes . . . maybe. But there are daughters and daughters, you know. Your two girls sound like little angels compared with mine. And I'm sure you're a perfect mother to them, aren't you?'

'I do my best. I try to spend as much time as I can with them, to make up for . . . what has happened. It can't have been easy for them, but they've managed to adjust to Craig leaving and the new baby and everything. I'll be glad to see them again tomorrow.' She gave a tender smile, not for Ben at that moment, but at the thought of her dear daughters.

'I'm sure they're lovely girls,' said Ben. 'I'm looking forward to meeting them.'

Lorna looked at him in some surprise. 'Oh . . . well, yes, of course.' She had not really given much thought to him meeting Karen and Joanne, or her parents, although she must have realised, deep down, that that would be inevitable if she were to carry on seeing Ben. 'You will meet them in time. But . . . let's just see how things go, shall we, Ben? We've had such a happy week here. It's bound to be different when we get back to reality. And there's your son to consider, too, you know. I'm sure he has a good relationship with you, doesn't he, with just the two of you living together?'

'Oh, Nick's no problem.' Ben answered airily. 'He does his own thing, as they say nowadays. Yes, we get on quite well . . . when we see one another.' He laughed. 'He's often out with his mates, or up in his room playing his records or watching telly.'

'And studying, surely? Didn't you say it was his O-level year?'

'Oh yes, studying. I suppose he does some of that, when he's a mind to. I keep reminding him he's to work hard, but

I don't believe in nagging. It's up to him to decide what he wants to do with his life.'

But he needs some guidance, doesn't he? thought Lorna, but she did not voice her thoughts. 'Just give me a few days when we get back,' she answered. 'I need some time with the girls, and I will be going back to work, of course. We'll exchange phone numbers and . . . we'll keep in touch? See if it's possible to arrange a meeting?'

'There's nothing more sure,' said Ben. 'I would move heaven and earth, if needs be, to see you again, Lorna.' He stared wonderingly into her eyes for a few moments until, a little bemused, she rose to her feet.

'Come on, Ben,' she said. 'We'd better be heading back to the hotel. Early start tomorrow, remember.'

'Yes, and I've got my last-minute packing to sort out,' he replied. 'OK, let's go.'

He put his arm around her as they walked through the square to the hotel, hidden away in a little street behind the cathedral. He kissed her goodnight outside her bedroom door. He had kissed her several times during the past week and she had responded to the tenderness and warmth of his embraces. But she had not sensed any passion or urgency in his kisses, and nor had he invited her to go into his room or suggested that he should enter hers. She decided she admired him all the more for that. After all, they had known one another for only a week, and he was obviously a man who strove to behave correctly and honourably.

When she alighted from the coach in Melcaster market square she felt as though it was a different world, not just another country or town. For a start, it was raining and had been ever since their arrival at Manchester airport. They had flown way above the clouds where the sun was shining in a blue sky, then they had descended through the layers of grey cloud and mist and rain for which Manchester was renowned.

She had phoned Robert from the airport, telling him the

approximate time of her arrival back in Melcaster. And there he was, parked across the road – good old Robert! – waiting for her. On seeing her alight he hurried across to assist with her luggage. She glanced up at the coach window, smiling and waving to Ben, who would be staying on the coach until it reached York.

Robert gave her a kiss and a friendly hug. 'I see you've made friends,' he remarked, 'and it's obvious you've had a good time, weather-wise at any rate.' Her fair skin was attractively flushed from the warmth of the continental sun, and there was a glow about her, too, that had nothing to do with the climate.

'Oh yes, it's all been great,' she replied. 'The weather . . . and everything else as well.'

Robert looked at her a trifle curiously. 'Well, it's good to see you safely back home again,' he said. 'Come on then, let's get this stuff into the boot and we'll get back home. The girls have been in for about an hour, and they're dying to see you.'

Indeed they were delighted to see her, both of them flinging their arms around her as she entered the house. They were pleased, of course, with the gifts she had brought – dolls in the national costume of the Lombardy region of Italy, little ceramic cats that resembled Tiger and Blackie, and packets of nougat and marzipan fruits – but she was gratified that they were even more pleased to see her and showed no resentment that she had been on holiday without them.

Rachel fussed around, insisting on Lorna and the girls staying for tea before returning to their own home. She would not let her daughter help at all, although the girls were enlisted to set the table. Lorna seized a moment to have a word with Robert whilst the others were out of the room.

'I met somebody on holiday,' she said in a quiet voice, but she was aware that her elation must be apparent. She had felt that she must tell someone about what had happened;

she was unable to keep it to herself any longer. 'The man that you saw waving to me . . . He's called Ben and he's an antiques dealer in York. He's really nice and I'm sure you and Mum will like him . . . but don't say anything to her just yet, will you?'

Robert looked perplexed. 'No, of course I won't say anything, but—'

'I know what you're thinking,' Lorna interrupted. 'It's OK, I know what I'm doing. I won't go rushing into anything, but . . . I really like him, Robert.'

'That's good then,' replied Robert, although he didn't really sound as though he thought it was good at all. 'Do be careful, though, Lorna. A holiday romance? They are not always—'

'I know, I know. I'll be sensible, I promise. It's early days yet and we'll have to see how things work out. But . . . I just wanted to tell you.'

'Well, thank you,' said Robert. 'I appreciate that. You know you're just like a daughter to me, don't you, Lorna? And I want everything to go right for you. Please, please . . . don't rush into anything . . . will you?'

'No . . . no, I won't,' said Lorna.

Robert, at that instant, felt what his mother called a goose walking over his grave. He gave an inward shudder of apprehension. My poor Adam, he thought.

Lorna decided she must wait until Ben phoned her. She was sure he would do so, but she was hardly able to contain her impatience as three days went by and she had not heard from him. She reminded herself, though, that she had told him she wanted a few days in which to sort herself out. They had returned from Italy on Thursday, so he must be waiting until after the weekend. Sure enough, he rang on the Monday evening.

'Lorna, how lovely to hear your voice again. Did you wonder why I hadn't rung sooner?'

'No, not really. Ben. I said to give me a few days, didn't I?'

'I didn't really want to do that, but there were one or two crises when I got back.'

'Oh dear . . . your son?'

'Oh no, Nick was OK. I knew he would be; he was staying with a mate. No, it was the shop. Alec got himself into a spot of bother with an order, and then an irate customer. Nothing to worry about, these things happen. But he needed a bit of calming down; he's inclined to get all hot and bothered, is Alec. Anyway, I'm sure you don't want to hear about all that. When can I see you? It has seemed ages . . . darling.'

It was the first time he had called her that, and it seemed as though he had been plucking up courage to say the word. 'Yes,' she replied. 'I've missed you too, Ben.'

It was not all that easy to arrange a meeting. Lorna had started back at work that day, only four mornings a week, but the girls were home from school soon after four o'clock, and she did not feel she could ask any more favours of her mother at the moment. Besides, Rachel often needed to stay late at her own school. But there were always Jim and Millie, her ex-in-laws. She had stayed in close contact with them and she was sure they would look after Karen and Joanne for once when they came out of school. She did not need to say exactly what she was doing, did she? she asked herself. Just that she was going to meet a friend in York.

It was arranged that she would travel to York by train on Thursday morning. Ben would meet her at the station and they would spend the whole day together. She preferred to visit his home and place of work first, before he came to Melcaster, as that would be rather more complicated.

When she spotted him standing at the station barrier she thought he looked different, somehow. Probably because he was no longer dressed in his holiday gear of sports shirts and slacks, but in a dark green anorak – the weather had turned very autumnal – and he appeared a little less carefree too. His smile lit up his face, though, when he caught sight of her. He kissed her gently on the lips.

'It's great to see you again, Lorna . . . darling. Do you

realise, it's a whole week since I said goodbye to you?'

'So it is,' she smiled. 'Good to see you too, Ben.'

He tucked her arm comfortably into his as they set off walking across the Lendal Bridge in the direction of the Minster. 'We'll go to the shop first,' he said, 'but I'm leaving Alec in charge today, and then we'll go to my home later. I'm going to cook you a slap-up meal; I've got it all prepared.'

'Gosh! That's great,' she said. 'I didn't know you could cook, Ben.'

'I'm a dab hand, my dear. I had to learn to look after myself when Christine left, and now I've become quite a keen chef. I'm good, too, though I say it meself.'

Ben's shop, Memory Lane, was tucked in between a second-hand bookshop and a gent's outfitters on a narrow street near to the Shambles. Although Lorna knew York fairly well she had not noticed the shop before, probably because she had never been all that interested in antiques, but she did not say so to Ben. A bell pinged as he pushed open the door and they entered a small space crammed from floor to ceiling with all manner of collectables. A youngish man popped up from behind the small counter at the back of the shop. He had a round, pinkish face and his shining scalp showed through his very short white-blond hair. He wore rimless glasses through which his blue eyes gazed curiously at Lorna. He reminded her of a startled white rabbit.

Ben introduced them. 'This is Alec, Alec Charlton, my right-hand man. And this is my special friend, Lorna Boothroyd, the lovely lady I met on holiday.'

They shook hands, saying, 'How do you do?' and Alec smiled pleasantly, revealing rather prominent teeth which made him appear even more rabbit-like. Lorna guessed he was about the same age as herself.

'Do you live locally, Miss . . . er, Mrs . . . Boothroyd?' he asked.

'It's Mrs,' she told him, to set the record straight, 'but call me Lorna, please. No, actually I live in Melcaster, not too far away.'

'Ah yes, I know it well. I have an aunt who lives there . . . Do excuse me, won't you?' A customer had entered and Alec became occupied reaching for a vase the lady had admired in the window.

'Have a look round, if you wish, Lorna, my dear,' said Ben, 'although I realise antiques may not be much in your line.'

'I've never really given much thought to them before,' she replied, 'but this all looks fascinating.'

Although the shop was filled to the brim it did not appear cluttered, nor dusty and grimy. Everything was arranged, according to its category, as neatly as was possible with so many articles to display. Lorna could imagine Alec tidying around in a fastidious manner, wielding a feather duster. There were cabinets and shelves containing glassware, both cut glass and coloured, including some pretty pinky-red pieces that Lorna liked particularly and which Ben told her were cranberry glass; porcelain and china figurines; commemorative ware depicting the reigns of several kings and queens, and including some of the wedding of Charles and Diana; silverware; brass and copper articles; pictures and clocks and mirrors and candlesticks . . . Myriad objects, far too many to take in on one visit. There were some larger pieces, too, of mahogany and rosewood furniture – an inlaid writing desk, a bureau, chairs, footstools and occasional tables.

'Goodness me! I'm quite bewildered by it all,' said Lorna when she had been looking around the shop for twenty minutes or so, occasionally asking questions of Ben or Alec. 'It's all so exciting, isn't it? I can see how you get hooked on antiques. I had never realised.'

'Yes, it gets into your blood, doesn't it, Alec?' commented Ben. 'Now, if you will excuse us, Alec, Lorna and I are going to have some time together. You'll see to everything, won't you? Good man.'

Ben had decided he would be a tourist that day, and although Lorna was no stranger to York either they did the things that first-time visitors liked to do. They walked along the city walls, lunched at an old inn overlooking the river, and visited the Castle Museum. Then it was time, Ben said, for them to go to his home. His car was parked quite a distance from his shop, in the nearest car park, driving being severely restricted in the ancient city centre.

His house was a couple of miles away, detached, and set back from the main road in a wooded garden. It was not visible from the road because of the abundance of trees and shrubs. Late Victorian, thought Lorna, seeing the old-fashioned shiny red bricks and the fancy embellishments on the woodwork, as Ben led the way up the path. Inside, however, beyond the stained-glass door and the tiled vestibule, the house had a much more modern appearance. The walls throughout were covered with pale, unobtrusive wallpaper, and the paintwork was white, to show off to greater advantage Ben's elegant furniture and the pictures and ornaments which adorned the rooms.

She sat on a gold velvet chaise-longue in the spacious lounge whilst he made a pot of tea, gazing round at her surroundings, at the crystal chandelier, the thick-piled carpet with its dainty design of yellow and brown leaves, the gold velvet curtains at the long windows, and the cabinets filled with leather-bound books, antique figurines and china tea services. When the tea arrived it was served on a silver tray and the cups and saucers were of the design that Lorna recognised as Old Rose.

Wow! she thought, wondering what Ben's reaction might be when he saw her humble cottage, her homely, countrified possessions and simple way of doing things. 'This is all very elegant,' she remarked. 'I'm impressed, Ben.'

He grinned. 'Well, that's what I'm trying to do, isn't it, to impress? I don't always go to such pains. A mug of tea in the kitchen, that's what I usually have.'

'And that would suit me fine,' said Lorna. 'Please . . . you mustn't stand on ceremony with me.'

'I won't, I promise.' He leaned forward in his chair, gazing at her intently. 'I'm an ordinary sort of bloke really; these are

377

just the trappings, part of the job, I suppose.'

'I can tell you like beautiful things, though, don't you?' said Lorna. Things that many of us can't afford, was what she was thinking.

'Well, yes, I do, but—' He stopped speaking at the sound of a key turning in the lock and then the front door opening and closing. 'That'll be Nick coming in from school. Nick . . .' he shouted. 'We're in here. Come and say hello to Lorna . . . I told him you were coming,' he added in an undertone.

The door was pushed open and the boy walked into the lounge. Lorna was struck at once by the likeness to his father, at least in features and hair colour, but apart from that there was no resemblance at all. Whereas Ben was always well groomed – quite immaculately dressed, even in an anorak or holiday gear – this lad could only be described as scruffy. His hair was almost shoulder-length, which was common to many teenage lads, but it was lank and greasy and looked as though it needed a wash. Lorna took in his scuffed shoes, his bedraggled anorak and trousers, his school tie knotted way below his collar and, above all, the surly expression on his face.

'Hi there, Nick,' said his father, greeting him pleasantly, despite the lad's sullen demeanour. 'This is Lorna – Mrs Boothroyd – the lady I met on holiday.'

'Hello, Nick,' said Lorna, in what she hoped was a bright and friendly voice. 'I've heard quite a lot about you.' She did not know whether or not to offer to shake hands with him, but decided against it. For one thing he looked grubby – she disliked herself for thinking that, but it was true – and she doubted he would have taken her hand anyway. His only answer was what sounded like a grunt.

'Huh . . .' Then he did manage to bethink himself suffi-ciently to say, 'Hi . . . yeah . . . pleased to meet yer.'

'Are you going to have some tea with us?' asked Ben. 'Take that disgusting coat off though, Nick, if you're going to sit down. I keep telling you to get a new one; I've given you the money for it.'

'No . . . I don't want no tea.' He shook his head. 'I've got stuff to do. See yer . . .' He shambled out of the room.

Ben looked at her apologetically. 'Don't take any notice of Nick. He's always like that. Can't be bothered to say more than two words at a time, not to me at any rate. I expect he's different with his pals.'

'He's going through a phase, I expect,' agreed Lorna, although, privately, she thought he must be one of the most unpleasant lads she had ever encountered. 'He's sixteen, isn't he?'

'Yes . . . almost.'

'Well, there you are then. It's a difficult age. I will have that to come in a few years' time with my two.' Although if Karen and Joanne turned out to be anything like that she would wipe the floor with them, she thought to herself. 'Perhaps he will join us for dinner, will he? Do you usually dine together?'

'Not much,' said Ben. 'He usually grabs a pizza or a pastie and eats it in his room. He's very unsociable recently – probably just a phase, as you say – but it's best to leave him alone. He'll come round in his own time.'

She did not see Nick again that day except, briefly, when he popped his head round the door to tell his father he was going out. 'Tara,' he said, nodding in her direction too, but did not add 'nice to meet you' or some such platitude. But then, neither did she.

Ben prepared a tasty chicken casserole which he served with mashed potatoes and mixed vegetables. She guessed the veg was from a packet, but it was all delicious and she was touched by the effort he had made on her behalf. He admitted that the apple pie was from Marks and Spencer, but he served it with fresh cream and then prepared real coffee – not the instant she usually made – in a percolator. He did not let her help at all, and she enjoyed having someone wait on her for a change.

They sat in the lounge after they had finished their meal, together on the settee, where he kissed her lovingly several times in between talking and listening to the records he selected: old Beatles classics, Andy Williams and Matt Munro.

He ran her to the station at nine o'clock to catch her train. He kissed her again and told her how much he would be looking forward to seeing her – and her girls – on Sunday, in only three days' time. That was what they had arranged.

She began to feel uneasy as Sunday drew nearer. She had told the girls the day after her visit to York that they would be having a visitor. 'I've got a friend coming to see me on Sunday; somebody I met on holiday. They'll be coming for dinner . . . and will probably stay for tea as well.' The ambiguous word 'they' did not disclose which sex the visitor would be. Lorna was not altogether sure whether or not that was her intention, but Karen, in particular, was not to be fobbed off.

'OK,' she said. 'Is it the person you went to see yesterday . . . in York?'

'Yes, that's right.'

'A lady, is it?'

'No . . . as a matter of fact, it's a man,' said Lorna. 'He's called Ben . . . You'll like him; I know you will.'

'Oh . . . all right then,' said Karen. 'If you say so . . .' She gave her mother a meaningful look. Or have I only imagined that? Lorna wondered. Then she turned quickly to her sister. 'Come on, Joanne. I want to show you something.'

The two of them disappeared upstairs to the bedroom they still shared, the cottage having only two upper rooms. This was another reason why Lorna wanted to move. She knew both girls would prefer to have a room to themselves, as she had always had when she was a girl.

What would her daughters really think about Ben? she wondered. It had been foolish of her to say, 'I know you will like him.' She had said that to Robert too, she remembered, almost as though she was trying to convince herself. But then Ben was a very likeable person. She decided it would be as well to tell her mother and Robert, too, about the forthcoming visit. She didn't want them to think she was being secretive. On the other hand, Lorna told herself, she was a grown-up woman, quite capable of making her own decisions without asking permission or advice of anyone else.

Ben arrived mid-morning on Sunday. He had found the farm without any difficulty, he told her. She was a little concerned to see that the immaculate green paintwork of his BMW was splashed with mud from the farm tracks – it had rained a lot recently – but he laughed and said he would get Nick to clean it for him. But not without promise of payment, she guessed.

Neither of the girls were at home at first. Karen had insisted that she had promised to go and help her dad, as the potato harvest had been somewhat delayed by the rain. Joanne had gone along with her. They liked to spend time together and Lorna felt she could not protest when they wanted to go and see Craig. She guessed, though, that it was an excuse to get away from the cottage that morning.

She had a leg of pork cooking in the oven and Ben insisted on staying with her as she prepared the meal. He liked watching her, he said. She noticed that he regarded her intently, his eyes following her as she went about her chores, and whenever she glanced at him he smiled at her adoringly. At least, that was how it seemed to her, but she reminded herself that it was still less than three weeks since they had first met.

When the girls returned at twelve-thirty – Lorna had impressed upon them that they must not be late back – Karen's dungarees and hands, and her face, too, were splattered with mud. Joanne was quite clean and Lorna surmised that, whatever they had been doing, she had stood on the sidelines.

Ben laughed. 'I can see you're a real farm girl,' he said to Karen.

'Yes, I am,' she replied. 'Me dad's a real farmer, you know,

381

and I help him. Sorry I can't shake hands with you; I'm all mucky.'

'Oh, I'm not bothered about a bit of muck,' said Ben.

It seemed to be the right thing to say because she did shake his hand, saying, 'How do you do?' as her mother had told her to do when meeting someone. And Joanne followed suit, a little more shyly.

The mealtime passed amicably enough, although neither of the children said very much. Lorna and Ben, too, found that conversation did not flow as easily between them in front of the girls. Lorna felt more relaxed when the meal was cleared away, the washing-up was done – a combined effort by the four of them – and Karen and Joanne went upstairs to change their clothes. They were going to Craig's parents' for tea. It wasn't very far up the road and they could be trusted to go on their own. Jim would bring them back later that evening.

Lorna breathed a sigh of relief as they ran off happily together, saying, 'Tara,' to Ben, as well as to her, without any ceremony. She felt guilty at wanting to be free of them, for the moment at any rate, but there was another obstacle to be faced. She and Ben were to have tea with her mother and Robert.

'Well, what did you think of him?' asked Robert, when their guests had departed soon after six o'clock, Lorna wanting to be back before the girls arrived home.

'He seems very nice,' said Rachel, although she realised as she said it that that meant nothing at all. 'I mean . . . he's polite and friendly. Yes, a very pleasant man altogether, I would say.'

'And he's worth a bob or two,' added Robert.

'Well, yes, he doesn't seem to be short,' agreed Rachel. 'I don't think our Lorna would be influenced by that, though.'

'It's to be hoped she won't be influenced by anything just yet,' said Robert. 'Good heavens! They've only just met. We don't want her rushing into another marriage, not after the way the last one turned out.'

'Who's talking about marriage?' said Rachel. 'You're jumping the gun a bit, aren't you, darling? As you say, they've only just met. Oh no, I reckon Lorna has her head screwed on a bit better than that.' All the same, she had noticed the way that Ben Frazer had looked at her daughter. The fellow was smitten all right.

'I do hope so,' said Robert. 'Oh dear . . . I do so want everything to go well for her.'

'It's early days yet,' said Rachel. 'Let's not go jumping to conclusions. You remember we advised her to wait when she first met Craig – in fact, we refused, didn't we, to let her marry him straight away? – but it still didn't work out. Anyway, she's a grown-up woman now. She should know what she's doing.'

'I certainly hope so,' said Robert again. 'I really do . . .' His thoughts were still with Adam, but he had decided not to mention that issue to Rachel, at least not just yet.

Karen and Joanne didn't seem to mind much either way about their mother's friendship with Ben.

'He's OK, I s'pose,' said Karen, when Lorna asked her if she liked him. 'What does it matter anyway? You're not going to marry him, are you, Mum?'

'Don't be silly, dear,' Lorna had replied. But that was at the beginning. As time went on she knew only too well what was in Ben's mind. He seemed to assume they would get married and that all minor problems – for that was how he saw her family and his – would fall into place.

Whenever Lorna visited the house in York, Nick was nowhere to be seen. If he did happen to appear he seemed to regard her as part of the surroundings, which was how he viewed his father, too. Lorna decided he was Ben's problem, not hers, and as he was not actually rude or abusive towards her, it did not matter very much.

'Lorna, you will marry me, won't you?' Ben asked her,

when they had known one another for about six weeks. 'It's silly us running backwards and forwards between York and Melcaster, when we could be together all the time . . . You could all come and live here, of course.'

She had known he would ask her, and she had known, too, that she would say yes. She was aware that they hadn't known each other for very long, but she liked Ben very much, and she had almost convinced herself that the liking was love. They enjoyed the same sort of things – music, television dramas, books, seeing interesting places – and she had recently become quite keen on what was the passion of his life – his love of antiques. Lorna liked the idea of living in York; she had always enjoyed visiting the city. The hills beyond the cottage were oppressive in the wintertime and the countryside was bleak. It would be good to get away from it all; besides, she did not want to live any longer in such close proximity to Craig and his family. And as she had been intending to sell the cottage anyway, everything seemed to be working out very well.

She looked round now, however, at the stylish furnishings in Ben's lounge where not a thing was out of place, and she tried to imagine her girls in such a setting. Like all children, they were constantly being reminded to tidy up.

'What about the children, though?' she asked, after Ben had kissed her ardently several times on hearing that she would marry him. 'They . . . well, they make rather a mess sometimes. And then . . . there are the schools to consider.' She was realising there was, in fact, quite a lot to consider.

'There are good schools here,' he replied. 'Excellent ones. And who's bothered about a bit of mess? I'm not. Anyway, there's bags of room here. They would each have their own bedroom. There now – they'd be thrilled at that, wouldn't they?'

She nodded. 'And Nick? What would he think about it?'

Ben shrugged. 'It doesn't really matter what Nick thinks, does it? He won't be here for ever. I'm hoping he'll go on to university in a year or two. Anyway, it's you and me who are important, darling. Now, let's see. How soon can we arrange a wedding?'

She had not realised he would want it to be quite so soon. Maybe next spring, she thought, but Ben seemed impatient. It was now the end of October.

'Let's wait until after the end of November,' she said. 'My brother will be back from the States by then. I would like him to be there.'

'Your brother?' queried Ben. 'I didn't know you had a brother. I haven't heard you mention him.'

'Oh, you must have done, Ben. Actually, he's my step-brother, Robert's son. But we were brought up together after my mum and Robert got married. No, maybe I haven't said very much about him, with him being away. He's on sabbatical in the USA. He's a journalist; he works for an evening paper in Leeds.'

Ben appeared disconcerted at this revelation. 'Really?' he said. 'No . . . I didn't know your step-brother was a journalist . . . To be honest, darling, I would like a quiet wedding; really quiet, I mean, with nobody there but you and me. And witnesses; we'd have to have those, of course. And . . . please don't ask me to wait until the end of November.'

He looked at her pleadingly, and she came to a sudden decision. Why not? She would do just as Ben asked. They would get married first, and tell everyone afterwards. A fait accompli. She knew very well that if she told them in advance, her mother and Robert would plead with her to wait a while. They had not said very much, but Lorna was aware of them – particularly Robert – looking at her anxiously when she and Ben called to see them.

'OK then,' she said. 'We'll get married now. Well, as soon as you can arrange it. Here in York, you mean? At the register office? I'll get in touch with my friend, Carol, in Leeds, and see if she can come and be a witness. I'll tell her to keep it to herself . . . but I must have somebody there who knows me.'

With a stab of conscience, she remembered her children.

But they were, after all, only children. They would do as they were told. And so long as she was there, as she always would be, to love and care for them, they would soon adjust to a different way of life.

Chapter 24

Adam had been in America for almost three months and now it was nearly time to return home. He had watched the weather change from unbearable summer heat to what was now freezing cold up in the White Mountains of New Hampshire. The first snows had arrived too, although the roads were kept clear and his journey back to Boston by hired car held no fears for him. He had become accustomed to driving on the broad highways, where the traffic kept to its correct lane and did not go switching back and forth as it did at home. The roads were comparatively empty, too, except close to the cities and larger towns, with none of the mile-long queues he was used to in England. It was, of course, a vast country, whereas the United Kingdom was a very small and crowded island.

Nevertheless, there was no place like home. 'God bless America,' said the citizens of what they believed to be the greatest nation on earth, but Adam knew that when he set foot on his native soil again he would say, 'Thank God for England.'

He had arrived in New York at the end of August in sultry, overpowering heat. Not the best time of year to be sightseeing, but he had viewed all the usual not-to-be-missed places and vistas. Wall Street, the Empire State Building, Central Park, Times Square, Chinatown and Greenwich Village, and what, to Adam, was the highlight of his time in the 'city that never sleeps', a night-time cruise around Ellis Island and the Statue of Liberty. Manhattan by night was truly breathtaking. There was only one thing which would have made his feeling of wellbeing complete, and that was to have had Lorna at his side.

From New York he had taken a Greyhound bus to Washington. This city was a must; once could not visit the States without see the Capitol Building, the White House and the Lincoln Memorial. But Adam's main purpose in coming to the USA was to see New England in the 'fall'; he had heard so much about it. And also to seek some peace and solitude in which to write his novel.

From Washington he flew to Boston. He spent a few pleasant days in what was thought of as the most English of American cities. He walked the Freedom Trail, then visited Harvard University, and Plymouth where the Pilgrim Fathers had landed. But it was time to press on, so he hired a car and headed northwards to the lakes and mountains of New Hampshire. He needed to find a place which he could make his temporary home for the next couple of months.

He found an ideal spot way up in the White Mountains. It was a hotel in what was really a ski resort and, therefore, not so crowded as it would be in the winter, but still quite busy with the tourists who were known as 'leaf peepers' – those who had come to see the glorious foliage of New England. He was delighted with the apartment he was allotted. It had a bedroom, sitting room, kitchen and shower room, with so many doors leading from one room to the next that he felt he needed a map to find his way around. Coffee- and tea-making facilities, too, in the kitchen, plus reasonably priced restaurants and bars on the same site. He had got it made!

Adam settled down and wrote and wrote, which had been his main intention. He cleared his mind of all the clutter and confusion of thoughts which had distracted him whenever he had tried, back in Leeds, to work on his novel. He did not forget his family – most particularly he did not forget Lorna – and he sent them postcards from time to time, but he began to feel as though they were part of another existence. They would still be there when he returned home, though.

Lorna would still be there . . . and one thing which would not change was his feelings for her.

He had met many friendly people during his travels, and here, in the White Mountain Resort, as it was called, his fellow guests and all the staff he met were unbelievably chatty and outgoing. A national characteristic, and one which Adam admired. He pondered that back home folk ignored their fellow human beings for much of the time – until there was a crisis, when they would pull together and become best mates. He had met some very pleasant young women too; he had conversed and laughed with some over a drink or a meal, but then had said goodbye without any regrets.

His novel, a murder mystery, which he hoped might be the first of a series, was almost completed. His policeman hero, DI Guy Summersby, had solved the crime, with the aid of his attractive assistant, DS Angela Ackroyd. All that remained now was a touch of editing and fine-tuning here and there, which he would do on his return, before trying his luck with a publisher.

He had kept his nose to the grindstone and his bottom glued to the seat of his chair for much of his stay in the White Mountains, but he had allowed himself to take trips out and about every so often. His mind was filled now with the sights he had seen, and the photographs he had taken would help him to recapture his memories when he returned, although he knew that no photographic image or picture could ever do justice to the wonder of New England in the fall. He recalled the beauty of the mountain slopes with trees of every autumnal shade and colour – russet, vermilion, golden yellow and orange, interspersed with the dark green of the conifer trees, like a giant chequerboard. The old Indian highways where the brilliant trees formed archways of colour, the dazzling light and dappled shade, the rocky rivers and covered bridges, and the shimmering blue of the lakes.

When the time came for his departure he drove back along the roads to Boston in a carefree and happy frame of mind. He would soon be saying goodbye to a wonderful country, but his heart was still back home amongst the hills and dales of his native Yorkshire.

Lorna usually had the whole of Thursday to herself, as it was not one of the mornings when she worked at Paige's. The members of her family were not surprised, therefore, when she said she would be spending the day in York with Ben. That was what she often did, arriving back in the early evening to collect her daughters from her mother's, or from Jim and Millie's, wherever they happened to be.

They might have been surprised, however, to see how she was dressed for the occasion, in her best pale blue woollen suit with the fashionable padded shoulders and short skirt. Feeling too nervous to drive, as she sometimes did, she left her car in the station car park and took the train. Ben would meet her at York station and they had arranged to meet their friends who were acting as witnesses – Carol, and Alec from the shop – outside the register office at a quarter to twelve. The ceremony was to take place at twelve o'clock.

Carol had shrieked down the phone at Lorna on hearing her news. 'What! You're getting married? To that Ben you were telling me about? But you've only known him five minutes . . .' Carol was now happily married to Neil, although she was still busy with her nursing career.

Lorna had tried to reassure her friend that she knew perfectly well what she was doing and that she had no doubts. Ben was a good man, trustworthy and kind; he was twelve years older than herself and he wanted, so much, to take care of her.

'But . . . do you love him?' Carol had asked.

'Well . . . yes, of course I do. I wouldn't be marrying him if I didn't. We knew straight away, when we met on holiday, that we were right for one another. But please . . . please, don't tell your mother, will you? Because she'd be sure to get in touch with mine, and then the fat would be in the fire.'

'All right, if that's what you want. But why the big secret?

They will have to know eventually, Lorna.'

'Yes, of course they will. But I have to do this my own way. I'll tell them afterwards and then there'll be nothing they can do about it. They would only make a great big fuss and try to put me off, and I can't stand all that again.'

'I should imagine they'll have quite a lot to say anyway, won't they, when they find out what you've done?'

'Yes, I'm sure they will.' Lorna sighed. 'But it will be too late by then, won't it? You will be a witness for me, won't you, Carol? You're my oldest friend and I do want you to be there.'

Carol had agreed that she would. She was on nights that week, so she didn't even need to change her hours.

Ben arrived at the station with a box of carnation buttonholes for the four of them to wear, and a posy of tiny pink carnations for Lorna to carry. He kissed her warmly, holding her close to him. 'In an hour's time you will be Mrs Frazer. You can't imagine how happy that makes me, my darling.'

Carol and Alec had already arrived and been introduced to one another. Both men looked very smart in dark grey suits with pristine white shirts, and Carol was wearing her best coral-pink suit.

Lorna had never been to a civil marriage ceremony before and had not known what to expect. She found it dignified and reverent, even without the religious overtones, and the woman registrar was friendly and put them all at their ease. The room was not a stark and bare office as she had expected. The panelled walls and mahogany furniture and the bowl of chrysanthemums and dahlias in autumn shades, which stood on the leather-topped desk, gave it a warm and friendly feel.

'There now, you may kiss the bride,' said the registrar when they had been made man and wife, and Ben did so, fondly but not passionately.

He had booked a table for the four of them at a hotel near to the Minster, having closed the shop for the day, or until Alec was able to return. They talked together, a little stiltedly at first, over a five-course luncheon.

'So . . . will you two be going off on honeymoon?' asked Carol. 'I don't mean now, but perhaps in a week or two?'

Lorna and Ben looked at one another. 'I don't think so,' Lorna replied. 'In fact, we won't even be together at all for a few days. I have to go back home tonight and sort things out at the cottage, and tell the girls and my parents . . .' Already she was feeling jittery at the thought of it.

'But it won't be your home for much longer, darling,' said Ben. 'Lorna and the girls are coming to live with me,' he told Carol and Alec. 'Next week, I hope.'

'What about your job?' asked Carol. 'Will you be leaving Paige's?'

'I shall have to,' said Lorna. 'I can't travel back to Melcaster every day. But I can work at home, like I used to do.'

'Yes, and she has promised to do some watercolours for us to sell in the shop, haven't you, darling?'

'Yes, that's right.' Lorna nodded. 'We shall all move here as soon as possible. And then the cottage will be sold, of course.' For the first time, she felt a tiny stab of apprehension at the thought of parting with the place which had been her home for the last twelve years. But she was Mrs Benedict Frazer now, and there was no turning back.

They said goodbye to Carol and Alec and drove back to Ben's home, soon to be Lorna's as well. For the first time ever, he showed her into the bedrooms. 'This will be our room,' he said, 'and you must feel free to make any changes you wish, my dear.'

But Lorna thought that the main bedroom, overlooking the wooded garden, would do very well as it was. She could not fault Ben's taste in either decoration or furnishings, all very elegant and stylish, although a few bits and pieces of her own would add a more homely touch.

The two smaller bedrooms which he had in mind for Karen and Joanne were only partially furnished, but Lorna intended to bring her own furniture and, in time, the rooms could be decorated in whatever colours or styles the girls might choose. Ben agreed that they must give her daughters a free hand.

'I won't show you into Nick's room,' he said, laughing, as he led the way downstairs again. 'I go in there as little as possible. If he wants to live in squalor, then it's up to him.'

'Oh dear,' said Lorna. 'Is it so bad? What about his washing? The bedclothes and that sort of thing?'

'He washes them himself when he thinks they need it,' replied Ben. 'Which isn't very often. He's old enough to use a washing machine, so I'm certainly not going to mollycoddle him.'

Oh dear, Lorna thought again. She had not taken to Nick at all, but now she was beginning to feel rather sorry for him. He was probably in need of a mother's love; she gathered it was about four years since Christine, Ben's first wife, had walked out on them. She decided she would try, hard though it might be, to befriend the lad and show him that there were people who cared about him.

To her amazement, Ben had never attempted to do anything other than kiss and embrace her, although he had told her, oftentimes, that he loved her. She had thought he might take full advantage, that afternoon, of the fact that they were now man and wife, but he made no move towards doing so.

'I'm sorry . . . that we can't have a honeymoon. Or at least – you know – a wedding night?' she said tentatively, when they were downstairs again.

'So am I,' agreed Ben. 'But we can't very well . . . not now. Nick will be home from school soon. Never mind, darling. It will be worth the waiting for. You go back to Melcaster and sort everything out. And then we'll be together – for always.'

As it happened, Nick did not come in from school. His father had no idea where he was when he drove his new wife back to York station to catch her train.

Lorna quickly changed out of her best clothes into her habitual trousers and a jumper before she went to pick up her daughters from Jim and Millie's bungalow. She guessed none of them would notice her shiny new wedding ring; she had continued to wear Craig's ring after the divorce, feeling naked without it. But she knew she must tell the girls, that night, before they went to bed. There would not be time in the morning when they were dashing around getting ready for school, and the longer she put it off, the harder it would be to break the news.

She decided it would be best to start on an upbeat note. 'I've got a surprise for you,' she said, when both girls were in their night attire and were sipping at mugs of hot chocolate. 'You know I'm going to sell the cottage, don't you, so that you can each have a bedroom to yourselves?' They both nodded, and she was aware of two pairs of eyes, one blue and one brown, staring at her intently. Karen, she recalled, had not been too keen on the idea of the cottage being sold. 'Well . . . I've decided that we're going to live in York, in a nice big house where there is plenty of room. Quite soon, I hope; maybe as early as next week.'

'York?' said Karen. 'That's where Ben lives, isn't it? That's where you've been today.'

'Yes, dear, of course it is. Well . . . Ben and I thought it would be nice if we were all to live together, then I wouldn't need to keep leaving you when I go off to York to see him.'

'You mean . . . to live with Ben?' asked Karen. Joanne, as yet, had not uttered a word. 'In his house?'

'That was the idea, yes . . .'

'But I don't want to.' Karen shook her head vehemently. 'I don't want to go and live in York, and I don't want to live with Ben.'

'Why not? I thought you liked him . . .' said Lorna, sounding a little feeble.

'He's all right. I've told you before, he's OK, I suppose. But it's you that likes him, not me and Joanne. And I shan't go and live there! You won't neither, will you, Joanne?'

The younger girl looked a little fearful. 'I don't know,' she replied. 'Have we got to, Mummy?'

Lorna felt her spirits sink lower and lower. But what had

394

she really expected? she asked herself. That her two daughters would jump for joy at the idea of leaving the cottage, their home ever since they had been born, to go and live in a strange town? Tell them, she said to herself. You know you've got to tell them the truth, right now.

'Well, yes, I'm afraid you will have to come with me if I decide to go and live in York. And this is what I have decided. You see . . .' she took a deep breath, 'Ben and I . . . we got married today, so I shall be going to live with him, because that is what husbands and wives do. Like your dad and Avril, you know? And you two will be coming with me.'

'Oh no, I won't!' yelled Karen, her blue eyes blazing with anger. She jumped to her feet and her cup of chocolate fell to the ground, splashing her dressing-gown and spilling on to the carpet. She paid no heed to it. 'What d'you want to go and get married for? We were all right like we were, you and me and Joanne, and now you've gone and spoiled it all.'

'Karen, love . . . just listen to me. Perhaps I should have told you, but you must have realised I was fond of Ben.'

'No, I didn't, I didn't! Not like that. And I won't go and live with him.' Lorna watched a look of pure defiance steal over Karen's little face, so like that of Craig. 'I shall go and live with me dad. In fact, I'm going right now. I'm going to tell him what you've done.'

She ran out of the room and out of the back door before Lorna could stop her. She knew it would be pointless to try to follow her. She ran to the door, though, to watch her racing down the lane in her bedroom slippers, her dressing-gown flapping around her ankles. It was not far to the farmhouse and, fortunately, it was not raining or muddy, nor were there usually any loiterers on the farm premises at night.

'Oh dear!' Lorna flopped down on the settee. 'I've made a right mess of everything, haven't I?' Joanne came and sat beside her, and Lorna put her arm around her.

'It'll be all right, Mummy,' said the little girl. 'Karen's cross, but I 'spect she'll get over it. I want to stay with you . . .

You won't go and leave us, will you?'

'Of course I won't, darling,' said Lorna. 'I've told you, we're all going to live in York . . . at least, that's what I had hoped.'

'But . . . if Karen doesn't want to go . . .'

'I'm afraid little girls have to do as they are told,' said Lorna, with more conviction than she was feeling. 'Mums and dads know what is best for them.' But do we always? she asked herself. And supposing Karen flatly refused to go, and insisted on staying with her father? Lorna had not envisaged her family breaking apart.

'I'll go with you, Mum,' said Joanne, 'but I want Karen to come as well.'

'I know you do, darling.' Lorna kissed the top of her blonde head. 'Let's just wait and see what happens, shall we? I expect your dad will be round shortly, or else he'll phone to find out what's going on. Oh dear . . . I'm sorry, Joanne.'

'It's all right, Mummy,' said the little girl.

Lorna reflected for a few moments on how different her daughters were growing up to be, not just in looks, but in temperament as well. Karen, who was the image of her father in outward appearance, had inherited her, Lorna's fiery nature. So how could she blame the child now, for reacting in the way she had done? Something was tugging at her memory. Had she, too, not been difficult when her mother had told her she was going to marry Robert? Yes, she had, and with no good reason because, even as a child, she had loved Robert as a father figure, and she still did. Karen, she realised, had far more reason to be making a fuss.

Joanne resembled Lorna in looks, being smallish, blonde and brown-eyed, but there the resemblance ended. The little girl's gentle nature and her striving never to upset anyone if she could avoid it reminded Lorna so much of her own mother, Rachel. Joanne, she guessed, would go with her to York and try to make the best of it, even though she might be feeling unhappy and all mixed-up inside. Oh, dear God, what have I done? Lorna felt herself asking. Nor was it an idle thought. If the Almighty could help her, then she prayed that He would.

Craig arrived at the cottage in less than fifteen minutes, as she had anticipated.

'Lorna, what the hell's going on?' he asked. 'Karen's told us some garbled tale about you getting married and going to live in York ... Hello there, Joanne love. Isn't it time you were in bed? Off you go, sweetheart, then your mum and I can have a chat.'

'Leave her, Craig,' said Lorna. 'We won't be saying anything I don't want her to hear. She knows, don't you, darling? And she's being a very good girl.'

'She knows what, exactly?'

'That Mummy's got married to Ben, today, and we're going to live in York,' said the child.

'What! You've actually married him ... already? I thought that was what Karen said, but I was sure she must have got it wrong. What on earth are you thinking of, Lorna?'

'I don't see that it's any of your business,' replied Lorna, 'and I'm not going to argue about it. You're right; Joanne must go to bed now – it's school tomorrow – and I'm tired as well. We'll talk in the morning. Karen can stay with you and Avril tonight, if that's OK with you?'

'Most certainly. I'll take her school clothes with me now, although I can't see her wanting to go to school, can you? She's very upset.'

'Yes, I know, but she'll calm down,' said Lorna. 'You know what she's like; she overreacts at times.' She knew she had handled things badly, but she was not going to admit that to Craig. All she wanted now was to get to bed, to sleep, if possible. There were more problems to be faced tomorrow.

She did not see Karen the next morning. Craig phoned to say that she had, surprisingly, agreed to go to school, but there were things he wanted to discuss with her, Lorna, as soon as possible. She drove Joanne to school and then went on to Paige's to inform Brian that she would no longer be working there. Her hours were flexible and she knew it would not be difficult to replace her in the office. The job had been more or less created for her because Brian Paige had always been fond of her, solely in an avuncular way. He was astounded to hear of her sudden marriage. He and all her former colleagues wished her well, wondering, though, why she had not told them earlier. They were not all that worried, however, about what she was doing; they all had their own problems to deal with. Brian was sorry to lose her, yet again, but not too concerned, provided she continued to send them samples of her latest art work. Her resignation, for Lorna, was only a minor hurdle, as nothing compared with what she would have to face later in the day – seeing her former husband and then her parents.

Craig and Avril, and baby Timothy, too, all came to see her in the early afternoon, after phoning to see if she was there. Craig came straight to the point.

'Karen has made up her mind that she wants to stay at the farm with me, and with Avril and the boys, of course. And we are quite willing to have her. In fact, we will make her very welcome, won't we, my dear?' He turned to Avril, who smiled, a little apologetically, at Lorna.

'Yes, we certainly will. It isn't as if she's not used to us. She gets on well with Simon and she loves our little Timmy. I know it will be a wrench for you, Lorna dear, but . . .'

'You mean . . . for good?' said Lorna. 'She wants to go and live with you, instead of me and Joanne?'

'You and Joanne . . . and Ben,' Craig pointed out, 'and in a strange town, Lorna. You knew how she felt last night. She was quite adamant about it.'

'But I thought she'd get over it. I didn't think she would really want to—' To her horror and shame – in front of Craig and his new wife – Lorna burst into tears.

Avril was at her side in an instant. 'Oh, my dear, I am so sorry. Now don't upset yourself. Karen loves you very much – she's told us she does – but she doesn't want to go and live in York. She loves the farm and she doesn't want to leave it.

Children are all so different, Lorna, as you know, and your Karen is a real farmer's girl. Far more interested in it than my Simon is.'

Lorna looked at Avril through tear-dimmed eyes. The woman was really very kind and she couldn't help but like her. She took hold of her hand. 'I know she is,' she said. 'I should have known what to expect. I don't want to lose her though. And Joanne will miss her.'

'We'll make sure they see one another, and you, very often,' said Craig. 'I'm sorry I flew off the handle last night, Lorna, but it was such a surprise. I hope you'll be very happy, though. You deserve to be happy, and we wish you all the best, Avril and me.'

'Indeed we do,' said Avril. 'I calmed him down. You know, reminded him of what he and I did. I know things haven't been easy for you, Lorna, and I hope you and Ben have a wonderful life together. I do, really.'

Lorna nodded. 'Thank you . . . I suppose it's for the best if Karen stays with you. Tell her not to worry.'

'You must tell her yourself,' said Craig. 'There must be no falling out about this. What do your parents say about you getting married?'

'They don't know yet,' replied Lorna, sniffing a little and dabbing at her eyes. 'I'm OK now. Thanks for being so kind, Avril . . . But I wonder if you would do me a big favour? Could you have Joanne at teatime, with Karen? Then I can go and break the news to my mother and Robert.'

'Of course we will,' agreed Craig. 'And the very best of British luck!' he added, smiling.

Lorna decided on a matter-of-fact approach. It would not do to be defiant or, on the other hand, apologetic. What she had done was her own business and no one else's. She was sorry about Karen, but had convinced herself by now that it was for the best, for the time being at any rate. It would be dreadful to live with an aggressive and resentful child, but maybe Karen would change her mind eventually.

She waited until five o'clock when she knew her mother would be home. Rachel was there, but Robert was still out working. 'How long will he be?' asked Lorna. 'I have some news for you, and I'd rather tell you both together.'

'Nothing too dreadful, I hope?' asked Rachel. Her daughter did not look exactly overjoyed.

'No, quite the opposite,' replied Lorna with a brightness which, to her mother, sounded a little forced. 'I hope you're going to be pleased about it.'

I know what it is, thought Rachel. She's getting engaged; she's going to marry Ben . . . 'I think I can guess what it might be,' she said. 'You know Robert and I want you to be happy, don't you, darling, but— Oh, there's Robert coming in now. Robert . . .' she shouted. 'Here's Lorna. She's got something to tell us.'

'You've guessed already, haven't you, Mum?' said Lorna. 'That Ben and I have decided to get married?' Well, that had made it a little easier. 'But what I have to tell you is . . . that we are married already.' She displayed her left hand with the broad shining gold band, topped by a superb antique ring of rubies and diamonds which Ben had given her at the same time as the wedding ring. She'd kept it in its box until she'd broken the news to the girls, but hadn't been able to resist slipping it on to her finger that morning.

'What!' Robert looked, and sounded, angry, but dumbfounded as well.

'Why? Why didn't you tell us? Oh, Lorna . . .' Her mother looked as though she was going to cry, and flopped down on to the nearest chair as though her legs would no longer support her. 'What on earth have you done?'

'Got married, that's all,' said Lorna. 'I've not committed a crime.'

'That's all?' repeated Robert. 'But why the secrecy? You should have told us.'

'And have you trying to put me off? That's why I didn't tell you, because Ben and I were sure, and we didn't want anybody else telling us what we should or should not do. I love Ben and he loves me – you must have realised that – and I'm going to live in his house in York. And . . . Joanne's coming with me.' She had said only the one girl's name knowing there would be a reaction.

'Joanne? And what about Karen?' asked Rachel. 'You have two girls . . .'

'Karen's going to live with Craig and Avril,' replied Lorna, just as though that was what she had intended all along. 'You know what a farmer's girl she is, and she'll be happier there. You mustn't worry about it; we're all quite happy and we have sorted everything out.'

'Yes, before telling us anything,' said Rachel. 'You mean . . . you are going to split up your family, separate your two lovely children, all for a man you hardly know? Oh . . . Lorna.'

'Don't keep saying, "Oh, Lorna!" ' she snapped. 'I hoped you'd be happy for me. I'm sorry you weren't at the wedding, but there was nobody there apart from Carol and a friend of Ben's. That was the way we wanted it, with both of us being married before. I thought you might understand that.'

'And . . . where is Ben now?' asked Robert dazedly.

'He's in York. He's coming here on Sunday, and then Joanne and I are going back with him on Monday. We're going to see an estate agent first and put the cottage up for sale, then we'll move my furniture to Ben's house and get settled in.'

'So you're not having a honeymoon or . . . anything?' asked Rachel.

'Sounds like a rum do to me,' muttered Robert. 'Living apart at the start of a marriage.'

'We had to,' said Lorna, 'so we could each get things sorted out.'

'Well, what's done is done, I suppose,' said Robert. 'But I do hope you know what you are doing, Lorna.'

'Let's hope you don't live to regret it,' added Rachel.

When Lorna left a few minutes later there was still a decidedly frosty atmosphere. She hated being out of friends with either of them. She and Ben must call there on Sunday, she decided, and show her mother and Robert just how happy they were together.

Rachel burst into tears as soon as Lorna had gone. 'The silly, stupid girl!' she cried. 'Of all the senseless things to do! I can't imagine what she was thinking of. And those poor little girls, Karen and Joanne. However must they be feeling?'

'Now, come along, darling,' said Robert, sitting at her side and wiping away her tears with his big white handkerchief. 'We must try and get things into proportion. As Lorna says, she hasn't committed a crime. And I'm sure she wouldn't do anything that would hurt her little girls. She's a very good mother and she thinks the world of them.'

'But this is thoughtless, to say the least,' replied Rachel. 'I can't see that she has considered them very much. I hate to say it, but Lorna has always been determined on getting her own way.'

'Well then, let's hope it works out for her,' said Robert. 'I don't like it any more than you do, but second marriages are sometimes all right. More than just all right,' he added with a chuckle. 'Look at ours. It's still wonderful, isn't it, after all these years?'

'It certainly is,' agreed Rachel. 'But I had known you a lot longer than she has known Ben. And our children knew one another, and they didn't mind about it. Well, Lorna made a bit of a fuss at first, but that was only to be expected, knowing Lorna . . .'

'And then there was the dreadful business with your mother dying,' Robert reminded her. 'It's no wonder Lorna was upset . . . And I would be very surprised if Karen hasn't kicked up about her mother marrying Ben. She's just like Lorna in her moods and the way she reacts. I can't see her taking it lying down.'

'No, I'm sure you're right,' said Rachel. 'It upsets me to think of those two girls being separated, but I must admit that Karen will probably be happier with her daddy on the farm. Oh dear! What a mess it all is. And I can't help liking Craig in spite of everything that has happened.'

Robert appeared lost in thought for a few moments. Then, 'Adam's the one I'm sorry for,' he said. 'I wasn't going to tell you this, Rachel love, but now . . . well, I think you ought to know.'

'Adam? What about him?' asked Rachel. 'He'll be surprised. In fact, he'll probably be very annoyed, like we are, when he finds out.'

'He'll be more than annoyed. Have you never realised, my dear, that Adam is in love with Lorna? He has been for . . . oh, for ages, for years and years.'

'Adam . . . and Lorna? No, he can't be. You must be mistaken. He's had lots of girlfriends. Anyway, he's her brother.'

'Rachel, will you stop saying that they're brother and sister? They're not, and you know it very well. They are no more brother and sister than . . . you and I are.'

'But they were brought up together after we got married. And they behaved like brother and sister. Don't you remember how they used to argue and fall out, just like real brothers and sisters do?'

'Yes, I know. But it's true all the same. I know, because Adam told me. He loves Lorna, not just as a sister; he is in love with her. He's known for a long time, even when she married Craig, but he tried to get over it. He was angry, for Lorna's sake, when Craig met Avril, but he must have thought there might be a chance for him at last.'

'But . . . why did he go to America then?'

'To sort himself out, I suppose. To clear his mind. And his sabbatical had been arranged for ages. I think he intended to say something to her when he returned. But now . . .'

'It's too late,' said Rachel. 'Oh . . . poor Adam! Yes, I can see it now. And of course they're not brother and sister. However are we going to tell him? He'll be home soon, won't he?'

'Yes, next week,' replied Robert.

By the time Ben arrived at Lilac Cottage on Sunday Lorna had made friends with Karen again. Hiding her true feelings, because she was really hurting at parting from her elder daughter, she told Karen that she wanted her to be happy, and it was obvious that living on the farm would be more congenial to her than living in York.

'I've decided I want to be a farmer when I leave school,' Karen told her mother, sounding very cheerful and excited. 'A real farmer, I mean, like Avril was, not just a farmer's wife. I shall go to agricultural college, like Dad did, and learn all about it.'

'Well, that's great then,' said Lorna. 'But you won't forget about Joanne and me, will you? You'll come and see us in York? Please, darling, I don't want to lose touch with you.'

'Of course I'll come, Mum. I'll come and stay, if you like. But I don't want to live there all the time.'

'And . . . you'll try to be nice to Ben, won't you, dear?'

''Course I will. I've told you, I think he's OK . . .'

Karen stayed and ate her Sunday dinner at the cottage with Lorna, Ben and Joanne. It was all quite friendly and sociable, almost like a real family, Lorna tried to tell herself. Then Karen said goodbye and went back to the farmhouse, which was now her home. Lorna was determined not to be downhearted. As she had planned, they went to see her mother and Robert, taking Joanne with them and all driving round in Ben's BMW.

Lorna was relieved that her mother and Robert seemed to have recovered from their annoyance at her hasty marriage. She guessed that the two of them had agreed to be pleasant to the newly married couple and to make the best of what they thought was a bad job. They both shook hands with Ben, and said it was a surprise, but that they wished them every happiness.

'You'll take care of her, won't you, Ben?' asked Robert. 'She's very precious to us, you know. And our little Joanne here.'

Ben assured them that he would. He smiled fondly at Lorna and at her daughter. Surely her parents could see that he was sincere? She, Lorna, trusted him implicitly.

'That wasn't too bad, was it?' said Rachel, after they had gone. 'I felt like tearing a strip off him, but we'd agreed, hadn't we, to be reasonable? And Joanne seems to be all right. That's one of my chief concerns. She was rather quiet, but then she always is.'

'Yes, all we can do is hope for the best,' said Robert. 'Hope . . . and pray.'

'He seems very fond of Lorna,' said Rachel. 'He'll look after her and Joanne. I'm sure he's very sensible and trust-worthy. A good man . . . I think.'

'Yes . . . possibly too good,' said Robert thoughtfully.

'What do you mean? In what way?'

'I'm . . . not sure. Just . . . something about him,' replied Robert. 'Let's hope I'm wrong. I'm prejudiced, of course, thinking about poor old Adam.'

'Yes, of course,' said Rachel. 'You're sure to be. I think Ben's very nice, and I expect we'll get used to him in time . . .'

Lorna lay wide awake in the darkness. Ben was asleep at her side, breathing heavily, but not too noisily. He had fallen asleep almost as soon as they had made love . . . if that was what you could call it.

She had been anxious and a little fearful too, that the first time they would come together would be in the bed where she and Craig had had so many wonderful moments, but it was just the way things had worked out. She had tried to banish such thoughts from her mind. She had even bought a new nightdress, which was pink satin with tiny shoulder-straps and a plunging neckline – not at all suitable for a November night, but she had wanted to look her best for Ben. And to encourage – even entice – him a little, too. He was an honourable man and he had not yet attempted to make love to her in the fullest sense.

He had admired her in her nightgown and told her she looked beautiful. He had taken her in his arms and they had lain down on the bed, for the very first time. But it was all over almost before it started. Then he had kissed her briefly on the lips, rolled away from her and fallen asleep.

We are both tired and a little on edge, she told herself. And this is not the right place for us. Tomorrow they would be moving to York and to the start of a whole new life. Things could only get better . . .

Chapter 25

'Why the hell didn't you let me know? Couldn't you have
written and told me, or phoned or something? To come back
and to find this; Lorna married . . . I just can't believe it.'

It was a week after the hasty marriage that Adam had
arrived back in Yorkshire. His father rang and asked him to
call and see him and Rachel as soon as possible as they had
some news for him; he gave no indication over the phone as
to what it was. Adam paled visibly with the shock of their
announcement, collapsing on the settee with his head in his
hands. He was not crying; he seemed too bewildered and
angry for tears.

'There was really no point in letting you know while you
were over there,' said Robert. 'She'd gone and married him
and there was nothing we could do about it.'

'But . . . I didn't even know she had a boyfriend. She hadn't
got one when I set off for the States. You could have written
to tell me about that.'

'I suppose we both hoped it would come to nothing,' said
Robert. 'There was no point in alarming you, son, not when
you were too far away to do anything. I hadn't told Rachel
then, you see, about your feelings for Lorna. You had told me
not to mention it to anyone, so I didn't even tell my wife. But
she knows now, of course.'

'Yes, and I'm truly sorry, Adam,' said Rachel. 'It wasn't
what we wanted for her at all, to marry this Ben fellow that
she hardly knew.'

'Who is he, anyway?' asked Adam. 'All you've told me is

that she's gone to live in York with this Ben character that she's married.'

'He's called Ben Frazer,' replied Robert. 'Short for Benedict, we believe, and he has an antiques shop in York, somewhere near the Minster. He doesn't live there though; he has a house on the Knaresborough Road ... What's the matter? Do you know him?'

Adam was frowning and nodding slightly, drumming his fingers on the settee arm as though trying to bring something to mind.

'The name rings a bell,' he said. 'You can't easily forget a name like that ... Let me think ... There was a court case ...'

'Oh dear! Not involving Ben, I hope?' asked Rachel fearfully.

'No ... it's no use. I can't quite remember,' said Adam, not wanting to worry Rachel. He realised he had said too much already. But the more he thought about it, the more the name of Benedict Frazer set not just one bell, but a whole cacophony of alarm bells ringing in his mind.

Lorna was extremely busy for the next few days. They called at the estate agent's in Melcaster on the Monday morning with the keys of the cottage, as he was to sell the property in Lorna's absence. Then, later that day they set off for York, each in their own car, after supervising the loading of the furniture on to the removal van, which set off at the same time as the cars. The van contained mainly bedroom furniture for Joanne, plus books, records and record players, china, pictures, cushions and odds and ends which would help them both to feel at home in a strange environment.

Lorna's chief concern was to make sure her daughter settled down, both in her new home and in a school. There was one not very far away, just back from the main road and within walking distance of the house. Mother and daughter went along there on the Tuesday morning, and Lorna felt much more contented about everything when she saw how

Joanne was welcomed by an affable headmaster and a very friendly woman teacher of a third-year junior class. She felt confident that Joanne would settle down well at school. She was quiet, admittedly, but not particularly shy and she did not find it hard to make new friends. It might have been more difficult for Karen, thought Lorna; the elder girl was much more bossy and inclined to throw her weight around. Maybe it was just as well that she was not required to change schools.

One of Lorna's greatest worries on coming to live in the house in York was what Nick's reaction to her and her daughter would be. Ben assured her that he had told his son of their marriage, but Ben's attitude seemed to be that it was not really any of Nick's business, and that he, Ben, lived his life in his own way and he left his son alone to get on with his. Lorna gathered that things had fallen apart since his first wife had walked out on them. His daughter, Chloe, had gone too, and Ben seldom saw her as she lived in Manchester where her boyfriend had a flat. Lorna had not yet met the girl. There seemed to be little stability in the family and Lorna hoped that she might be able to mend a few fences, with Nick at any rate.

He had greeted her quite civilly when he came home from school, quite early for once, on their first day in York. 'Hiya,' he said, 'Er . . . congratulations, an' all that. Me dad told me about . . . yer know.'

'Thank you, Nick,' she said. 'That's very kind of you. This is my daughter, Joanne. She'll be living here as well. I expect your father has told you?'

'Yeah . . . He said summat about it. Hiya, kid.' To Lorna's surprise, he smiled at the little girl quite pleasantly.

'Hello,' she said. 'But I'm not a kid.'

Good for you! thought Lorna.

'Yeah, well . . . whatever. Hi Joanne. I'll see you later. I've got stuff to do.' That was what he always said when he ambled off to his room.

'Nick . . .' Lorna called after him. 'Come and have a meal

with us later, will you? I'm cooking something a bit special, with it being our first meal here.'

'Yeah . . . OK, then. See yer . . .'

'It's quite an achievement to get Nick to dine with us,' remarked Ben when they were all seated at the table. Lorna would have preferred the boy to have worn something other than his shabby tracksuit bottoms and a holey jumper, but at least his hands and face looked clean. He tucked into the pork and mushrooms in wine sauce, and the sherry trifle, with relish. A pleasant change from his usual diet of chips or pizza, she presumed.

She and Ben did most of the talking, but she was pleased to see that Nick did pass an occasional remark to Joanne.

'D'you like listening to music? Records an' that?'

'Yes, sometimes,' Joanne answered politely. 'I have my own record player, actually. I've brought it with me.'

'Oh yeah? Right . . . I've got a stereo system. You can come and listen to it, if you like.'

Lorna smiled to herself. She doubted that Nick's choice of music would be the same as her daughter's, but it was nice of the lad to try and make her feel at home. She was beginning to change her mind about him, just a little. All the same, she was not too happy about the little girl going into Nick's room, chiefly because of what Ben had told her about it. She decided she would, quite soon, venture into the room herself to change the bed linen and to have a bit of a tidy-up. It couldn't be much fun for the lad, having to do his own washing.

She discovered that Ben had a cleaner, Mrs Jarvis, who came on two mornings a week to do the dusting, hoovering and polishing, the cleaning of windows and any ironing that needed to be done.

'I daresn't go into t' lad's room,' she told Lorna, when they first met on the Wednesday morning. 'Well, I went in once, but he carried on at me summat awful for touching his things. So, I says to meself, Never again! He can rot in his muck!'

We'll see about that, thought Lorna. She would not be told what to do and what not to do in the place which was now her home as well as Ben's. After all, she was the mistress of the house, and it was her job to see that all the rooms were kept clean and tidy. Mrs Jarvis came on Wednesdays and Thursdays, so it was on Friday that Lorna took her first foray into the room.

It was the smell she noticed first; it hit her as soon as she opened the door. How on earth could anyone live in such a fetid atmosphere? But he was probably so used to it that he didn't even notice it. There was an odour of unwashed socks and underpants, several of which lay discarded on the floor, and a dusty smell which told her that the place had not been cleaned or dusted for ages, even before she noticed the thick layers of grime on every surface that was not littered with magazines, records, unwashed mugs or discarded chocolate and toffee wrappings. There was an unmistakable aroma of cigarette smoke as well and . . . something else, unless she was very much mistaken. She was surprised Ben had not had something to say about that. Maybe he had, or maybe the lad had only recently started the habit.

She had expected the walls to be covered with posters, as were the bedroom walls of most teenagers. There were pictures of groups that she knew vaguely, and some she had never heard of – weird-looking characters clad in black leather from head to toe, clutching guitars or mikes and gyrating wildly, with spikey hair all colours of the rainbow and silver studs glistening from ears, noses and lips. Mostly males, she guessed – the bearded ones certainly were – although it was difficult to tell. There were pictures of girls, too, very scantily clad, which left nothing to the imagination. Not what you could truly call pornographic, she pondered, but the couple of magazines lying on the bed most definitely were.

Whew! She was tempted to go out and close the door on it all. Let him live in his squalor, which was what Ben had said, but she was not a quitter. She knew it was a sense of

411

devilment, though, that drove her on, as well as determination. She yanked off the sheets, after she had first removed the jumble of articles that lay on top of the bed: the soiled shirts and jumpers, records, tapes, half-empty packets of crisps and pop bottles, even a beer can, and the offending magazines. The duvet cover was grimy too, so she removed it, then ran downstairs to bung the whole lot – duvet cover, sheets and pillowcases – into the washing machine. The dirty clothing would have to be a separate load. Then she went back upstairs, armed with dusters, cloths, polish, Windowlene and disinfectant, to begin her mammoth task. She did not stop for lunch – neither Ben nor Joanne were coming home at midday – and it took her until two in the afternoon to get some semblance of order and cleanliness into the room. She was pleased with her efforts when she had finished.

She suspected, however, that Nick would not be pleased. She purposely kept out of his way when she heard him come in from school, but it was not long before he came looking for her. He stormed into the sitting room where she was pretending to read a book.

'What the effing hell d'you think you're doing, going into my room? Nobody goes in there but me, see. Even me dad knows better than to go in. Just mind yer own bloody business and keep yer effing hands off my things, right?'

She was shocked at his language, the like of which she had seldom heard before. None of the men she knew well swore, at least not like that, and Nick was only a lad. She was determined to stand her ground.

'Don't you swear at me!' she retaliated. 'I live here now, as well as you. This is my home and I will not allow one of the rooms in my home to remain in such a filthy state as yours was. Your dad doesn't go in because he has decided to let you live in your muck. But I don't agree with him. No one can want to live in squalor like that and . . . quite honestly, Nick, I don't think it was fair of him to expect you to do your own washing.'

412

'I'm OK. We was both OK, me dad and me. Why d'you have to come along and stick yer nose in? I'll see to me own stuff without any help from you.'

'But you haven't done, have you? Those bedclothes hadn't been washed for ages. Months, it seemed like to me.'

'Well, what of it? What's it got to do with you, eh? You keep yer hands off my things, or else—'

'Or else . . . what? Don't you try to threaten me, Nick! Just listen to me. Either you work along with me to keep your room reasonably clean – I said reasonably. I don't mind a bit of mess and clutter – or else . . .' She paused ominously. 'Or else I shall tell your father that you've been smoking pot.' She saw the lad quake visibly, but he covered it up immediately with a show of bravado.

'So what! He knows . . .'

'Are you sure about that, Nick? Can you look me in the face and tell me, truthfully, that your dad knows you've been smoking cannabis?'

'Yes! Er . . . no, he doesn't. But it's no big deal . . .' He suddenly seemed to shrink and to lose his tough-guy act. 'You won't tell him, will you? It was some lads at school; they got me into it.'

'Yes, it's always somebody else, isn't it? No, I won't tell him, Nick, not so long as you keep your part of the bargain. I want us to get along, you know; I would like us to be friends. I realise things can't have been easy for you since . . . since you were on your own with your dad.'

'Yeah, she walked out on us, the bitch! And me effing sister's not much better.'

'Don't swear, please,' she said quite mildly. 'At least, don't do it in front of me. I'm not used to it and I find it offensive. As I've said, I want us all to get on together. I appreciate you trying to make friends with my Joanne. She's missing her sister at the moment and she's a little bit wary of you, but she'll come round. You'll move those magazines, though, won't you? And some of those pictures, if she goes into your room. She's only nine, you know.'

413

'Yeah . . .' He grinned sheepishly. 'She's only a kid, isn't she? A nice little kid, though. OK, I'll tidy me room up a bit – just a bit, mind – if you'll do me dirty washing.'

'OK, it's a deal,' replied Lorna. He had not apologised for his loutish behaviour, but at least she felt that they understood one another a little better now.

There had been no suggestion that Lorna should find a job in York, apart from doing her art assignments from home. It took several days for her to get acclimatised in her new home and surroundings, but she found she quite enjoyed living on the fringe of a big city where traffic was continually passing by on the main road and in close proximity to houses and shops. There was a row of local shops not far away where she could buy everyday requirements. If she wished to visit York she discovered it was easier to travel on the bus than by car. The traffic in York was horrendous, vehicles being restricted in the city centre, and the car parks were gigantic places situated quite a distance from the main shops and facilities.

She worked out a timetable for herself, allowing two or three hours during the day when she could work undisturbed at her painting, avoiding the times when Mrs Jarvis came to clean. She was a very loquacious woman who hardly ever stopped to give her tongue a rest.

She was working on the set of paintings of the Italian Lakes from sketches and photos taken on that memorable holiday. These were to be offered to Paige's for their greeting cards, but Ben had persuaded her to do a series of paintings of their own city for sale in the shop, depicting the lesser-known spots and hidden-away corners rather than the usual views of the Minster and the Shambles. There were quiet stretches of the old Roman wall, ancient churches and hidden alleyways aplenty, and over the next few weeks she worked on her preliminary sketches. Ben said he knew of a good printing firm and they could, eventually, have the paintings reproduced as limited-edition prints, no more than a hundred of each. They should sell well in the shop. They were not antiques, of course, but he did occasionally deal in more modern high-class products.

She called a halt to the sketching as Christmastime drew near, partly because she was busy with other things and partly because she was colder than she had ever been in her life. She was used to the harsh Yorkshire climate, but York was renowned for its damp and biting cold which crept through every street and alleyway, having its source in the deep and murky River Ouse which flowed through the city.

She had not been looking forward to Christmas and found herself wishing it was over before it had begun. She knew that her marriage to Ben had caused a good deal of trauma in the family, therefore it was up to her to see that everything ran as smoothly as possible. Craig brought Karen to York on Christmas Eve, and she spent Christmas Day with her mother and Joanne, Ben and Nick. She returned home on Boxing Day, and Joanne went too, to spend a day or two with her father. The sisters were happy to be together again, and Nick was on his best behaviour – for him, that was, because he was never what could be called really pleasant or gracious. Lorna realised he was trying, though, in his usual half-hearted, grudging manner, to make Karen feel at home. The girl stared at him as though she was unable to make head nor tail of this strange lad, but Lorna heard Joanne whisper to her, 'Take no notice; he's always like that. But he's OK really, when you get to know him.'

It had seemed more appropriate, under the circumstances, for Lorna to visit her parents – including Derek and Sylvia – with just Joanne and not her new husband. So the two of them did their festive visiting a few days before Christmas and again at New Year. Perhaps by next year, thought Lorna, they might all be able to meet more congenially. She had seen Adam only once since his return from the USA and he had not yet met Ben. He had congratulated Lorna on her marriage but, like the rest of the family, had been unable to hide his disapproval. Robert said that his son was very busy, trying to find a publisher for his book, and with that and his work for the newspaper he had little time to spare.

It was after the New Year – 1984 – that Lorna started to help out in the shop occasionally, particularly on Alec's half-day. She had come to like Alec very much, and after his initial wariness of her, she thought that he liked her too.

'He's ... er ... gay, isn't he?' she said to Ben, soon after their marriage.

'Yes, of course,' replied Ben. 'That goes without saying. I thought you would have known that straight away. Why? Does it worry you?'

'No, why should it?' she said. 'I think he's a very nice chap, and he gets on well with the customers, doesn't he? They like him because he's so helpful and friendly.'

'Yes, he's quite a gem is our Alec,' said Ben, with what she thought was a touch of sarcasm. 'Very high-principled and honest. Rather too much for his own good at times,' he added.

'What do you mean, Ben?' she asked. 'If he's honest, then that's what you want, isn't it? You don't want somebody who is deceitful working for you, do you?'

'No, of course not, my dear. Just forget I said it. I didn't mean anything.' But Lorna did not entirely forget.

It did not worry her that Alec was gay, although it was the first time she had really had any dealings with someone who was that way inclined. She wondered if he had a friend. There was no one sharing his flat, that was for sure. An awful thought had occurred to her. Could it be that Alec ... and Ben? No. She had dismissed that thought almost immediately as being ludicrous, and as the weeks went by she decided that Ben was definitely not 'like that'. She had to admit, though, to herself, that sex was not very high on his list of priorities. They made love a couple of times a week, with tenderness, but without a great deal of passion. It was better than the first time, but still not memorable enough to think about the next morning and to look forward to the next time. Not like it had been with Craig . . . but she knew she had to rid her mind of such futile thoughts. She had married Ben for better or for worse, and on the whole it was . . . quite good. He loved her, that was certain, and he would never do anything to hurt her.

As well as the customers who wished to buy the goods on sale, and many more who just wished to browse, there were others who had articles to sell. Lorna had watched Ben now and again dealing with these people, talking in what seemed like hushed tones, fearful that anyone should overhear. He told her that she must never undertake such a transaction on her own if she was alone in the shop – something that rarely happened – but must tell the man or woman to come back later 'when Mr Frazer is in'.

It was on Alec's half-day, when Ben had gone to see a dealer friend in Harrogate, that a woman came into the shop. She had a collection of commemorative ware for sale, she told Lorna, starting to delve into her shopping bag and place the newspaper-wrapped articles on the counter before Lorna had a chance to tell her that Mr Frazer was not there. Lorna had studied the cabinet of royal souvenirs in the shop and, by so doing, had learned a good deal she had not previously known about the reigns of the various sovereigns. The woman glanced at the cabinet now.

'I see you already have a lot of commemorative items,' she remarked, 'but some of these that I have, I think are quite valuable.'

There were a few mugs and a cup and saucer dating from 1952, the date of the present Queen's accession, and a couple of much more recent ones commemorating the Silver Jubilee of 1977. Nothing unusual there, as far as Lorna could see, but some of them were made by well-known pottery firms: Wedgwood, Aynsley and Spode.

'And this one is George the Sixth,' the woman went on, 'and these two are Edward the Eighth; he was never crowned, you know – although you are too young to remember, of course – so I'm sure they must be quite

417

valuable. Don't you think so?'

'Oh yes, I should imagine they are,' replied Lorna. 'Especially this one.' She picked up an ornate mug with the royal crest and a gilded handle and looked at the maker's stamp on the base. 'Crown Derby. Yes, I think that should be worth a bob or two, as they say.' She smiled at the woman, then remembered, rather belatedly, what Ben had said, that she must never do a deal on her own. 'Actually,' she said, 'I'm afraid I can't help you, not at the moment. My husband, Mr Frazer, is in charge and he isn't here just now. I don't know enough about them, but if you could come back tomorrow? Why do you want to sell them?'

'Oh, they were left to me by an aunt,' said the woman. 'They're not much in my line, nice as they are. I would find the money much more useful. Yes, thank you, I'll call back when Mr Frazer is here.'

Lorna was not there when the woman returned, but she had to face her husband's wrath when he told her, that evening, about the transaction. It was the first time he had ever been angry with her.

'You very nearly messed things up for me, good and proper,' he told her, 'telling that woman that her items were valuable.'

'I didn't say that,' retorted Lorna. 'She thought they were, and I was agreeing with her, sort of . . .'

'But you must never do that; admit to a punter that their items are valuable.

'But I thought they were. Two of the mugs were Edward the Eighth, Ben – the uncrowned king.'

'Then that shows how very little you know.' His voice was scornful. 'Edward the Eighth may not have been crowned, but all the souvenirs had been made months in advance; they always are. In fact, there were more of them than there were of his brother, George the Sixth, the one who was crowned instead of him. They're not valuable at all . . . at least, not all of them.'

'I'm sorry; I didn't know.'

'No, you didn't, so please keep your pretty little nose out of things that don't concern you.' He seemed to have calmed down a little; he was even smiling. 'I told the woman what I've just told you, that they're nothing out of the ordinary. But, actually, one of them was a Crown Derby, one of a limited edition. The number underneath didn't mean anything to her and she was quite happy to sell it to me for twenty pounds. That was a fair price, I told her, and she seemed very satisfied. I should be able to sell it for . . . oh, in excess of a hundred, maybe a hundred and fifty pounds. I gave her seventy-five for the lot. A good afternoon's work in the end, but in future remember what I've told you and keep your mouth shut.'

'But . . . that's cheating!' cried Lorna. 'That poor woman! You've diddled her out of hundreds of pounds.'

'It's business, my dear,' replied Ben.

'It's sharp practice,' countered Lorna. 'It's . . . dishonest.'

Ben laughed. 'Find me an antiques dealer who isn't. We have a living to make, Lorna.'

'Conning the unsuspecting public . . .'

'Oh, come down off your high horse, darling. It's not like that at all. In this trade you win some and you lose some. Occasionally I've bought a piece, paid the earth for it, then discovered it was a fake. That was when I was starting out, of course. I'm more wary now; in fact, you could say the boot is on the other foot.'

'What do you mean?'

'Oh, it's sometimes hard to tell the difference between a fake and the genuine article, to the untrained eye, that is. But I've had years of experience . . . Now, I don't want you to concern yourself with what I'm doing. It's all above board, I can assure you. I'm glad of your help in the shop, but your job is to look pretty and to encourage the customers to make a purchase. OK? Do you understand?'

'Very well, Ben,' she replied. But she was not at all happy to discover that her husband was not a hundred per cent honourable, as she had believed he was.

★ ★ ★

Adam was in a quandary when he first started to look into the background of Benedict Frazer. If Lorna was really and truly happy with him, if she loved him – and how it hurt Adam to think that she might do so – and if the fellow had turned over a new leaf and was now going straight, then maybe he should leave things alone. He knew it was partly jealousy and just a touch of vindictiveness that was driving him, but he had to know. If Frazer was still involved in shady dealings, then it should be brought to light; far better for Lorna to find out now than to suffer years of misery in another unhappy marriage.

How he loved her, and how his hopes had been shattered when he had heard the devastating news on his return from the USA. He cursed himself for being such a fool as to embark on his sabbatical without saying something to her. There had been times – very occasionally – when he had almost persuaded himself that she might have feelings for him other than those of a sister for a brother. When he had first started seeing her friend, Carol, for instance, Lorna had seemed very disgruntled. But that was ages ago, and she had been going steady with Craig at the time. It was all water under the bridge anyway, but remembering his past mistakes and the way he had let her slip through his fingers only served to spur him on now to find out whatever he could.

He remembered Benedict Frazer . . . from somewhere. He had recognised the name at once, but he could not at first recall the exact circumstances. He searched in the archives, the newspapers dating from two or three years ago, some of which were now stored on microfilm and easier to peruse. All the same, it was painstaking, headaching work, but at last he found what he was looking for.

Eighteen months ago, not so long ago as Adam had thought, Benedict Frazer had been brought to court on a charge of receiving stolen goods. Adam remembered him now; a handsome and charming fellow with a smooth tongue that had, somehow, convinced the jury. He had denied all knowledge of where the goods – silverware and paintings – had come from. Yes, they had been found in his shop, but he had bought them in good faith. He was acquitted, but the other two men, Jake Caldicott and Reggie Brooks, who were known crooks with previous convictions, were each sentenced to two years' imprisonment.

Adam reckoned they should now be getting near the end of their time. In fact, they could be out very soon with remission for good behaviour. Pay-back time? He hoped not. Lorna could well be in danger if these characters were to go after her husband seeking revenge. It could, of course, be true that Frazer was innocent, but Adam, who had attended the trial, had his doubts. Especially as he had later discovered that there had been other instances of shady dealings in which the antiques dealer had been involved. Dealing in fakes – high-class figurines, but with a forged maker's mark. Ben had been fined that time – for the one and only time – several years ago, but since then he had kept his nose clean. At least, there was nothing that could be proved.

Adam was known to be an honest journalist, and, as such, he had made a few friends in the police force. They were inclined to look upon newspaper men as being economical with the truth, if not downright liars, but Adam's reputation had gained him the confidence of two police officers in particular. They were only too pleased to do some sniffing around with regard to Frazer. They agreed he was a smooth talker and it was hard to pin anything on him.

He had been suspected, in the past, of doing what was known in the trade as 'knocking', calling at houses, usually in middle-class or poorer-class areas, and persuading old people to part with their treasures for a pittance. The more reputable antiques dealers would have nothing to do with this despicable practice, and it had to be said that Ben Frazer had not been involved in it recently. His assistant, Alec Charlton, was said to have no time for such trickery. Knocking, of course, was not a crime and was very hard to prove.

As for Jake Caldicott and Reggie Brooks, Adam's friend, PC Hollingworth, was soon able to inform him that they would be free in a month's time – that would be in May – and that, according to his 'snout', they were both hot for revenge. It was also said that Ben Frazer had already had a call from a former inmate, a mucker of Jake and Reggie, warning him that they would soon be on his tail and he must co-operate, or else . . .

Adam confided in his father about his discoveries, but they agreed it would not be right to say anything to Rachel or Lorna whilst there was no real evidence that Ben was still involved in criminal activities.

Robert was shocked and horrified. 'She's not in any danger, is she?' he asked. 'I mean . . . he's been up to his neck in it in the past, or so it seems. He's not violent, is he? He wouldn't harm her?'

'I have no reason to believe so,' said Adam. 'He was more of a gentleman crook. No, he was never involved in rough stuff. If there was any fear of that I would go and sort him out right now, believe me!'

'But . . . when these two characters get out . . .'

'I shall be watching their every move, don't worry, or someone else will be doing so on my account. I have some influential friends, Dad. No harm will come to Lorna. I would like to barge in and rescue her now, you know I would, but it wouldn't be the wisest move. I may have a word with Alec Charlton, though, on the QT, and ask him to keep his eye on things.'

'Do you know him?'

'No, but I can make it my business to get to know him. A decent chap, from all accounts. Maybe he has helped to keep Frazer on the straight and narrow . . .'

'Take care, Adam, won't you? You're not a tough guy, you know. And your leg still troubles you now and again, doesn't it? I can't help noticing you are limping a little.'

'Hardly at all, Dad; only a twinge occasionally when I get

overtired, and I have been doing a fair bit of dashing about.'

'You still haven't met Ben Frazer, have you? Do you know, I always suspected there was something fishy about him. I know it's easy to say that now, but I did. I said to Rachel that he was too good to be true. He's a charmer, all right.'

'No, I haven't met him, not since he married Lorna. I thought it was best to keep my distance. I doubt if he would remember me, but on the other hand, he might. Lorna's sure to have told him that I work for the *Courier*. But I shall meet him sooner or later, I am quite sure.'

And when he did meet him he hoped, also, that he would be able to prove Benedict Frazer's guilt and not his innocence. Vindictive? Yes, maybe it was, but he had waited a long time for Lorna. And he knew that, in the long run, she could never be happy with such a man, whether he was guilty or innocent.

Chapter 26

It was on a morning in mid-April, when both Nick and Joanne had returned to their schools following the Easter break, that Lorna heard a knock at the front door. She cursed to herself and was tempted not to answer – it was probably somebody selling something, or Jehovah's witnesses – as she had just started painting. However, as the knocking persisted, she threw down her brush and went to the door.

'I thought you were never coming,' said the girl on the doorstep. 'What took you so long, eh? I suppose you must be Lorna?'

Lorna stared at her. She did not know the girl from Adam . . . or Eve. She looked about nineteen years of age, although it was difficult to tell. Her black hair was highlighted here and there with purplish-red streaks and stuck up from her head in jagged spikes. Her lips were a splash of magenta in a dead-white face, and her eyes were outlined in black with silver lids. There were silver studs, several of them, not only in her ears, but in her nose as well and she was dressed in a shaggy fake fur coat with red high-heeled boots.

'Yes, I'm Lorna,' she replied. 'But . . . who are you?'

'I'm Chloe,' said the girl. 'Hasn't me dad told you about me? And aren't you going to ask me in?'

'Er, yes . . . of course,' said Lorna, standing back. 'Come in. I'm . . . pleased to meet you. It's rather a surprise, though. Your father didn't tell me you were coming.'

'No, of course he didn't, because he didn't know, did he? Where are we going? In here?' She pushed open the sitting-room door. 'I used to live here, you know.'

'Yes, come in and sit down. Take your coat off and . . . and I'll make us a cup of coffee.'

The girl took off her coat, revealing a brief leather-look black mini-skirt and a tight black sweater. Her legs, what could be seen of them above the knee-length boots, appeared to be bare. She plonked down in an easy-chair, stretching her long legs out in front of her.

Make yourself at home, why don't you? Lorna thought to herself, but she asked the girl politely, 'Have you come to see your father? He's at the shop all day as I suppose you know, but you are very welcome to stay until he comes home.'

'I'm hoping I'll be welcome to stay for good,' replied Chloe.

'What!' exclaimed Lorna. She had made the remark automatically, without stopping to consider that it might sound rude. This, after all, was Ben's daughter. 'I mean . . . I hadn't realised . . .'

Chloe laughed. 'That took the wind out of your sails all right, didn't it? Go on and make us that coffee and I'll tell you all about it. In fact, I'll come with yer.'

She accompanied Lorna to the kitchen, stopping at the adjacent dining-room door and poking her head round. 'Ooh . . . are you an artist? This is yours, is it?' She nodded appreciatively at the half-finished painting of one of York's hidden alleyways, with a cat, Lorna's favourite animal, lounging on the cobblestones. 'I'm impressed. D'you do a lot of this sort of stuff?'

'Yes,' replied Lorna. 'This one is part of a series. I've already done three, and your father has had them made into limited-edition prints to sell in the shop.'

'Oh, I say, you clever thing! He's fallen on his feet all right, marrying you. I heard he'd got married. I thought he might've invited me to the wedding, but I suppose that was too much to expect. We'd fallen out, him and me, and he can

425

be a right awkward bastard when he's that way out. Won't admit he's wrong . . . but then I suppose I'm like that an' all.'

'You don't need to feel upset about the wedding,' Lorna told her. 'There was nobody there except us and two witnesses – a friend of mine and one of Ben's. Your father wanted it that way. We didn't tell anybody till afterwards . . . Come on, let's see to this coffee.'

'Oh . . . right. What about me brother, then? My darling brother, Nick? Didn't he know about it?'

'Not till it had happened, but he was quite all right about it.'

'How d'you get on with him?'

'OK. We don't see much of him. He spends a lot of time in his room playing his records, or he's out with his mates. I think he really should be spending more time studying.'

'Tell me about it! Dad was always on at the pair of us to study, then he got fed up nagging at us and left us alone. Me and Nick never got on. He won't half get his knickers in a twist when he knows I've come back.'

She lounged against the kitchen cupboards whilst Lorna boiled the kettle and put the coffee in the beakers. Instant would have to do for now. She couldn't be bothered with the percolator. She reached for the biscuit tin.

'Not for me, thanks,' said Chloe. 'I'm on a diet. Are we going back in the lounge?' She led the way, carrying her beaker. Lorna hastily placed a silver coaster on the coffee table.

Chloe laughed. 'Still as posh as ever, ain't it? Not a thing out of place. It used to get on me bloomin' nerves, me dad and his pernickety ways. Don't worry; I won't mark yer precious table.'

Lorna was beginning to lose patience with this bold girl who had turned up out of the blue. 'I think you had better tell me why you have come, Chloe,' she said. 'From what your father says, he hasn't set eyes on you for over a year, and now you just come back and expect—'

'I've been kicked out, haven't I?' said Chloe. 'Jason, the

426

bastard, the bloke I was supposed to be marrying, he's chucked me out. And I've nowhere else to go.' At that moment she looked very young and vulnerable, far less than her nineteen years, and Lorna began to feel sorry for her.

'Have you no friends in Manchester who could have helped you out? That was where you were living, wasn't it, in Manchester? And what about your job?'

'Oh, I can easy find another job,' said Chloe airily. 'I'm a typist. I did do some studying, see, but now they're wanting computer skills an' all. But I'm not worried; summat'll turn up. Yes, I've got a few friends in Manchester, but I wanted to get right away from the place. Jason's done the dirty on me, see. I found him in bed with another girl an' I went mad at him. Well, at both of 'em. Nearly killed 'er, I did. But it's his flat, see, when all's said and done. I haven't got a leg to stand on. He pays the rent and everything. So . . . I've come here. Can I stay . . . please, Lorna?'

'It isn't really for me to say, is it?' said Lorna. 'It's your father's house . . .' She realised as she said it, and not just for the first time, that the house was in Ben's name, and although he had said he would alter it to both their names, he had not yet done so. 'You will have to ask him, won't you? Why didn't you go there first, to the shop, instead of coming here?'

'Wanted to see what you were like, didn't I?' The girl grinned so cheekily that Lorna could not help but smile.

'And what am I like?' she asked. 'Meet with your approval, do I?'

Chloe nodded. 'I reckon we'd get on OK. I'd be no bother, honest. And there's room for me, isn't there? I could have my old room.'

'My daughter lives here as well,' Lorna told her. 'Didn't you know?'

'Gosh, no! I didn't realise you had any kids.'

'Actually, I have two daughters. Joanne, who's nearly ten – she's the one who lives here – and Karen, who's two years older. She stayed with her father.'

'Oh, I see. She didn't like the ideal of living with me dad, eh?'

'No, it wasn't like that,' said Lorna. 'My ex-husband is a farmer, and Karen is a real country lass. She's far happier there than she would be here.'

'Don't you miss her?'

'Yes, of course I do. But she visits quite often. It's all working ... quite well. But you really must ask your father, Chloe, if he will agree to you coming back. And if he says yes, then it's all right with me.'

'Thanks, you're a star.' The girl beamed. 'Which room has your little girl got? Can I go and see?'

Together they went upstairs and it turned out, fortunately, that the room which was vacant was the one that Chloe had previously occupied. There was a bed in it and a chest of drawers, but little else.

'I see me dad's got rid of some of the stuff,' Chloe commented. 'There was a wardrobe and a desk and a knee-hole dressing-table; all dead old-fashioned. I expect they've gone to his precious antiques shop. I kept telling him I wanted fitted furniture, but he took no notice.'

'Mm, perhaps ... if you stay, we could think about it ...'

When they were downstairs again Lorna told her, 'I think it might be as well if you go to the shop and explain everything to your father. I can phone him and tell him you are coming, if you like, then he will be expecting you. Now, shall I make us both some lunch, and then you can be on your way?'

'OK then, I'll go, but never mind about lunch. I'll get a pizza in town. You can ring him, though. Cheerio then, Lorna. See yer later.' She grabbed her shaggy coat and dashed away.

Ben agreed, although a trifle grudgingly, that his daughter could come back, for a trial period, he said.

'What else can I do?' he said to Lorna. 'She is my daughter, and maybe I'll get on better with her now you are here. She seems to like you a lot.'

Lorna had no wish to act as a mediator if there were any disagreements, but she was quite willing to give Ben's daughter a chance.

Chloe and Nick, as the girl had said, did not hit it off at all. 'What the hell are you doing here?' had been his only comment when he first saw his sister, and that was a foretaste of their relations from then on.

Fortunately, they both liked Joanne. Chloe was surprisingly kind to the little girl and Joanne seemed fascinated and not at all fazed by two such unusual – Lorna would have said weird – persons living in the same house as herself. Neither of them were like Ben, Lorna often thought. There was a facial resemblance, but that was all. They were both so outlandish in appearance. Chloe did care about what she looked like, and spent ages on her clothes and make-up, even though she often ended up looking a freak, whereas Nick was just untidy and scruffy and didn't give a toss. There could not be a greater contrast to his offspring than Ben, every inch the antiques dealer in his neat suits and shirts and silk ties. Lorna wondered if they had inherited the larger share of their genes from their mother, Christine, who had walked out on them several years ago.

Adam was a man with a mission. The consensus of opinion amongst his friends in the know was that Frazer was going straight for the moment, but a careful eye was being kept on him. It was believed that he was crafty, and smooth-tongued enough to con a lot of folk, but that he might be easily swayed if pressure was put upon him.

Adam phoned Alec Charlton at his flat above the shop, during the evening, when he knew that Ben Frazer would not be there. Alec was hesitant at first to talk about his boss, but when he knew he was talking to Lorna's brother – or step-brother, to be correct – he was a little more forthcoming.

'Oh yes, Lorna's a lovely lady,' he enthused. 'Not just beautiful, she's charming and friendly – a real lady.'

'Yes . . . well, I'm worried about her,' said Adam. 'You know Frazer has been involved in . . . er . . . criminal activities in the past, do you?'

'Yes, I did . . . but I believe nothing was ever proved.' Suddenly the timbre of Alec's voice changed. 'Actually, Mr Blundell, I'm glad you've rung. I've been wanting to talk to somebody. There's something fishy going on and I didn't want to tell the police, not on the little evidence I've got. And I've been a bit worried about Mrs Frazer, too. Such a lovely lady . . .'

They agreed to meet at a hotel near the railway station on Alec's next half-day.

'How long have you worked for Mr Frazer?' asked Adam, when they were comfortably seated in the lounge bar, each with a pie and a pint.

'Oh, eighteen months and more it must be now,' said the well-spoken young man. From his accent Adam guessed him to be a southerner. 'Let me see . . . It was just before Christmas, the one before last. I'd moved up here because I had a friend who was already living here. But it's all over between us now . . . you understand?'

'Perfectly,' replied Adam. 'You didn't know about Frazer's brush with the law, then?'

'No, not when he first employed me. It had happened a month or so before, I believe. I heard about it later, on the grapevine, of course, and then Ben told me himself. But he swore he was innocent.'

'Yes, so he would,' said Adam. 'But there was always some doubt. Anyway, those two villains that were convicted, Caldicott and Brooks, are due out anytime now. That's why I'm so concerned about Lorna.'

'And you are right to be,' said Alec. 'That's what I wanted to tell you. He's already had a visit – not from one of them; they're both still inside. But a very shady-looking character came in the shop and Ben took him into the back room, where we make our cups of tea, you know.'

'When was this?'

'Oh, about ten days ago. I couldn't hear everything they were saying; in fact, I heard very little. I was busy with a customer most of the time, more's the pity. I was dying to get my ear up against the door. But from what I heard I got the impression it was something to do with . . .' he paused dramatically, '. . . with drugs.'

Adam was shocked. 'Surely not,' he said. 'Couldn't you be mistaken? I've not heard that he's ever been mixed up in anything of that sort.'

'Oh, I do hope I'm wrong, Mr Blundell,' said Alec. 'Or . . . may I call you Adam?'

'Yes, why not?'

'Well, Adam, I certainly heard some very suspicious-sounding words. Gold dust – that's heroin, you know – and "sniff" and "snort", which refer to inhaling—'

'Yes, I know what they mean,' said Adam grimly. 'This is far worse than I thought, if you're right.'

'Oh, I think I am, because Ben has seemed frightened of his own shadow ever since. And talk about irritable!' He flapped his hand in the air. 'I asked him what was wrong, but he said it was just a family thing. His daughter's come back home to live and I gather they don't exactly hit it off. And as for his son, well really, Adam, he's nothing more than a lay-about.'

My poor Lorna, thought Adam. What on earth has she got herself into?

'And you didn't ask him about the strange visitor?'

'Oh no, I thought it best to mind my own business. He wouldn't have told me anyway. The thing is, Adam,' his blue eyes looked confidingly into Adam's, 'though I say it myself, I felt I was rather a good influence on Ben. I know he hasn't been mixed up in anything too crooked whilst I've been here.'

'I'm sure you're right,' said Adam sincerely.

'I vowed to myself that I would leave if I ever discovered anything—'

'Please don't,' said Adam. 'I will feel happier if you are

431

there. Not that I am happy at all, thinking of Lorna.'

'Oh, don't worry. I shall stick to my post and keep my eyes and ears open, and if I hear so much as a whisper I shall let you know. Anything to help your nice sister . . .'

When Adam left the hotel he could not resist the urge to see Lorna. Besides, he felt that she should now be told, if not everything, then a little of what was going on. She was in charge of the shop as it was Alec's half-day and Ben was said to be visiting a client. That in itself worried Adam; he did not like the idea of her being left alone. He walked briskly over the Lendal Bridge and made his way to Memory Lane. He had sussed it out before, but had never been inside.

Lorna smiled when she saw him enter, dashing forward to kiss his cheek. 'Hello there, stranger. Long time no see. To what do I owe this honour?'

Adam kissed her cheek, resisting the temptation to gather her into his arms. 'Oh, I had some business to attend to in York, so I thought I would drop in and see you. Your . . . er, husband, Ben, is he out?'

'Yes, he's negotiating a deal with a client and it's Alec's half-day, so I'm in charge. You might be able to meet Ben; he shouldn't be too long. It's odd that the two of you haven't met yet, but I know you've been very busy. Robert tells me all about what you're doing. Have you found a publisher yet?'

Adam grinned. 'Fingers crossed. I've not exactly found a publisher, but I've got an agent and that's the next best thing. She seems very impressed.'

'She? It's a woman?'

'Oh yes, I'm no male chauvinist. I never underestimate what a woman can do. Actually, though, Lorna . . . I wanted to have a quiet word with you about something else. Now, I don't want you to get all upset or to fly off the handle, but . . .'

'But . . . what?'

'But there's something I think you should know . . . about Ben.' An obstinate look came over her face, one he remembered so well from when she was a little girl.

'What about him?' she asked.

432

'Well . . .' He paused. 'A couple of years ago he was involved in something shady; receiving stolen goods, as a matter of fact, but he claimed he was innocent.'

'There you are then! I'm sure he was.'

Adam sighed. 'There was always some doubt, Lorna. And now . . . to put it in a nutshell, the two fellows who were sent down for the offence are due out of prison. And it's believed that Ben has already had a visit from an unsavoury character. He may well be involved in something . . . well . . . illegal, to say the least.'

'Oh, I see.' Lorna stared at him defiantly. 'And where have you heard this cock-and-bull story?'

'From a reputable source, I can assure you. And I wouldn't have told you, except that I'm very, very concerned about you. Lorna, you must be careful.'

'Oh, you newspaper chaps, you're all alike. You get a whiff of a story and you blow it up out of all proportion. I don't believe a word of it, whatever it is you're trying to warn me about. I know my husband and he is as straight as a die. How dare you come here and—'

The doorbell jangled and a man and woman came into the shop. Lorna quickly assumed a smile of greeting. 'Please, excuse me,' she said to Adam. 'I have some customers . . .'

Adam knew he had got his marching orders and that his meeting with Benedict Frazer would have to wait until another time. All he could do now was keep his ear close to the ground and hope and pray that Lorna would not be in any danger.

Lorna did not tell Ben about Adam's visit. Her step-brother was hardly ever mentioned, and Lorna had thought it strange that the two men had never met; it was almost as though they were avoiding one another. Although she had refused to heed Adam's story, she was, nevertheless, a little disturbed by it. She had noticed that her husband had seemed nervy and a trifle irritable for the last week or two, but she had put it down to the arrival of Chloe in their midst.

It was easy to see, now that the girl had been with them for a few weeks, why Chloe and her father had fallen out previously. Nick was untidy and scruffy, but at least the mess was confined to his own room, and he had more or less kept to his side of the bargain by keeping the clutter under control. But Chloe made her presence felt everywhere.

She had not yet found a job, and spent several hours of the day mooning around the house. She did not rise till mid-morning, when she would make breakfast, if she felt so inclined, then leave the dirty pots in the sink to be washed later, by someone else, if she was lucky. And the someone else was invariably Lorna, who could not abide a messy kitchen. She knew she should have words with the girl about it rather then complain to her husband, but she did not want to fall out with her so early in their relationship, and it was clear that Chloe had a very short fuse. It upset Lorna's routine to have her there in the middle of the day. This was her time for painting and the presence of someone else in the house made it difficult for her to concentrate.

Chloe tried to be friendly by asking Lorna, now and again, to join her in the lunch she had prepared. She did so occasionally, not wanting to appear stand-offish, but she was appalled at the number of pans the girl used to make even the most simple meal. Bacon, eggs and baked beans, for instance, were cooked in three separate pans, and all left for Lorna to wash up afterwards, to say nothing of the coating of grease left behind on the cooker and the work surfaces. Chloe usually insisted that she had somewhere important to go, chasing after jobs which never materialised.

She had been away from York for well over a year, but she soon looked up some of her old friends from school and from a pub in the town where she had once been a barmaid. The young women, three or four of them, soon started to congregate in Chloe's room before going out on the town, or would choose to stay in, playing loud music and smoking and drinking beer straight from the can. It was debatable which was the scruffiest room, hers or Nick's, but Lorna was learning to close the door on the clutter. She would do their washing, but nothing else.

Ben, to her annoyance, did not reprimand either of them, although she knew he deplored slovenly behaviour. The only time he rebuked Chloe was when she infiltrated herself into their sitting room, which he liked to keep spick and span at all times. Nick hardly ever sat foot in there, but Chloe was no respecter of persons or privacy. The room which had once been meticulously tidy and scrupulously clean was now littered with magazines, discarded articles of clothing, chocolate wrappers, fag ends and beer cans and the polished surface of the coffee table stained with ring marks from damp glasses. An irate word from her father did not seem to have any effect.

But the day of reckoning came when Chloe had been with them for almost a month, and Lorna found one of Ben's small Worcestershire figurines lying in pieces in the waste-paper bin.

'Sorry, I knocked it with me arm, didn't I?' said Chloe, when Lorna tackled her. 'What does me dad expect with his bits and pieces cluttering the place? You can't move for 'em. Don't tell him . . . please, Lorna. He might never notice.'

But Ben did notice, that same evening, and Lorna was forced to tell him what had happened. She had thought of saying she was to blame for the breakage, but had then changed her mind. Why should she? The girl had come back uninvited and must learn to take responsibility for her actions. Ben had spoken to his daughter before, but not as sternly as he might have done, not wishing to upset her, Lorna surmised, when she had been back only a short time. But this time it was different; he almost raised the roof as he shouted at her. Lorna could hear snatches drifting down from the room above.

'Don't think you can come back and use the place as you did before . . . a disgrace . . . not paid a penny piece since you arrived . . . no respect for me or my possessions . . . or my wife . . . a job by the end of the week, or else . . .'

435

'Don't worry, I shan't stay in this . . . this flamin' museum a minute longer than I can help. It's not a home; it's more like a bloody mausoleum . . .' A few seconds later there was the sound of Chloe's feet running downstairs, then the slam of the door as she went out.

Ben came into the lounge and sat down on the settee, his head in his hands. 'Well, that's done a fat lot of good,' he said. 'She doesn't listen to a word I say. She never did.'

Lorna knew there was no point in trying to defend the girl. Although she could not help liking her, she had realised by now that Chloe, as her father had stated, was rather a nuisance. 'No, I see what you mean,' she replied. 'She is certainly a handful. I thought I was, when I was a teenager, but I was quite angelic compared with her.'

'I'm so sorry, darling,' said Ben. 'I know it's given you a lot of extra work having her here . . . And I've been short-tempered too. I know I have. It's not just because of Chloe . . . There are one or two problems at the shop that I'm having to deal with.'

'Oh . . . I see.' He was looking at her concernedly, as though there was something on his conscience. She thought back to what Adam had said. 'Would you like to tell me about it, Ben?' she asked gently. 'You know what they say about a trouble shared.'

'No . . . no, it's all right, my dear. I'll sort it out in my own good time. I don't want you to be worried at all, not about anything.'

All the same, Lorna was worried, not just about what Adam had told her, but about the situation in which she now found herself. She had not bargained for this, for sharing a house with two difficult teenagers who were really nothing to do with her, and Ben, who was not turning out to be at all as she had expected. She did not doubt that he loved her, but more as a doting father would, it seemed, than as a husband. Already he was behaving as though they had been married for twenty years or more, not just six months. And, all the time, she was missing her elder daughter and wishing so

436

much that they could all be together again.

Oh, dear God, what have I done? she asked in moments of despair. One of these moments had descended upon her when Ben refused to share his problems with her. She had been so off-hand with Adam, downright rude to him, in fact, even though she had suspected there might be some truth in what he was saying. Now she was frightened that Ben really was involved in something shady, and there was nothing she could do about it.

She cheered up a little when she remembered that Karen was coming to visit them the following week. It was the annual Wakes Week in Melcaster, a holiday dating from the times when all the mills and factories used to close down, and a tradition which had carried on into modern times in several of the mill towns. Karen would be staying for several days, so that was something they could all look forward to.

The situation had improved a little by the end of the week as Chloe had found a job. She had obviously heeded her father's words and came home full of the news that she had found employment at a burger bar in the city centre. It was a far cry from her former secretarial work, but Lorna guessed that beggars could not be choosers. She breathed a sigh of relief that the girl would now be away from the house for a larger part of the day. It was shift work, however, so there were still times when she was at home, but fortunately not messing up the kitchen as the burger bar provided all the meals she might require.

Lorna drove over to Melcaster on the Sunday evening with Joanne, to pick up her elder daughter from the farm. She never had much conversation with Craig on such occasions; they were coolly polite with one another. And when she called to see her mother and Robert she put on a brave face, assuming a happy smile and a carefree voice to assure them that all was well. Robert, though, was clearly concerned about her, and Lorna concluded that Adam had been talking to him.

'You'll let us know if you ever want anything, won't you?' he said to her. 'I mean ... if you ever find you are in any trouble, or if you're worried about anything.'

She smiled, trying to hide the anxiety that was with her for most of the time of late. 'You've been listening to Adam, haven't you? Everything's fine, honestly, but I'll let you know if I have cause to be worried. Tell Adam ... I'm sorry I was so rude to him. I didn't mean to be.'

'He's just concerned about you, Lorna love, that's all,' replied Robert. 'As we all are—' He stopped talking when Rachel came back and Lorna assumed that her mother knew nothing of Adam's worries, whatever they might be.

Joanne's school was closed for the week, too, so the girls were able to spend a happy few days together. Because Chloe was occupying the fourth bedroom the sisters shared Joanne's room, squashing up together in the three-quarter-sized bed, which they thought was great fun. Ben had told Lorna that she did not need to go into the shop at all that week, and she gave herself a break from her painting, too, to spend as much time as possible with her daughters.

They found York tiring in the warmth of early June, and when they had seen most of what the city had to offer they took a boat trip along the River Ouse with scores of other tourists. Lorna drove them to Knaresborough, to Harrogate, and to Ripon, to visit their grandad and Aunty Sylvia. Sylvia still had the shop near the cathedral and Derek was still working as a sales rep for Whittakers. The girls thought that the shop, with its trendy clothing and its array of flimsy – and sometimes saucy – lingerie, was a wonderland. Sylvia had branched out and now sold stylish tops and jumpers, for both day and evening wear, as well as much more provoca-tive undies. One range of tops was for teenagers and slightly younger children, and Karen and Joanne came away delighted with the garments that Sylvia had given them. Lorna, too, was pleased with the sweater that Sylvia had insisted she must accept as a gift – a summery top with a bold pattern of appliquéed flowers and fruit.

On the Friday afternoon Lorna decided she must do her weekend shopping, and as this was not of particular interest to the girls they chose to stay at home. Nick had lent them some of his records and they decided to have a rare old time playing Led Zeppelin and The Rolling Stones at full volume whilst no one was there to tell them to be quiet. The house was detached, so there would be no irate neighbours either.

Lorna had been pleasantly surprised at how well both the girls got on with Nick. He had invited them into his room a few times and, apart from the fact that they had both developed a liking for his more way-out music, she could see no harm in their being there, especially as he was keeping the more dubious of his posters and magazines out of sight. Maybe there was a pleasanter side to him that only surfaced when he was with those of his own peer group, or younger. She had no qualms about leaving them on their own that afternoon. She did not intend to be too long at the super-market or on the other errands she had to do. Nick should be in before four o'clock and Chloe soon afterwards as she was on a day shift, from nine till four.

Karen and Joanne were singing along loudly with Status Quo when they heard the front door bang and footsteps on the stairs.

'That'll be Nick,' said Joanne, jumping off the bed. She opened the door. 'Hi, Nick. We're playing your records. D'you want to come and join us?'

'Yeah ... Why not? No ... you come to mine. There's more room, and my equipment's tons better than what you've got.'

Joanne was quite proud of her Dansette record player that had once belonged to her mum, but she did not argue. It was true that Nick's ghetto-blaster was something else.

'Hang on, I'll go and get us some Coke from the fridge,' he said. 'D'you want some, both of yer?'

The drink, he meant, Coca-Cola, not the hard stuff. He knew he had to be on his best behaviour when he was with those two kids. Not that he had ever experimented with coke, not yet. The odd whiff of pot was as far as he had gone, and he had been careful about that since Lorna had come on the scene. And now his sister was here as well, but how she felt about drugs he didn't know. He didn't get on well enough with her to find out.

In spite of the brash front he adopted, Nick knew himself to be immature compared with a lot of his pals. That was why he had tried pot and he had found it did give him more self-confidence. His mates had never seemed to notice he was lacking in any way, and he boasted along with the rest of them about how he had scored with the birds. If he were honest, girls frightened him to death, and beyond the occasional kiss or furtive fumble in the bushes behind the school, he was completely lacking in experience. Girls did not seem to find him attractive or interesting. They tired of him after a few moments' acquaintance. That was why he liked being with Joanne, and particularly with her elder sister, Karen. Those two girls were a receptive audience and they lapped it up when he talked knowledgeably about the various groups and how he and some of his mates were going to form a band of their own.

He felt in fine fettle when he went upstairs with the cans of Coke. He and a couple of the lads had had a crafty drag in the bushes before making their way home, leaving him with a laid-back feeling of euphoria. Joanne was sitting on the floor of his room, and Karen was seated on his bed, sprawling back against the pillow, her hands behind her head and her long legs stretched out in front of her. He had noticed already how she had matured since the last time he saw her. She was a well-built girl for her eleven years. Her budding breasts were outlined by the thin fabric of her sweater, and her bare legs were already tanned by the sun. He knew she liked living on the farm and spent a good deal of her time helping her father. Nick thought she was one of the prettiest girls he had ever seen, with her dark curly hair and blue eyes, her rosy cheeks and tempting red lips that looked as though they were just longing to be kissed.

'What d'you think you're staring at?' Karen's voice brought him out of his reverie.

'What, me? Nothing,' he said. 'I just thought you were making yerself at home on my bed, that's all.'

'Well, why shouldn't I? You told us to, didn't you?' she said, swinging her long legs down to the floor. She reached out for a can of Coke. 'Ta very much.'

Nick continued to watch her as she tipped back her head, drinking the Coke straight from the can, as he had taught both her and her sister to do; he had told them it was decidedly uncool now to drink out of a glass. He put a tape of his choice into his cassette player, 'Stairway to Heaven' by Led Zeppelin, one he knew Karen liked too, then sat on the edge of the bed at the side of her, nodding his head in time to the beat of the music. No one spoke for the duration of the track, then, as it was drawing to its close, there was the sound of the front door opening and closing.

'That'll be Mum,' said Joanne, jumping to her feet. 'You'd better turn that down a bit Nick, you know what she's like. Shan't be a minute; I want to see if she remembered to get those biscuits we like.'

It was not Lorna, however, but Chloe, back from her stint at the burger bar. 'Hi there, kid,' she called, as she saw Joanne coming down the stairs. 'Come and see what I've got. I've been treating meself.'

Joanne followed her into the sitting room and watched whilst she opened a rainbow-coloured plastic bag and drew out a sleeveless top. Black as usual, Chloe's garments were invariably black, but this one was more loose-fitting than she usually wore and decorated with silver and white spangles in the semblance of a tiger's head.

'That's fab,' said Joanne. 'But won't it be too big for you?'

'It's meant to be loose,' said Chloe. 'Anyroad, I've put a lot of weight on since I started at Billy's. Too many burgers and chips.' She patted her stomach. 'What yer doing, eh? Listening to music with our Nick? Never mind him, eh?

441

Stay and talk to me for a bit.'

Joanne did so. She was fascinated by this older girl – a grown-up really, she supposed – who took an interest in her and did not treat her as though she was a baby.

Nick turned the volume down and drew closer to Karen. She stiffened a little as he put his arm round her, but then she relaxed. 'You're growing up fast,' he told her. 'Your little sister, she's just a kid, but you're . . . I think you're lovely, Karen.'

She stared at him in amazement, her red mouth a little open. 'Hey, give over, Nick. What d'you think you're playing at?'

'I'm not playing; I mean it,' said Nick, feeling a stirring in the pit of his stomach. 'Have you got a boyfriend?'

''Course I haven't,' she laughed. 'I'm only twelve . . . well, nearly.'

'Yeah . . . I know. But nobody'd think so.' Daringly he put out his hand and stroked her cheek.

She drew back, as much as she could, because his other arm was holding her close to him. 'Stop it, Nick; I don't like it.'

'Have you never been kissed?'

'No, I haven't, and I don't want to be neither. Give over, or I'll shout for me mum.'

'Your mother's not here. It was only me sister coming in. Come on, Karen. You'll like it, I know you will . . .'

His mouth came down on hers and he pushed her back on the bed.

Karen acted instinctively, unaware of the effect it would have on her assailant. All she wanted to do was to get this dreadful, disgusting lad away from her. She raised her knee, thrusting it into his flesh as hard as she could. The next minute he had rolled away from her with a shriek of agony.

'Ow . . . ow! You stupid little bitch.' He fell off the bed, clutching at himself and yelling.

'Help me,' cried Karen, jumping off the bed and rushing to

the top of the stairs. 'Chloe, come quick . . . Nick's going bonkers . . . He's been trying to kiss me.'

Chloe, bounding up the stairs and entering the bedroom, with Joanne following behind her, summed up the situation at once.

'Nick, what the hell do you think you're playing at?' She realised he had been kicked where it hurt most, and it served him damn well right. Good for Karen, she thought. But she also took in his bleary eyes and dilated pupils. 'And you've been smoking, haven't you? And not just an ordinary ciggy neither.'

'Only a bit; it weren't much. And I was only wanting to kiss her, the vicious little bitch!'

'He pushed me on to the bed. He kissed me . . . and I don't like it!' cried Karen, whilst Joanne stood by, open-mouthed with shock.

Chloe took hold of her brother and shook him. 'I always knew you were a waste of space,' she yelled, 'but this beats everything. Whatever is Lorna going to say about this, and our dad?'

'They don't need to know, do they, unless you tell 'em? And that'd be just like you, wouldn't it, you sneaky cow?'

'I shall tell me mum anyway,' said Karen. She seemed to have recovered and was standing her ground.

'Aw, Karen, you wouldn't, would you?' wheedled Nick. 'I didn't mean to hurt you, honest. I don't know what got into me.'

'But I do,' said Chloe. 'It's the weed, isn't it? And how you manage to do it without Dad finding out beats me. He'd go berserk if he knew.'

'Huh! Don't you be so sure,' scoffed Nick. 'He wouldn't care. And d'you know why? Because he's up to his neck in it himself.'

'Up to what? What the hell are you on about?'

'You know – the hard stuff – dealing. He's caught up in summat. I know he is.'

'What a load of codswallop! Of course he isn't. Our dad?

443

You must be out of your tiny mind.'

'I'm not. I heard him on the phone, the other day. He thought he was in on his own, but he weren't 'cause I was there, earwigging. Surprising what you learn when you keep yer eyes and ears open.'

'You're talking a load of baloney...' Chloe suddenly became aware of Karen and Joanne still standing there, listening intently. 'But whatever crazy idea you've got in your head, we shouldn't be talking about it now. I still haven't made up my mind what to say to Lorna and me dad. You're a no-good waster, Nick Frazer, and you deserve all you get. You'll get found out, and if I don't tell them, then—'

There was the sound of footsteps coming up the stairs and then Lorna's voice. 'What's all the shouting about?' She marched into the bedroom, staring at the four bewildered faces.

'What on earth is going on?' she said.

Chapter 27

There was no way of hiding the truth from Lorna. At the sight of her mother Karen burst into tears and the whole story came out, between sobs and hiccups and interruptions from Nick of, 'I didn't mean it . . . Don't tell me dad.' Even, 'I'm sorry . . .'

'Chloe, take the girls downstairs and make them a cup of tea,' said Lorna. 'Stronger than usual and with more sugar in. And I'll have a word with him!' She nodded severely at Nick. 'Thanks very much, Chloe, dear.'

She smiled at her, gratified to see that the young woman had already been trying to shield the girls, and her castigation of her brother had to be heard to be believed. Which was another reason to get her daughters out of the way; they were not used to such strong language. But Lorna was discovering a side to Chloe that was much softer and kinder.

Nick, by now, was in tears, but Lorna could not find it in her heart to feel any sympathy for him. He sniffled and moaned and said it wasn't his fault; his mates had forced him to take a whiff of cannabis and it had knocked him senseless.

'Not so senseless that it stopped you frightening my daughter to death,' said Lorna. 'She's only a child, Nick. Couldn't you stop to think what this might do to her?' She was so angry that she threatened at first to tell his father, and she meant it too.

However, she agreed, against her better judgement, that she would not say anything to her husband. But neither of the girls would be allowed to set foot in Nick's room in future, and would never be left alone in the house with him again. She decided that Ben already had enough on his plate if Adam's suspicions – whatever they might be – were true, and as for her, Lorna, it was one more worry added to those she had already encountered since she married Ben Frazer.

She drove Karen home the next day, taking Joanne with her. The sale of Lilac Cottage was going through – there was a board to that effect in the garden – otherwise she felt she might have been tempted to stay there. Her heart was heavy as she drove back to York, but she tried to behave normally with Joanne. The little girl did not fully understand what had happened between her sister and Nick. Lorna had told her the two of them had been having a silly fight and it had got out of hand.

She had impressed upon both the girls that it might be as well not to say anything to their father about what had taken place. 'Don't worry, I shan't, Mum,' said Karen,' and you won't either, will you, Joanne?'

Joanne had nodded solemnly, and already it seemed that both girls were trying to put the whole thing to the back of their minds.

That night Lorna awoke, after midnight, screaming and terrified. Her childhood nightmare, which she had not experienced for years and years, had returned. She sat bolt upright in bed, trembling and shouting, just as she had done when she was a little girl.

'Help! Oh, please . . . Help! There's something there, behind the curtain . . . It's coming to get me . . .'

Ben was awake at once and he put his arms around her. 'Hush . . . hush . . . My darling, what is it? I'm here with you. See – there's nothing to be frightened of.' He switched on the bedside light as she gave a long, shuddering sigh and collapsed against him.

'Oh . . . Ben, I was so scared. I thought . . .' She shook her head dazedly. 'It's a nightmare, like I used to have when I was a child. I haven't had it for years.'

'Yes, that's all it is. It's a bad dream.' He looked at her

lovingly. 'All right now? Shall I go and make you a cup of tea?'

'Yes . . . please,' she replied, her fears gradually diminishing in the light of reason, 'and I'll take some aspirins.' When he returned with the tea, she smiled at him. 'Thank you . . . I've been worried about you, Ben. You would tell me, wouldn't you, if there was anything troubling you? Anything . . . I ought to know?'

'There's nothing, darling,' he said. 'Nothing you need to worry about at all. I admit there was a little problem at the shop, but I'm dealing with it. It's all under control now. We can't have you being frightened to death like this, now can we? Take your tablets, there's a good girl, and go back to sleep.'

And so she did, but the niggling anxiety at the heart of her would not go away. She felt as though she was on the edge of a precipice, but she did not know exactly why she had this feeling of dread. A few weeks went by, and as all seemed to be going on normally she began to wonder if she had imagined it. Ben did not appear as anxious as he had been, Alec was going about his work cheerfully and as though he hadn't a care in the world, Chloe seemed to be enjoying her job . . . and Nick was keeping well out of Lorna's way. Maybe Adam had imagined it all, too. He had not been in touch with her, and that, for some reason, made her sad.

Joanne went back to stay in Melcaster during the long August break from school. She would stay there a couple of weeks, at the farm with her father and his family and part of the time with her gran and Grandad Rob. Lorna missed her – she missed both of the girls – but she knew she had made her bed, as the saying went, and now she must lie in it. She tried to rid herself of the sadness and the niggling doubts that still haunted her by throwing herself into her work.

She had completed the series of York scenes, which were now all on sale in the shop, and had started on some imaginative and avant-garde illustrations of Hans Christian Andersen's fairy tales. She had finished 'The Ugly Duckling' and was now engaged on 'The Little Mermaid', which gave her a chance to allow her creativity full rein.

On Wednesdays, though, Alec's half-day, she worked in the shop, and it was very busy during the summer months. She arrived promptly at one o'clock one afternoon in mid-August to find the shop door closed and locked. This was very unusual. Occasionally, when they were not too busy, Ben might allow himself an hour or so for a lunch break and would close the shop, but never at the height of the season. She rattled at the door, but there was no answer. It was difficult to see through into the interior as the door was almost entirely covered with adverts, for local amateur productions and visiting choirs, for professional plays at the local theatre, and notices telling of the various exhibitions and shows to be seen in the city. She peered through a chink and could make out, in the dim light, the shapes of two figures. One was Ben, and the other was a man she had not seen before. He appeared to be backing her husband up against the cabinet of silverware which stood against the back wall.

She ran as fast as she could, jostling her way through the crowds of tourists and shoppers thronging the narrow streets, round a corner and into a back alley where she found the rear entrance to the shop. Fortunately the back door was not locked. She pushed it open, entering the room where stock was kept and where there was a gas ring and a sink. She paused just a moment to shout up the narrow stairway. 'Alec . . . Alec, if you're there, can you come down, please? It's Lorna. I think you might be needed . . .'

She had not stopped to consider how foolish or downright dangerous her actions might be. All she could think of was that her husband was being threatened – or so it seemed – and she had to do something to help him. She barged into the shop which was in semi-darkness. She had already noticed that the window blind had been partially lowered, but whether by her husband or someone else she did not know. Ben was still cowering – at least, that was how it looked to her – against the cabinet of silverware.

'Lorna!' he cried, on seeing her. He raised his arms. 'Keep out of it, please! This has nothing to do with you. I've told you; I'm sorting it out.'

The other man swung round and Lorna had a glimpse of a stubbly beard on a pock-marked face and the reddest hair she had ever seen, before all hell broke loose. Ben made to come towards her at the same time as his assailant lunged at him.

'Brought in the heavy mob, have you, Frazer?' he scoffed. 'A fat lot of good she'll do you.'

'Don't you dare touch him!' cried Lorna. Somehow she got herself between the two of them, and the blow intended for Ben hit her on the side of the head. Ben tried to grab her as she fell, but he was too late. She tumbled to the floor, her head receiving another glancing blow from the corner of a chest of drawers.

'Lorna!' he cried, falling on his knees at her side. 'Lorna . . . Oh God, what have I done to you? Lorna, speak to me . . . This is all your fault, Brooks.'

'Don't start blaming me. You know what I want. It serves you bloody well right, and her an' all for interfering. I'm telling you, Frazer, if you don't do as we say then there'll be worse to come. And the little lady may not be as lucky next time . . .' Already Lorna was stirring and starting to open her eyes. 'I'll leave you to it. Think on now, and don't say you've not been warned.'

Lorna came round from a momentary spell of unconsciousness to see the ginger-haired man retreating through the door and to feel Ben's arm holding her in a tight grasp. Her head hurt, it hurt like mad, and her arm as well. And at the same time there was the sound of a voice, Alec's voice, and his footsteps coming down the stairs.

'Sorry, Lorna,' he was calling. 'Couldn't manage it any sooner. Actually, I was in the loo! What was it you wanted?' His pink face appeared round the door, then his pale blue eyes behind the rimless glasses opened wide with shock. 'What in heaven's name . . .?' He, too, knelt on the floor at Lorna's side.

449

'Lorna ... Ben ... What the dickens is going on?'

'An unwelcome visitor,' said Ben grimly. 'What you might call a ... contretemps between the two of us, and Lorna, unfortunately, got in the way.'

'So I see ... Who was it?'

'You don't need to know that. I've got rid of him. It's ... sorted.'

'An unwelcome visitor, eh? You've had one or two of those lately, haven't you?' Alec was looking at him suspiciously and Ben did not like to be quizzed.

'I might have done, but it's my business, not yours. There's nothing I can't handle on my own.'

'Very well. If you say so.' Alec's eyes narrowed in a calculating way that Ben did not like at all. 'But the main thing now is to see to your wife, isn't it?' Ben had managed to get her to her feet and she was now sitting in a small boudoir chair, with his arm still around her, listening, but not speaking. 'It looks to me as though she should go to hospital. You never know with bumps on the head. There's a bruise there already, and a lump appearing.'

'I know, I know,' replied Ben, 'and I couldn't be more sorry.' He stooped and kissed her forehead. 'But I'll look after her. There's no need to go to hospital. If the bruise is coming out ... then there's nothing to worry about. She's had a shock, though, and so have I. I'll close the shop for the rest of the day and take her home. Listen, Lorna darling ... I'm going to fetch the car and take you home. Don't worry, my dear, I'll take care of you ... Alec, will you look after her, please? I won't be long.'

'It will be a very great pleasure,' said Alec. 'I hope you know what you're doing, Ben. I still think she should go to hospital.'

Ben did not reply.

'Alec ...' said Lorna, bewilderedly, as she saw her husband go out of the door. 'What's going on? What's Ben up to?'

'I don't know ... exactly, and that's the honest truth,'

replied Alec. 'But there's something, that's for sure. Listen, Lorna, I don't want to scare you, but . . .'

'Don't worry about that, Alec,' she said, giving a shudder. 'I'm scared already.' She was beginning to feel sick and dizzy, longing to get home and into bed, to sleep and to forget. But she knew that would not be possible. She could not ignore what was happening.

'I'm afraid you might well have reason to be scared,' he said. 'Keep well away from the shop in future. I'm here to watch what's going on. And . . . get in touch with your brother.'

'My . . . brother?'

'Yes, Adam. He's your step-brother really, isn't he? We've kept it a secret, Adam and me, but he came to see me, quite a while ago. He was worried about you and he asked me to keep my eye on things, but I still can't fathom out exactly what's going on.'

'You . . . and Adam. I had no idea you knew him.' She shook her head dazedly. 'But . . . doesn't Ben try to involve you in . . . whatever it is?'

'No, he knows I won't touch anything . . . shady.'

Lorna recalled, hazily, how Ben had once said that Alec was too honest for his own good.

'Yes, I'll tell Adam,' she said. 'Adam . . . he's always been such a good friend to me . . .' Suddenly she was tired and did not feel like talking any more. She closed her eyes.

She became aware of Alec shaking her. 'Lorna . . . Lorna, don't go to sleep. Not yet.' She roused herself with difficulty and managed to stay awake until Ben returned.

'Don't let her nod off again,' said Alec, sounding agitated. 'You'll have to be careful with her, Ben, after a bump on the head. Take her to the doctor, there's a good chap.'

'For God's sake, Alec, stop fussing!' retorted Ben, in a harsh whisper. 'She's my wife. Surely you can trust me to look after her? Come along, darling, let's get you home. You're going to be all right; don't worry about a thing . . . Lock the door when we've gone, Alec, and put a notice up to say we're closed for the rest of the day.'

Lorna perked up a little in the fresh air, and the few minutes' walk, with Ben's arm around her, to where his car was parked in an alleyway, seemed to clear her head of its muzziness. It was still aching like mad where she'd been hit, but she no longer wanted to go to sleep. Neither did she want to talk, so it was a very quiet drive home.

Ben fussed around her when they arrived back at the house. 'Now, let's make sure there are no bones broken. Oh dear! Your poor arm; it's badly bruised . . . Can you move it up and down?'

Lorna found that she could. She guessed she would be black and blue the following day, but she assured Ben that she did not need to see a doctor. He seemed relieved, agreeing with her too readily. But she could not complain of his care for her. She was plied with cups of tea and painkillers, and he made a quick meal of spaghetti bolognese of which she managed to eat a small portion. Chloe showed concern when she came home from work, but seemed satisfied at the explanation that Lorna had sustained some nasty bumps falling off a ladder at the shop, and Nick neither knew nor cared.

She was loath to discuss what had happened with her husband, nor did she even try to find out, now, what sort of bother he had got mixed up in. All she could think about was getting through this coming night, then, the following day, she would contact Adam, as Alec had advised her to do. Adam would know what to do. She went to bed early after taking another dose of pain-killers, and it was the thought of Adam that lulled her to sleep. Adam would take care of her . . .

A glance in the mirror the next morning revealed to Lorna what she had feared. The bump over her right eye had gone down a little, but the whole area was purple and black. She had a lump on the back of her head where it had hit the floor. Her right elbow and arm, and her hip and upper leg were discoloured too.

'Stay in today, darling,' said Ben, regarding her anxiously. 'In fact, I don't think you will be going anywhere for several days. Oh dear! Are you sure you will be all right if I go to the shop as usual?'

'Of course I will,' she replied. 'It looks worse than it is; bruises always do.'

'I could come home at lunchtime . . .'

'No,' she answered, almost too quickly. 'No . . . thank you. I'll be OK, honestly. I'm feeling a little better. My head isn't aching quite as much . . .' It was not true. She felt ghastly, but all she wanted, now, was for him to go.

'Very well then, if you're sure . . .' He kissed her lovingly. Even now, she did not doubt that he loved her, but she could not respond.

As soon as he had backed the car out of the garage and she had heard him zoom off along the road she went to the telephone. Chloe had already left for work and Nick was still in bed, and she did not expect him to surface until lunchtime or even later.

'Adam? Oh, thank goodness you're there,' she said, on hearing his voice. 'I thought you might have left for the office.'

'No, I've got the day off . . . Lorna, what is it?'

'Oh, Adam . . . Can you come, please? Now, as soon as you can. I'm in the most awful trouble. At least . . . I think Ben is . . .'

'I'll be with you in less than an hour,' said Adam. 'You're at home, I take it? I mean . . . at Ben Frazer's place?'

'Yes. D'you know where it is? You've never been . . .'

'No, but I've sussed it out; I know where it is. Don't worry, Lorna. I'll be with you just as soon as I can.'

That, indeed, was in less than an hour, as he drove at top speed the twenty-five miles between Leeds and York. She greeted him at the door, opening it before he even rang the bell, knowing she was unable to hide her injured face.

'Lorna . . . oh, my darling! Whatever has happened to you?' The endearment, one he had wanted to use for so long, came

453

instinctively as he put his arms around her, holding her close and feeling that he never wanted to let her go. He stroked her hair. 'Is it Ben Frazer? Has he done this to you? I'll kill him! By God, if I get my hands on him ... But I never expected this. I never thought he was violent. Oh, Lorna ...'

'He isn't, Adam,' said Lorna. 'He's not violent. It wasn't Ben. I got caught up in something ... We'd better go inside and I'll tell you.'

With his arm still around her they moved into the sitting room. He took hold of her arms, gazing into her lovely brown eyes. Her poor face was badly marked, but she was still beautiful, and still the only woman in the world he had ever wanted. 'Now ... tell me.' He led her to the settee. 'What has been happening?'

He was horrified to hear of the brawl she had been involved in. 'A ginger-haired fellow?' he said. 'Yes, that's Brooks. Reggie Brooks. I remember him from the trial.' He told her, now, things he had hesitated to tell her previously, knowing of her – undeserved – loyalty to her husband. 'They're planning something, Brooks and Jake Caldicott. They've only been out a few months and already they're at it again. Their time inside hasn't reformed them, but then it rarely does ... And it's my belief that they're determined this time to involve ... er, your husband. I told you, didn't I, that he was implicated before, but he talked his way out of it?'

'Another robbery, you mean?'

'Most likely ...'

'How do you know?'

'Friends in the police force, Lorna. They've got their eye on things, but they don't know where or when.'

'How can they be sure?'

'Informers; snouts, they call them. Some villains are only too ready to grass on their comrades for ... well, a monetary reward, I suppose.'

'A dangerous game ...'

'Most certainly. And one that I don't want you involved in,

not to the slightest degree. I've been out of my mind with worry ever since you married him. Listen, Lorna, you've got to get away from him, right now.'

'But how can I? I'm married to Ben, and I can't just turn my back on him . . . can I?'

'Tell me, Lorna . . .' It hurt him to ask. 'Do you love him? Have you ever loved him?'

'I thought I did, once,' she replied. 'But not any more. No, I don't love him. But I'm pretty sure he loves me, Adam. He really does. Not . . . not in the way you might think, though . . .'

'You mean . . . you don't make love?' It was agony for him to ask this as well.

'Hardly ever, and it's not . . . satisfactory, you know? He treats me more like a father would. He . . . cherishes me, I think. Is that the right word? As though I'm a precious possession, like one of his antiques.'

Adam gave a dry laugh. 'You've just about summed it up. I think he wanted to possess you, for you to belong to him. Yes, maybe he does love you, but he's a weak man, Lorna. He's got himself into a mess and doesn't know which way to turn. But there is nothing we can do to help him. He has done you nothing but harm, and you have to get away. I'll take you home, to your mother . . . and my father.'

'I have something else to tell you, Adam,' Lorna said.

He listened, shocked, as she told him about Nick and how he had behaved with Karen. 'Then there's no question about it at all,' he said. 'You can't let Joanne live in the same house as that . . . lunatic boy. You don't know what he may try next. Come on. Pack a couple of suitcases and we'll get away as soon as we can. We can come back for the rest of your things some other time.'

'But . . . what about my car?'

'You are in no fit state to drive. It will come to no harm in the garage until you decide you need it.'

'But I must leave a message for Ben.'

'By all means.'

'Isn't it rather pathetic, though? I mean, running off home to my mother. And . . . shouldn't we try to stop Ben getting into further trouble?'

'It's gone too far, Lorna, take it from me. He's in it up to his neck and there's no turning back. And it's my guess that he will be glad to have you out of the way . . . out of danger.'

'Yes, maybe you're right . . .'

She was just remembering something. It was coming back to her now, the remark she had heard the ginger-haired fellow make as she was coming round. 'The little lady might not be so lucky the next time . . .'

'You're right, Adam.' She smiled at him, realising how glad she was that he was there.

Rachel cried out in alarm when she saw her daughter's face. 'Oh, my darling, whatever have you done? And . . . Adam? What's this all about?'

It would not be right to say her fears were soon laid to rest. Rachel listened in horror as her daughter and her step-son, between them, told her as much of the story as was necessary.

'Thank God you rescued her, Adam,' she said. 'If I had known she was in such danger . . . You and Robert should have told me. This is my daughter. Didn't I have a right to know?'

'I didn't believe it myself until just recently,' said Lorna. 'Don't blame Adam or Robert. I refused to accept what Ben was really like.'

'And I didn't guess, either,' said Rachel sadly. 'I trusted him, Lorna, to look after you, even though I knew in my heart that you were making a big mistake.'

'Mistakes can be put right, Rachel,' said Adam, putting his arm protectively around Lorna's shoulders. Rachel could see the love in his eyes. She only hoped her daughter would feel the same way.

Chapter 28

Joanne accepted the explanation that her mother had been hurt in an accident at the shop, which was more or less true, and that the two of them would be staying at her grand-parents' home to allow Lorna to recover from the shock she had suffered. Karen was pleased to have her mum back in Melcaster, and when Lorna saw how happy and carefree her elder daughter was, living on the farm, she knew that that was the right place for her to be.

As for herself, she wondered why she had ever left. How could she have been such a fool as to rush into such an unsuitable and ill-advised marriage? At the same time, she was an honourable woman, not one to renege on promises she had made. Even in the hasty civil marriage ceremony she had made a vow to stay with her husband, 'for better or for worse'. How spineless it was, therefore, to hide away at her parents' home and let Ben bear his burdens on his own.

'Troubles he has brought upon himself,' both Adam and Robert reminded her.

'And I guess he would rather not have the added worry of having you there,' Adam told her again. 'From what you have told me I am sure he loves you . . . in his own peculiar way. Whatever offences Ben Frazer had committed, he won't want you to be in any danger.'

'Then he should have thought about that when he married me, shouldn't he?' said Lorna. 'And I shouldn't have been such an idiot as to be flattered by him. Oh, whatever have I done?' She must have asked the same question of herself and her immediate family a hundred times. 'Even now, we're only guessing – aren't we – that Ben's involved in something criminal?'

'There seems to be little doubt,' Adam told her. 'After all, he hasn't begged you to go back to him, has he?'

That was true. She had left a note for Ben, which had seemed to her a very cowardly thing to do, saying that her step-brother had come to visit her and had insisted on her going to stay with her mother for a while, as she had been quite badly hurt in that fall. When she had phoned him that evening, still a little remorseful and fearful as to what his reaction might be, she had heard the relief in his voice as he told her she had made the right decision.

'Stay where you are, my dear, and have a good rest. Your mother will take care of you. You know how very sorry I am, don't you, about your accident? I wouldn't want to hurt you for the world . . . so it's best that you stay there, in Melcaster. It might not be for long.'

'No, maybe not, Ben,' she replied, but she felt in her heart that she would not be returning to the house in York.

'Your step-brother . . . that's Adam Blundell, isn't it?' asked Ben, and she could hear the wariness in his voice. 'The reporter . . . from Leeds?'

'Yes, that's right,' she answered. 'I told you about him.'

'Yes, so you did . . .' She knew from his suspicious tone that he remembered Adam from a previous encounter. 'Do you need your car, my dear? Shall I ask Alec to drive it over for you?'

She told him it did not matter. She would have the use of her mother's Mini, if she so wished, and she would collect her car all in good time.

Adam was a frequent visitor to his father and Rachel's house. He drove over two or three evenings a week and stayed overnight at the weekends, sleeping on the settee in the sitting room.

One day he brought some good news. In the midst of all the recent traumas and crises he had almost forgotten about his detective novel, so the phone call from his agent telling him of its acceptance by a publisher was all the more welcome and a very pleasant surprise. And already they were wanting him to think up further crimes for his hero, DI Guy Summersby, to solve, in what they hoped would become a popular series.

At the moment, though, Adam had more important things on his mind. He and Lorna had little time on their own, and he was still waiting for the right moment to declare his feelings for her. Added to that was the problem that she was still married.

Lorna's bruises gradually faded, and so did her fears, and the spasms of tension that had gripped her so frequently at first. She felt as though she were in a state of limbo, knowing that something momentous was about to happen, but almost convincing herself at other times that life was normal and that she had imagined it all. She busied herself with her art work. Her painting equipment had been amongst the essential items she had brought with her, and her make-believe world of fairy-tale scenes brought her solace and helped to divert her mind.

Rachel returned to her school at the beginning of September, and so did Karen. Joanne went back to her previous school, although the headteacher was told it might only be a temporary arrangement, whilst her mother was recovering from an accident. It began to feel, to Lorna, as though they had never been away.

It was during the second week in September that the crisis came, the culmination of all Lorna's fears and forebodings. It was with a feeling of relief, as well as dread, that she saw Alec's pinker than usual face and startled blue eyes as she opened the door. It was mid-afternoon and she was in on her own.

'I had to come and tell you before you saw it in the paper,' he gabbled as she ushered him into the house. 'Oh, Lorna, my dear . . . I don't know how to tell you. I really don't . . .'

'Then just . . . tell me!' she almost shouted. 'Alec, what is it?'

'It's Ben. He's been arrested! He's . . . in prison!'

It was no more than she had expected, deep down, but at the same time it was a shock to hear it. 'Your brother will be coming later to tell you everything, but he's working right now to catch tonight's paper, so I said I'd come and warn you. Oh, Lorna dear, it's far worse than I thought.'

'Tell me, Alec,' she said again. 'Whatever it is, I have to know.'

It transpired that Brooks and Caldicott had been planning a larger-scale robbery for quite some time, even before they had been released from jail, and this time they were determined that Ben Frazer would be involved as well. It was he who had wriggled his way out of the last lot, and had been responsible for getting them both banged up for a two-year stretch, or so they believed, although they had never been able to prove it. The robbery had taken place two nights before at a large house on the road to Leeds. It had been carefully planned, some of the details, though by no means all, being known in advance by the police, thanks to informers. A duplicate set of keys had easily been made by a bogus workman, as the elderly couple had never bothered to have up-to-date locking devices installed, nor to have a burglar alarm fitted. They were said to be worth almost a million in assets, and the haul, if it had come off, would have been considerable. Silverware, china, oil paintings, jewellery, and a collection of coins and war medals.

The couple who owned the house were on holiday in Tenerife, and all would have gone well for the burglars had their getaway not been disturbed by the man who lived next door. A strange fellow, so neighbours said afterwards; he lived alone and was given to bouts of sleeplessness when he would wander around his garden after midnight. It was his misfortune that he had done so that evening, although it did lead to the burglars' subsequent arrest. Piecing the bits of the puzzle together, the police assumed he had challenged the intruders, and that one of them had coshed him on the head, then pushed him back into his house through the door, which he had left open. He had been found there, in the hallway, by the cleaning woman the following afternoon.

'And some of the loot was discovered in our shop,' said Alec, his voice getting higher and shriller. 'Some Dresden figures and silver and jewellery. There were pictures as well, and coins and medals, but I think they would already have a buyer for those, overseas, no doubt. Oh, you have no idea what goes on, Lorna dear! And so Ben was arrested. I could tell that he knew the game was up . . .'

'But he'll get bail, won't he?' said Lorna. 'They can't keep him in prison, can they? I mean, he's not dangerous or anything like that?'

'I haven't finished,' said Alec, shaking his head sorrowfully. 'You see . . . the old man next door, the one who disturbed the thieves, he was dead when the cleaner found him, poor old chap. So it's a charge of murder, not just robbery.'

'Oh! Oh, this is dreadful,' cried Lorna. 'Poor Ben . . . I mean, he's done wrong, I know, but he's not a wicked man, is he? From what I know of him, he wouldn't harm a fly.' But she knew he had, in truth, caused a lot of harm in other ways. 'And . . . what about you, Alec? I know you are not involved, but didn't the police suspect that you . . . might be?'

'No, apparently not. And Ben, to give credit where it's due, he said at once that I was not implicated and that I knew nothing about it. And I swear to you, Lorna, that I didn't. I knew something was afoot, as I told your brother, but I didn't know what it was. You can be sure I will speak up for your husband if I get the chance. He's been a good employer, very fair in his dealings with me, and if there's anything I can do to help . . . But I'm afraid it looks bad for him. There's something else I haven't told you yet . . .'

Lorna wondered how she was going to face yet more revelations. Surely nothing could be worse than a charge of murder, even though it was obvious that Ben was in no way responsible for that.

'They came with sniffer dogs,' said Alec in a hushed voice. 'Honestly, I didn't know where to put myself, Lorna, the shame of it.'

'Sniffer dogs?' she repeated. 'You mean . . . they were looking for . . . drugs? In the shop?'

'Yes, apparently they had known for some time that there were some small-time dealers involved in a much larger racket. And . . . I'm afraid Ben was one of them.'

'You mean they found . . . What was it? Heroin?'

'Yes, only in small amounts. And – I shall have to tell you this, Lorna; it's only right that you should know – it was hidden in the frames of the lovely pictures you had painted.'

'What! My scenes of York? But those have been selling all summer, to all sorts of people. Visitors and American tourists . . .'

'There were several of them kept separate, hidden away on a high shelf. I swear I had no idea. In fact, when I first found out what he'd done I felt as though I wanted him to rot in prison! He deserves all he gets, I thought. But . . . I can't be like that. I'll have to try and defend him as best I can.'

'You're a good man, Alec,' said Lorna. 'A really good man.'

'I try. I always try my best to be. But Ben was avaricious. Working with all those beautiful objects made him greedy; he wanted more and more . . . And now he's lost everything.'

'When was he arrested?' asked Lorna.

'Late this morning. He will be allowed a phone call, won't he? I expect he will ring you.'

'Yes, unless he is too ashamed. I don't know what to think, Alec, or what I ought to do. I am completely . . . bewildered.'

Oh, somebody . . . please, please help me! she cried inside herself. Poor Alec was really just as stunned by events as she was. She knew that Adam would be with her as soon as he could, but at that moment she felt very alone. She had almost forgotten her mother and Joanne, but it was the two of them who arrived, fortuitously, together, a few moments later.

'Lorna, whatever's the matter?' cried Rachel, a question she seemed to have asked so many times of late. 'And who's this?'

'It's Alec from the shop, Grandma,' cried Joanne. 'Alec, what are you doing here?'

'Oh, I've just come to fill your mum in on the latest news,' said Alec. He turned to Rachel. 'And you must be Lorna's mother? I'm delighted to meet you.'

'I've heard a lot about you, Alec,' she said, 'and I'm glad to meet you at last. Now ... has my daughter not even made you a cup of tea?'

'It doesn't matter, Mrs Blundell, honestly. I didn't intend staying long.'

'Nonsense, Alec. You must stay and have a meal with us. You don't have to dash back for anything, do you?' Lorna asked.

'No, I've closed the shop for the rest of the day, and I'm free tonight.' He sounded so much like Mr Humphreys from *Are You Being Served?* – but so completely unaware of it – that she smiled to herself in spite of her anxieties. 'Thank you so much,' he went on. 'That's a very kind offer, and I will be pleased to accept.'

Six of them, including Adam and Robert, eventually sat down to a hastily prepared meal of salads, cold meats and new potatoes, although it was quite a sombre occasion, by no means a tea party. Joanne, who had guessed there was something wrong, was told as much and as little of the truth as her mother deemed necessary; that Ben was in prison – just temporarily, she stressed – because he had become involved with robbers who had planted stolen goods on him. Goodness knows, there were enough police dramas on the television for the little girl to be aware of what went on, and she had to realise that sometimes these things happened in real life as well.

'Poor Ben,' she said. 'I hope he gets out soon.' She was a tender-hearted girl and never liked to bear a grudge against anyone.

It had been all the more necessary for her to be told about what was happening because, during the preparation of the meal, there had been a phone call for Lorna, from Ben.

'You know where I am, do you?' he asked. 'Has Alec been to see you? Yes . . . York prison. Oh, the shame of it, Lorna. I'm so terribly sorry, my dear. I didn't mean to involve you in all this mess.' She could hear the anguish in his husky voice, and guessed he was trying hard not to break down. In spite of everything she felt more sorry than ever for him now. But what could she say to him? It's all right, Ben? Because it most certainly was not all right.

'And I'm sorry, Ben,' she replied, 'that all this has happened. You should have told me . . . well, some of it at least.'

'How could I, my darling? I was too ashamed. I'd got caught up in something far too big for me, and now . . . Oh, Lorna, I'm scared. Whatever is going to happen to me?'

'I don't know,' she replied. It would be futile to tell him not to be afraid or not to worry, as he was sure to do both. 'Alec will speak up for you. He has said so.' Then she plucked up the courage to ask, 'Would you like me to come and see you, Ben?' although it went very much against the grain. But she was his wife, so what else could she do?

'Oh, Lorna, my dear, would you? I thought it was too much to ask, but I would love to see you—'

The call ended abruptly then, and Lorna came away from the phone with tears in her eyes.

Ben had been allowed two phone calls from prison, one to his wife, and one to his daughter and son at his home in York. It was Chloe who answered and she sounded shocked to hear that her father was being held in prison.

'But why? What on earth for, Dad?' she shouted. At the same time she remembered Nick's garbled tale about drugs, which she had dismissed at the time as being just another excuse that her useless brother had invented to get himself out of bother. Maybe there had been some truth in it after all.

'Read the evening paper,' said Ben. 'It'll all be in there. I'm sorry, Chloe; I've brought such shame on you ... and to Nick. Try to look after him, won't you, although I know you don't get on too well. And get in touch with Lorna if you can. She's a lovely lady, far too good for me, and I know she'll want to help you. She was the best thing that ever happened to me, and look what I've done to her, what I've done to you all.'

'Dad, for God's sake, stop feeling so bloody sorry for yourself!' she cried. 'You're not going to be banged up in there for ever, are you?'

'I don't know. Read the paper and see what you think.'

'I think you've been a bloody fool,' retorted Chloe, 'but we'll do our best to get you out of it. Chin up, Dad. I'll come and see you if it's allowed. Cheerio then. Never say die.'

After reading the evening paper she realised, from the little the reporters had been allowed to disclose, that the prospect did not look good. Robbery, receiving stolen goods, a murder charge – although her father, surely, could not be implicated in that? – and drug-dealing. She took the paper up to her brother's room and thrust it under his nose.

He roused himself sufficiently from his doze to cast his bleary eyes over it. 'Serves him effing well right,' he said.

Lorna visited Ben, as she had promised to do, in the prison in York. Adam accompanied her, but waited outside. Only one visitor was allowed; besides, Adam Blundell would be the last person Ben would want to see. Ben was pale and a little unshaven, and although he was clean and tidily dressed he was not the immaculately handsome man she remembered from her first meetings with him. The regulation sleeveless tunic of red cotton, worn over the prisoners' own clothes, was what distressed her the most. Her husband was a prisoner amongst all those felons – robbers, embezzlers, maybe even rapists or murderers – whereas all he had done was get mixed up in something too hot for him to handle. He was devious and not always truthful, she was realising that

465

much now, and that he was, fundamentally, a weak man, but she could not see him as a hardened criminal.

They found they had little to say to one another. He assured her he was not being badly treated. His cell mate, with whom he got on quite well, was being held on charges of misuse of funds and bribery, but, like Ben, he was still awaiting a trial. He was a decent enough bloke, Ben said, and Lorna supposed he was, compared with some of the others. She said she would go to see him again, but she knew that her visits could only be duty ones. All the affection and regard that she might once have had for him had now gone, and all she could feel was pity.

Lorna had contacted Chloe by phone, and the young woman told her she was carrying on as well as she could, trying to keep the house in some sort of order in her father's absence, and also to keep an eye on Nick. Apparently he still spent most of his time, when he was not at school, up in his room. Lorna could imagine the chaos, not only there, but in the rest of the house as well. Despite what Chloe said about keeping it in order, she was sure it would be neither clean nor tidy, especially as Mrs Jarvis, the cleaning lady, had stopped going there when she had heard the news. There was no mention of Lorna returning to live there, but she promised she would call and see Chloe before very long, when she returned to pick up her car.

It was an evening in late September when Adam and Lorna set off, in Adam's car, on the short journey to York. On the return journey she would drive her own Mini and Adam would drive his car. She also had a few belongings, winter clothing and various odds and ends, to pick up from the bedroom she had used. She was not looking forward to the visit, although Chloe had sounded pleased on the phone when she heard that Lorna was coming over, saying that she had a surprise for her. She would not say what it was, but Lorna felt she had had enough surprises – or shocks – recently to last her a lifetime.

They could see a reddish glow through the gathering dusk from quite a distance away.

'A fire,' said Lorna. 'It looks like quite a big one as well.'

'And it seems to have taken hold,' added Adam. 'Oh no . . . Surely it can't be. Look, Lorna. Is it . . .?'

'Oh no . . . please don't let it be,' cried Lorna. 'Oh God . . . No!'

But as they drove nearer they could see that it was, indeed, Ben Frazer's house that was ablaze. They were unable to get very near as the police had already arrived, and a fire engine and ambulance as well. Adam hastily parked in an avenue off the main road, then he and Lorna ran towards the scene.

There was a cordon around the danger zone and they stood there, stupefied, for a few moments, with a gathering crowd of onlookers, watching the scarlet and orange flames shooting from the upper windows and the firemen playing their hoses on the inferno.

'If there's anyone still in there, then they've had it all right,' said a lugubrious voice in the crowd.

'Aye, look, there's a fireman going up there now. Rather him than me.'

The fireman stood on the ladder, breaking the glass of the side window which Lorna knew opened on to the upstairs landing. But it was the sight of two firefighters carrying a stretcher out of the front door that made Lorna break through the cordon and run into the midst of the mêlée, with Adam following.

'Hey, stop! You can't go any nearer, miss,' cried a policeman, barring her way.

'But I must,' cried Lorna. 'I used to live here. I must see who's on the stretcher.'

The policeman opened his mouth to protest, then he recognised Adam. 'Oh, I see. OK then, but you mustn't be long. This is a bad do, Adam. Bad for Frazer, on top of everything else. I think it's the young lady they've brought out. Frazer's daughter, is she?'

It was, indeed, Chloe who was lying on the stretcher, covered almost entirely by a red blanket. She was unconscious and breathing, only just, it seemed, through an oxygen mask.

'Chloe!' cried Lorna, rushing towards her, but both Adam and an ambulance man restrained her.

'We'll do our best for her, miss,' said the man, 'but we've got to get her to hospital as fast as we can. Sorry an' all that . . . Relation of yours, is she?'

'My . . . step-daughter,' replied Lorna.

With Adam's arm around her she went back behind the cordon. There was nothing they could do but watch and wait. The flames were dying down now, but it was clear that the upper part of the house was gutted, consisting of nothing but blackened and rotting timbers, and already the roof was caving in.

'Nick . . .' said Lorna, in a whisper. 'What do you think has happened to him?'

Adam did not answer.

A few moments later the brave fireman who had smashed the window and ventured inside reappeared. 'It's too late,' they heard him say to his colleagues, sounding utterly weary and dispirited. 'There was nowt I could do. We'll not be able to get him out neither, till this lot's cleared.'

'Nick . . .' said Lorna again. 'Oh, Adam . . . the poor boy's gone.'

'It sounds like it,' said Adam grimly, and then in a quieter voice he added, 'I guess he may have started it too. Not deliberately . . . but if he was high on drugs, he may not have known what he was doing. The poor lad.'

'I would never have wished him any harm,' said Lorna. 'Although he was . . . well, I couldn't really take to him. But he didn't deserve this! Oh, Adam, I can't bear it. Take me home, please . . .'

Adam asked for compassionate leave from the newspaper, and the next morning he drove Lorna to the hospital in York where Chloe had been taken. A phone call late the previous night had set their minds at rest. They were informed, on confirming that Lorna was a relative of the young woman, that Miss Frazer was out of danger and was as well as could be expected.

They were pointed in the direction of the ward and they followed the signs and arrows along endless corridors and flights of stairs until they arrived at Ward 20.

'Would it be possible to see Miss Frazer?' asked Adam of the nursing sister who sat at the desk. 'I know it might not be visiting hours, but we are rather anxious about her, and this lady is her step-mother.'

'Yes, of course, that's no problem,' replied the nurse. 'Of course you may see Miss Frazer, and the baby, too, if you wish.'

'Baby?' repeated Lorna. 'No, I don't think so. Miss Chloe Frazer. She was injured in a fire last night.'

'Yes, that's right,' smiled the nurse. 'And a few hours ago she gave birth to a little girl. Come along and I'll take you to see her.'

Chloe was in a little side ward on her own, leaning back against the pillows. Her eyes were closed and Lorna could see that her hands were bandaged and there was a covering of lint and gauze over part of her face as well. Her hair was scorched and singed and much of it had been cut away. She opened her eyes as she sensed their presence.

'Lorna! Oh . . . how lovely to see you. And . . .?' She looked a little questioningly at Adam.

'This is Adam, my step-brother,' said Lorna. 'I know I've told you about him, but you've never met.'

Chloe grinned at him in the irrepressible way that Lorna remembered. 'Hi, Adam. Pleased to meet you. But just my luck to be looking like this when I meet a good-looking bloke!' She turned to Lorna. 'I've given you a shock, eh? Did she tell you about the baby?'

'Yes, the nurse told us,' replied Lorna. 'Shock isn't quite the word. I was . . . flabbergasted! But very pleased for you . . . Where is she, though?'

'In the baby unit. They're keeping her there 'cause she was premature, see, only seven months. It was the shock of the fire and everything that brought it on . . . I've been very lucky, I suppose.' She looked sad and her eyes were filling up with tears, and yet she looked happy at the same time, if that were possible.

'Yes, you have,' said Lorna, going to her and putting her arms around her. 'And we are so very glad you are safe . . . Have they told you about Nick?'

'Yeah . . .' said Chloe. 'The doctor told me, just before you came. But I'd guessed anyroad. Poor Nick . . . but it must've been him that started it. Not on purpose, but he'd no doubt be stoned out of his mind. He'd been worse since Dad was put away. I'd warned him and threatened him, but he took no notice . . .'

'You have to think about yourself now,' said Lorna, 'and the baby. But . . . I had no idea. How did you manage to hide it . . . and why?'

'I don't know why. I wasn't sure when I came back to York, but when I knew I was pregnant . . . well, I suppose I thought you might chuck me out.'

'Honestly, Chloe, as if I would!'

'Well, not you, but p'raps me dad. So I managed to disguise it, wearing loose clothes, and I had the excuse I was putting weight on with working at the burger bar. Then – I suddenly realised I must tell you – that was the surprise I was on about – but it all happened at once. The fire and the baby and our Nick . . . Had anyone told me dad?'

'I expect so,' said Adam. 'I'm sure the police will tell him . . . everything. We're so sorry, Chloe, and if there is anything that Lorna and I can do to help you, then we will.'

'Yes, of course,' agreed Lorna. 'What are you going to do, Chloe? I mean, where will you go? The house will be in no fit state to live in. What about the baby's father?'

'Oh, him! It's that wastrel, Jason – you know, him I was living with in Manchester. He doesn't know, and it's better that way. I want no more to do with him. I 'spect the Social'll find me somewhere to go, and afterwards ... I may go to stay with my mother in Canada.'

'Your mother?' asked Lorna. 'But I thought ... you were estranged, that you had no contact with her. That was what your father said.'

'And it was true, for a while,' said Chloe. 'Oh, she did wrong, I know that, and she knows it too, abandoning us all like that, but she had her reasons. Anyway, she wrote to me a couple of years back, real remorseful, like, and I've kept in touch with her ever since. After all, she is me mum. She wrote to Nick as well, but he didn't want to know.'

'And does your father know?' asked Lorna.

'No, there's a lot he doesn't know ... that I know.' She looked meaningfully at Lorna.

Lorna was puzzled. 'What happened between them?' she asked. 'What went wrong?'

'I'm not sure really,' said Chloe. 'I was only a kid. But I know me mum liked to have a good time, to go out and enjoy herself; she was a lot like me, I suppose. And me dad, well, you know what he's like, don't you? A bit stiff and starchy, and then he got so involved with his bloody antiques and deals and auctions and all that carry-on that I think she just got fed up. Then along comes this Nigel fellow, and she fell for him good and proper. He whisked her off to Canada and they've been there ever since.'

'So she married him over there, did she?' asked Lorna.

'No ... she didn't,' replied Chloe. 'They didn't get married, and when she wrote to me she said they still weren't married. There's no need, she said. They're sure of one another so there's no point.'

'Well, that's up to them, isn't it?' said Lorna, feeling it was really none of her business. 'But your father divorced her, didn't he? I mean ... he must have done ...'

Chloe was looking at her strangely.

'What is it?' said Lorna. 'Is there something I ought to know?'

Chloe nodded slowly. 'I would never have told you, Lorna, but now, with him in prison and everything . . . well, I've got to say. When you and my dad got married I assumed he was divorced. In fact, I tackled him about it when I came back home, and he said yes, of course he was divorced, what sort of a man did I think he was, an' all that. But I remembered what my mother had said, so I wrote and asked her. And she said – guess what? – that she was still officially the wife of Ben Frazer. So . . .'

'So . . . he's a bigamist,' said Adam in a whisper. 'On top of everything else . . . he's a bloody bigamist!'

'Then he and I . . . we are not married at all?' said Lorna. 'But I can't believe it . . . It's just not possible . . .'

'If you knew my dad as well as I do,' said Chloe, 'then you would realise that it is. He's sly, Lorna, he's a schemer . . . but he is my father, God help me! If I were you, I would be thankful he is not my husband.'

After that revelation Adam was finding it difficult to control his feelings, to not throw his arms around Lorna, but this was neither the time nor the place. The arrival of the nurse, hinting that they had stayed long enough, cut short their visit. They said goodbye to Chloe with a promise that they would visit her again soon. A peep through the window of the baby unit revealed a glimpse of a tiny red-faced and wrinkled baby with just a wispy covering of darkish hair on her blue-veined scalp. Tears came into Lorna's eyes.

'This may be just what Chloe needs,' she whispered, 'to set her world to rights. I know there's a wealth of love and caring in that young woman. She just needs something to put her back on the right track.'

When they were back in the car Adam could not wait any longer and gathered Lorna into his arms. 'Lorna . . .' he said softly. 'Have you any idea how I feel about you.?'

'I think I might have . . . now,' she replied. The look of wonderment that was appearing in her eyes told him that she understood.

472

'I love you, Lorna,' he said simply.

'And I love you too, Adam,' she replied. 'Oh . . . why didn't I realise?'

His lips came down on hers in a tender and loving kiss.

'Oh, Adam . . . I can't quite believe it. We've found each other at last. But there is so much sadness as well. Ben in prison, and goodness knows what will happen to him, and Nick . . . poor mixed-up Nick . . . I feel I have no right to be happy.'

'Let's just take one day at a time, darling,' said Adam.

They kissed again, more fervently this time. As he held her close she knew that this was where she belonged, for always. Their immediate future was uncertain, full of problems and fears to be faced, but this was where she felt safe and loved. She was filled with an overwhelming feeling of joy and contentment. Her long-term future, the years and years ahead, lay with her beloved Adam. There would be many obstacles to overcome, but they would face them, together.

Epilogue

Announcement in the *Melcaster Evening News*, two years later:

BLUNDELL. Adam and Lorna are delighted to announce the safe arrival of twins, on 25th September, Kevin Andrew and Katherine Amy, a welcome brother and sister for Karen and Joanne. Mother and babies are all doing well. Our grateful thanks to the doctor and midwives at Melcaster Hospital.

Rachel still had not come down to earth. 'How wonderful!' she kept saying to her husband. 'Twins! One of each! Your first grandchildren, Robert.'

'Don't forget Karen and Joanne,' said Robert. 'You know I've always thought of them as mine as much as yours.'

'Yes, I know, darling,' replied Rachel. 'But what makes these so special is that they really and truly belong to both of us. These two are little Blundells, through and through. Oh, my darling, I am so happy, and so, at last, is my Wednesday's child.'